#5

BATTLE STATION PRIME
THE ZOMBIE WARS

AN UNOFFICIAL GRAPHIC NOVEL
FOR MINECRAFTERS

CARA J. STEVENS

ILLUSTRATED BY SAM NEEDHAM

SKY PONY PRESS
New York

This book is not authorized or sponsored by Microsoft Corp., Mojang AB, Notch Development AB or Scholastic Inc., or any other person or entity owning or controlling rights in the Minecraft name, trademark, or copyrights.

Sky Pony Press books may be purchased in bulk at special discounts for sales promotion, corporate gifts, fund-raising, or educational purposes. Special editions can also be created to specifications. For details, contact the Special Sales Department, Sky Pony Press, 307 West 36th Street, 11th Floor, New York, NY 10018 or info@skyhorsepublishing.com.

Minecraft® is a registered trademark of Notch Development AB.

The Minecraft game is copyright © Mojang AB.

Visit our website at www.skyponypress.com.

10 9 8 7 6 5 4 3 2 1

Library of Congress Cataloging-in-Publication Data is available on file.

Series design by Brian Peterson
Cover and interior artwork by Sam Needham

Print ISBN: 978-1-5107-5332-7
Ebook ISBN: 978-1-5107-5333-4

Printed in China

BATTLE STATION PRIME
THE ZOMBIE WARS

MEET THE

PELL: A boy with a talent for getting lost and for making the best of every situation.

LOGAN: Pell's best friend, who is an expert hacker and redstone programmer.

MADDY: Logan's very smart little sister, who has a talent for enchanting objects.

UNCLE COLIN: Pell's uncle, who is an excellent politician and leader.

CHARACTERS

MR. JAMES: The leader of Battle Station Prime.

NED: A great chef who has a mysterious past.

BEN FROST: A programmer who has a talent for inventing clever solutions.

CLOUD, ZOE, AND BROOKLYN: Residents of Battle Station Prime.

INTRODUCTION

When you live in a battle station, you expect war to come knocking at your gates every hour of every day. For a long time now, Battle Station Prime has faced daily attacks from waves of armed skeletons. Our heroes have given up all thoughts of play time, sleep, regular meals, and even school as they fight tirelessly against the unending stream of skeletons.

We rejoin our friends as they formulate a risky plan that could eventually free the battle station from endless warfare. Will the kids succeed in holding back the tide of skeletons? Will they finally discover the source of the skeleton attacks, or will their counter-attacks open the door to new, even bigger threats? Even if their plan works, the kids know that Herobrine may be true to his threat and return to defeat Battle Station Prime once and for all.

Our story resumes far from Battle Station Prime, in a small cave in the middle of nowhere, where an almost-forgotten child guards a very precious artifact . . .

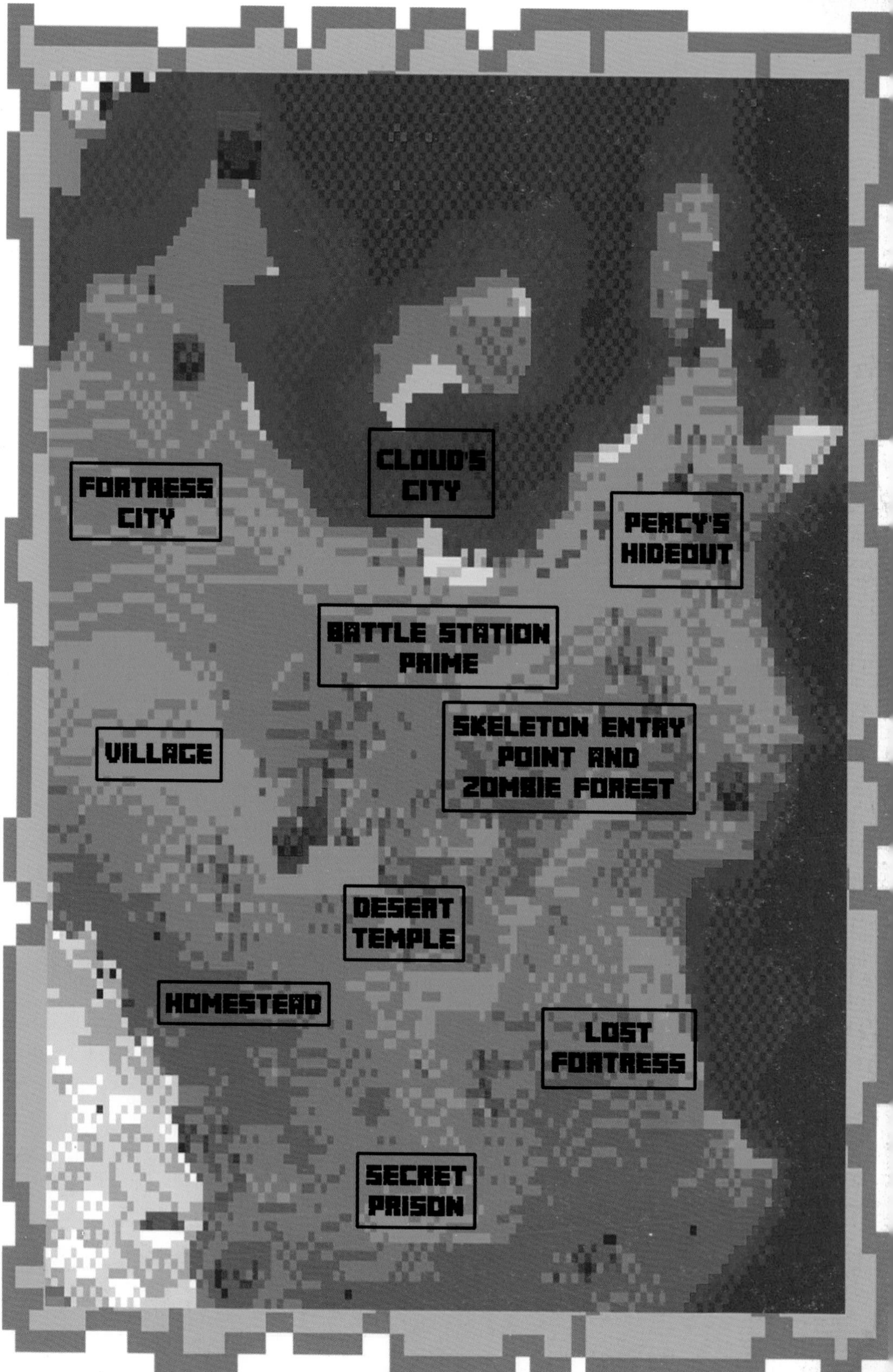

FORTRESS CITY
CLOUD'S CITY
PERCY'S HIDEOUT
BATTLE STATION PRIME
VILLAGE
SKELETON ENTRY POINT AND ZOMBIE FOREST
DESERT TEMPLE
HOMESTEAD
LOST FORTRESS
SECRET PRISON

PROLOGUE

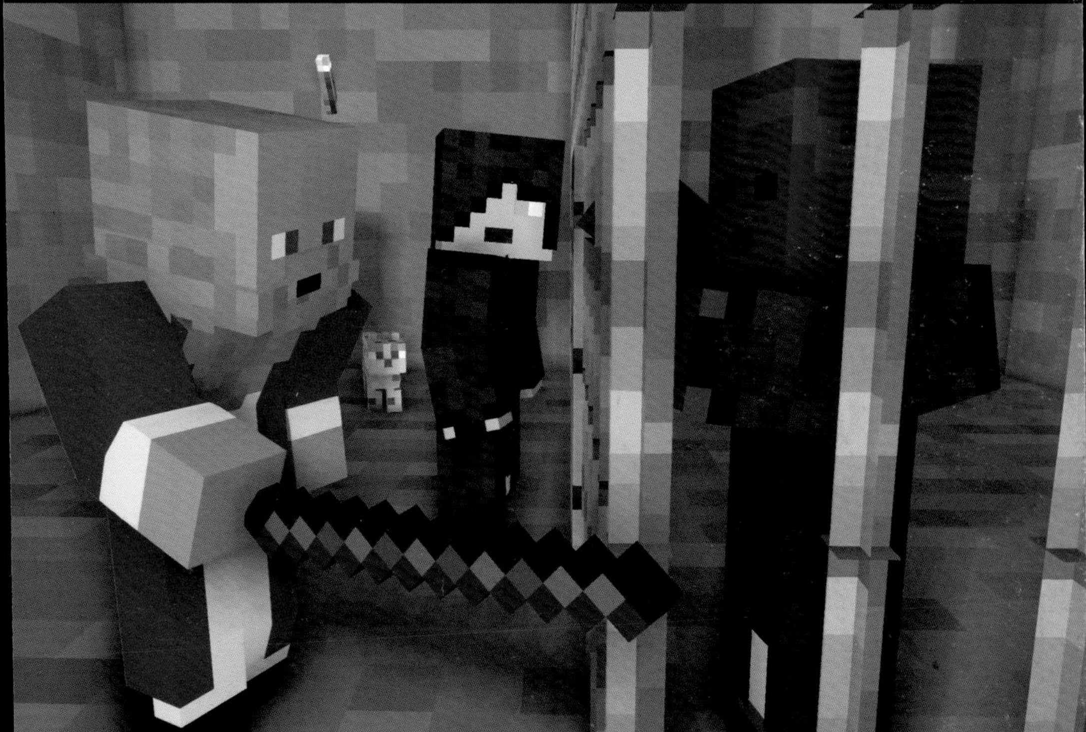

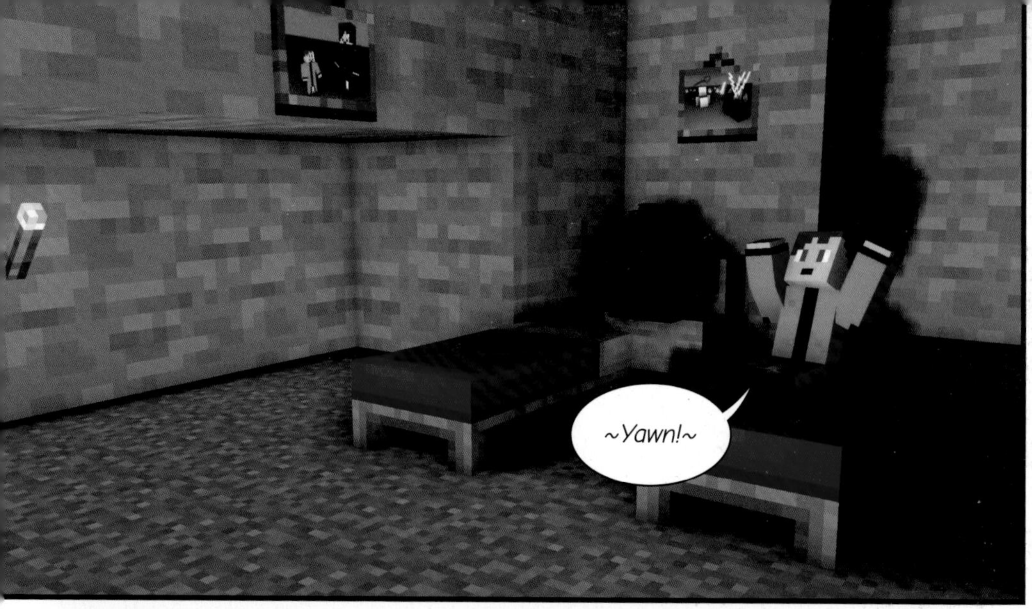
~Yawn!~

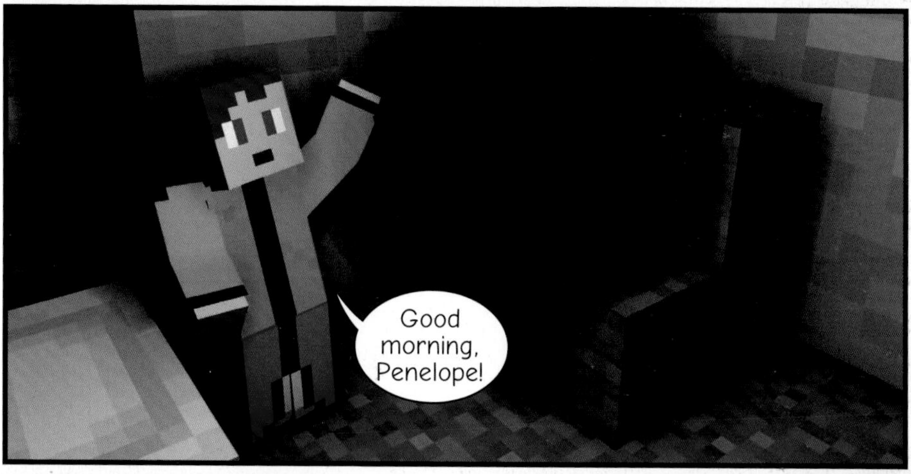
Good morning, Penelope!

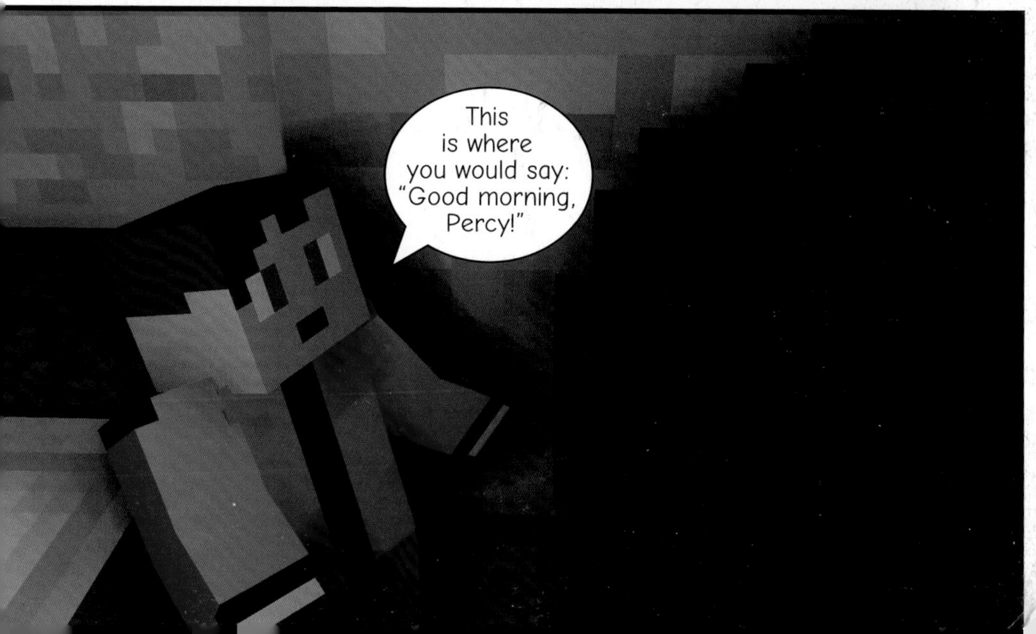
This is where you would say: "Good morning, Percy!"

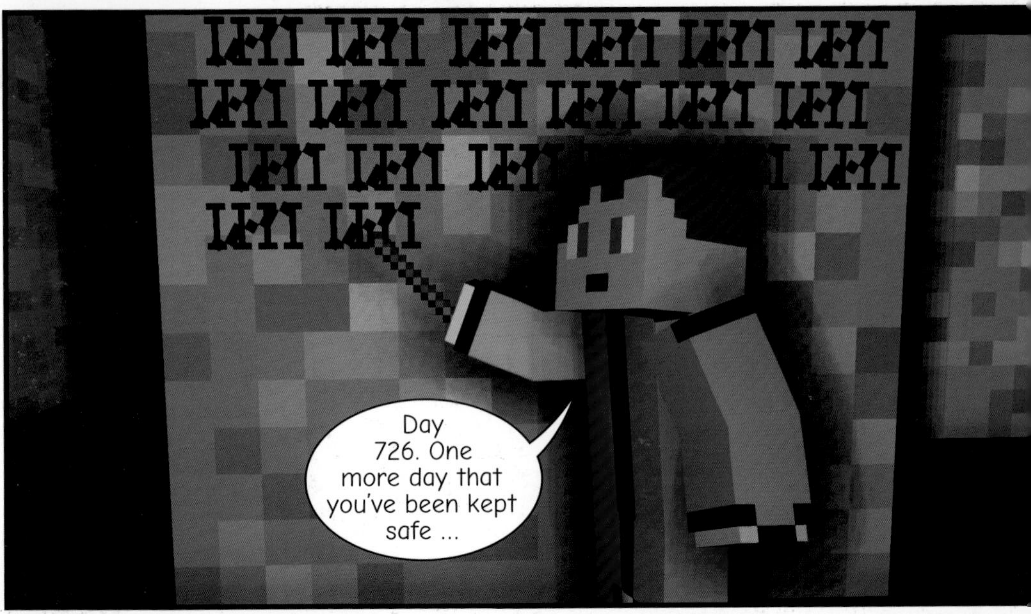
Day 726. One more day that you've been kept safe ...

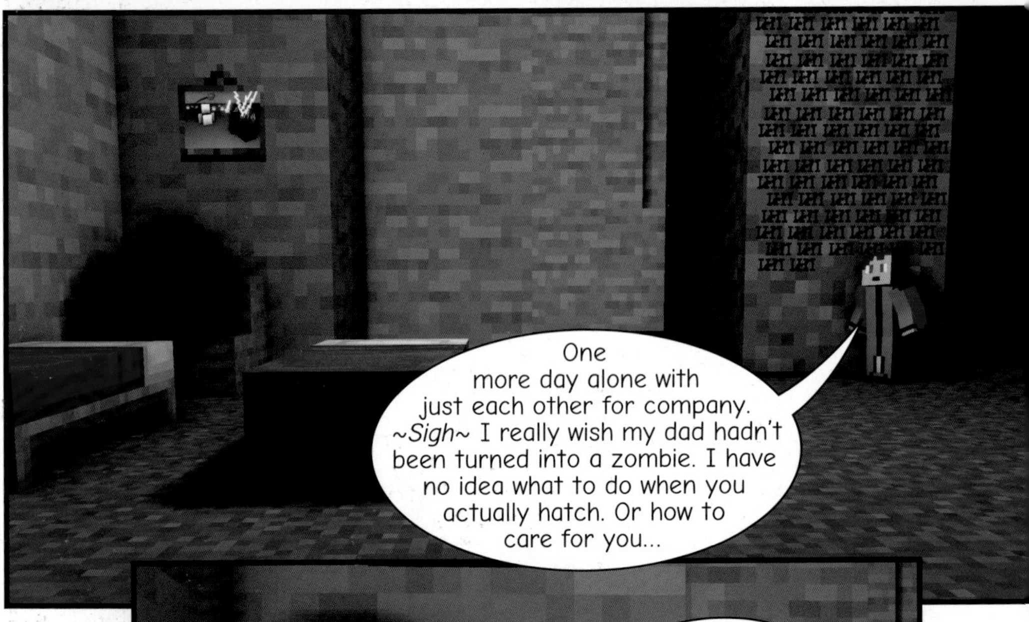
One more day alone with just each other for company. ~*Sigh*~ I really wish my dad hadn't been turned into a zombie. I have no idea what to do when you actually hatch. Or how to care for you...

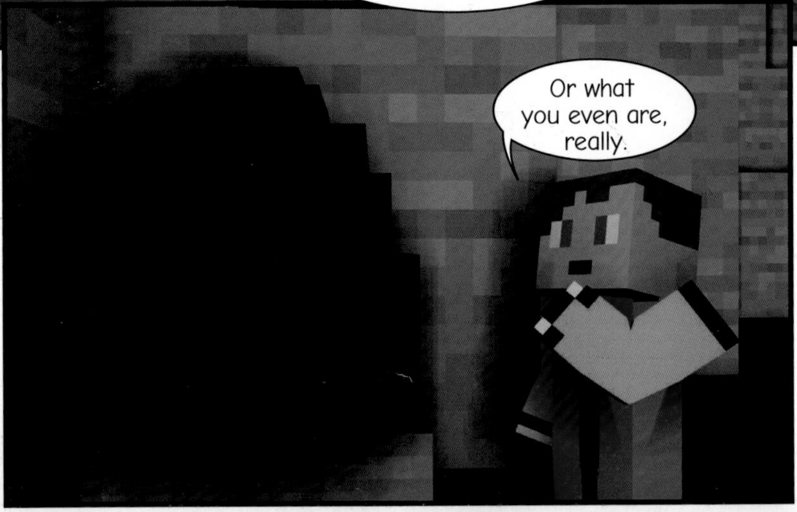
Or what you even are, really.

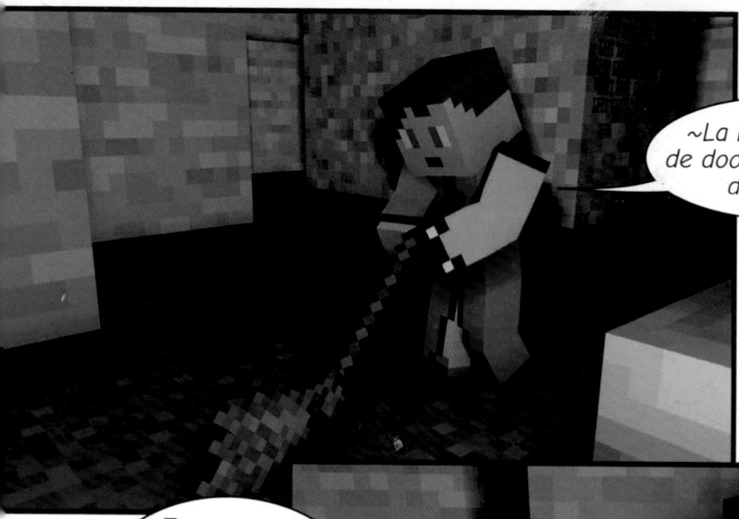
~La la la. Doooo de dooo doo doo da dooooo~

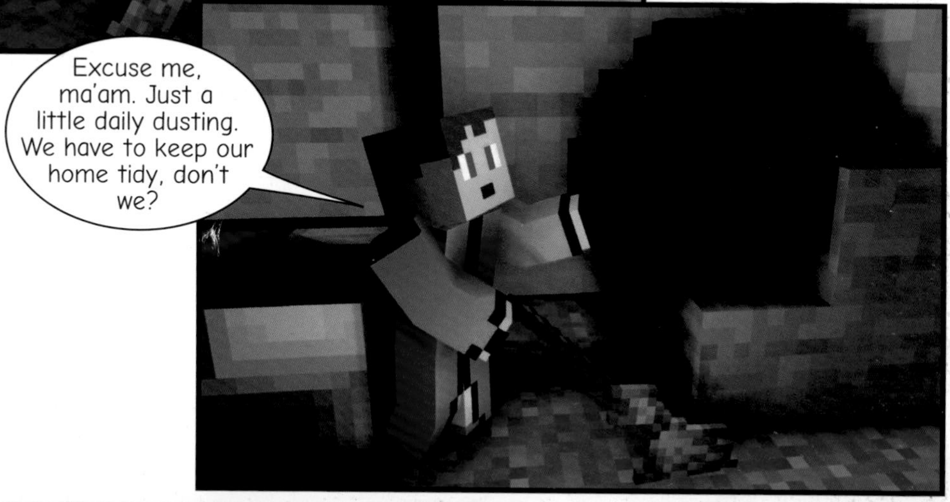
Excuse me, ma'am. Just a little daily dusting. We have to keep our home tidy, don't we?

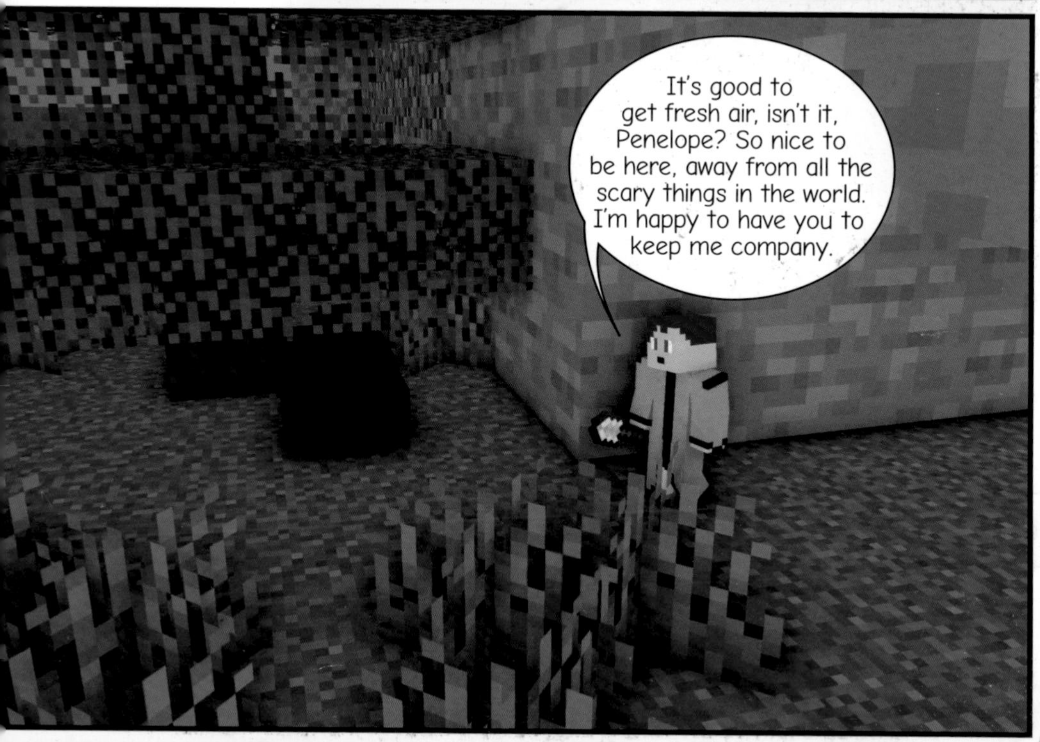
It's good to get fresh air, isn't it, Penelope? So nice to be here, away from all the scary things in the world. I'm happy to have you to keep me company.

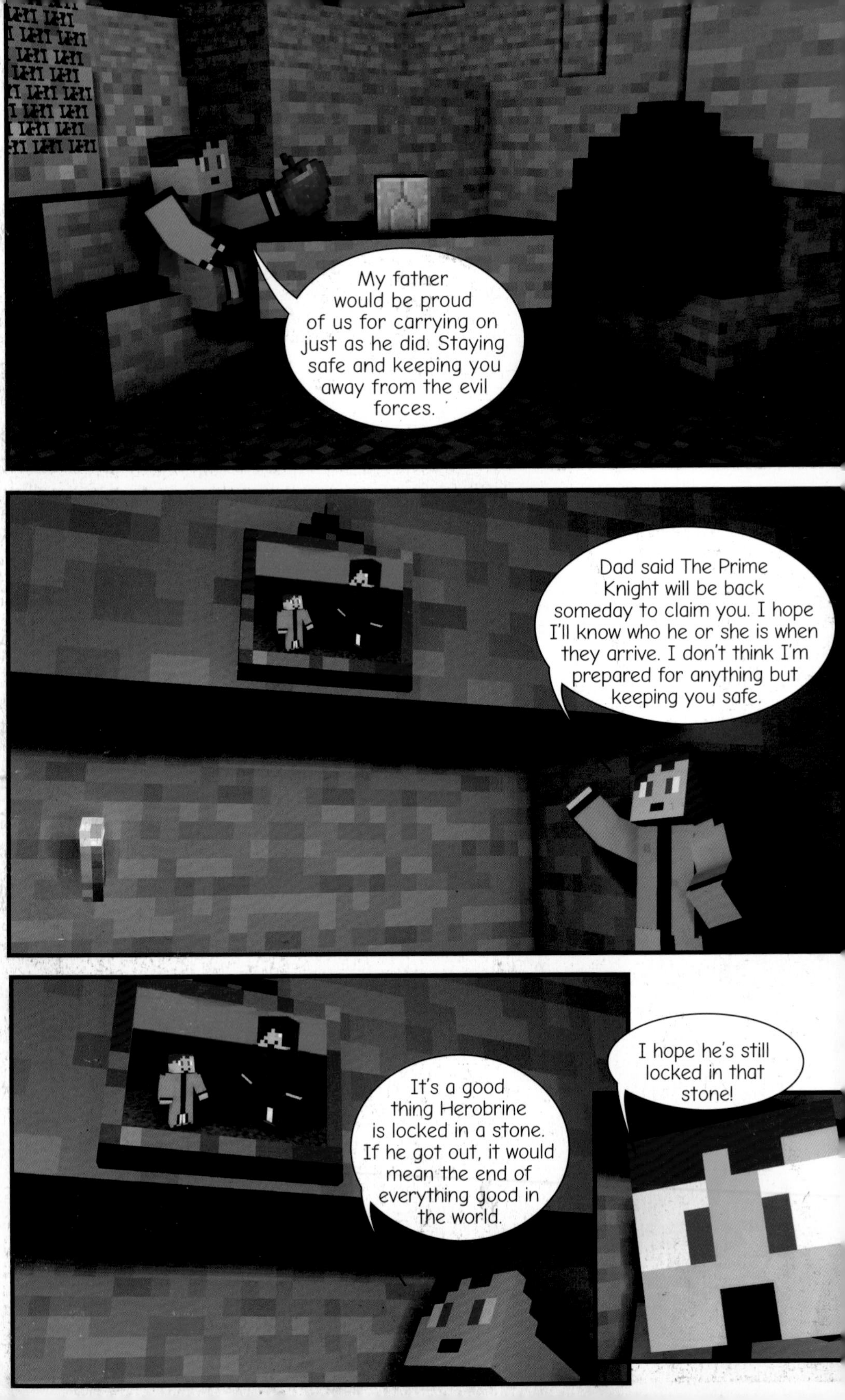

My father would be proud of us for carrying on just as he did. Staying safe and keeping you away from the evil forces.
Dad said The Prime Knight will be back someday to claim you. I hope I'll know who he or she is when they arrive. I don't think I'm prepared for anything but keeping you safe.
It's a good thing Herobrine is locked in a stone. If he got out, it would mean the end of everything good in the world.
I hope he's still locked in that stone!

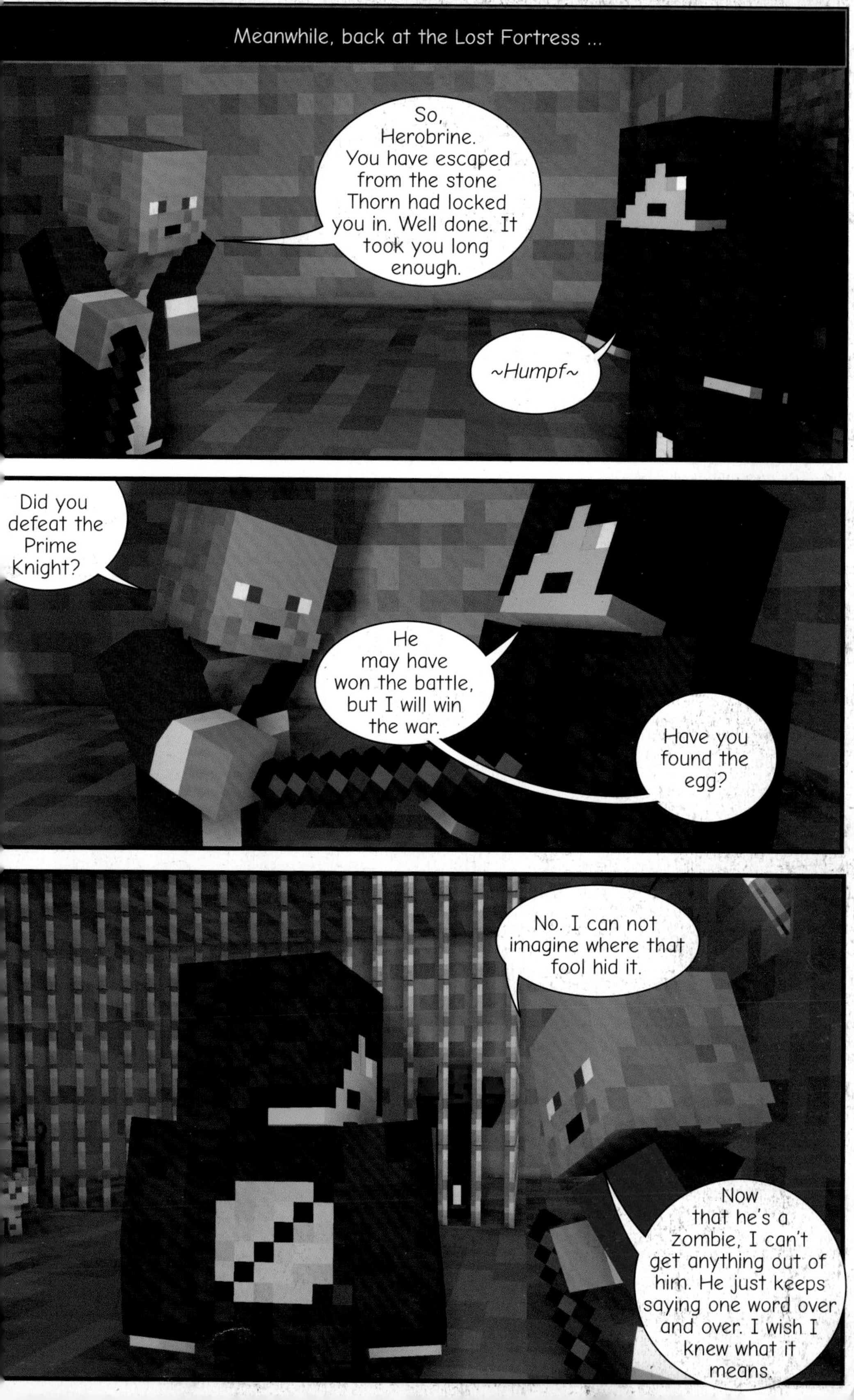
Meanwhile, back at the Lost Fortress ...
So, Herobrine. You have escaped from the stone Thorn had locked you in. Well done. It took you long enough.
~Humpf~
Did you defeat the Prime Knight?
He may have won the battle, but I will win the war.
Have you found the egg?
No. I can not imagine where that fool hid it.
Now that he's a zombie, I can't get anything out of him. He just keeps saying one word over and over. I wish I knew what it means.

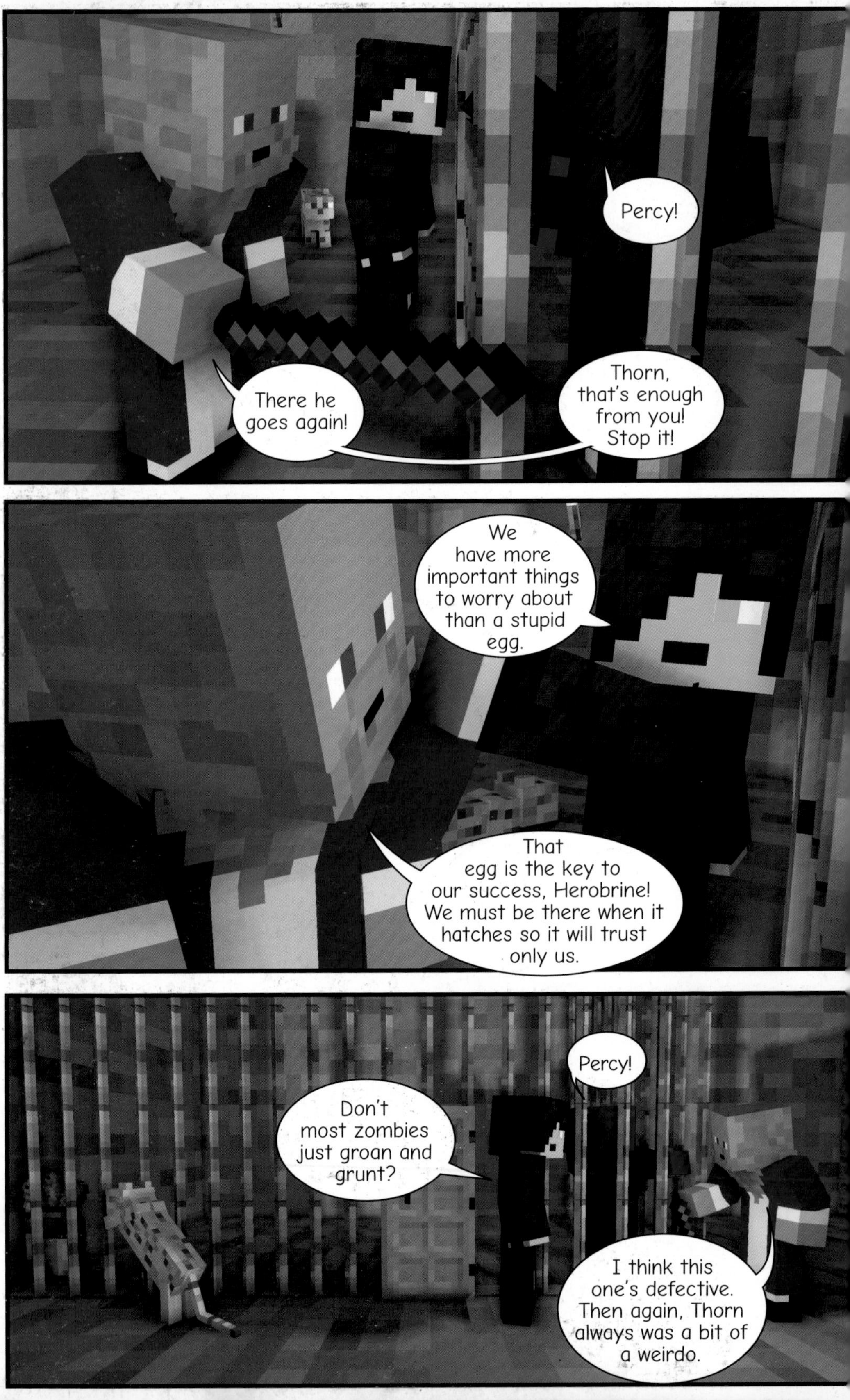
Percy!
There he goes again!
Thorn, that's enough from you! Stop it!
We have more important things to worry about than a stupid egg.
That egg is the key to our success, Herobrine! We must be there when it hatches so it will trust only us.
Percy!
Don't most zombies just groan and grunt?
I think this one's defective. Then again, Thorn always was a bit of a weirdo.

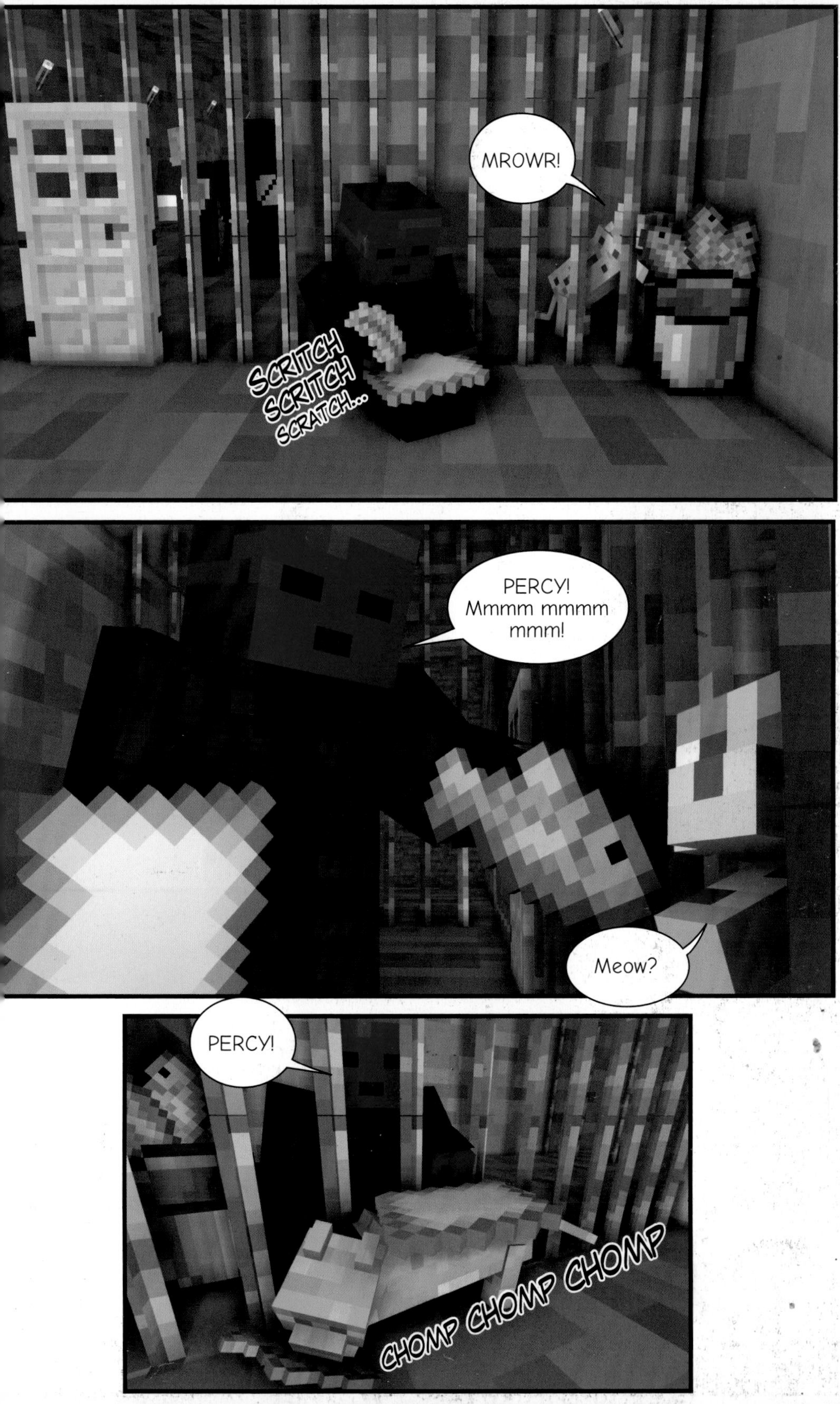
MROWR!
SCRITCH
SCRITCH
SCRATCH...
PERCY! Mmmm mmmm mmm!
Meow?
PERCY!
CHOMP CHOMP CHOMP

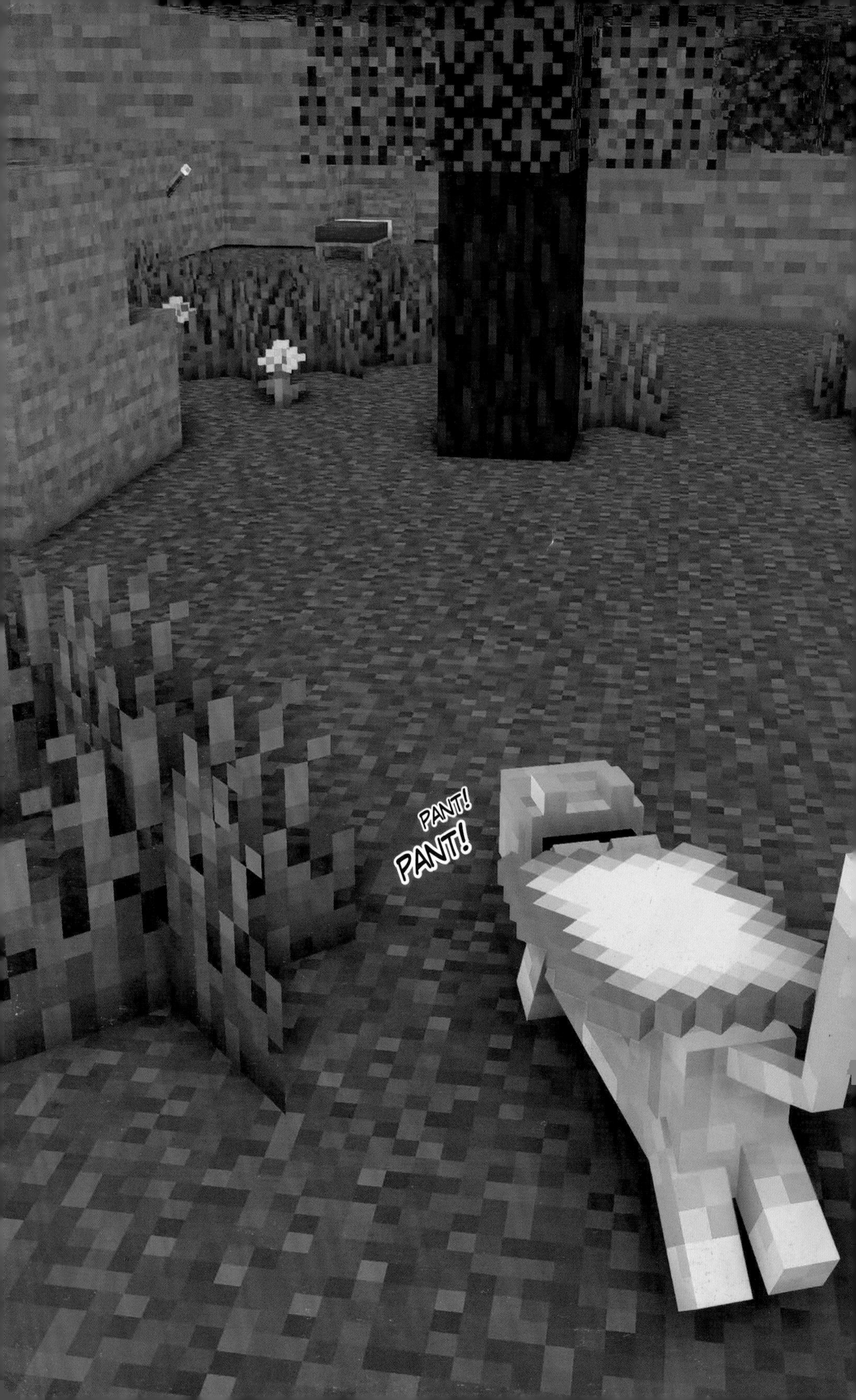
PANT!
PANT!

CHAPTER 1

A NEW ERA

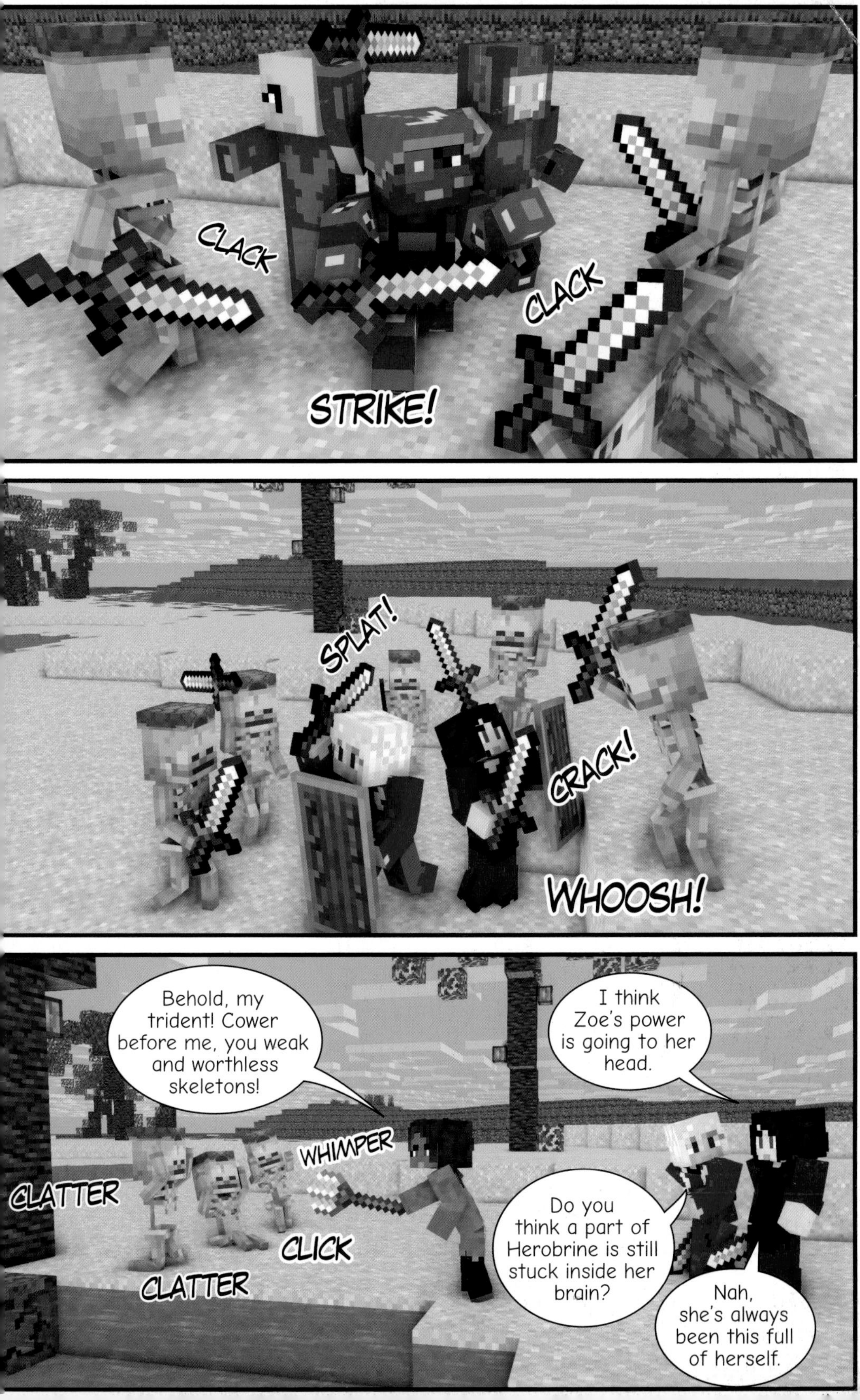
CLACK
CLACK
STRIKE!
SPLAT!
CRACK!
WHOOSH!
Behold, my trident! Cower before me, you weak and worthless skeletons!
I think Zoe's power is going to her head.
WHIMPER
CLATTER
CLICK
CLATTER
Do you think a part of Herobrine is still stuck inside her brain?
Nah, she's always been this full of herself.

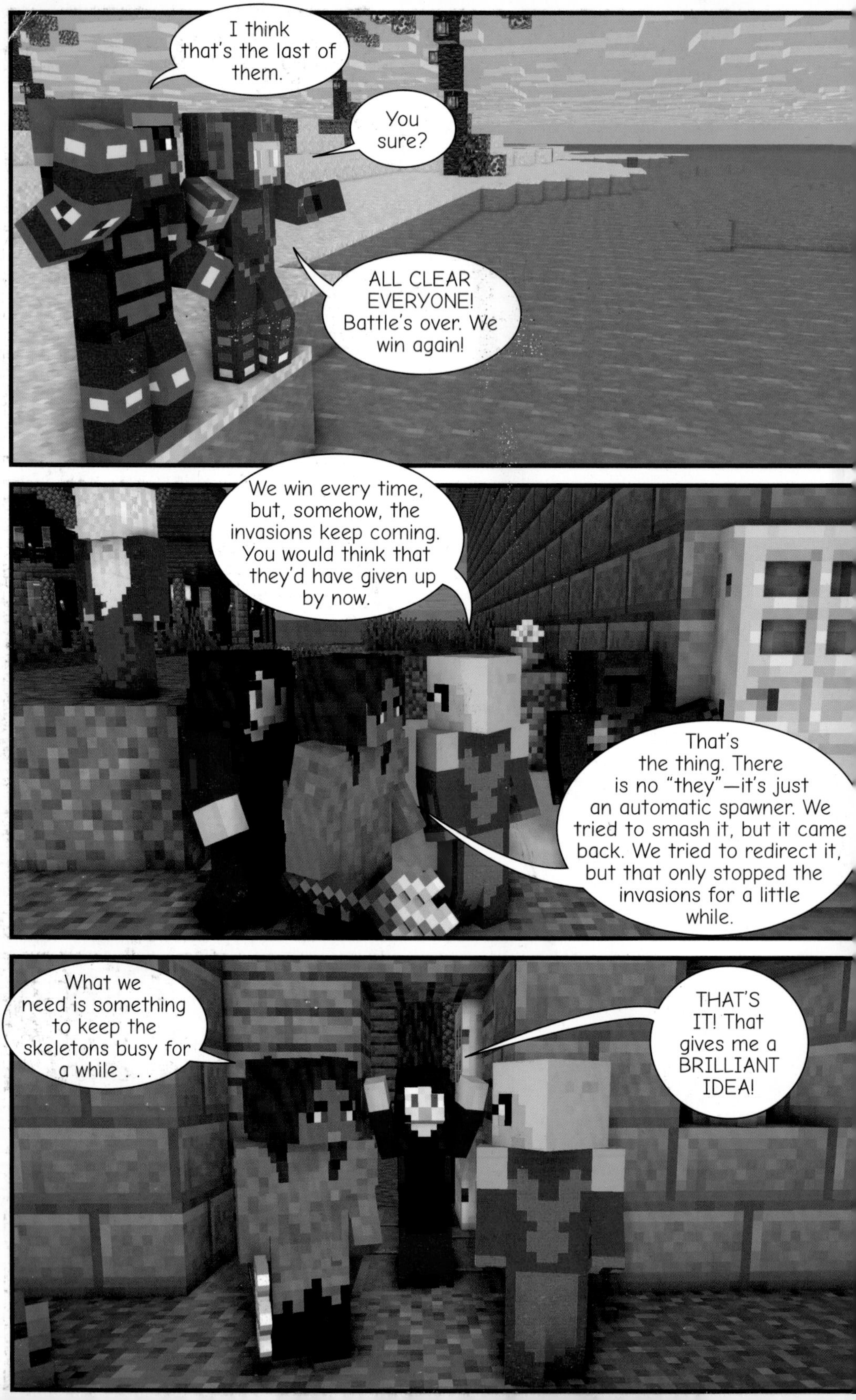
I think that's the last of them.
You sure?
ALL CLEAR EVERYONE! Battle's over. We win again!
We win every time, but, somehow, the invasions keep coming. You would think that they'd have given up by now.
That's the thing. There is no "they"—it's just an automatic spawner. We tried to smash it, but it came back. We tried to redirect it, but that only stopped the invasions for a little while.
What we need is something to keep the skeletons busy for a while . . .
THAT'S IT! That gives me a BRILLIANT IDEA!

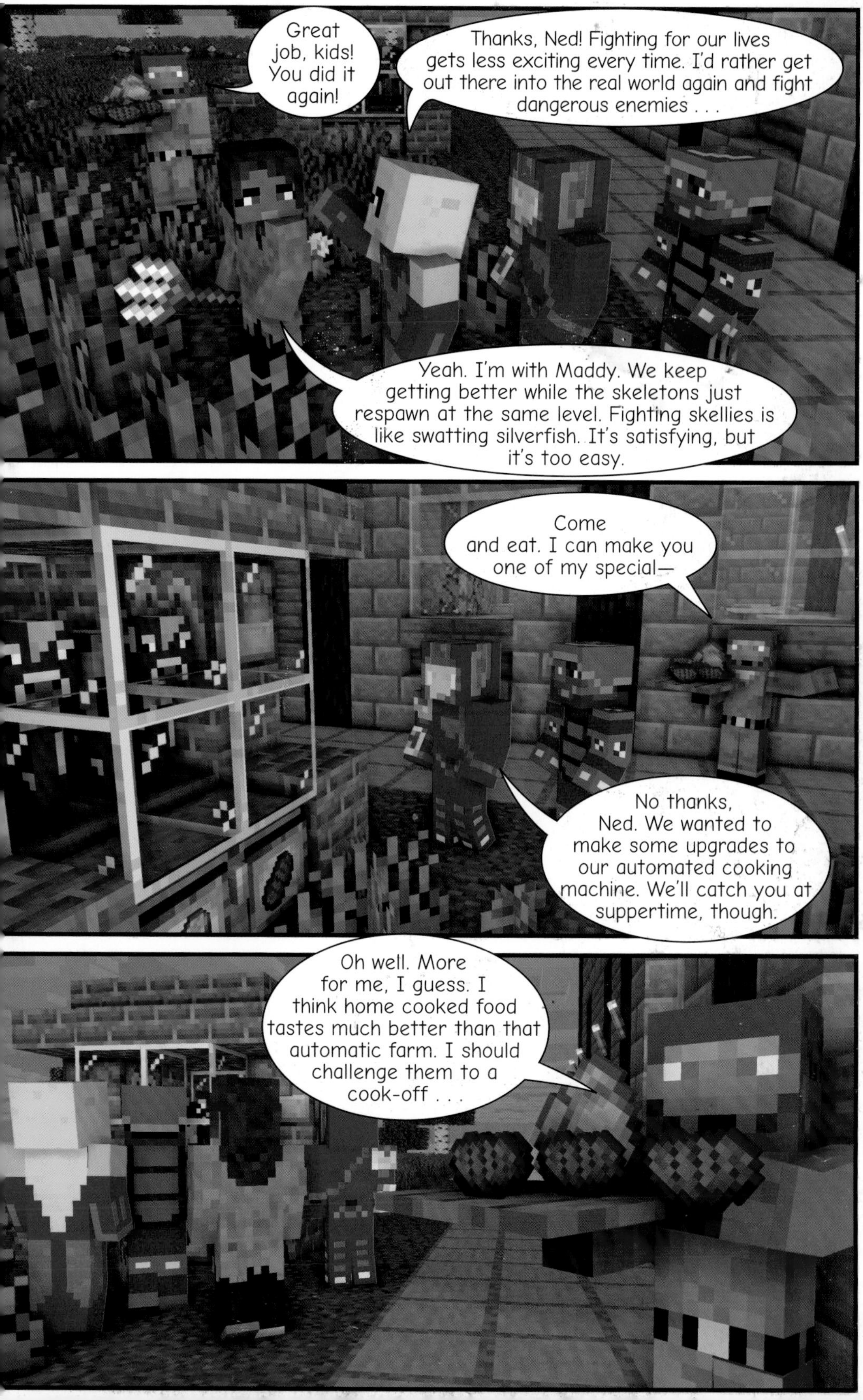
Great job, kids! You did it again!
Thanks, Ned! Fighting for our lives gets less exciting every time. I'd rather get out there into the real world again and fight dangerous enemies . . .
Yeah. I'm with Maddy. We keep getting better while the skeletons just respawn at the same level. Fighting skellies is like swatting silverfish. It's satisfying, but it's too easy.
Come and eat. I can make you one of my special—
No thanks, Ned. We wanted to make some upgrades to our automated cooking machine. We'll catch you at suppertime, though.
Oh well. More for me, I guess. I think home cooked food tastes much better than that automatic farm. I should challenge them to a cook-off . . .

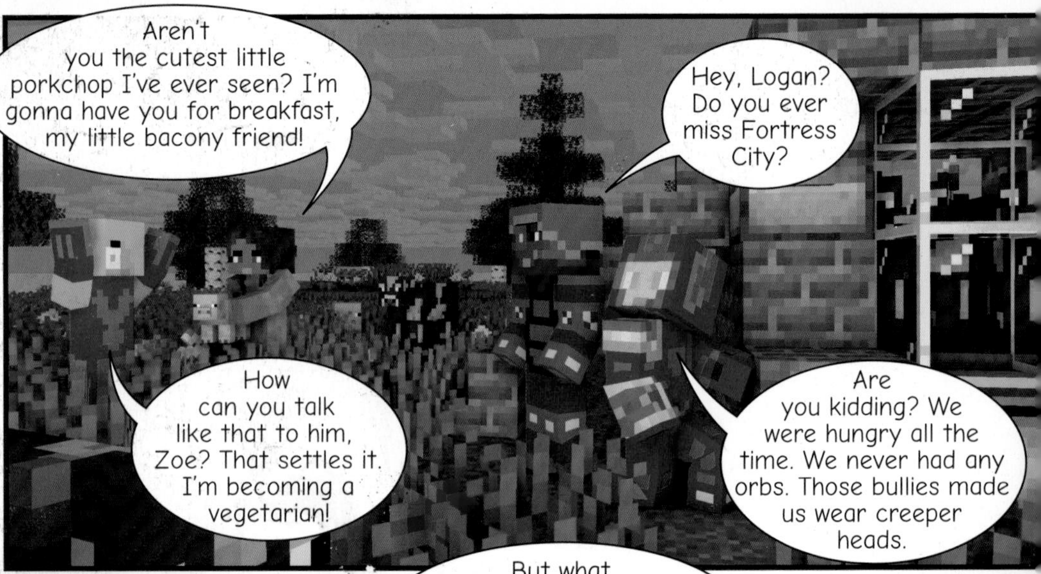
Aren't you the cutest little porkchop I've ever seen? I'm gonna have you for breakfast, my little bacony friend!
How can you talk like that to him, Zoe? That settles it. I'm becoming a vegetarian!
Hey, Logan? Do you ever miss Fortress City?
Are you kidding? We were hungry all the time. We never had any orbs. Those bullies made us wear creeper heads.

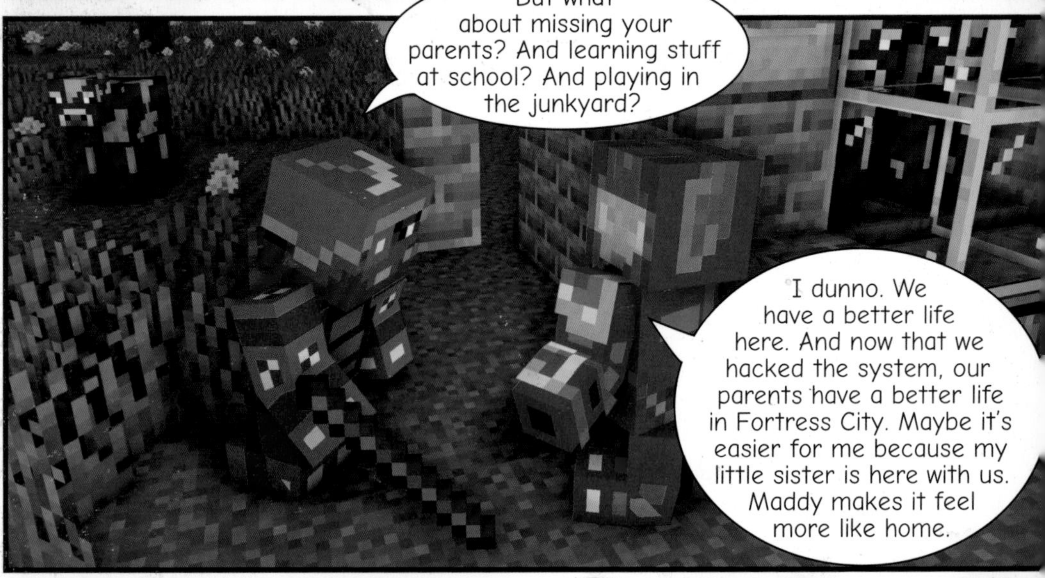
But what about missing your parents? And learning stuff at school? And playing in the junkyard?
I dunno. We have a better life here. And now that we hacked the system, our parents have a better life in Fortress City. Maybe it's easier for me because my little sister is here with us. Maddy makes it feel more like home.

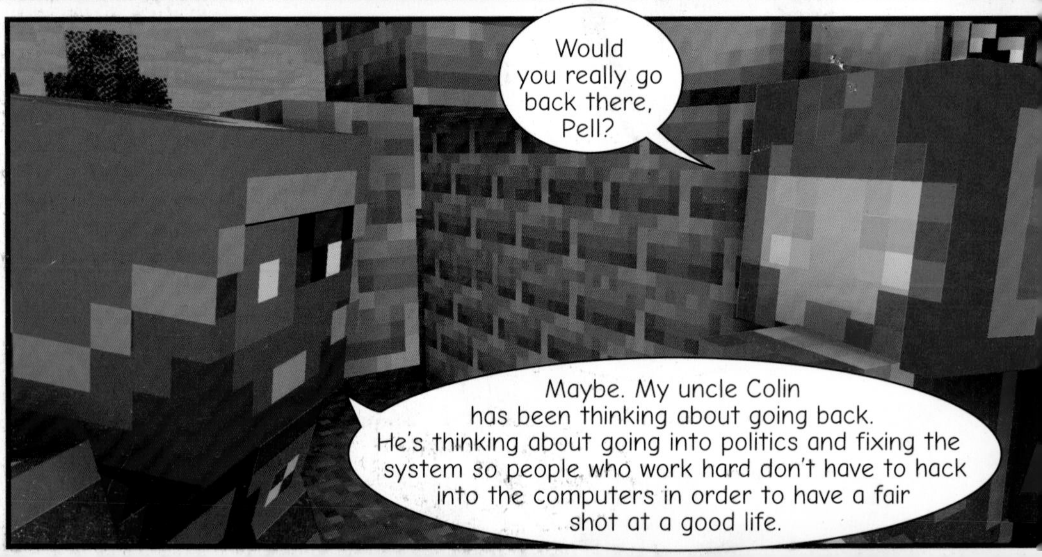
Would you really go back there, Pell?
Maybe. My uncle Colin has been thinking about going back. He's thinking about going into politics and fixing the system so people who work hard don't have to hack into the computers in order to have a fair shot at a good life.

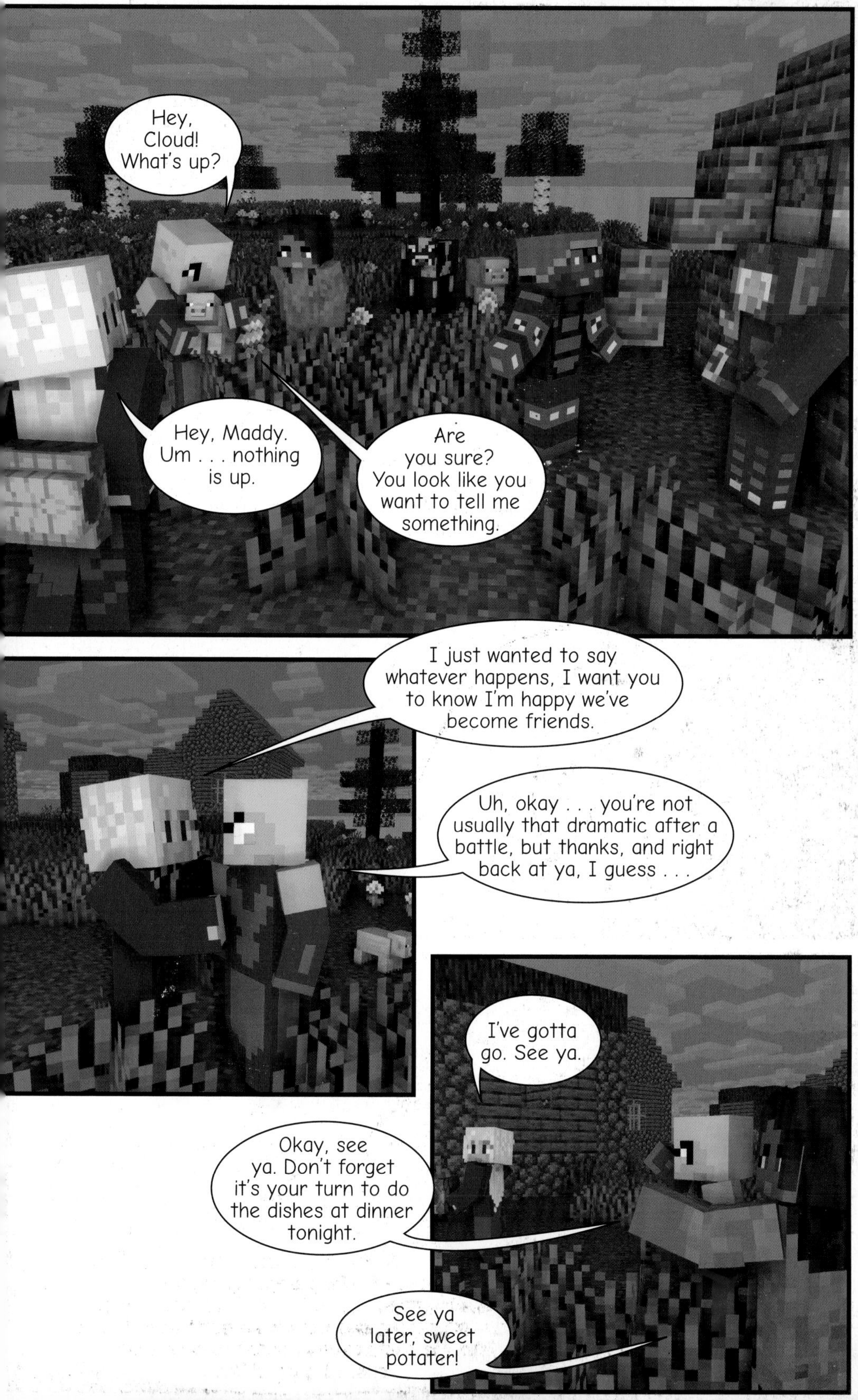
Hey, Cloud! What's up?
Hey, Maddy. Um . . . nothing is up.
Are you sure? You look like you want to tell me something.
I just wanted to say whatever happens, I want you to know I'm happy we've become friends.
Uh, okay . . . you're not usually that dramatic after a battle, but thanks, and right back at ya, I guess . . .
I've gotta go. See ya.
Okay, see ya. Don't forget it's your turn to do the dishes at dinner tonight.
See ya later, sweet potater!

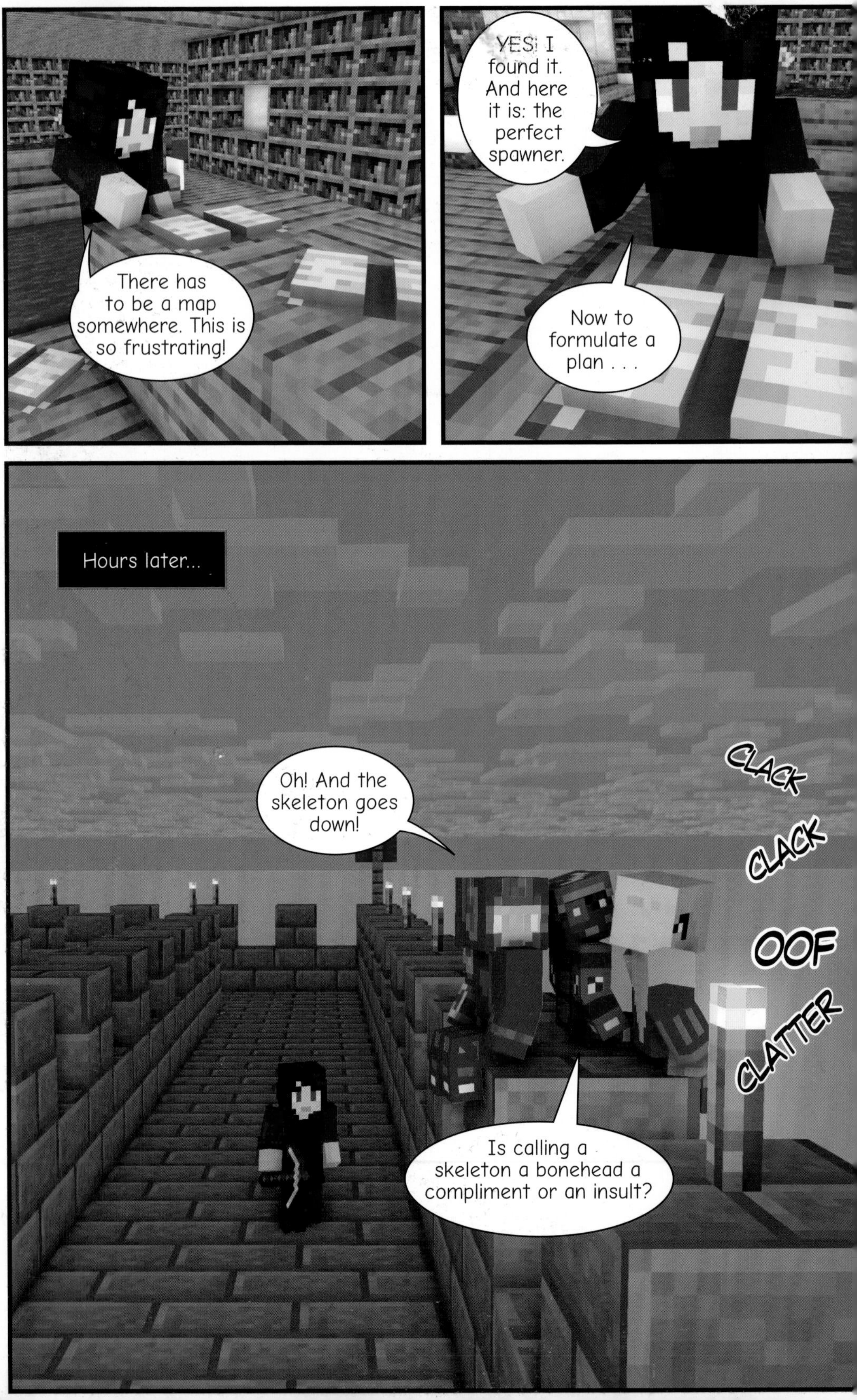
There has to be a map somewhere. This is so frustrating!
YES! I found it. And here it is: the perfect spawner.
Now to formulate a plan . . .
Hours later...
Oh! And the skeleton goes down!
CLACK
CLACK
OOF
CLATTER
Is calling a skeleton a bonehead a compliment or an insult?

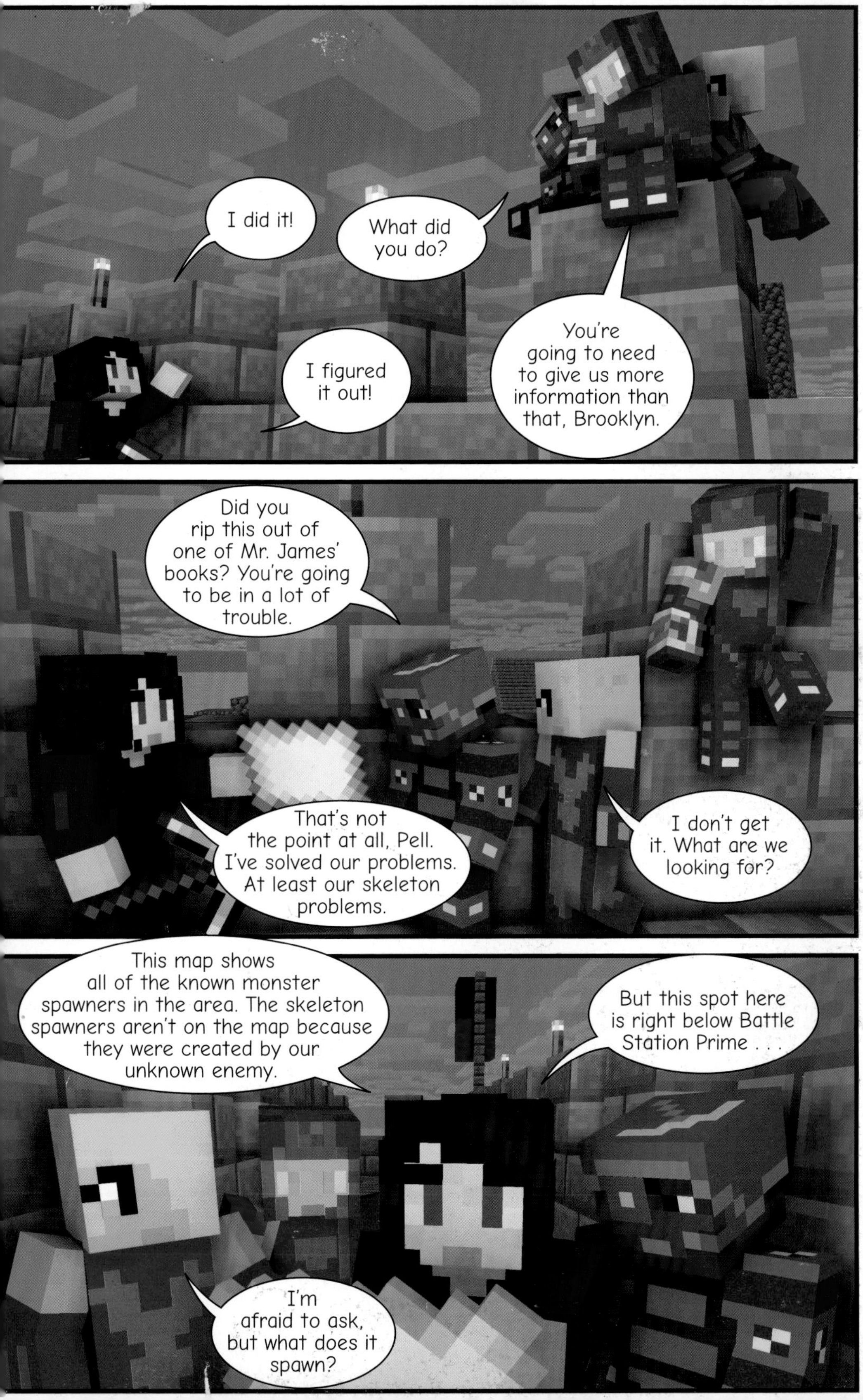
I did it!
What did you do?
I figured it out!
You're going to need to give us more information than that, Brooklyn.
Did you rip this out of one of Mr. James' books? You're going to be in a lot of trouble.
That's not the point at all, Pell. I've solved our problems. At least our skeleton problems.
I don't get it. What are we looking for?
This map shows all of the known monster spawners in the area. The skeleton spawners aren't on the map because they were created by our unknown enemy.
But this spot here is right below Battle Station Prime . . .
I'm afraid to ask, but what does it spawn?

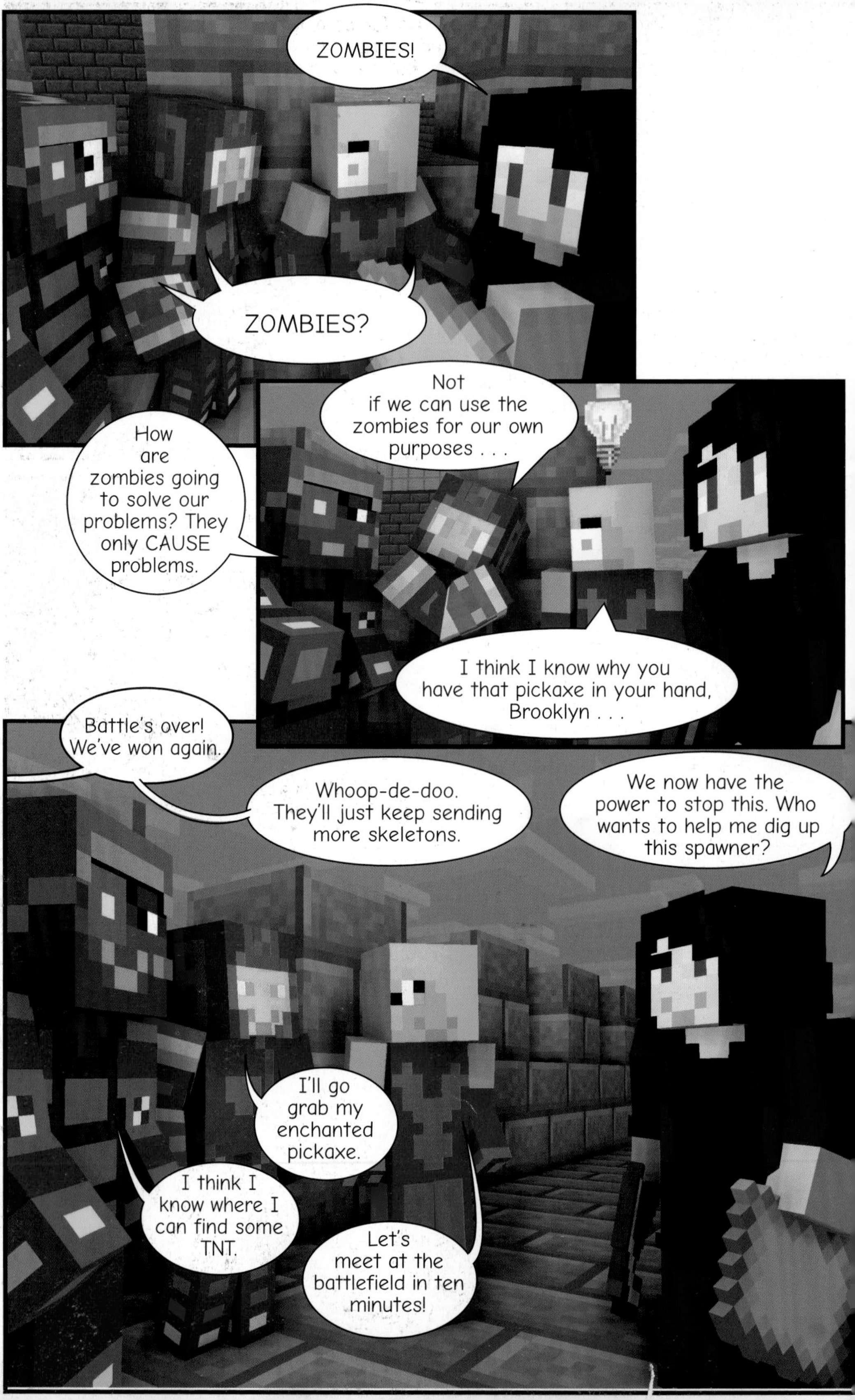
ZOMBIES!
ZOMBIES?
How are zombies going to solve our problems? They only CAUSE problems.
Not if we can use the zombies for our own purposes . . .
I think I know why you have that pickaxe in your hand, Brooklyn . . .
Battle's over! We've won again.
Whoop-de-doo. They'll just keep sending more skeletons.
We now have the power to stop this. Who wants to help me dig up this spawner?
I'll go grab my enchanted pickaxe.
I think I know where I can find some TNT.
Let's meet at the battlefield in ten minutes!

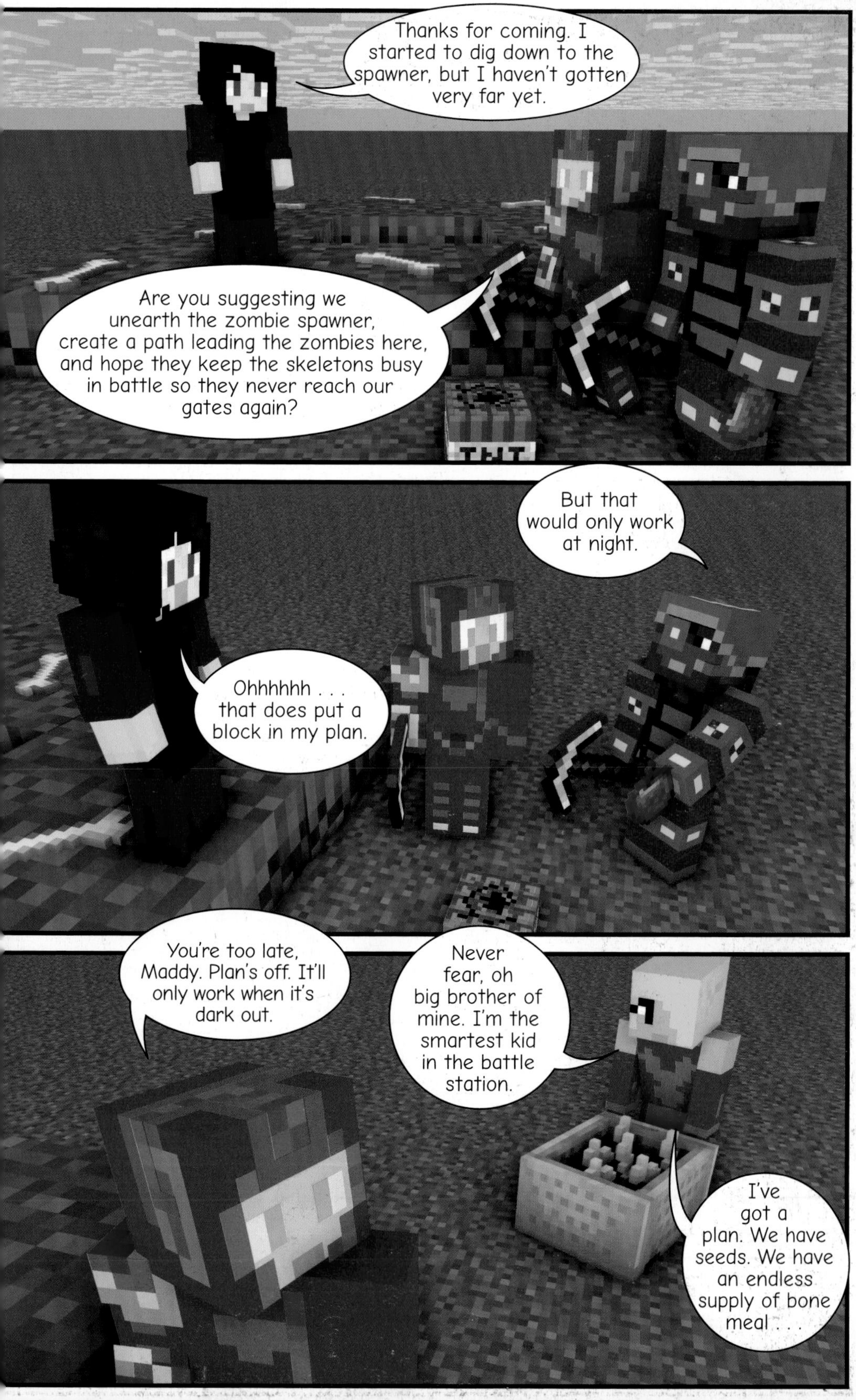
Thanks for coming. I started to dig down to the spawner, but I haven't gotten very far yet.
Are you suggesting we unearth the zombie spawner, create a path leading the zombies here, and hope they keep the skeletons busy in battle so they never reach our gates again?
But that would only work at night.
Ohhhhhh . . . that does put a block in my plan.
You're too late, Maddy. Plan's off. It'll only work when it's dark out.
Never fear, oh big brother of mine. I'm the smartest kid in the battle station.
I've got a plan. We have seeds. We have an endless supply of bone meal . . .

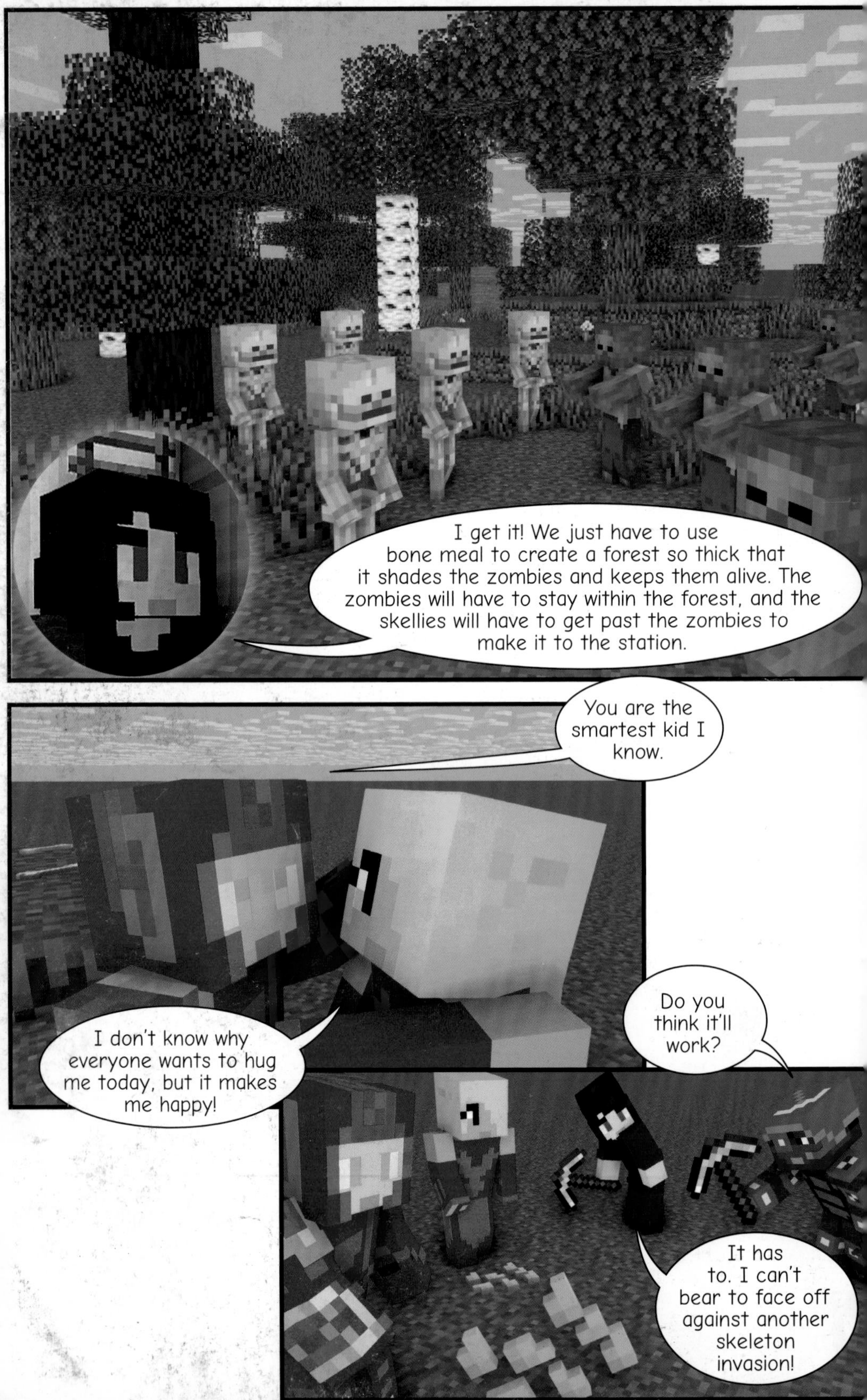
I get it! We just have to use bone meal to create a forest so thick that it shades the zombies and keeps them alive. The zombies will have to stay within the forest, and the skellies will have to get past the zombies to make it to the station.
You are the smartest kid I know.
I don't know why everyone wants to hug me today, but it makes me happy!
Do you think it'll work?
It has to. I can't bear to face off against another skeleton invasion!

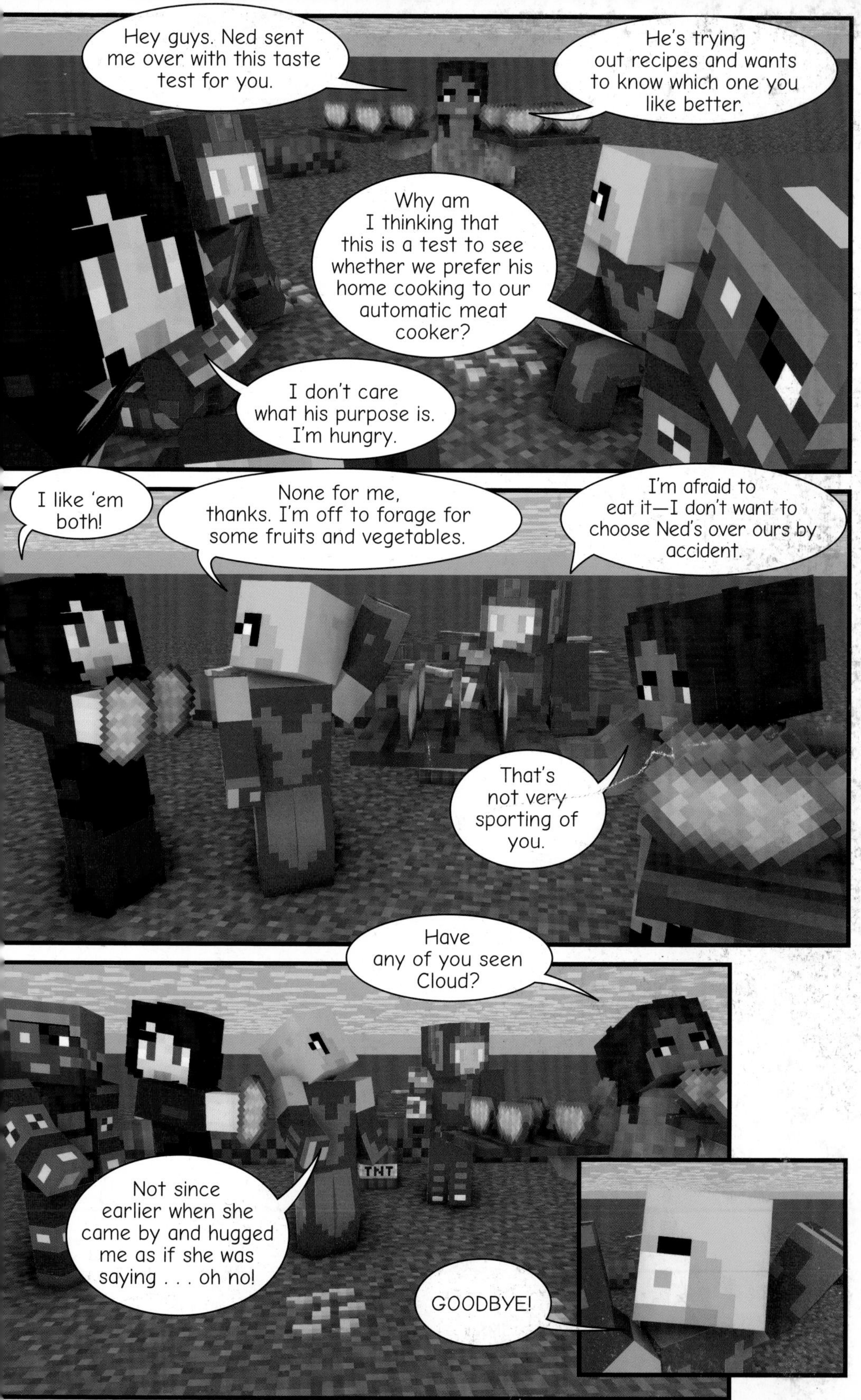
Hey guys. Ned sent me over with this taste test for you.
He's trying out recipes and wants to know which one you like better.
Why am I thinking that this is a test to see whether we prefer his home cooking to our automatic meat cooker?
I don't care what his purpose is. I'm hungry.
I like 'em both!
None for me, thanks. I'm off to forage for some fruits and vegetables.
I'm afraid to eat it—I don't want to choose Ned's over ours by accident.
That's not very sporting of you.
Have any of you seen Cloud?
Not since earlier when she came by and hugged me as if she was saying . . . oh no!
GOODBYE!
TNT

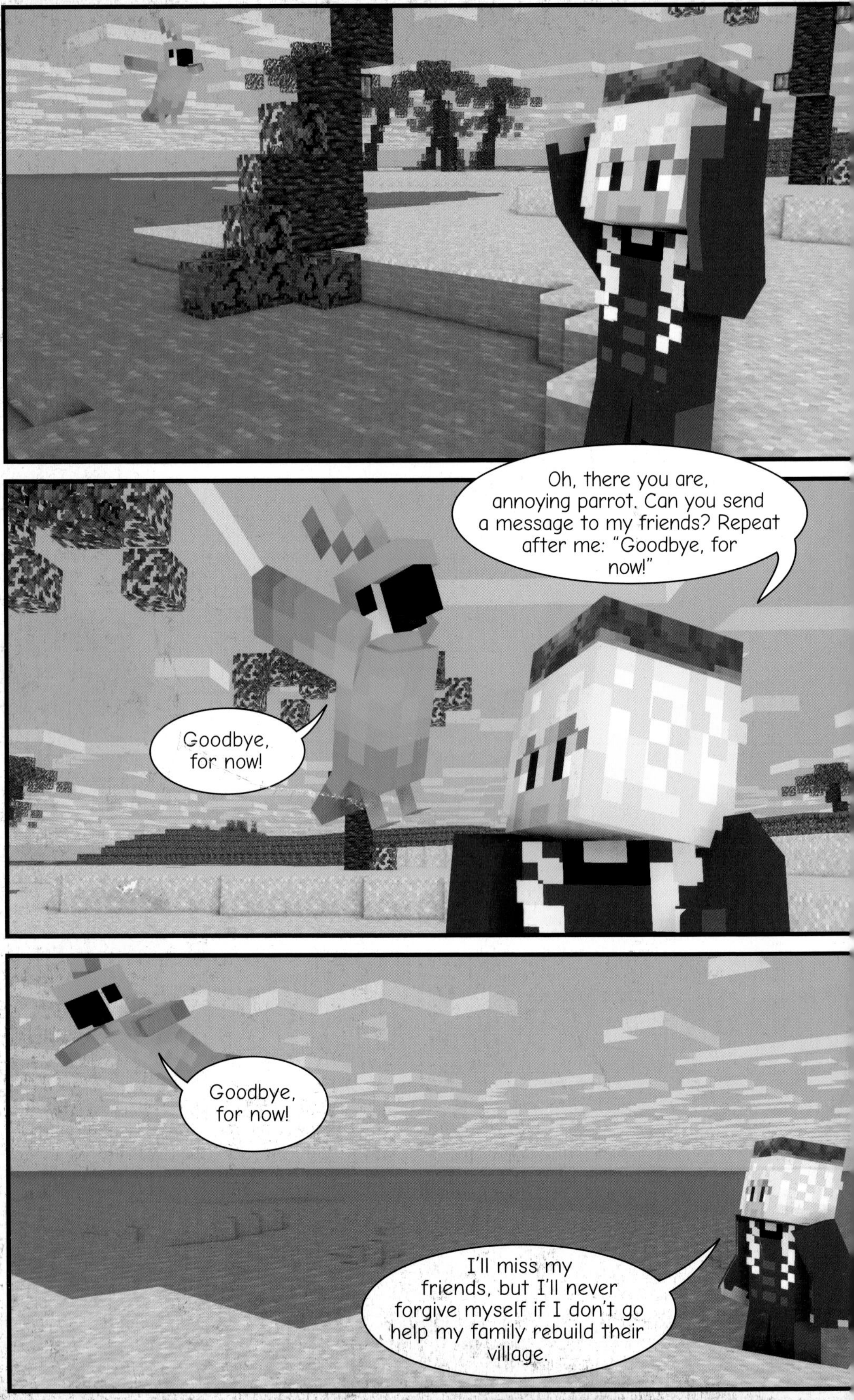
Oh, there you are, annoying parrot. Can you send a message to my friends? Repeat after me: "Goodbye, for now!"
Goodbye, for now!
Goodbye, for now!
I'll miss my friends, but I'll never forgive myself if I don't go help my family rebuild their village.

CHAPTER 2

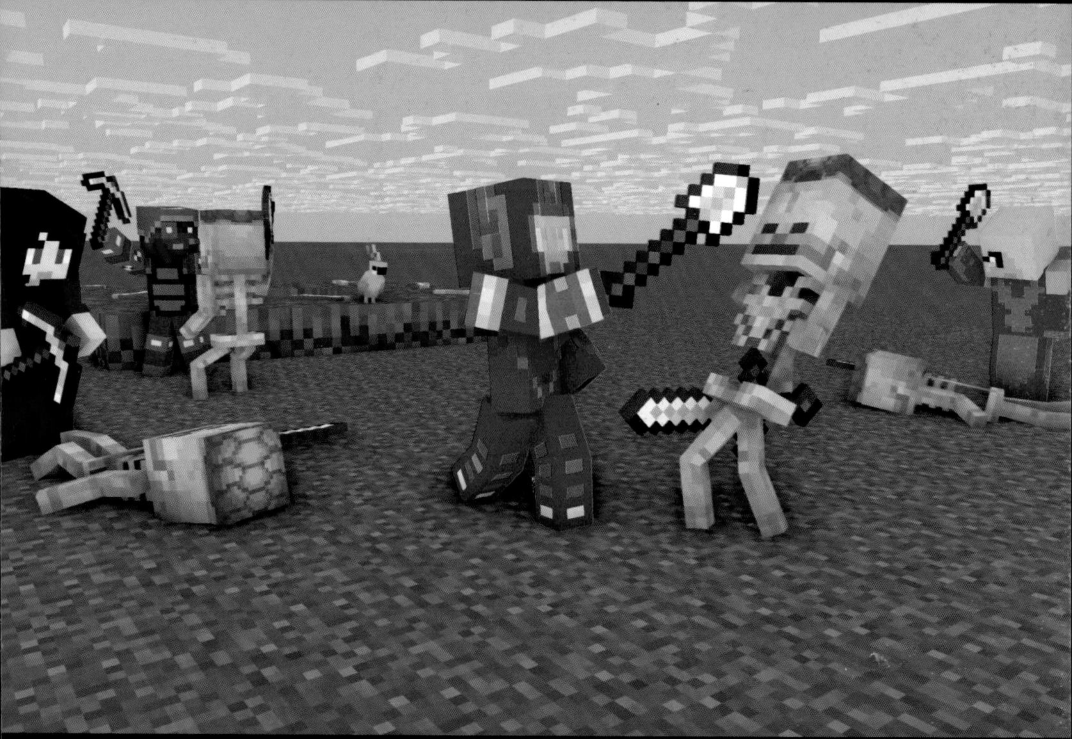

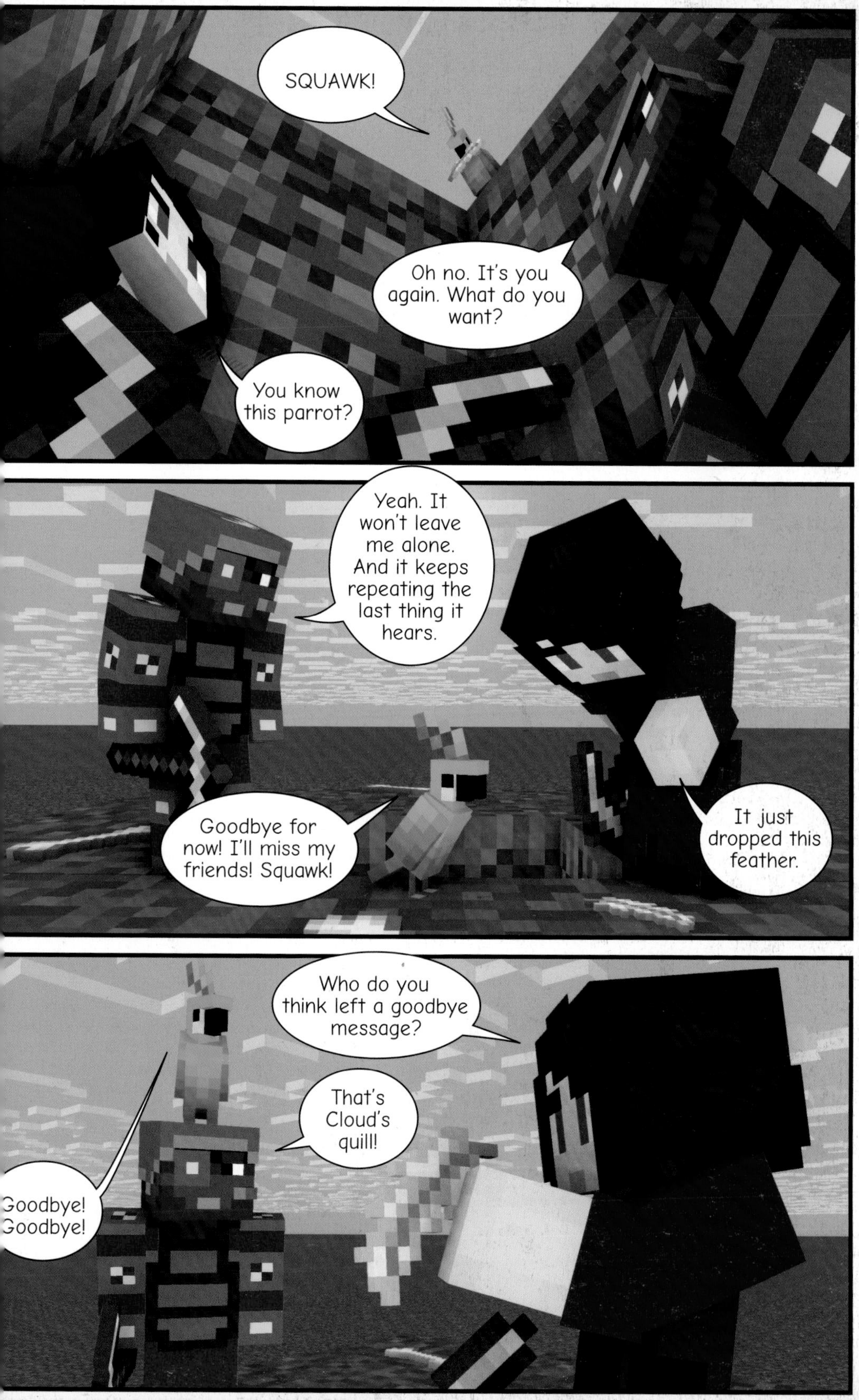
SQUAWK!
Oh no. It's you again. What do you want?
You know this parrot?
Yeah. It won't leave me alone. And it keeps repeating the last thing it hears.
Goodbye for now! I'll miss my friends! Squawk!
It just dropped this feather.
Who do you think left a goodbye message?
That's Cloud's quill!
Goodbye! Goodbye!

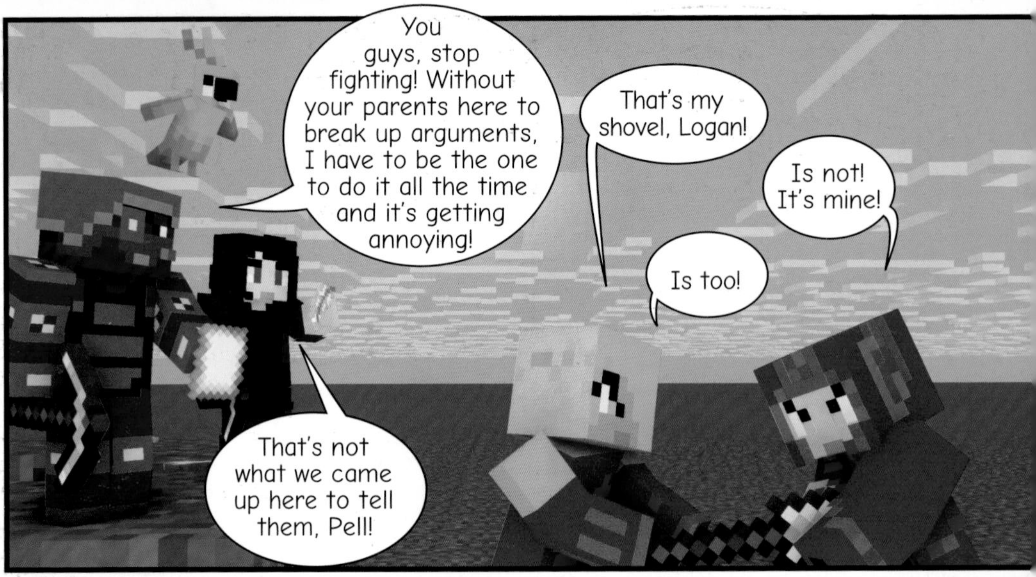
You guys, stop fighting! Without your parents here to break up arguments, I have to be the one to do it all the time and it's getting annoying!
That's not what we came up here to tell them, Pell!
That's my shovel, Logan!
Is too!
Is not! It's mine!

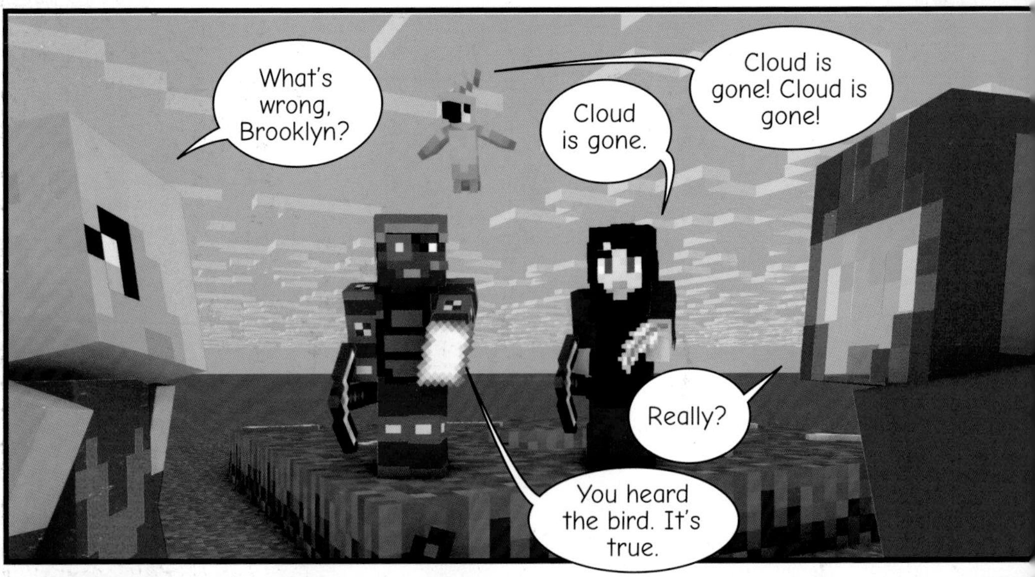
What's wrong, Brooklyn?
Cloud is gone! Cloud is gone!
Cloud is gone.
Really?
You heard the bird. It's true.

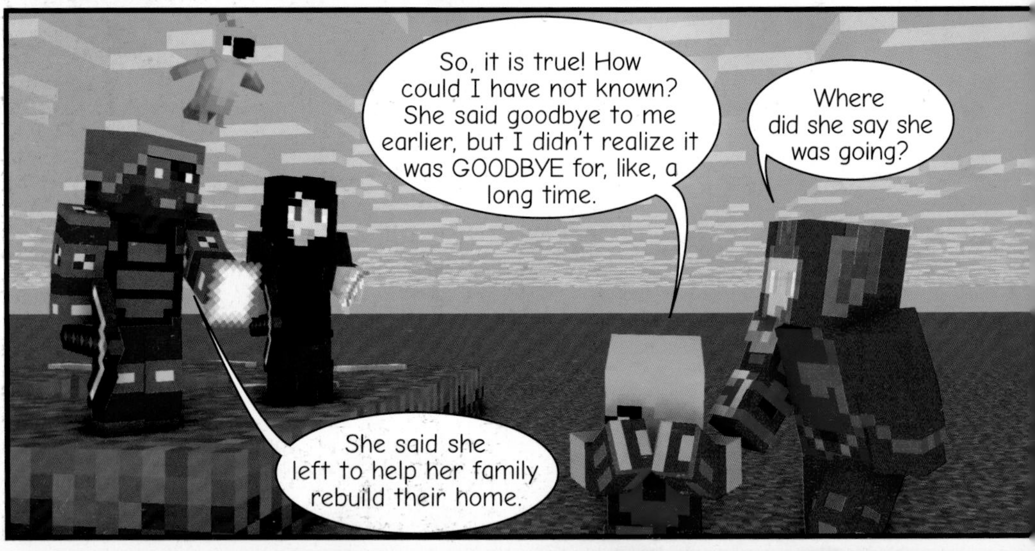
So, it is true! How could I have not known? She said goodbye to me earlier, but I didn't realize it was GOODBYE for, like, a long time.
Where did she say she was going?
She said she left to help her family rebuild their home.

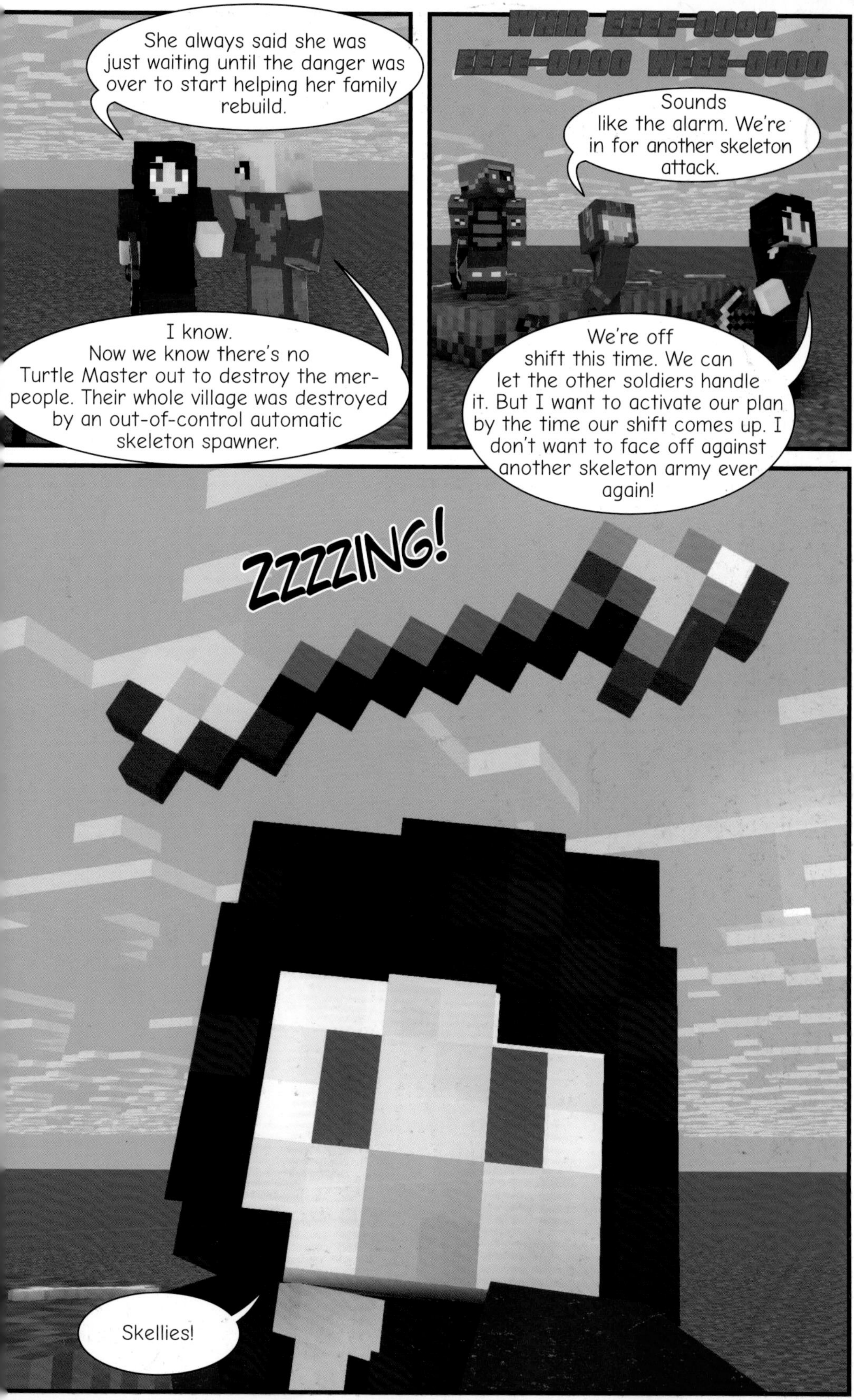
She always said she was just waiting until the danger was over to start helping her family rebuild.
I know. Now we know there's no Turtle Master out to destroy the mer-people. Their whole village was destroyed by an out-of-control automatic skeleton spawner.
WHIR EEEE-OOOO EEEE-OOOO WEEE-OOOO
Sounds like the alarm. We're in for another skeleton attack.
We're off shift this time. We can let the other soldiers handle it. But I want to activate our plan by the time our shift comes up. I don't want to face off against another skeleton army ever again!
ZZZZING!
Skellies!

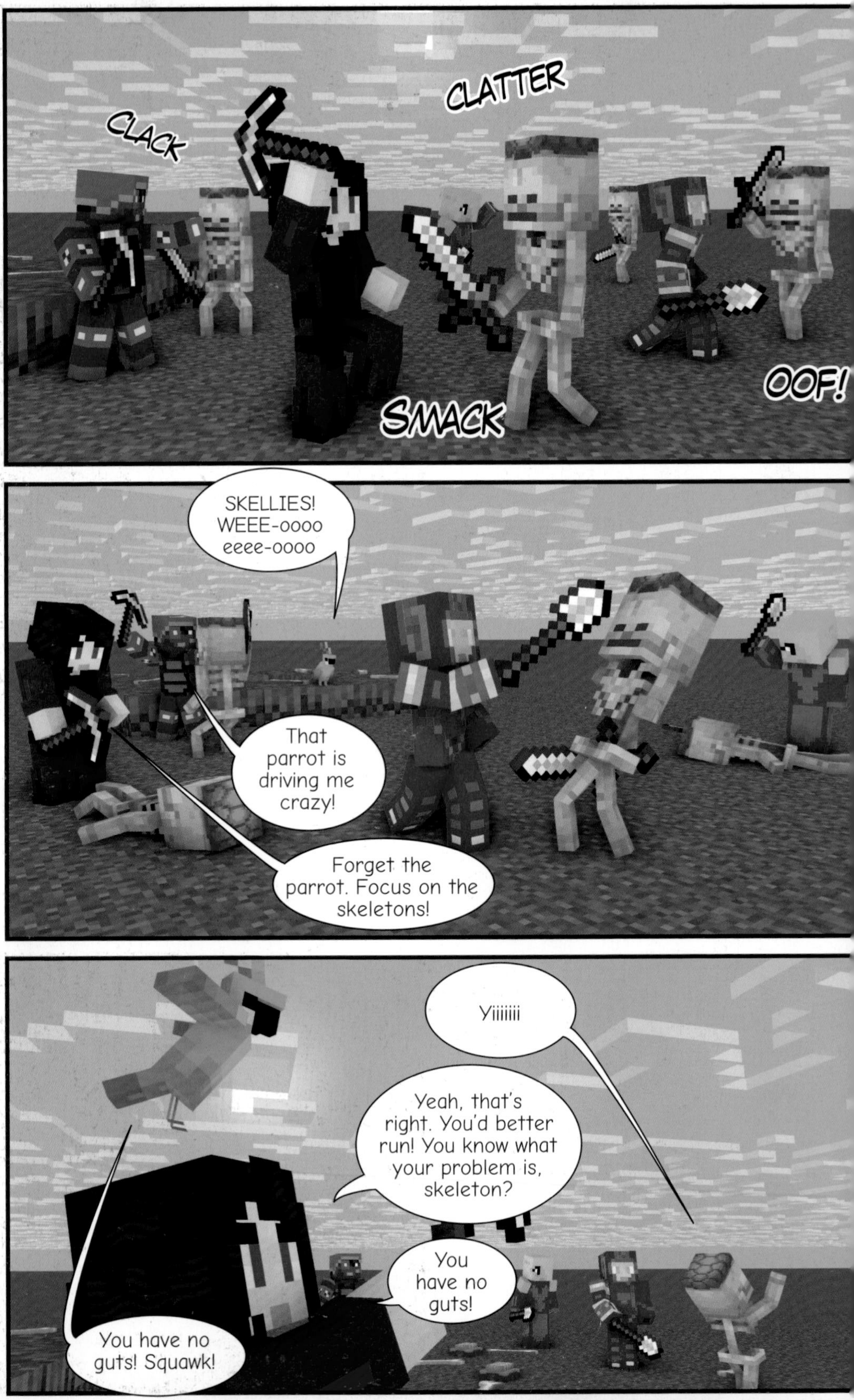
CLACK
CLATTER
SMACK
OOF!
SKELLIES! WEEE-oooo eeee-oooo
That parrot is driving me crazy!
Forget the parrot. Focus on the skeletons!
Yiiiiiii
Yeah, that's right. You'd better run! You know what your problem is, skeleton?
You have no guts!
You have no guts! Squawk!

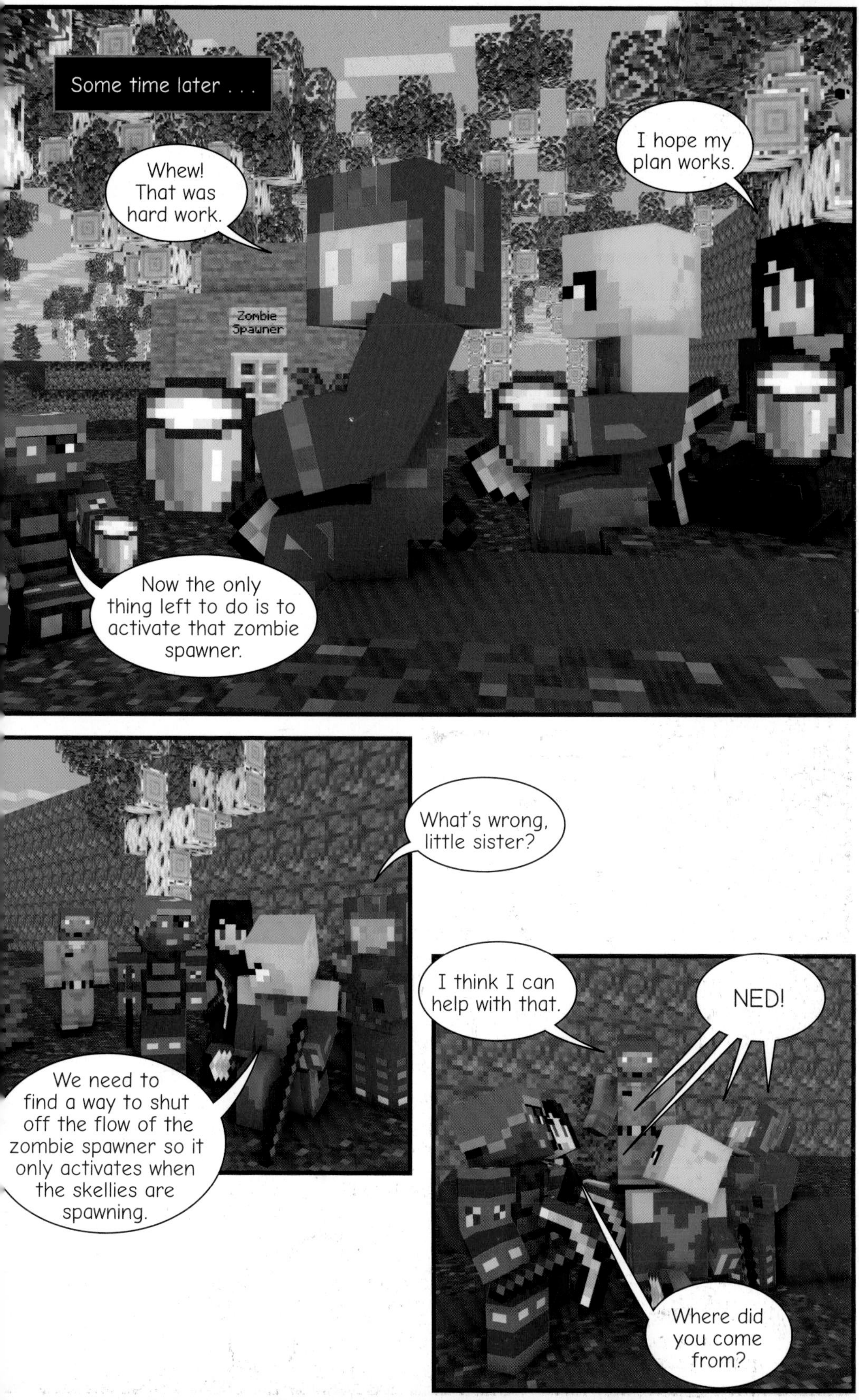
Some time later . . .
Zombie Spawner
Whew! That was hard work.
I hope my plan works.
Now the only thing left to do is to activate that zombie spawner.
What's wrong, little sister?
We need to find a way to shut off the flow of the zombie spawner so it only activates when the skellies are spawning.
I think I can help with that.
NED!
Where did you come from?

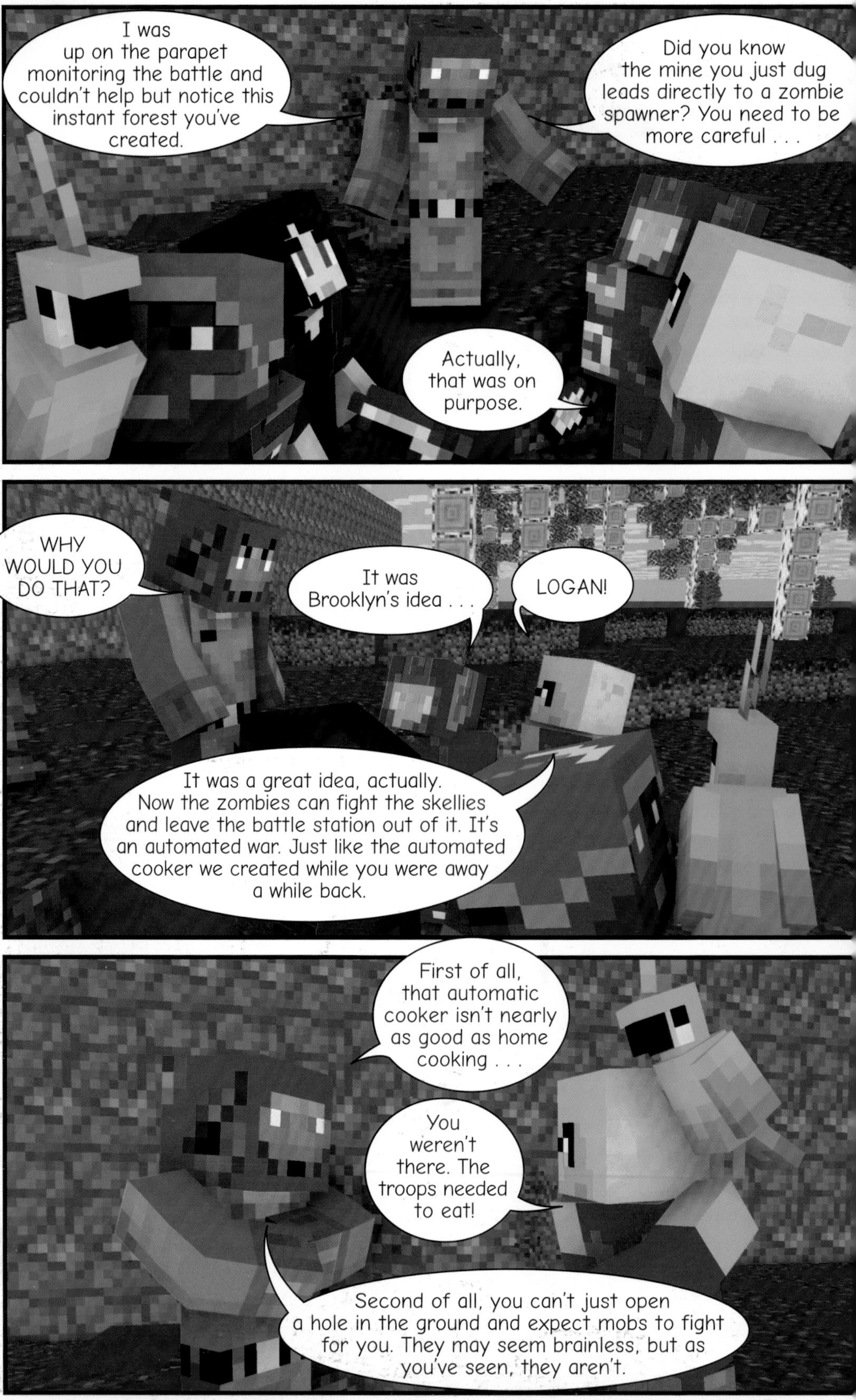

I was up on the parapet monitoring the battle and couldn't help but notice this instant forest you've created.
Did you know the mine you just dug leads directly to a zombie spawner? You need to be more careful . . .
Actually, that was on purpose.
WHY WOULD YOU DO THAT?
It was Brooklyn's idea . . .
LOGAN!
It was a great idea, actually. Now the zombies can fight the skellies and leave the battle station out of it. It's an automated war. Just like the automated cooker we created while you were away a while back.
First of all, that automatic cooker isn't nearly as good as home cooking . . .
You weren't there. The troops needed to eat!
Second of all, you can't just open a hole in the ground and expect mobs to fight for you. They may seem brainless, but as you've seen, they aren't.

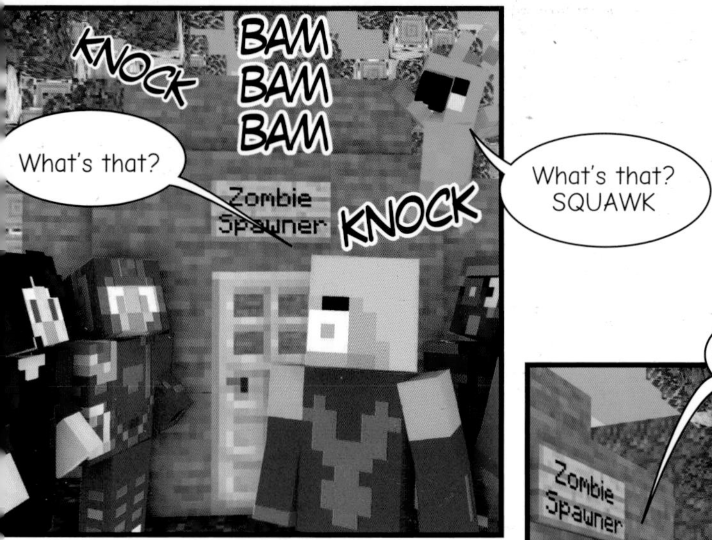
KNOCK
BAM
BAM
BAM
What's that?
Zombie Spawner
KNOCK
What's that? SQUAWK

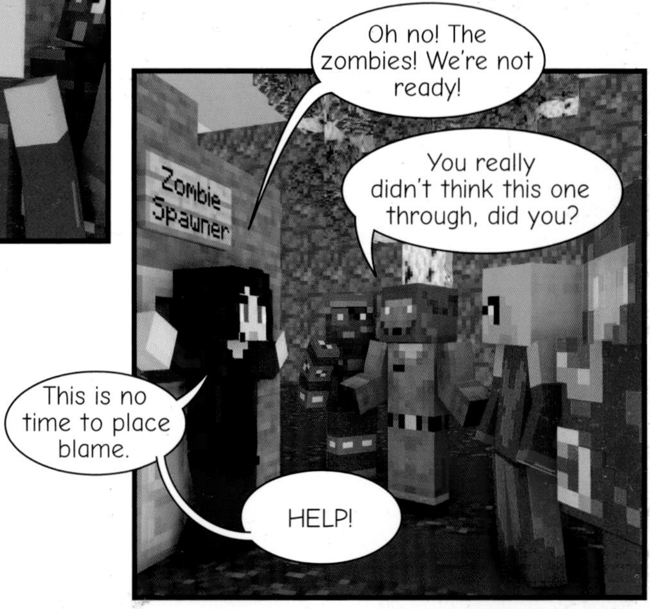
Oh no! The zombies! We're not ready!
Zombie Spawner
You really didn't think this one through, did you?
This is no time to place blame.
HELP!

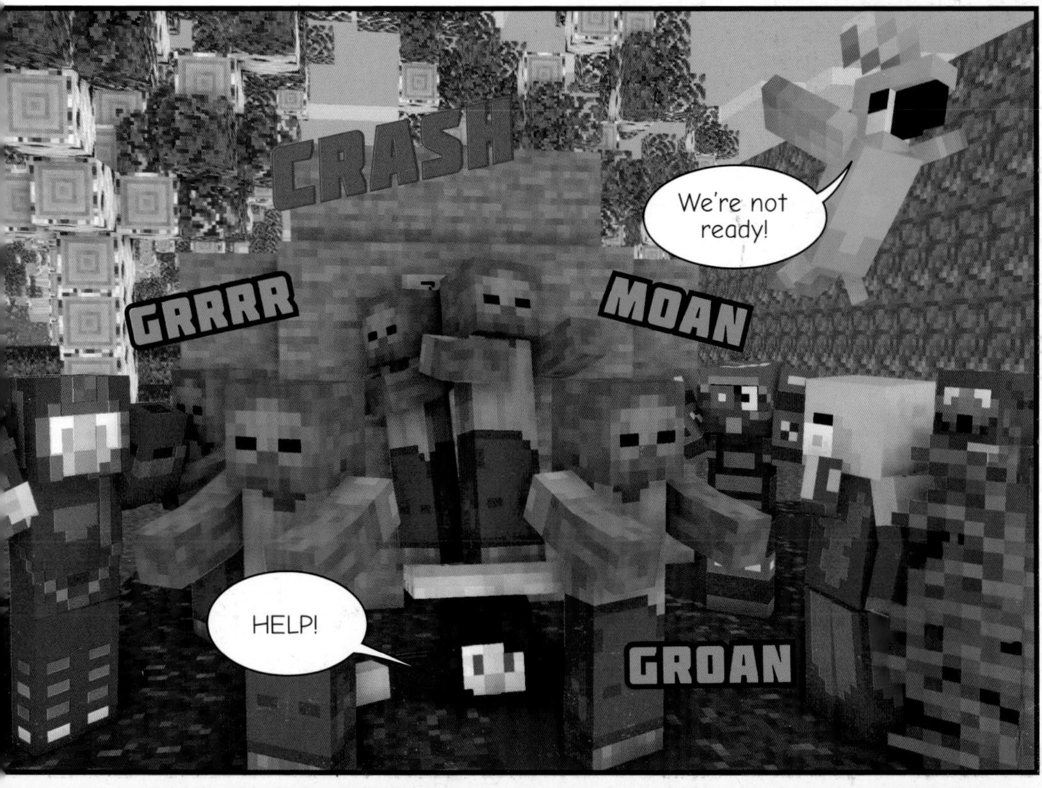
CRASH
We're not ready!
GRRRR
MOAN
HELP!
GROAN

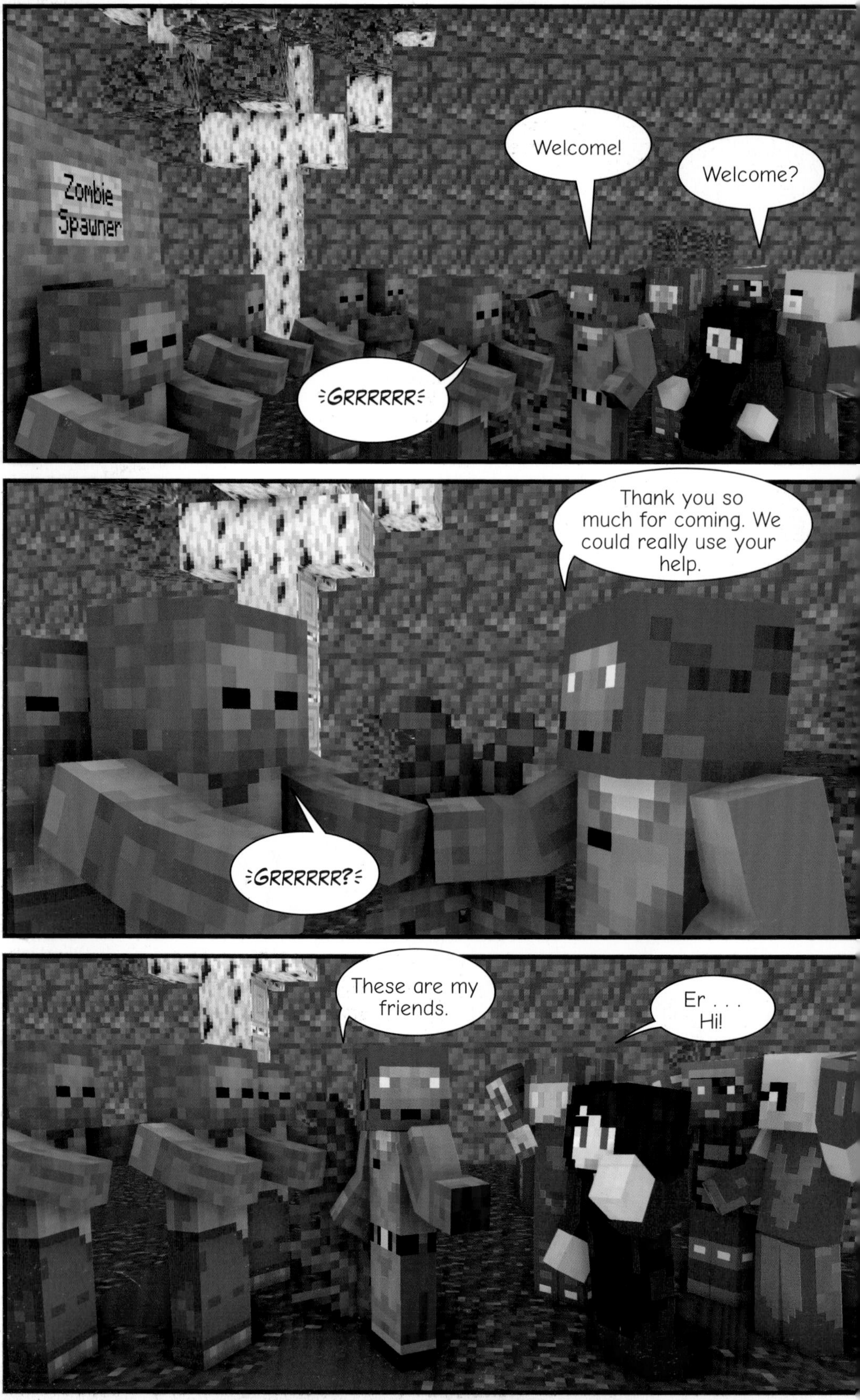
Zombie Spawner
Welcome!
Welcome?
GRRRRRR
Thank you so much for coming. We could really use your help.
GRRRRRR?
These are my friends.
Er . . . Hi!

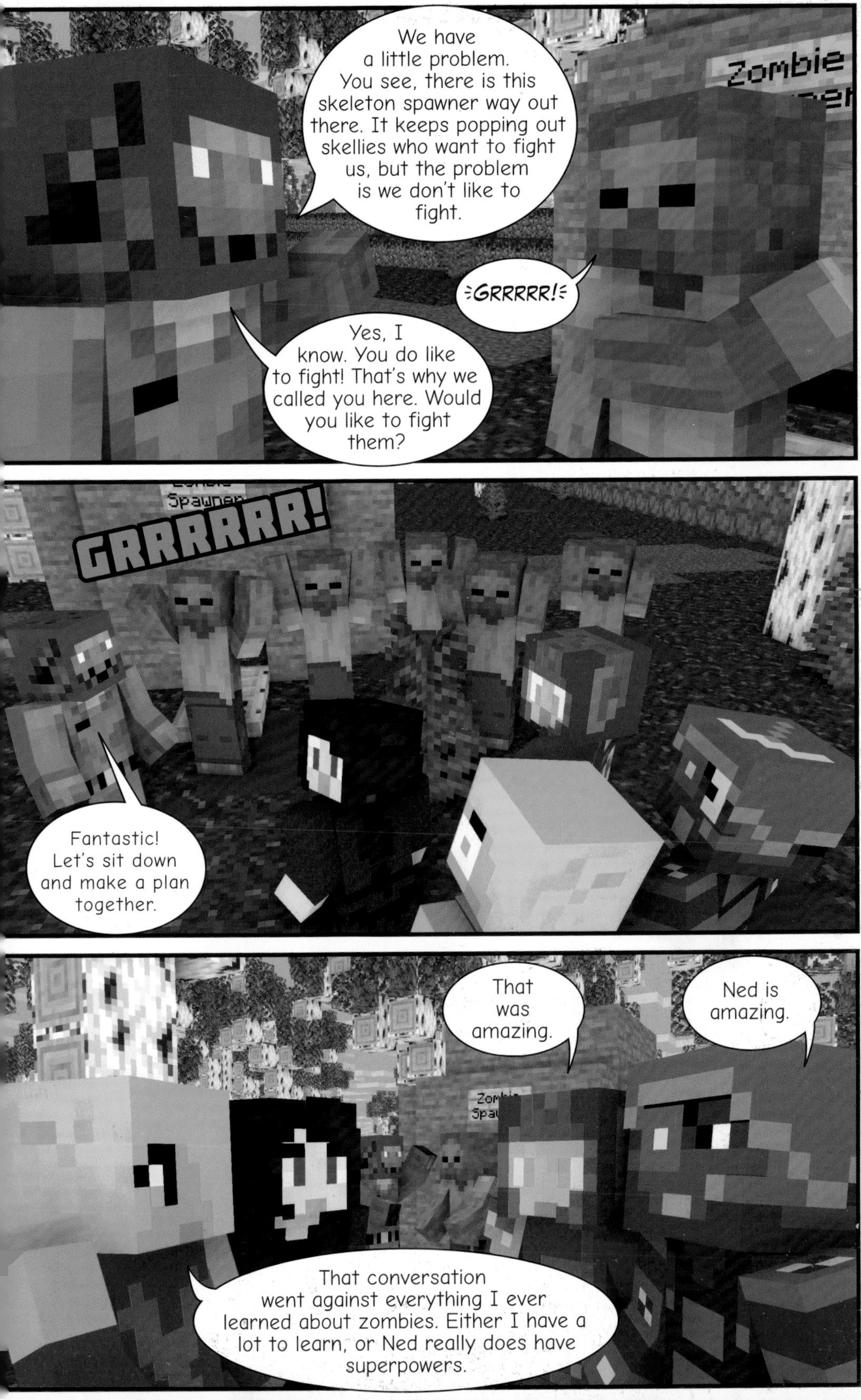
Zombie
We have a little problem. You see, there is this skeleton spawner way out there. It keeps popping out skellies who want to fight us, but the problem is we don't like to fight.
GRRRRR!
Yes, I know. You do like to fight! That's why we called you here. Would you like to fight them?
Spawner
GRRRRRR!
Fantastic! Let's sit down and make a plan together.
That was amazing.
Ned is amazing.
That conversation went against everything I ever learned about zombies. Either I have a lot to learn, or Ned really does have superpowers.

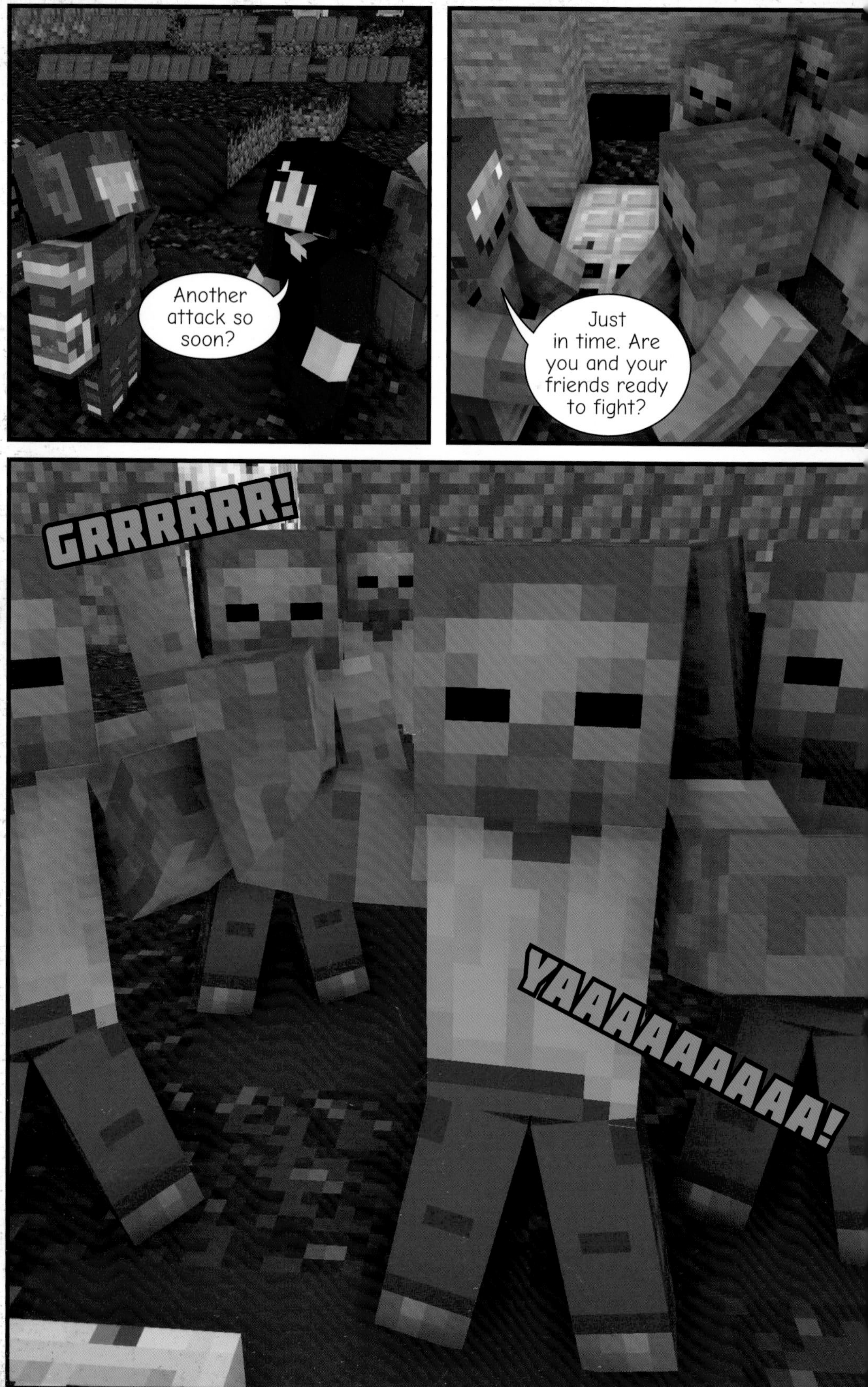
Another attack so soon?
Just in time. Are you and your friends ready to fight?
GRRRRRR!
YAAAAAAAAA!

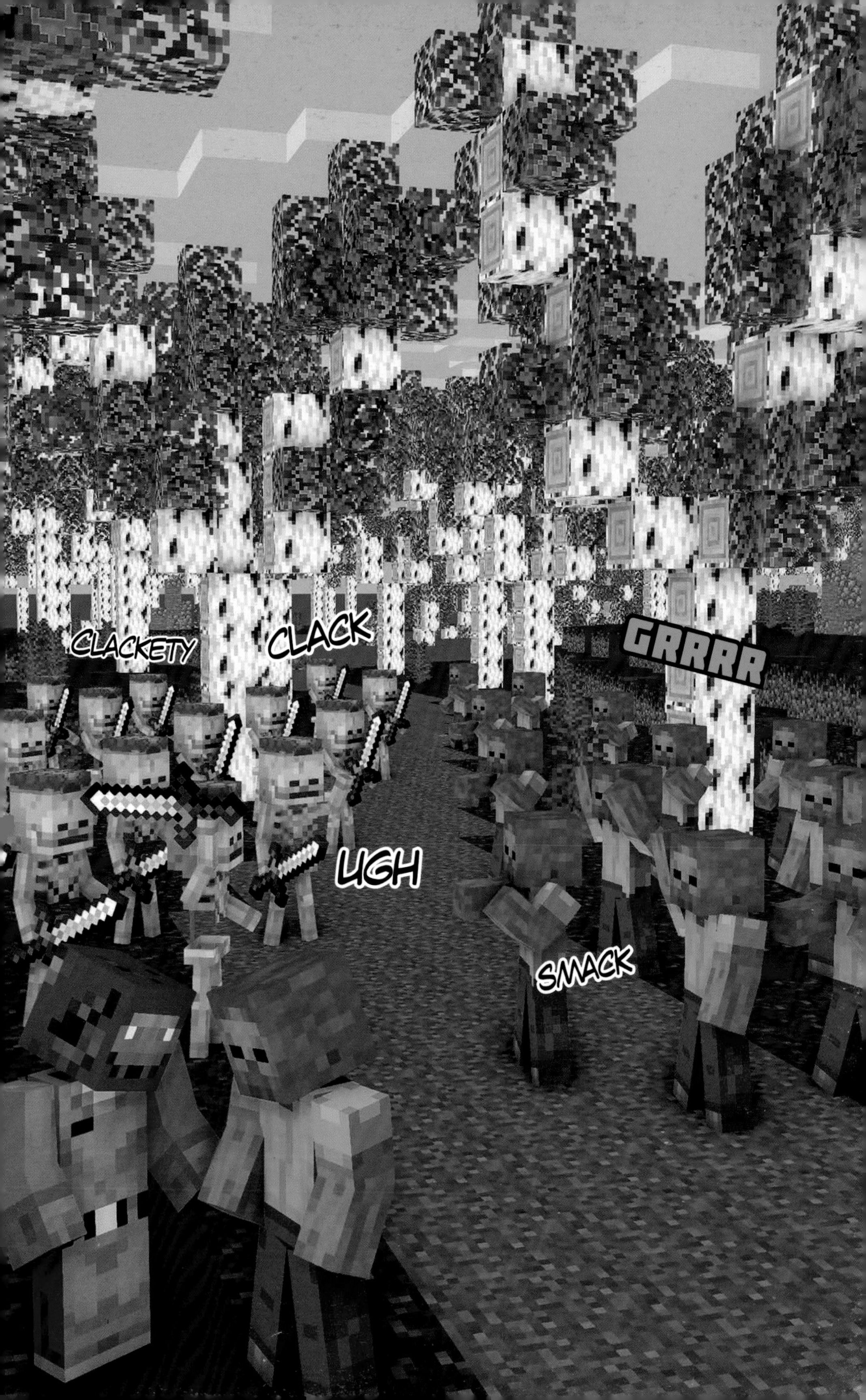
CLACKETY
CLACK
GRRRR
UGH
SMACK

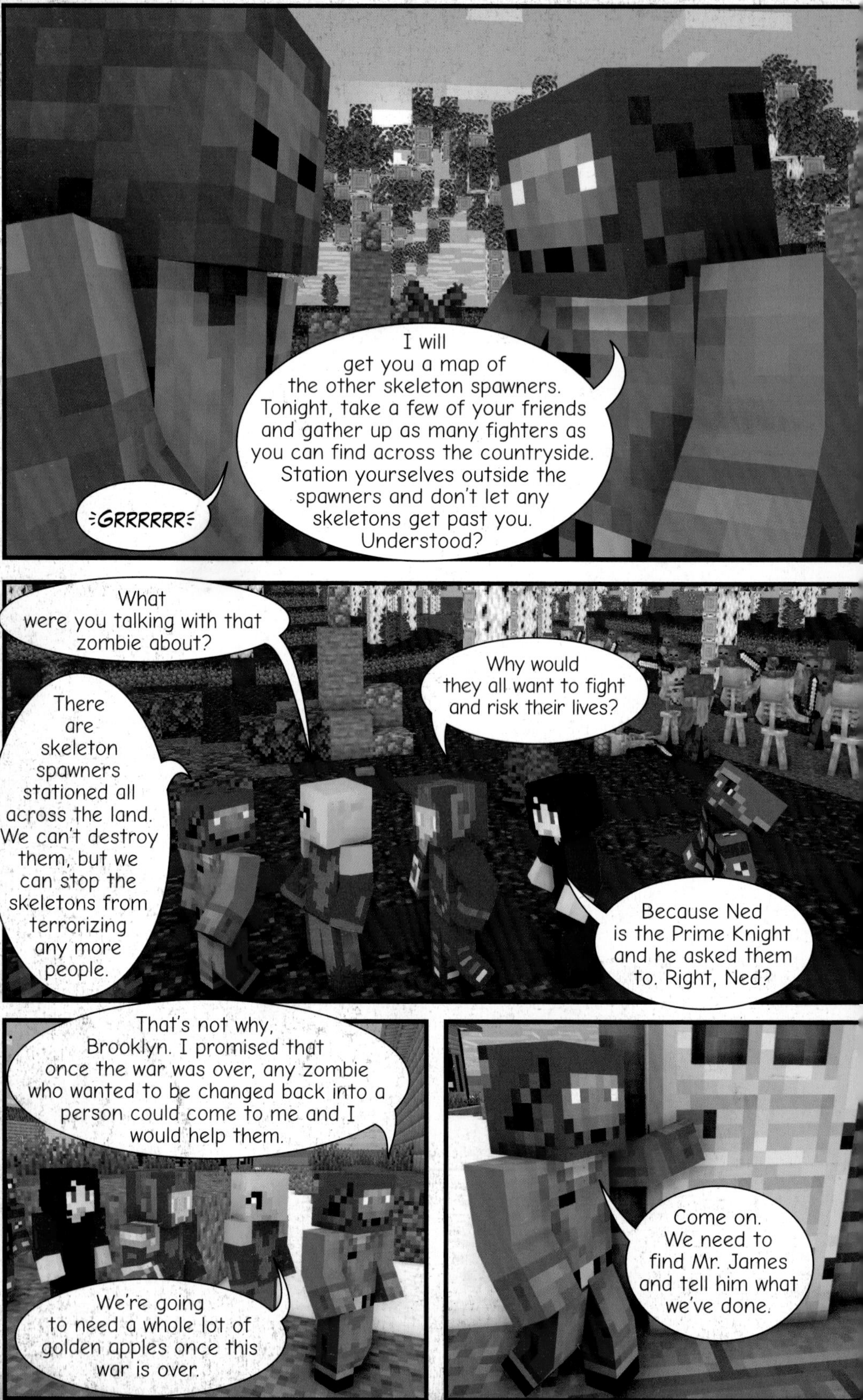
I will get you a map of the other skeleton spawners. Tonight, take a few of your friends and gather up as many fighters as you can find across the countryside. Station yourselves outside the spawners and don't let any skeletons get past you. Understood?
GRRRRRR
What were you talking with that zombie about?
There are skeleton spawners stationed all across the land. We can't destroy them, but we can stop the skeletons from terrorizing any more people.
Why would they all want to fight and risk their lives?
Because Ned is the Prime Knight and he asked them to. Right, Ned?
That's not why, Brooklyn. I promised that once the war was over, any zombie who wanted to be changed back into a person could come to me and I would help them.
We're going to need a whole lot of golden apples once this war is over.
Come on. We need to find Mr. James and tell him what we've done.

CHAPTER 3

ENDINGS AND
BEGINNINGS

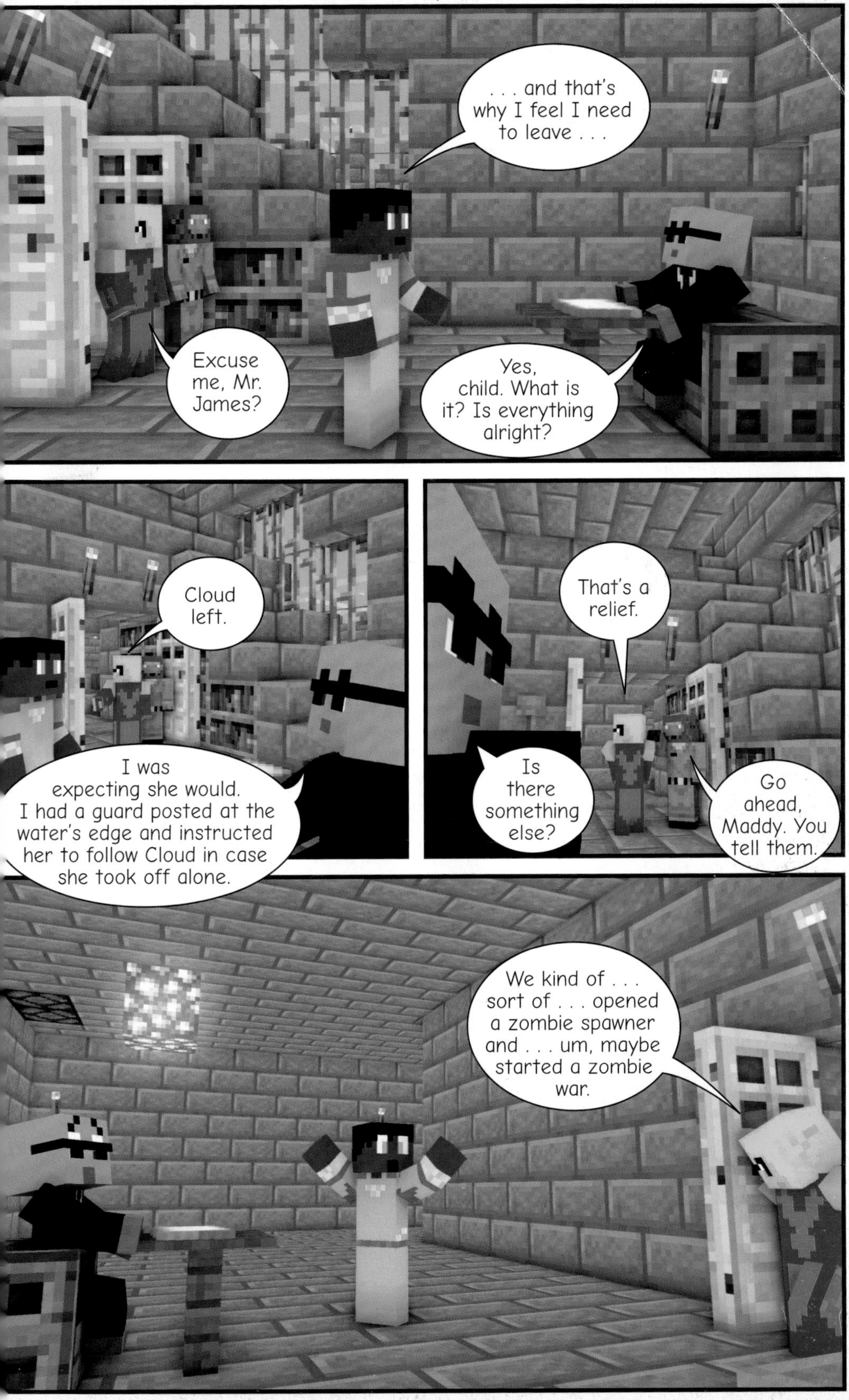
. . . and that's why I feel I need to leave . . .
Excuse me, Mr. James?
Yes, child. What is it? Is everything alright?
Cloud left.
I was expecting she would. I had a guard posted at the water's edge and instructed her to follow Cloud in case she took off alone.
That's a relief.
Is there something else?
Go ahead, Maddy. You tell them.
We kind of . . . sort of . . . opened a zombie spawner and . . . um, maybe started a zombie war.

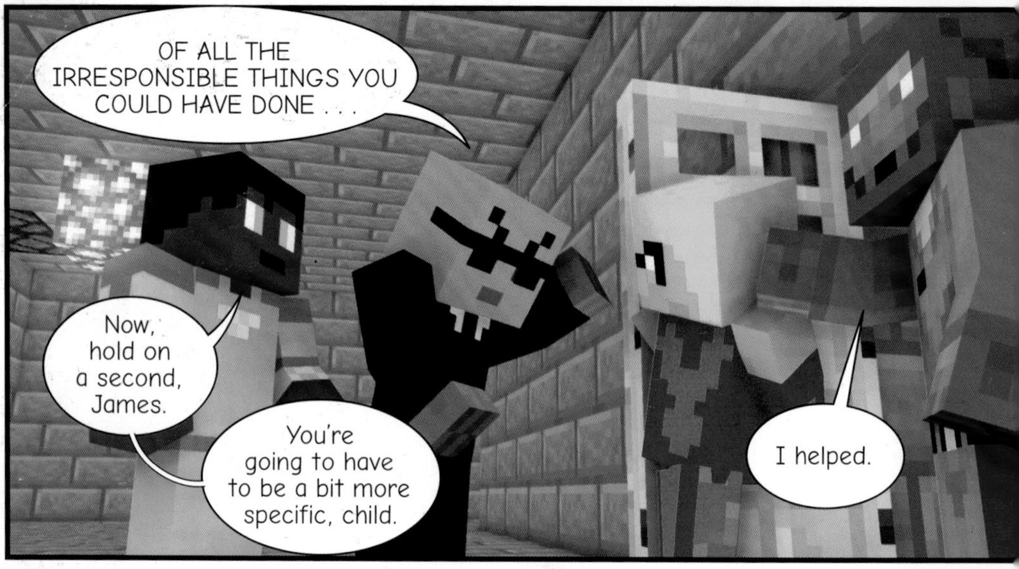
OF ALL THE IRRESPONSIBLE THINGS YOU COULD HAVE DONE . . .
Now, hold on a second, James.
You're going to have to be a bit more specific, child.
I helped.

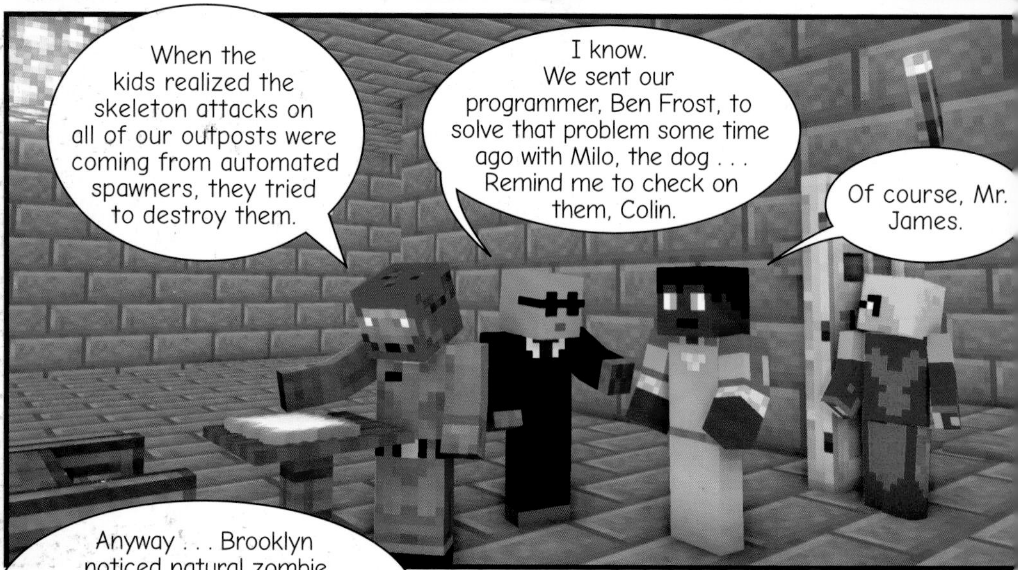
When the kids realized the skeleton attacks on all of our outposts were coming from automated spawners, they tried to destroy them.
I know. We sent our programmer, Ben Frost, to solve that problem some time ago with Milo, the dog . . . Remind me to check on them, Colin.
Of course, Mr. James.

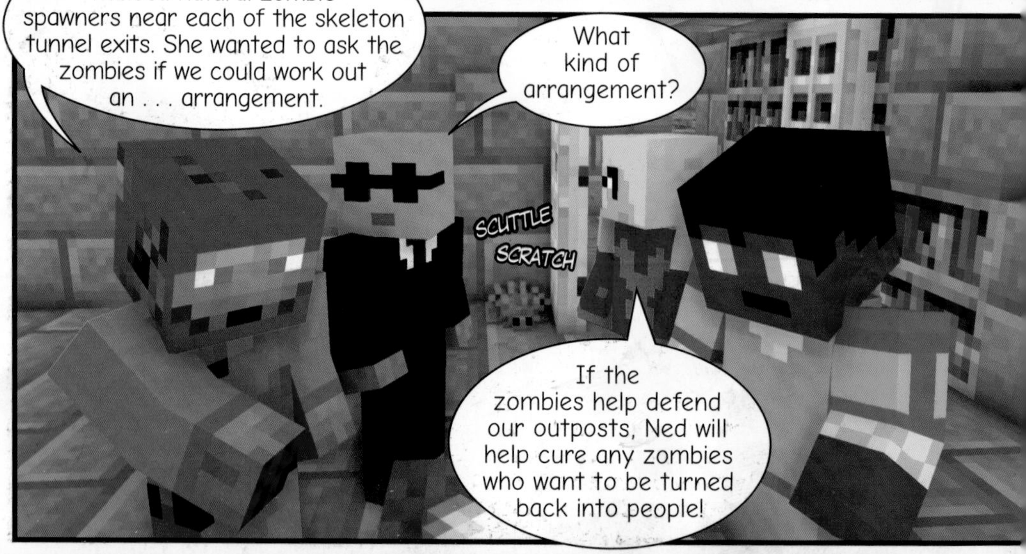
Anyway . . . Brooklyn noticed natural zombie spawners near each of the skeleton tunnel exits. She wanted to ask the zombies if we could work out an . . . arrangement.
What kind of arrangement?
SCUTTLE
SCRATCH
If the zombies help defend our outposts, Ned will help cure any zombies who want to be turned back into people!

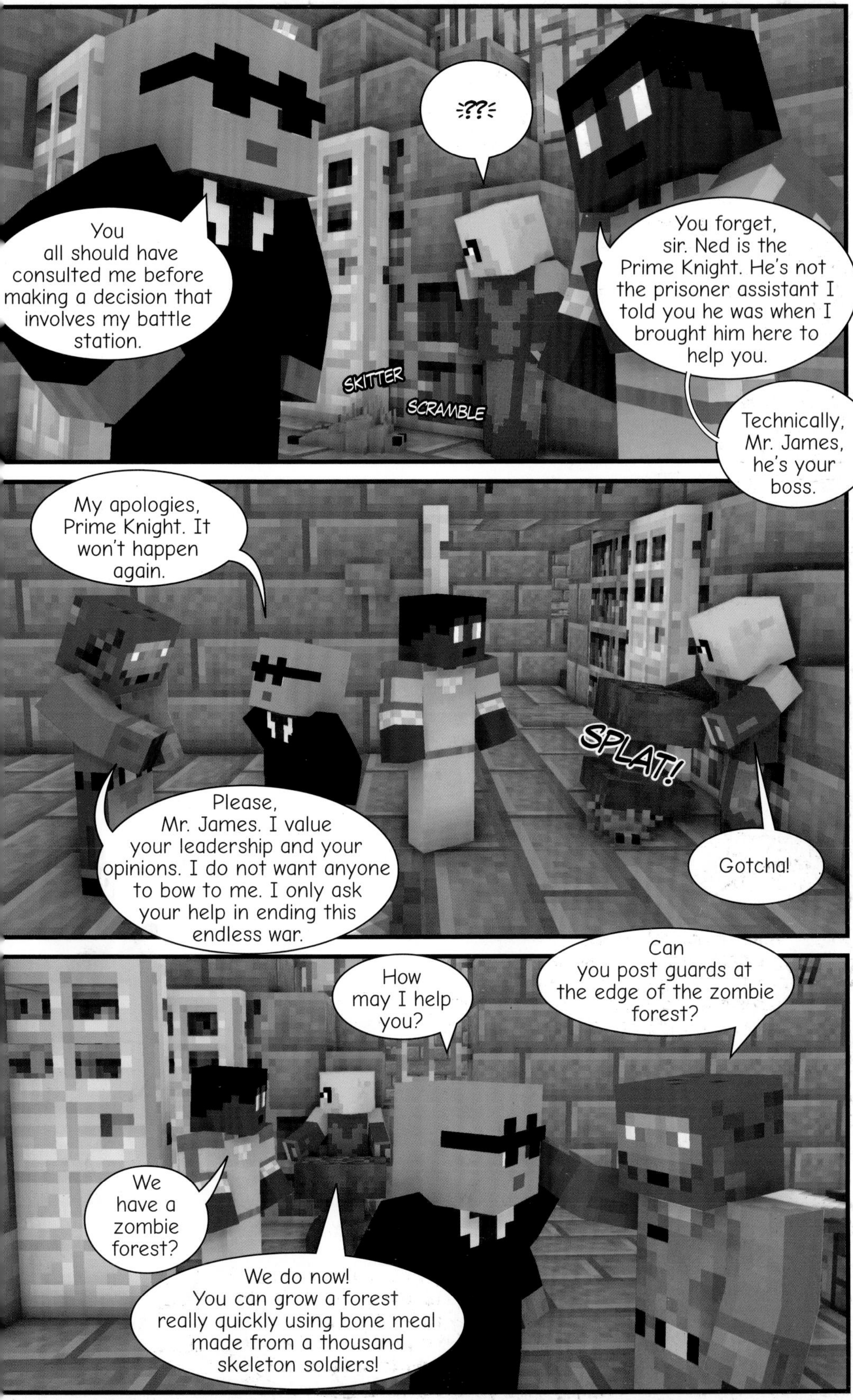
You all should have consulted me before making a decision that involves my battle station.
???
SKITTER
SCRAMBLE
You forget, sir. Ned is the Prime Knight. He's not the prisoner assistant I told you he was when I brought him here to help you.
Technically, Mr. James, he's your boss.
My apologies, Prime Knight. It won't happen again.
SPLAT!
Please, Mr. James. I value your leadership and your opinions. I do not want anyone to bow to me. I only ask your help in ending this endless war.
Gotcha!
How may I help you?
Can you post guards at the edge of the zombie forest?
We have a zombie forest?
We do now! You can grow a forest really quickly using bone meal made from a thousand skeleton soldiers!

Tell us all about it over lunch.

I'll cook!

I made a batch of cakes this morning.

I love your cakes, Pell's Uncle Colin!

Just "Colin" is fine, Maddy.

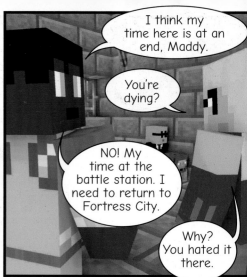

I think my time here is at an end, Maddy.

You're dying?

NO! My time at the battle station. I need to return to Fortress City.

Why? You hated it there.

I received a letter from my sister, Tia. She wants to start a revolution. Thanks to you kids, people are ready for change.

I'll lead our secret operations from a back room in my bakery.

If you go back, you can help make sure people are treated fairly.

That's right. No more bullies. Now, I have to figure out how to tell the others.

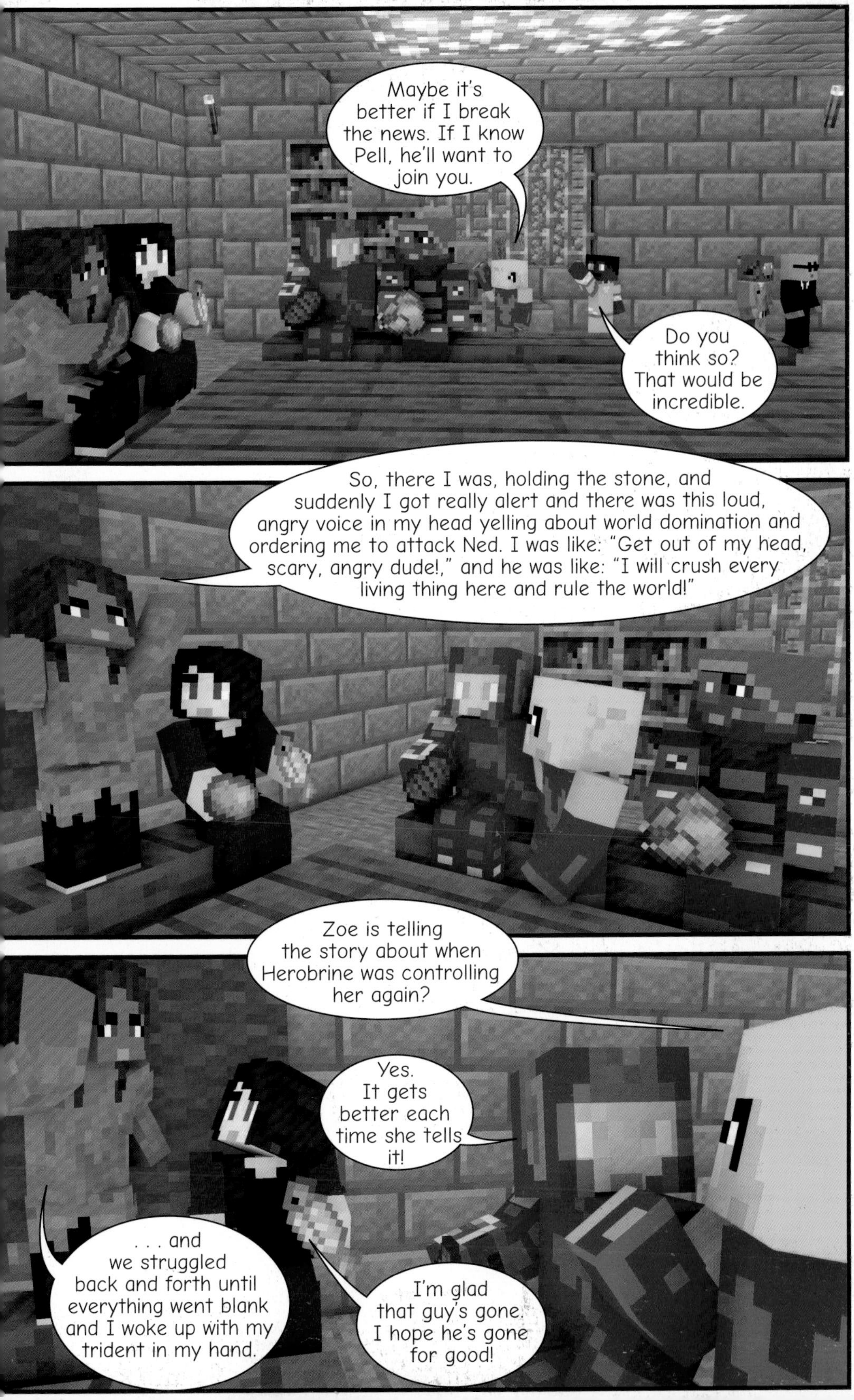
Maybe it's better if I break the news. If I know Pell, he'll want to join you.
Do you think so? That would be incredible.
So, there I was, holding the stone, and suddenly I got really alert and there was this loud, angry voice in my head yelling about world domination and ordering me to attack Ned. I was like: "Get out of my head, scary, angry dude!," and he was like: "I will crush every living thing here and rule the world!"
Zoe is telling the story about when Herobrine was controlling her again?
Yes. It gets better each time she tells it!
. . . and we struggled back and forth until everything went blank and I woke up with my trident in my hand.
I'm glad that guy's gone. I hope he's gone for good!

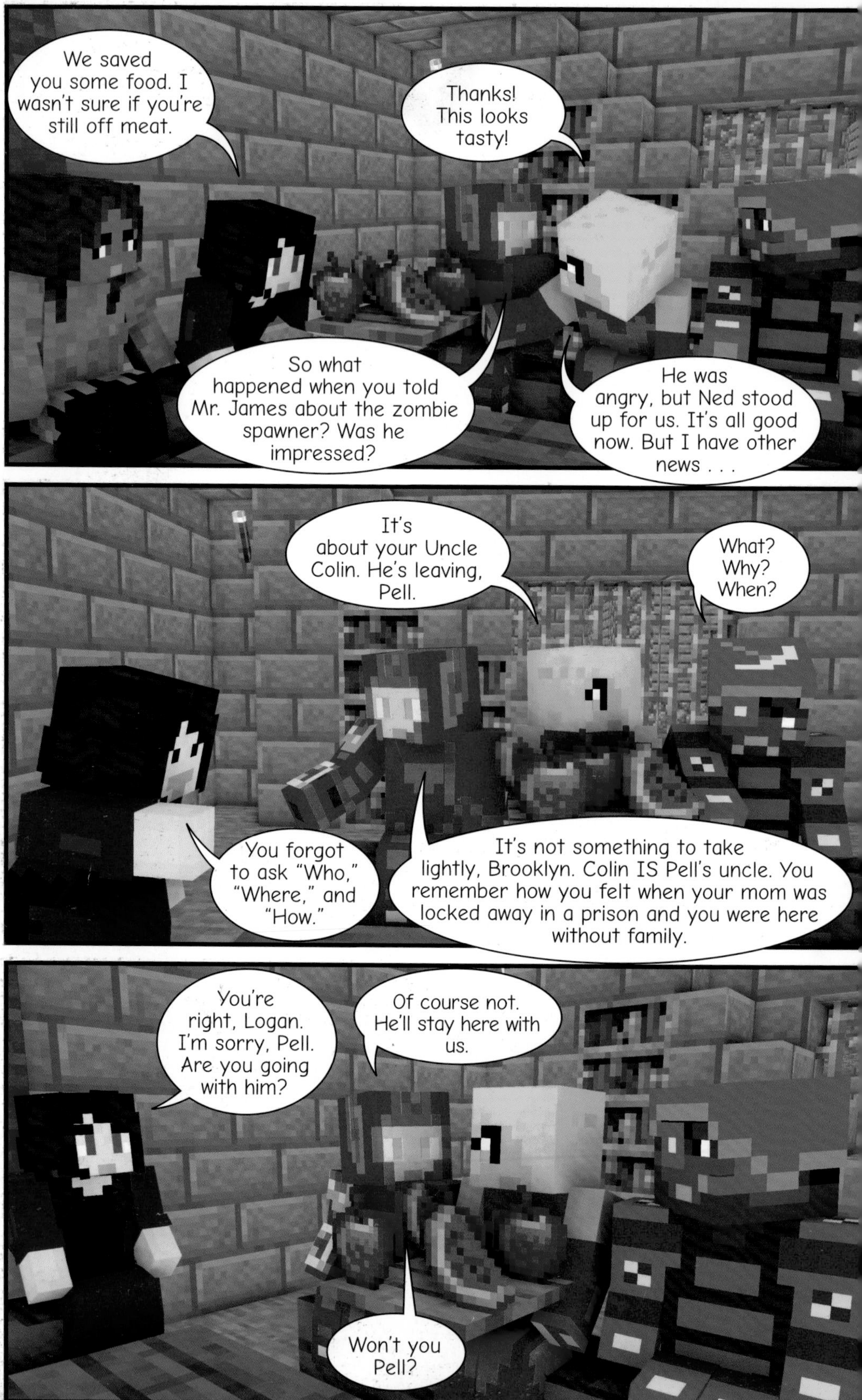

We saved you some food. I wasn't sure if you're still off meat.
Thanks! This looks tasty!
So what happened when you told Mr. James about the zombie spawner? Was he impressed?
He was angry, but Ned stood up for us. It's all good now. But I have other news . . .
It's about your Uncle Colin. He's leaving, Pell.
What? Why? When?
You forgot to ask "Who," "Where," and "How."
It's not something to take lightly, Brooklyn. Colin IS Pell's uncle. You remember how you felt when your mom was locked away in a prison and you were here without family.
You're right, Logan. I'm sorry, Pell. Are you going with him?
Of course not. He'll stay here with us.
Won't you Pell?

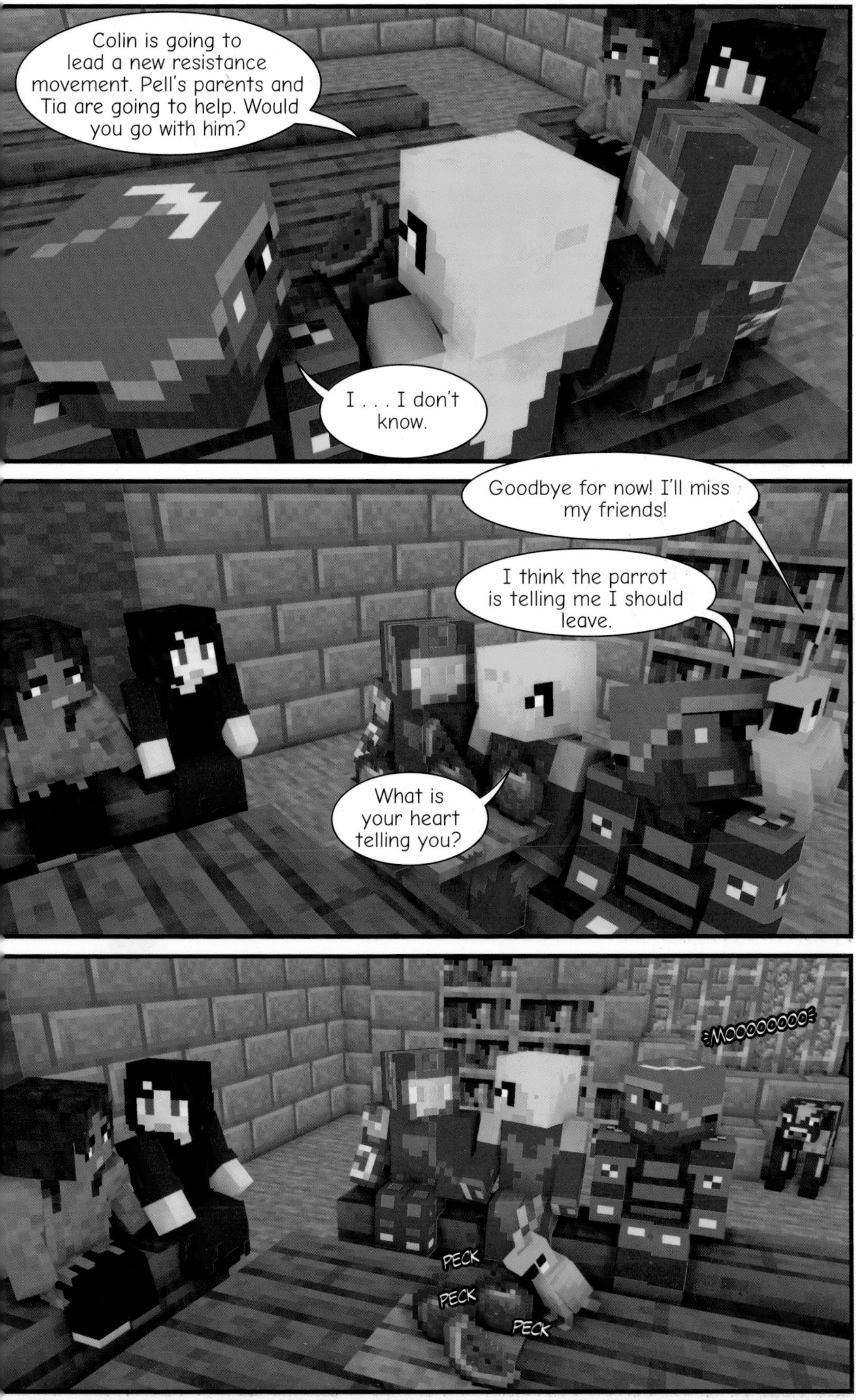
Colin is going to lead a new resistance movement. Pell's parents and Tia are going to help. Would you go with him?
I . . . I don't know.
Goodbye for now! I'll miss my friends!
I think the parrot is telling me I should leave.
What is your heart telling you?
MOOOOOOOO
PECK
PECK
PECK

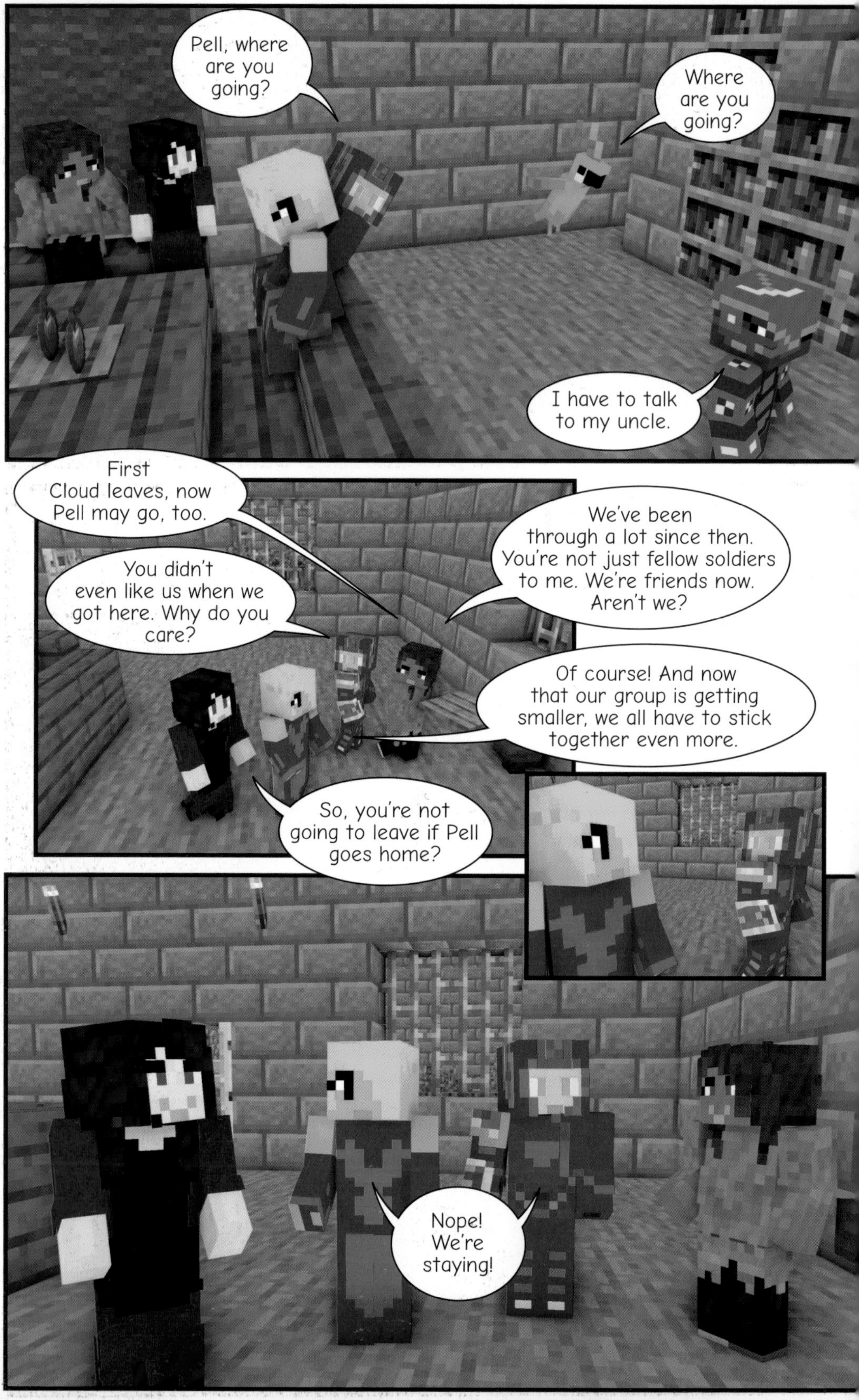
Pell, where are you going?
Where are you going?
I have to talk to my uncle.
First Cloud leaves, now Pell may go, too.
You didn't even like us when we got here. Why do you care?
We've been through a lot since then. You're not just fellow soldiers to me. We're friends now. Aren't we?
Of course! And now that our group is getting smaller, we all have to stick together even more.
So, you're not going to leave if Pell goes home?
Nope! We're staying!

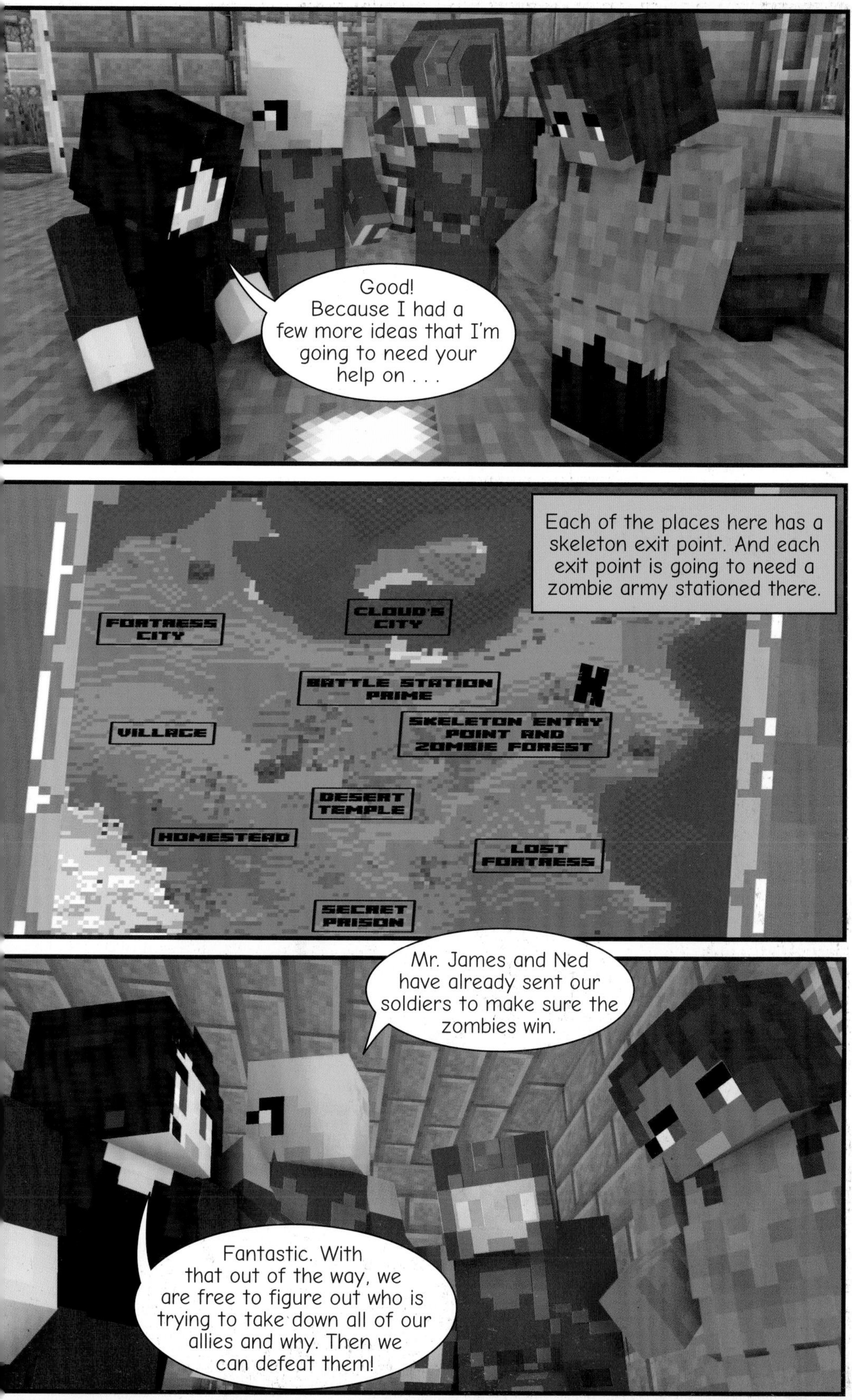
Good! Because I had a few more ideas that I'm going to need your help on . . .
Each of the places here has a skeleton exit point. And each exit point is going to need a zombie army stationed there.
FORTRESS CITY
CLOUD'S CITY
BATTLE STATION PRIME
VILLAGE
SKELETON ENTRY POINT AND ZOMBIE FOREST
DESERT TEMPLE
HOMESTEAD
LOST FORTRESS
SECRET PRISON
Mr. James and Ned have already sent our soldiers to make sure the zombies win.
Fantastic. With that out of the way, we are free to figure out who is trying to take down all of our allies and why. Then we can defeat them!

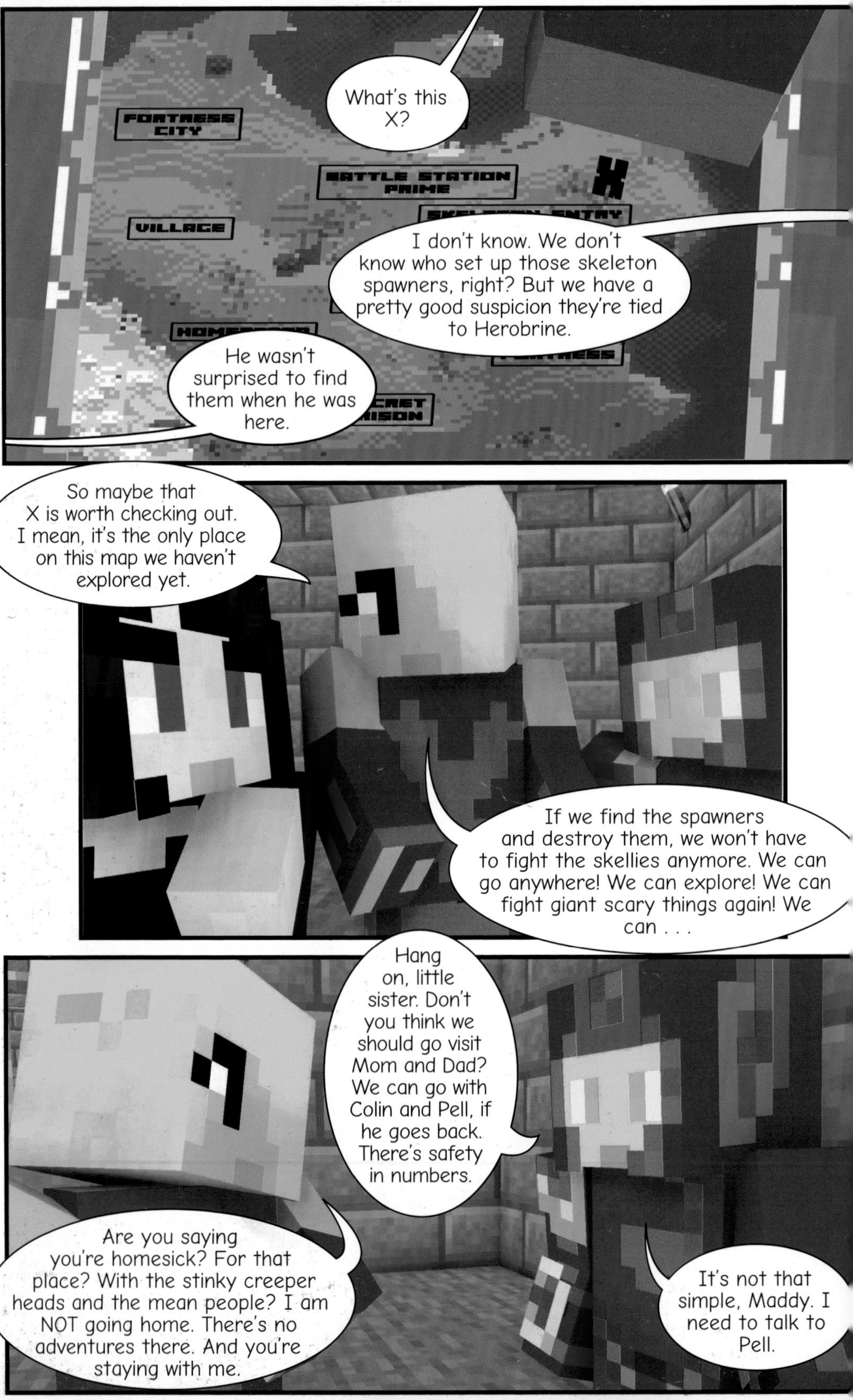
FORTRESS CITY
BATTLE STATION PRIME
VILLAGE
X
What's this X?
I don't know. We don't know who set up those skeleton spawners, right? But we have a pretty good suspicion they're tied to Herobrine.
He wasn't surprised to find them when he was here.
So maybe that X is worth checking out. I mean, it's the only place on this map we haven't explored yet.
If we find the spawners and destroy them, we won't have to fight the skellies anymore. We can go anywhere! We can explore! We can fight giant scary things again! We can . . .
Hang on, little sister. Don't you think we should go visit Mom and Dad? We can go with Colin and Pell, if he goes back. There's safety in numbers.
Are you saying you're homesick? For that place? With the stinky creeper heads and the mean people? I am NOT going home. There's no adventures there. And you're staying with me.
It's not that simple, Maddy. I need to talk to Pell.

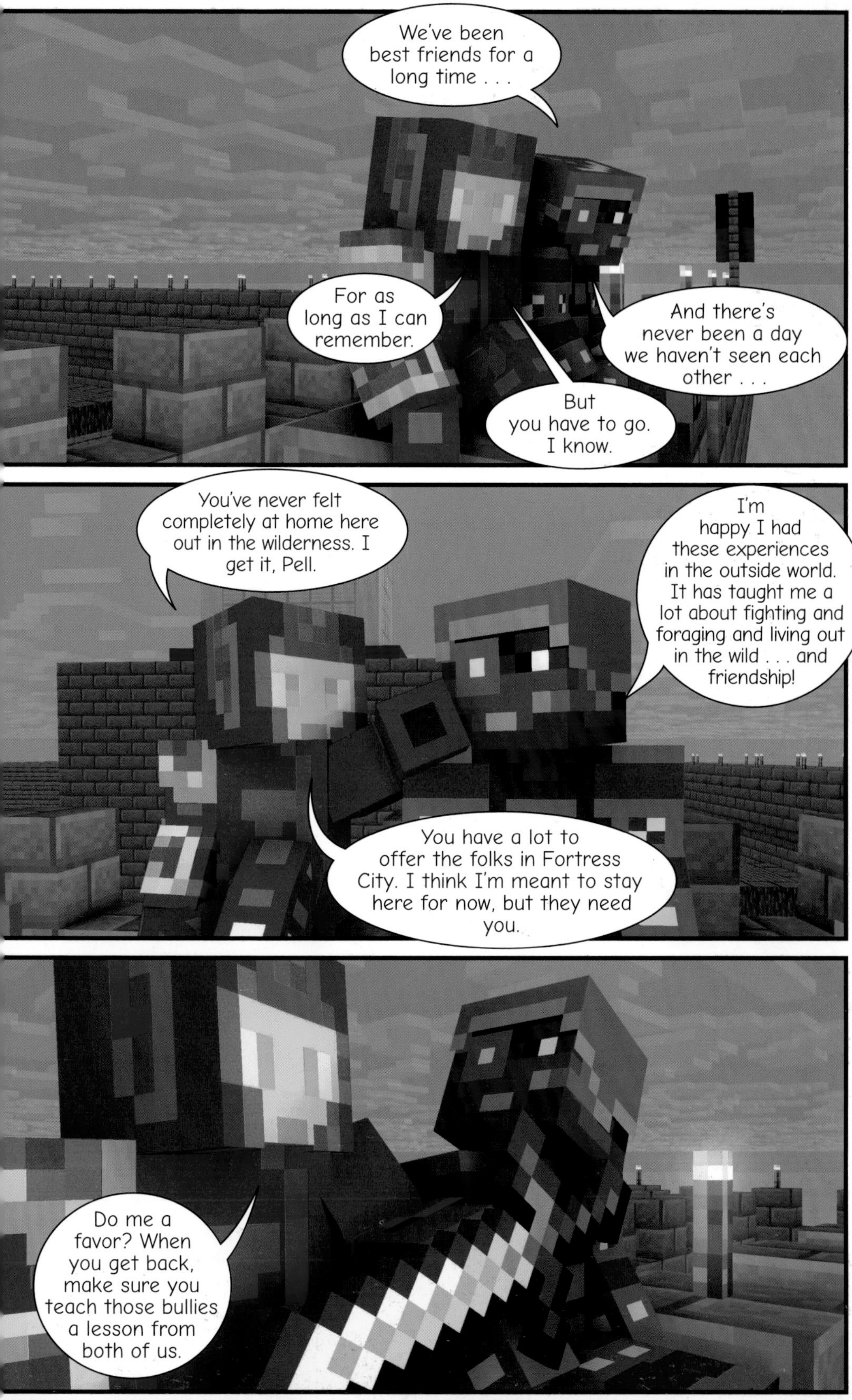
We've been best friends for a long time . . .
For as long as I can remember.
And there's never been a day we haven't seen each other . . .
But you have to go. I know.
You've never felt completely at home here out in the wilderness. I get it, Pell.
I'm happy I had these experiences in the outside world. It has taught me a lot about fighting and foraging and living out in the wild . . . and friendship!
You have a lot to offer the folks in Fortress City. I think I'm meant to stay here for now, but they need you.
Do me a favor? When you get back, make sure you teach those bullies a lesson from both of us.

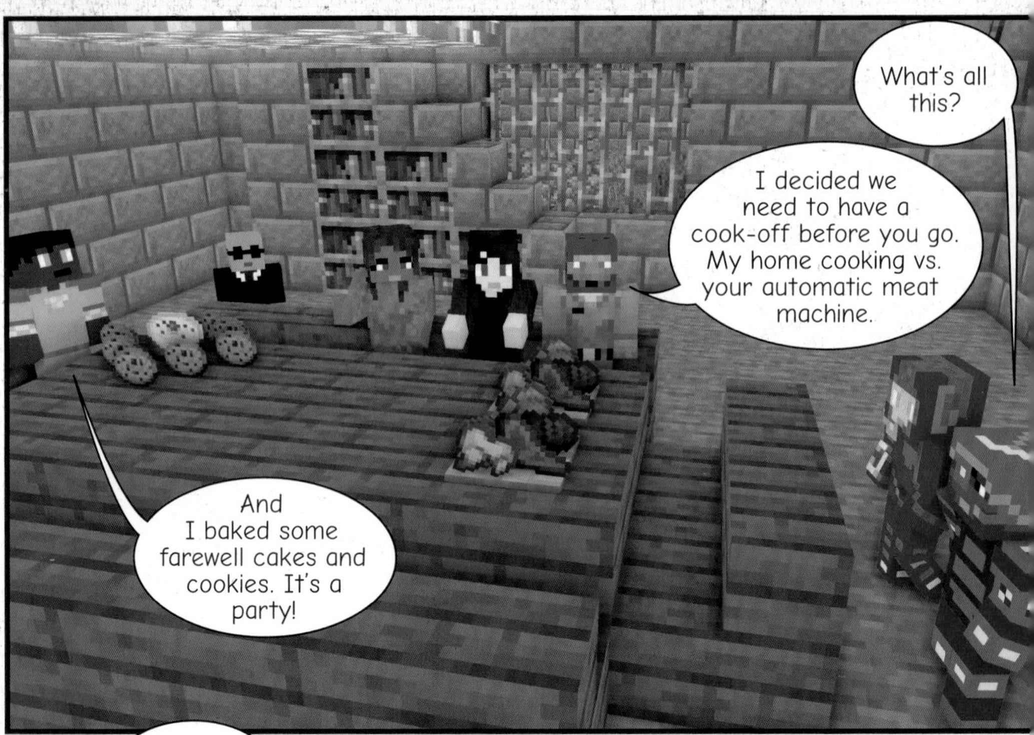
What's all this?
I decided we need to have a cook-off before you go. My home cooking vs. your automatic meat machine.
And I baked some farewell cakes and cookies. It's a party!

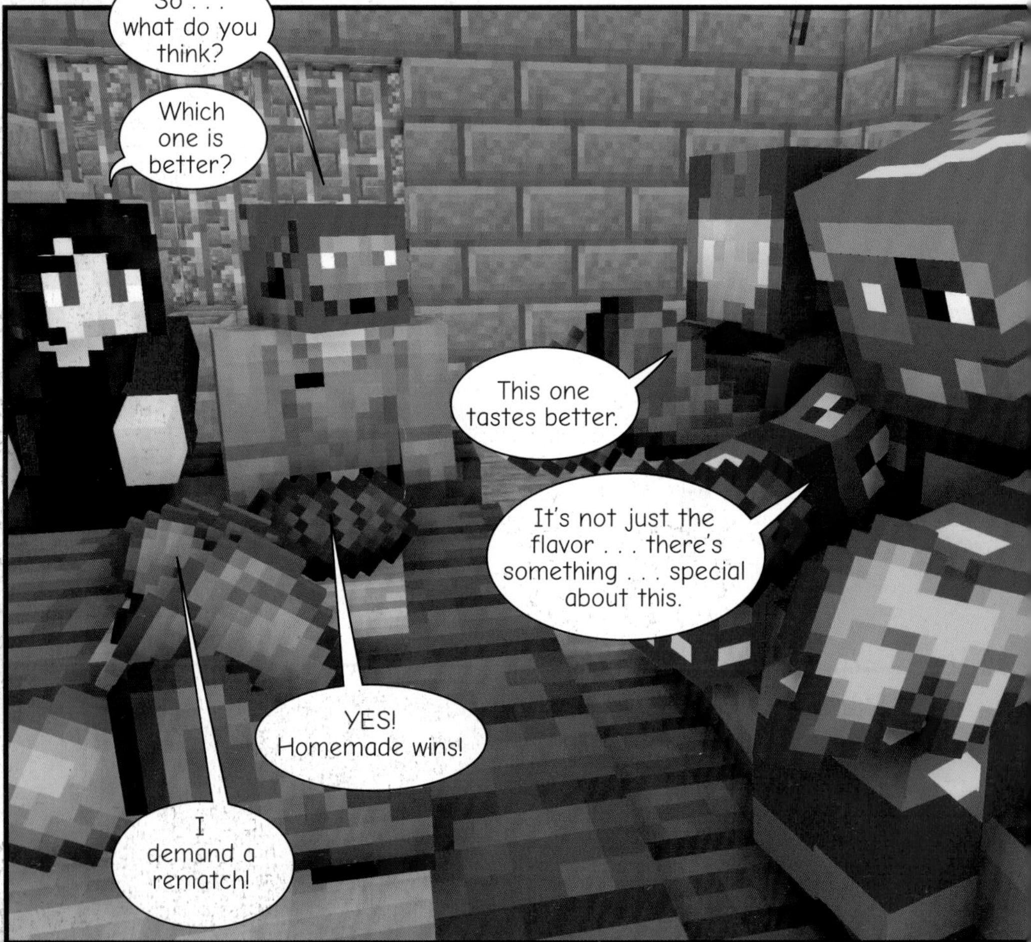
So . . . what do you think?
Which one is better?
This one tastes better.
It's not just the flavor . . . there's something . . . special about this.
YES! Homemade wins!
I demand a rematch!

CHAPTER 4

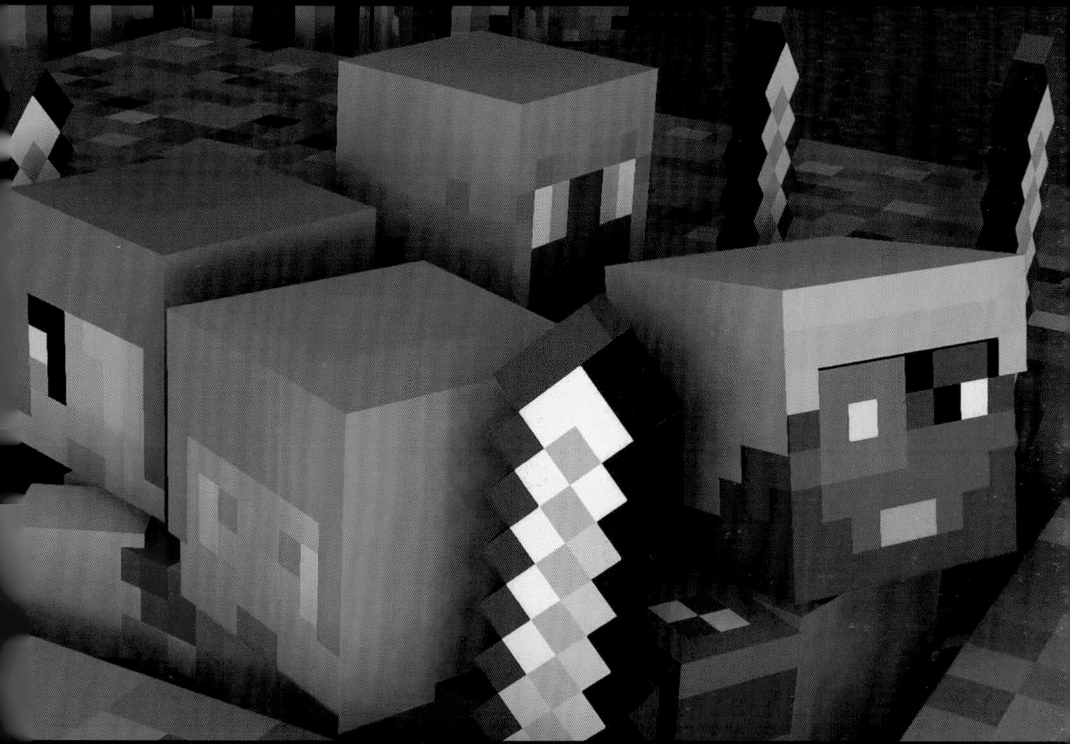

FORTRESS CITY

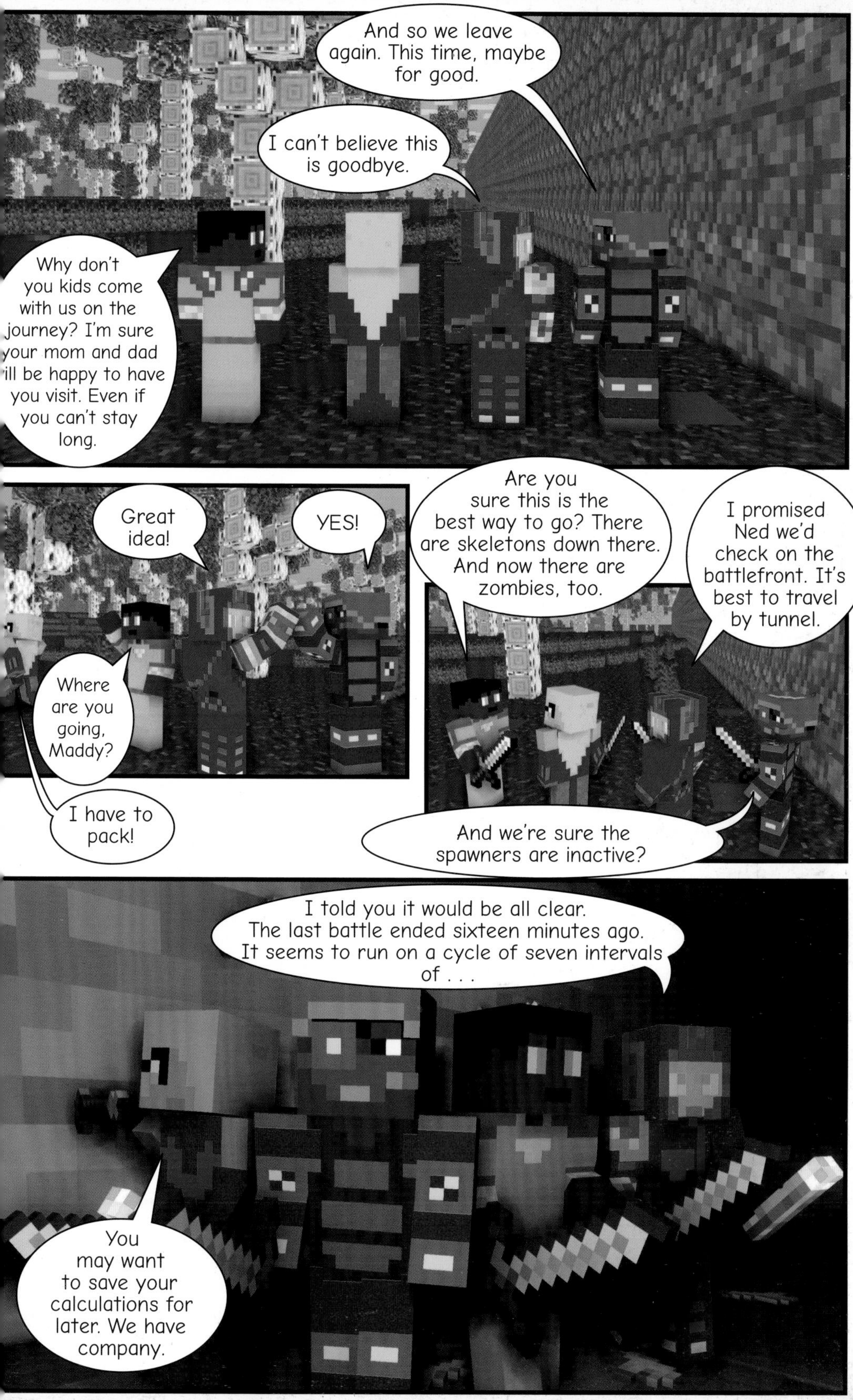
And so we leave again. This time, maybe for good.
I can't believe this is goodbye.
Why don't you kids come with us on the journey? I'm sure your mom and dad ill be happy to have you visit. Even if you can't stay long.
Great idea!
YES!
Where are you going, Maddy?
I have to pack!
Are you sure this is the best way to go? There are skeletons down there. And now there are zombies, too.
I promised Ned we'd check on the battlefront. It's best to travel by tunnel.
And we're sure the spawners are inactive?
I told you it would be all clear. The last battle ended sixteen minutes ago. It seems to run on a cycle of seven intervals of . . .
You may want to save your calculations for later. We have company.

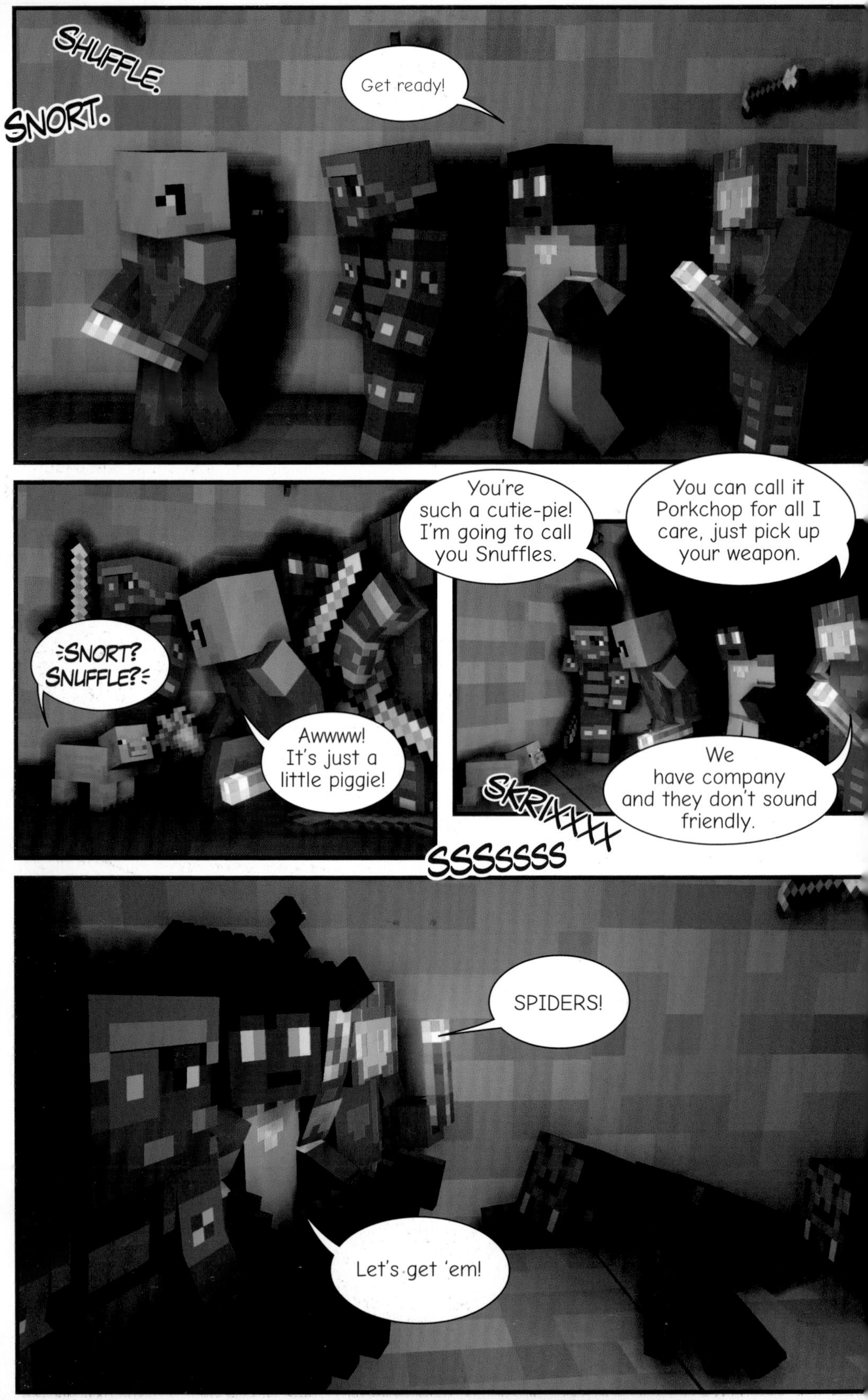
SHUFFLE.
SNORT.
Get ready!
SNORT? SNUFFLE?
Awwww! It's just a little piggie!
You're such a cutie-pie! I'm going to call you Snuffles.
You can call it Porkchop for all I care, just pick up your weapon.
We have company and they don't sound friendly.
SKRIXXXX
SSSSSSS
SPIDERS!
Let's get 'em!

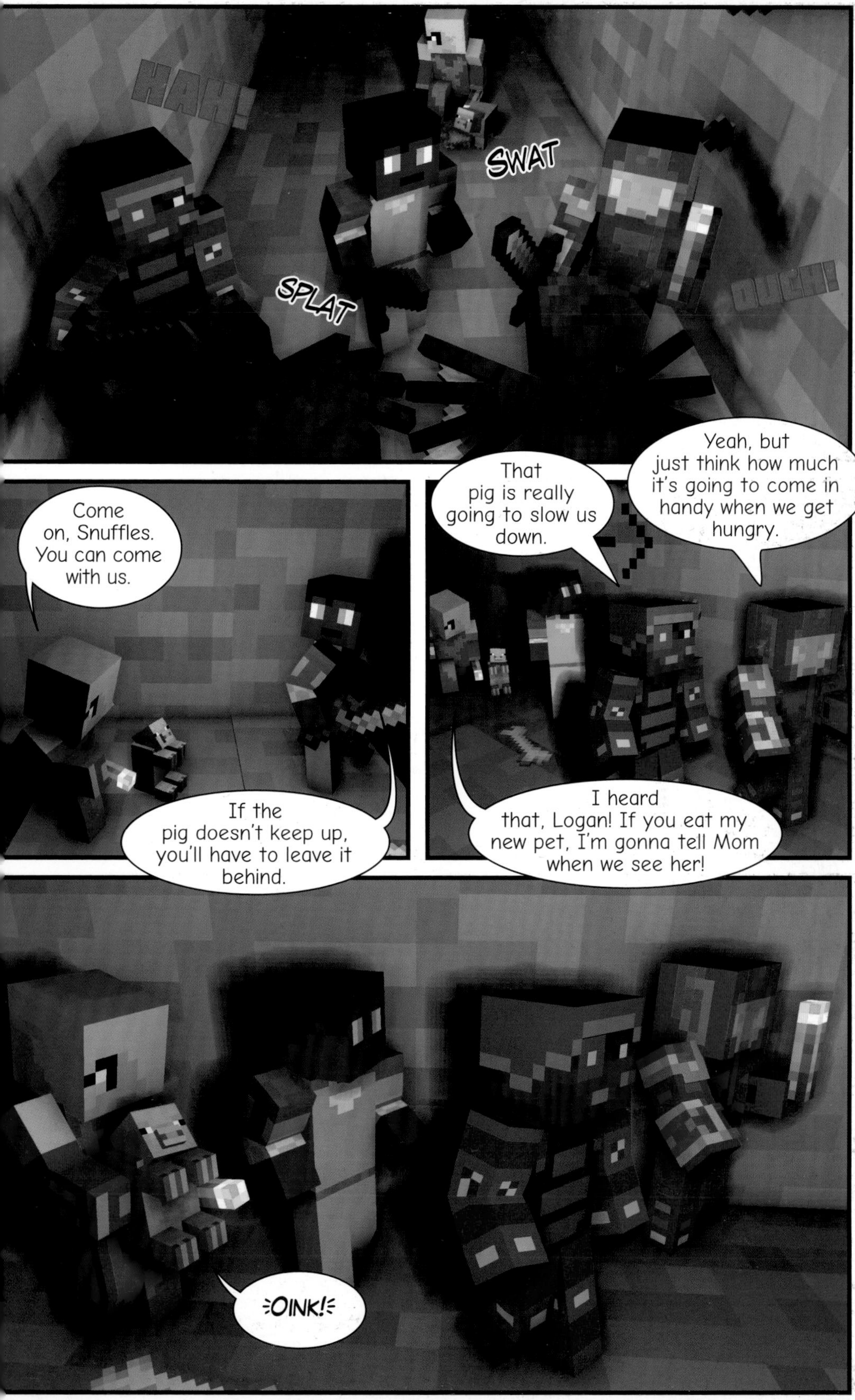
HAH!
SWAT
SPLAT
OUCH!
Come on, Snuffles. You can come with us.
If the pig doesn't keep up, you'll have to leave it behind.
That pig is really going to slow us down.
Yeah, but just think how much it's going to come in handy when we get hungry.
I heard that, Logan! If you eat my new pet, I'm gonna tell Mom when we see her!
OINK!

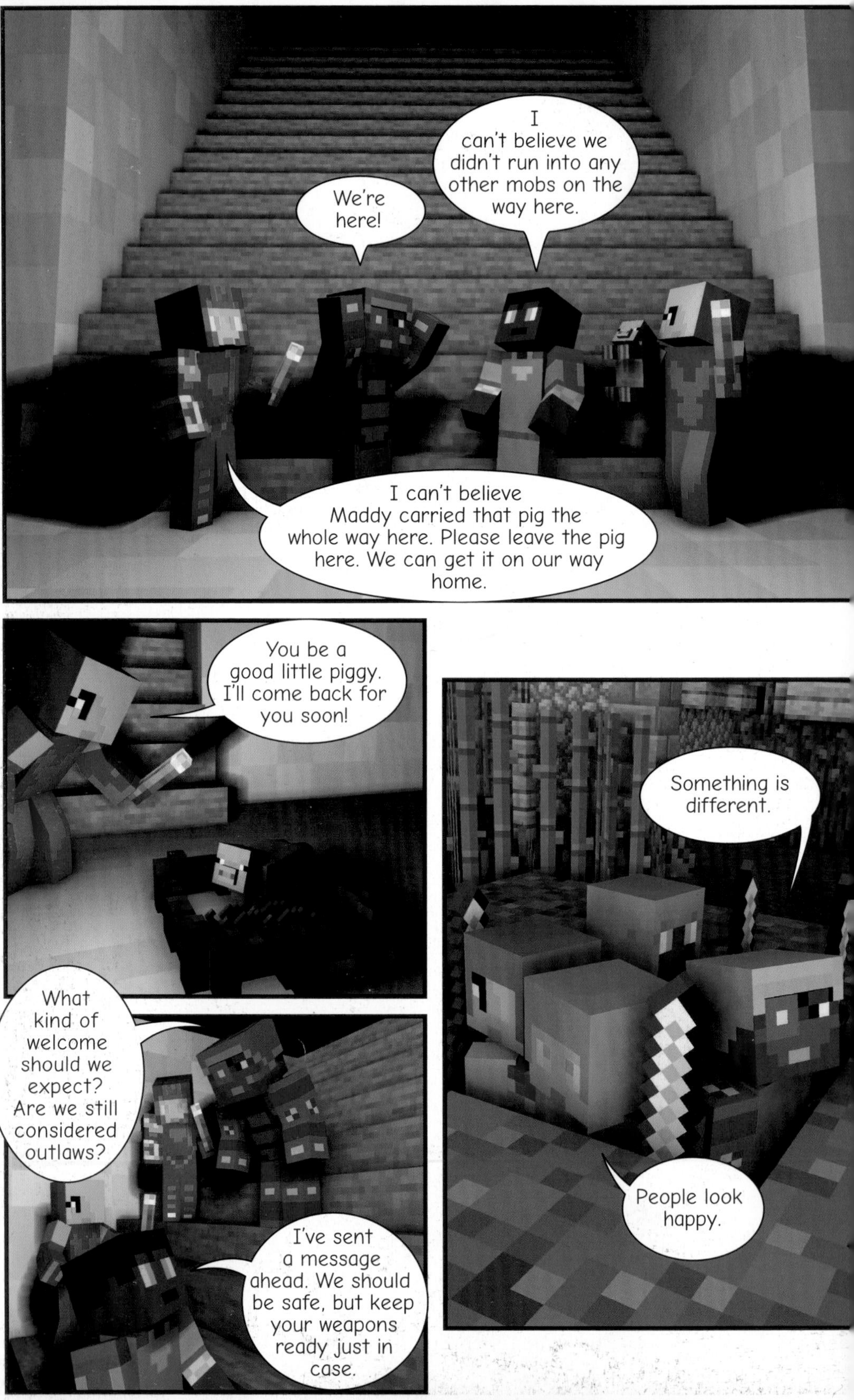

We're here!
I can't believe we didn't run into any other mobs on the way here.
I can't believe Maddy carried that pig the whole way here. Please leave the pig here. We can get it on our way home.
You be a good little piggy. I'll come back for you soon!
What kind of welcome should we expect? Are we still considered outlaws?
I've sent a message ahead. We should be safe, but keep your weapons ready just in case.
Something is different.
People look happy.

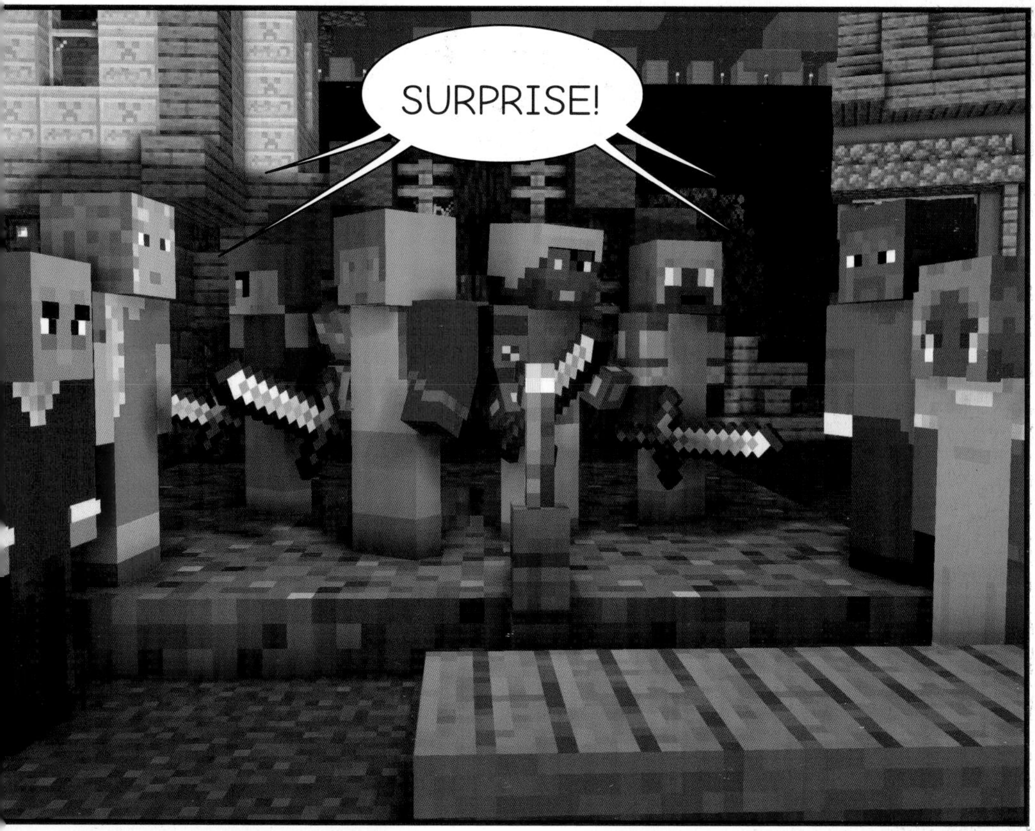
SURPRISE!

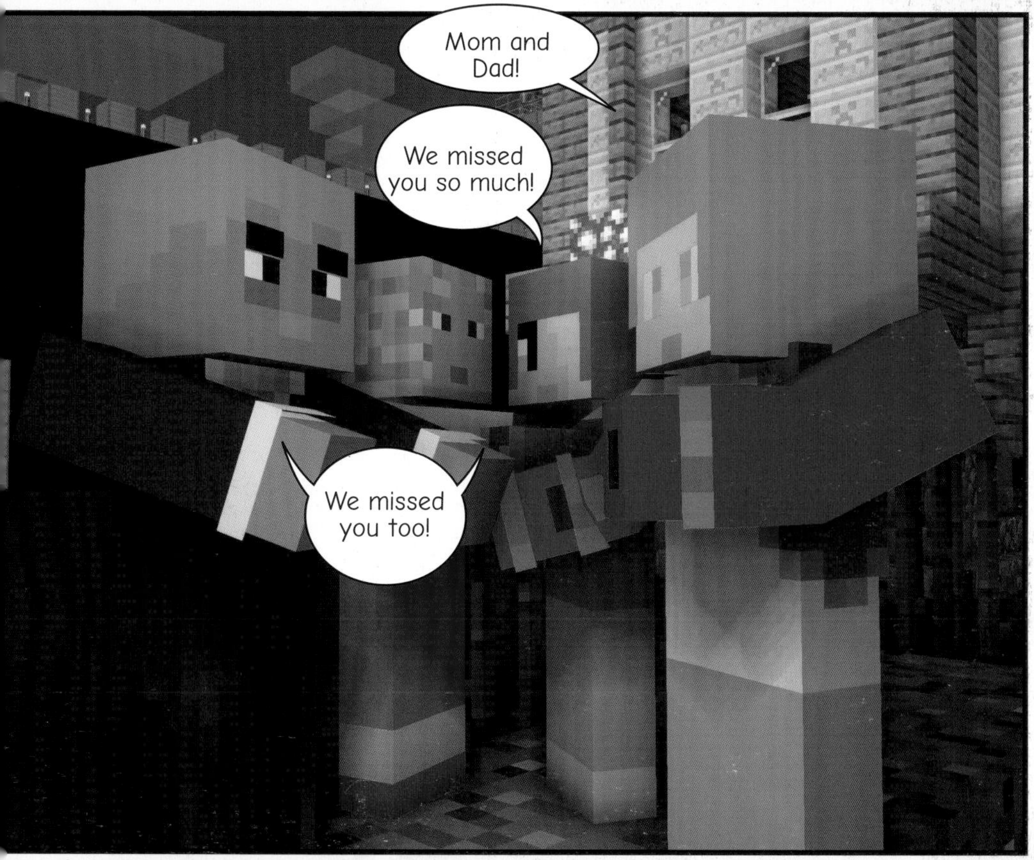
Mom and Dad!
We missed you so much!
We missed you too!

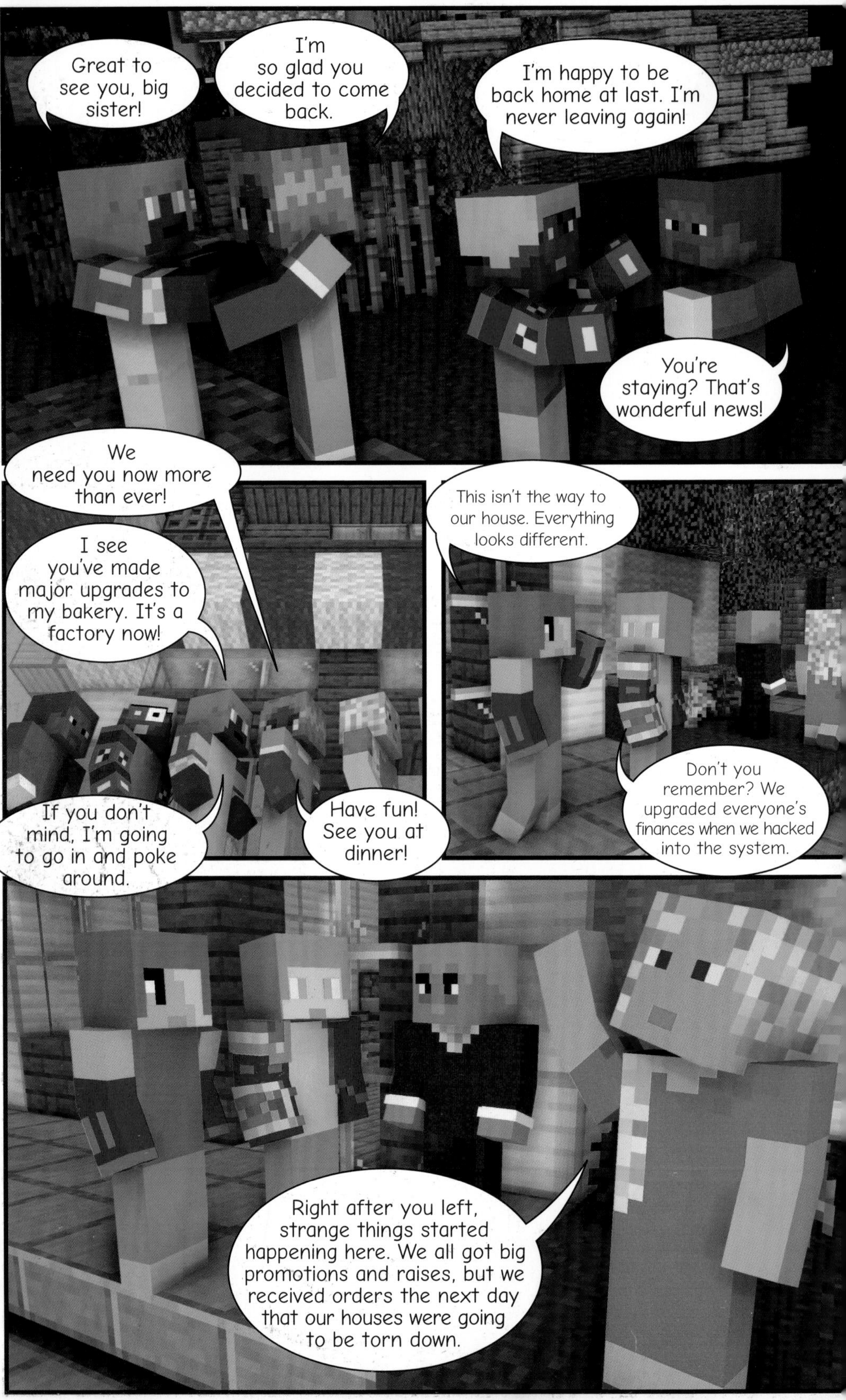
Great to see you, big sister!
I'm so glad you decided to come back.
I'm happy to be back home at last. I'm never leaving again!
You're staying? That's wonderful news!
We need you now more than ever!
I see you've made major upgrades to my bakery. It's a factory now!
If you don't mind, I'm going to go in and poke around.
Have fun! See you at dinner!
This isn't the way to our house. Everything looks different.
Don't you remember? We upgraded everyone's finances when we hacked into the system.
Right after you left, strange things started happening here. We all got big promotions and raises, but we received orders the next day that our houses were going to be torn down.

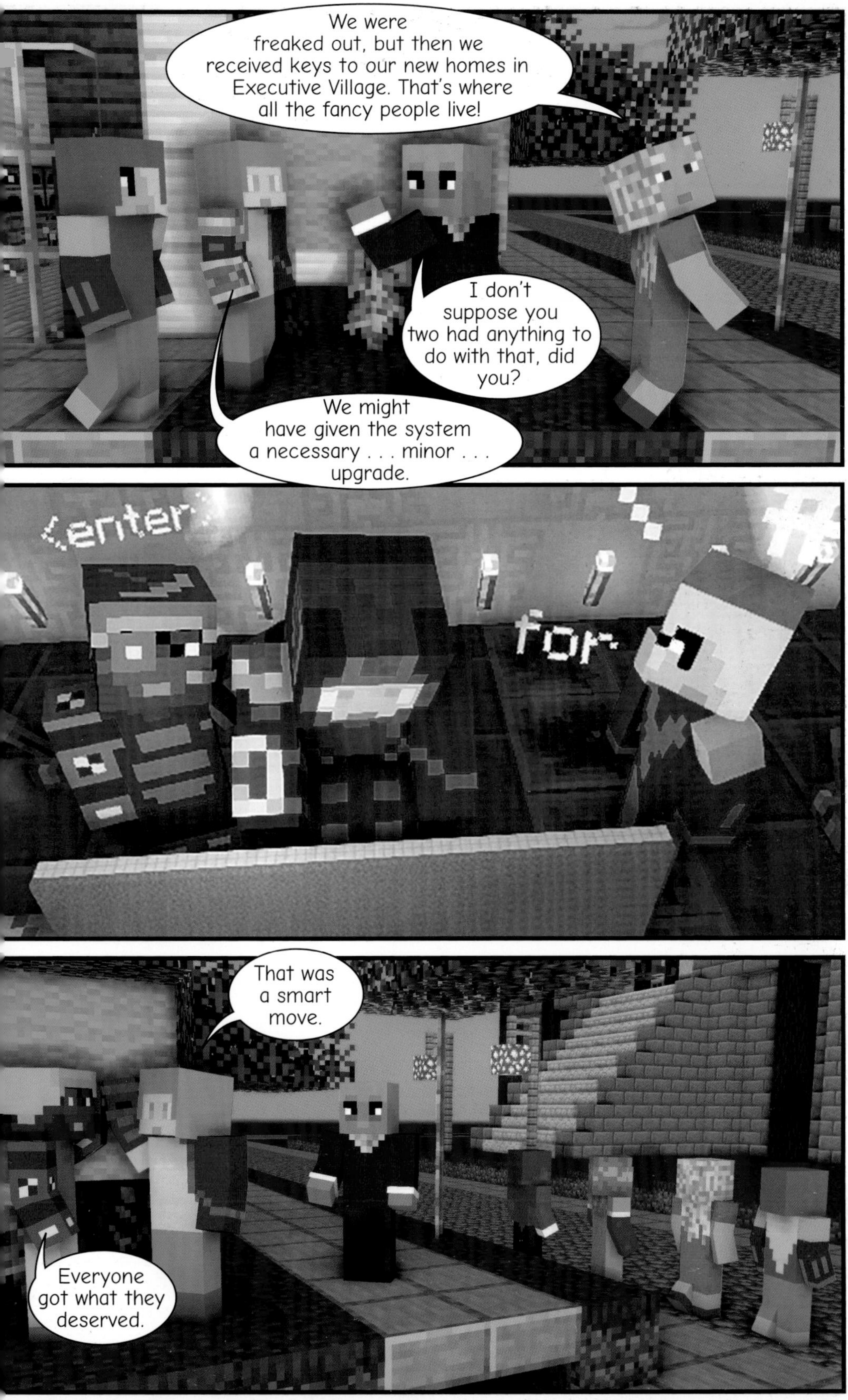
We were freaked out, but then we received keys to our new homes in Executive Village. That's where all the fancy people live!
I don't suppose you two had anything to do with that, did you?
We might have given the system a necessary . . . minor . . . upgrade.
for
That was a smart move.
Everyone got what they deserved.

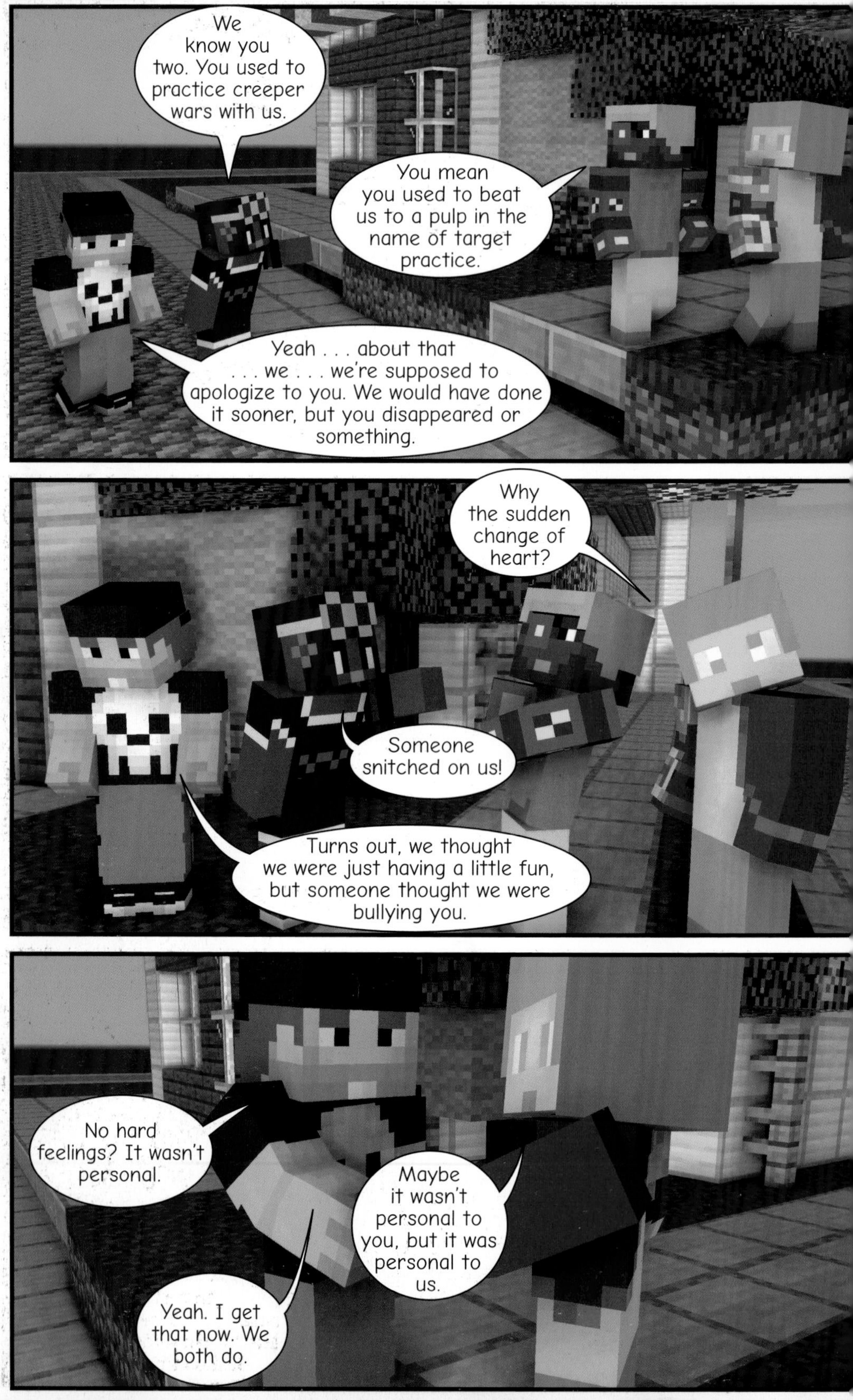
We know you two. You used to practice creeper wars with us.
You mean you used to beat us to a pulp in the name of target practice.
Yeah . . . about that . . . we . . . we're supposed to apologize to you. We would have done it sooner, but you disappeared or something.
Why the sudden change of heart?
Someone snitched on us!
Turns out, we thought we were just having a little fun, but someone thought we were bullying you.
No hard feelings? It wasn't personal.
Maybe it wasn't personal to you, but it was personal to us.
Yeah. I get that now. We both do.

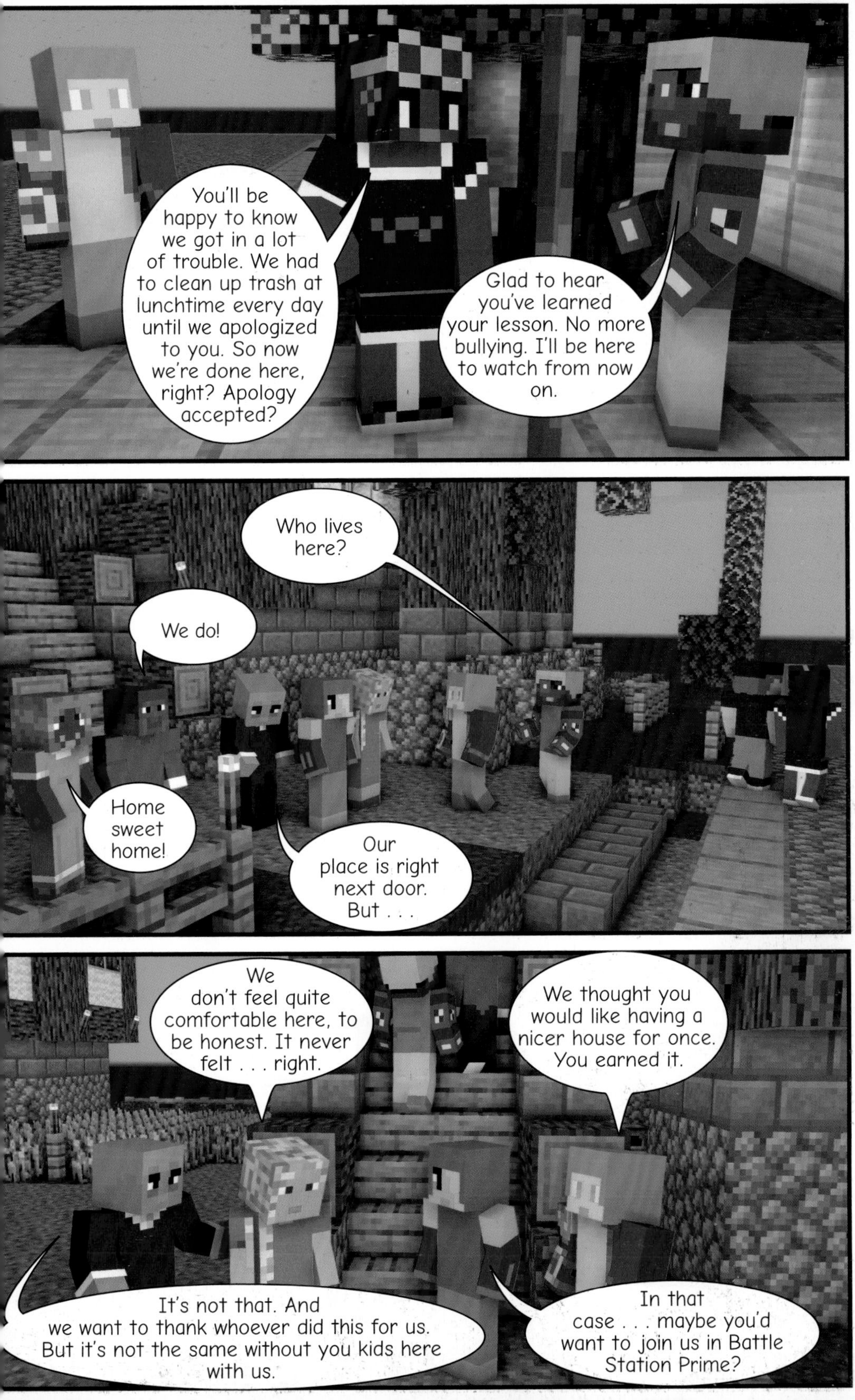
You'll be happy to know we got in a lot of trouble. We had to clean up trash at lunchtime every day until we apologized to you. So now we're done here, right? Apology accepted?
Glad to hear you've learned your lesson. No more bullying. I'll be here to watch from now on.
Who lives here?
We do!
Home sweet home!
Our place is right next door. But . . .
We don't feel quite comfortable here, to be honest. It never felt . . . right.
We thought you would like having a nicer house for once. You earned it.
It's not that. And we want to thank whoever did this for us. But it's not the same without you kids here with us.
In that case . . . maybe you'd want to join us in Battle Station Prime?

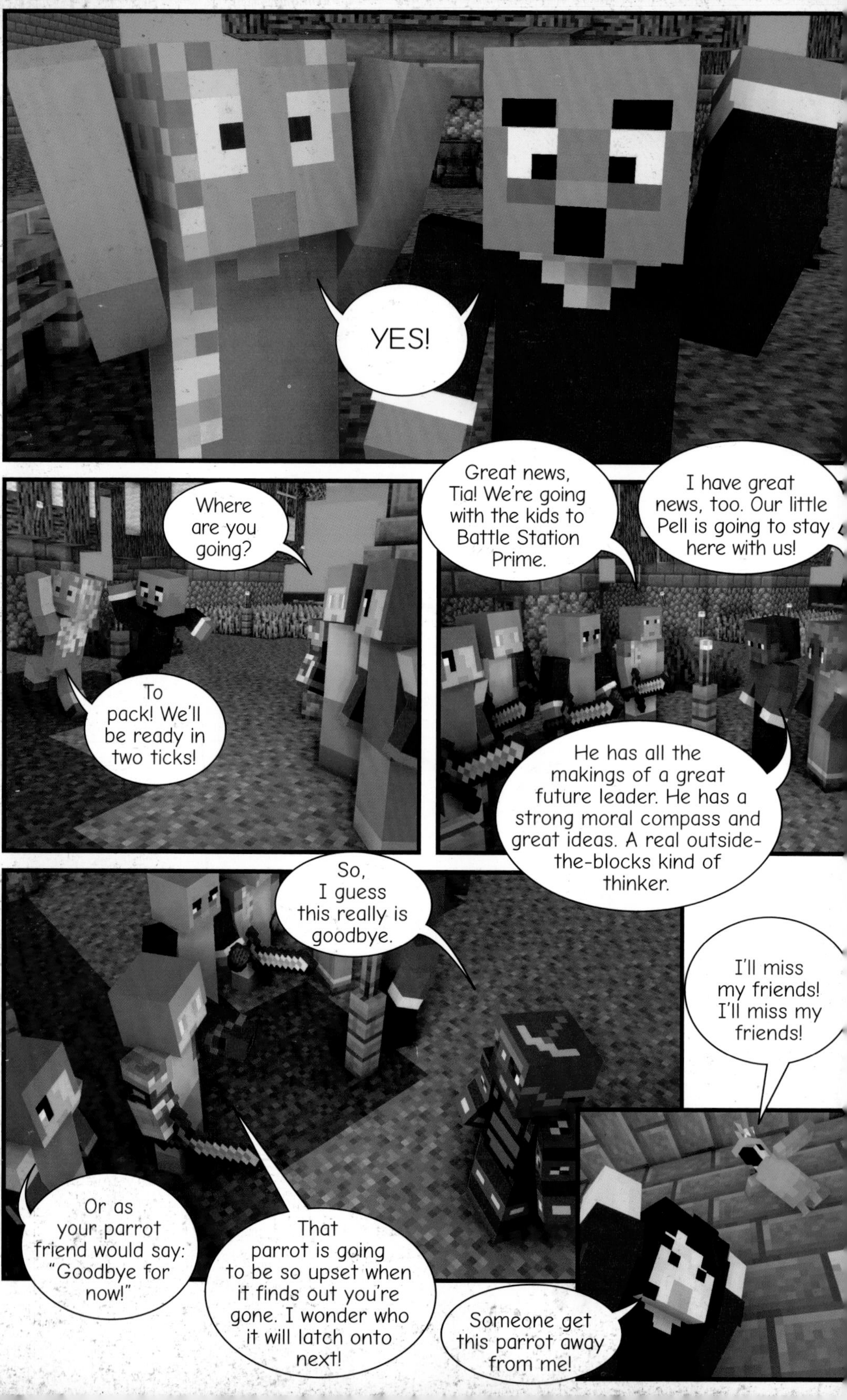

YES!
Where are you going?
To pack! We'll be ready in two ticks!
Great news, Tia! We're going with the kids to Battle Station Prime.
I have great news, too. Our little Pell is going to stay here with us!
He has all the makings of a great future leader. He has a strong moral compass and great ideas. A real outside-the-blocks kind of thinker.
So, I guess this really is goodbye.
Or as your parrot friend would say: "Goodbye for now!"
That parrot is going to be so upset when it finds out you're gone. I wonder who it will latch onto next!
I'll miss my friends! I'll miss my friends!
Someone get this parrot away from me!

CHAPTER 5

EMBARRASSING PARENTS

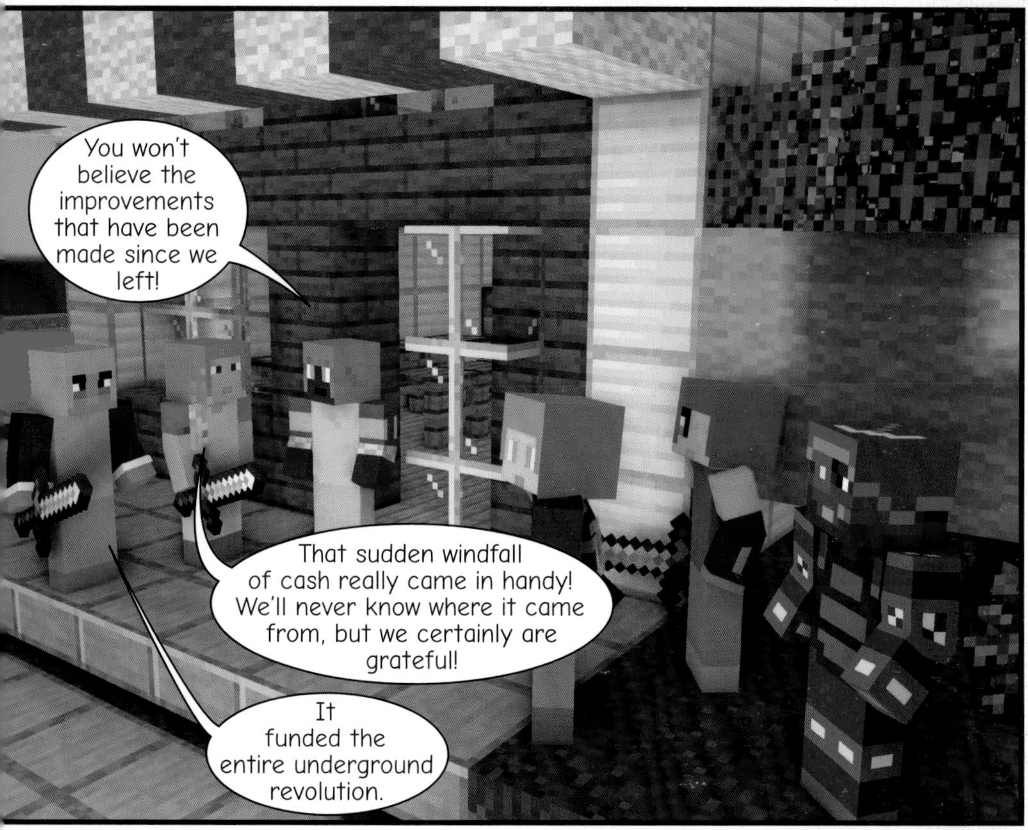
You won't believe the improvements that have been made since we left!
That sudden windfall of cash really came in handy! We'll never know where it came from, but we certainly are grateful!
It funded the entire underground revolution.

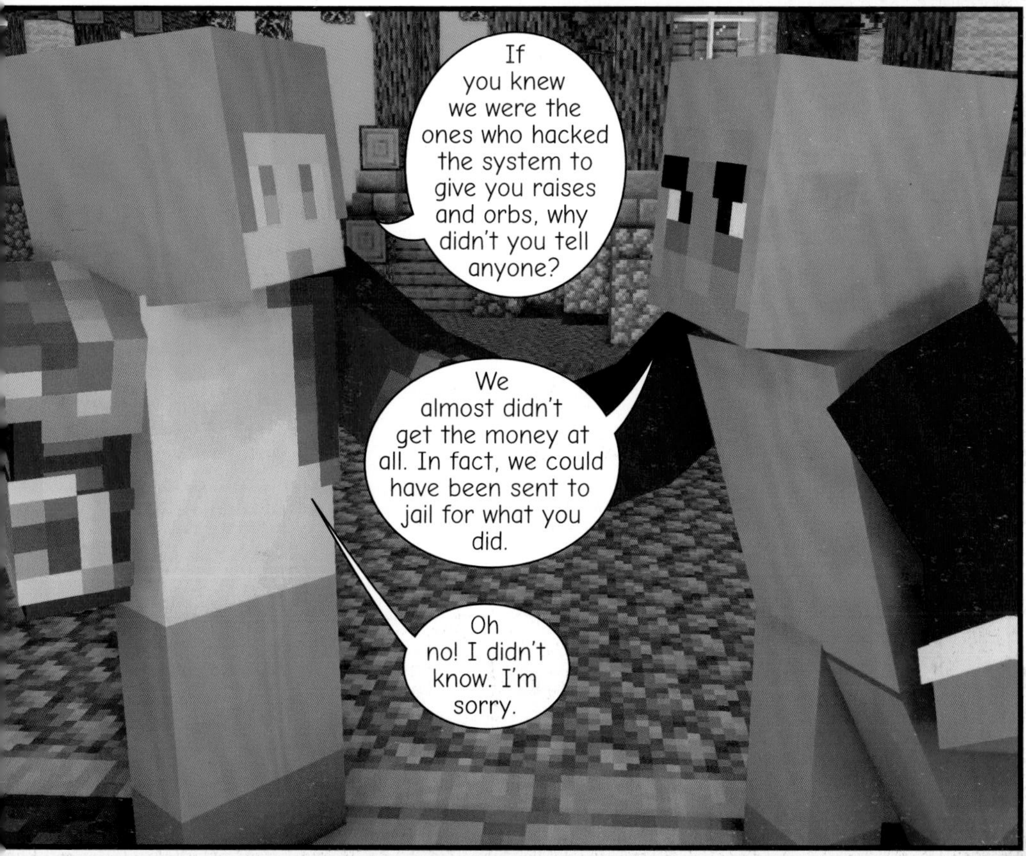
If you knew we were the ones who hacked the system to give you raises and orbs, why didn't you tell anyone?
We almost didn't get the money at all. In fact, we could have been sent to jail for what you did.
Oh no! I didn't know. I'm sorry.

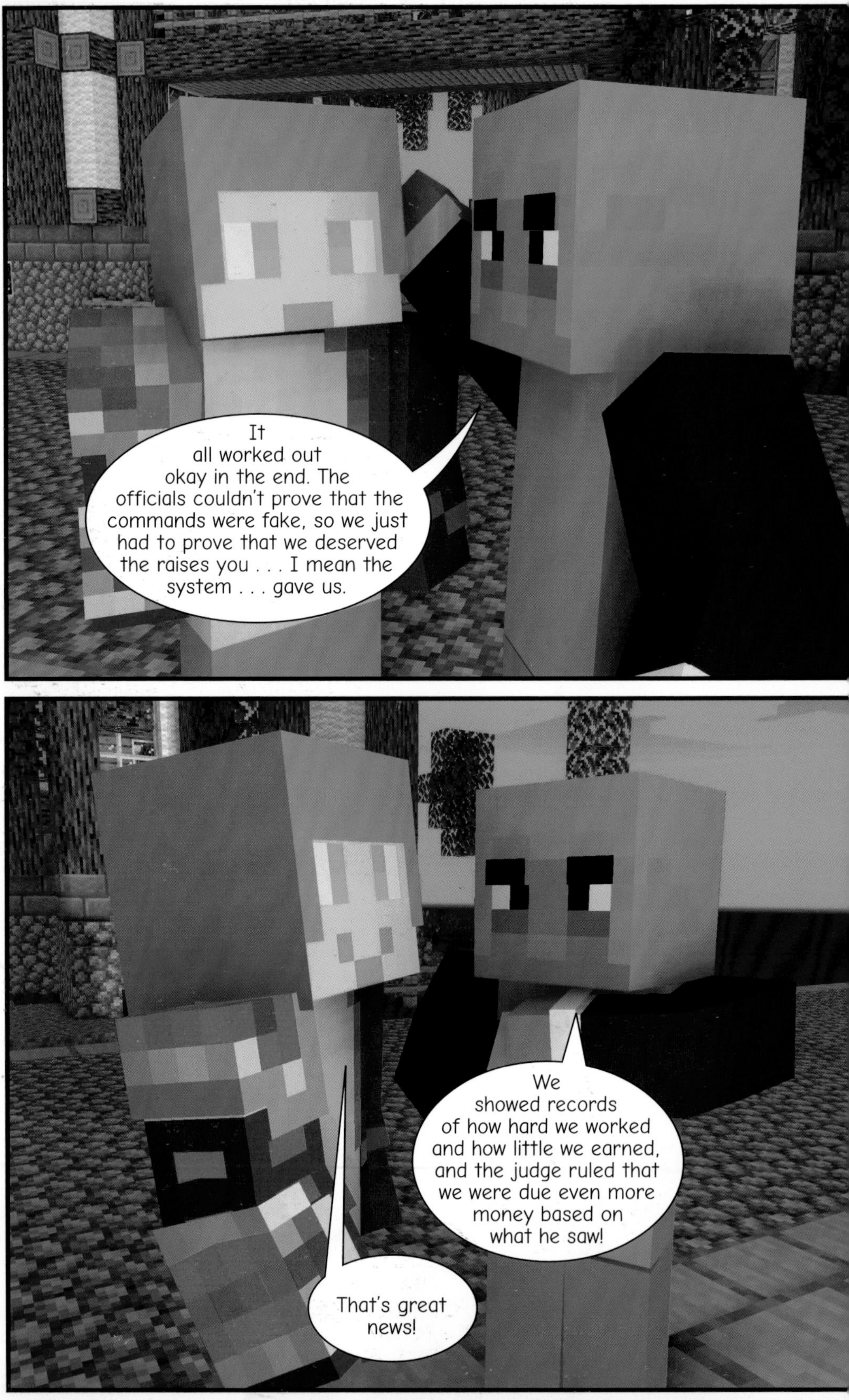
It all worked out okay in the end. The officials couldn't prove that the commands were fake, so we just had to prove that we deserved the raises you . . . I mean the system . . . gave us.
We showed records of how hard we worked and how little we earned, and the judge ruled that we were due even more money based on what he saw!
That's great news!

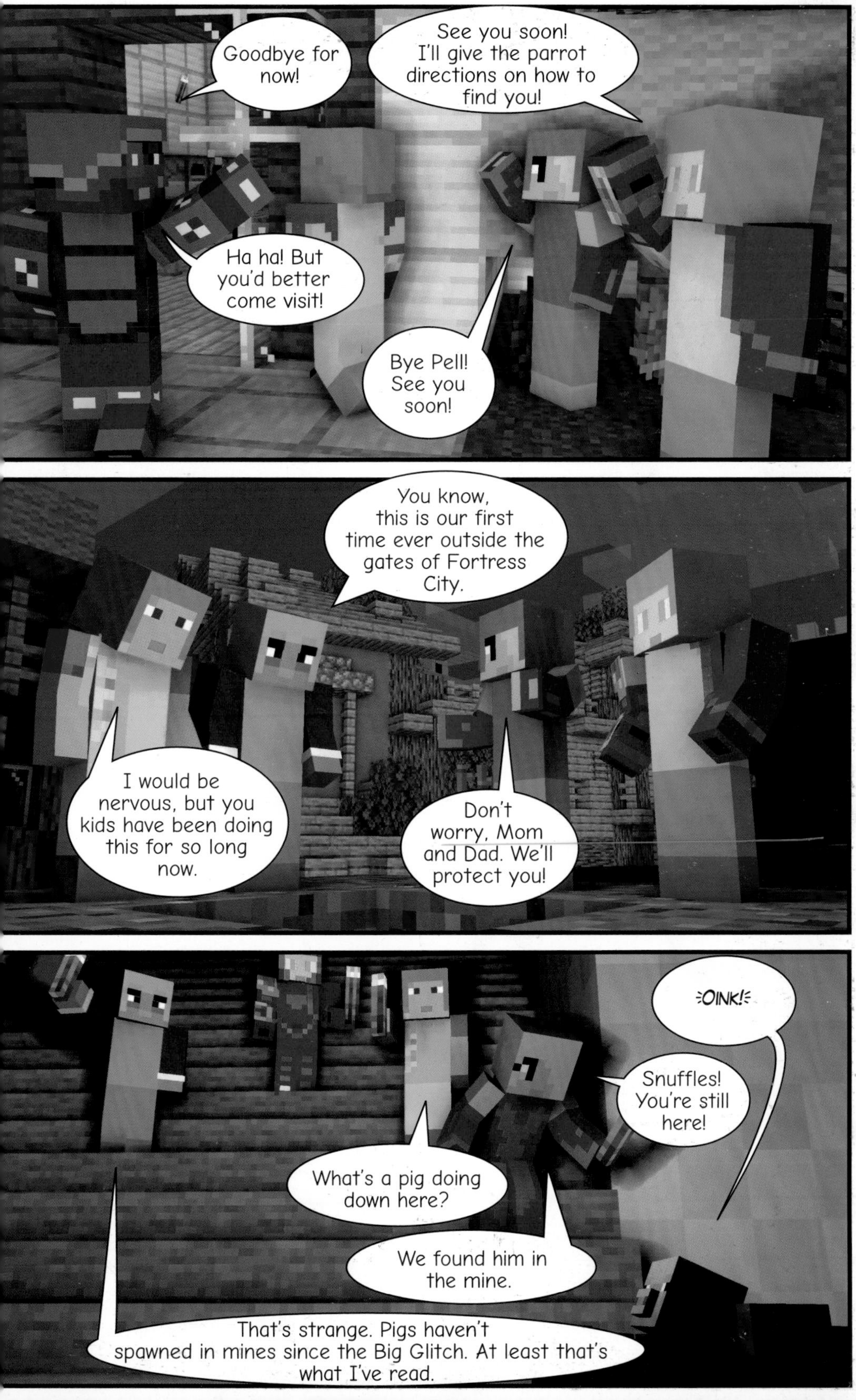
Goodbye for now!
See you soon! I'll give the parrot directions on how to find you!
Ha ha! But you'd better come visit!
Bye Pell! See you soon!
You know, this is our first time ever outside the gates of Fortress City.
I would be nervous, but you kids have been doing this for so long now.
Don't worry, Mom and Dad. We'll protect you!
OINK!
Snuffles! You're still here!
What's a pig doing down here?
We found him in the mine.
That's strange. Pigs haven't spawned in mines since the Big Glitch. At least that's what I've read.

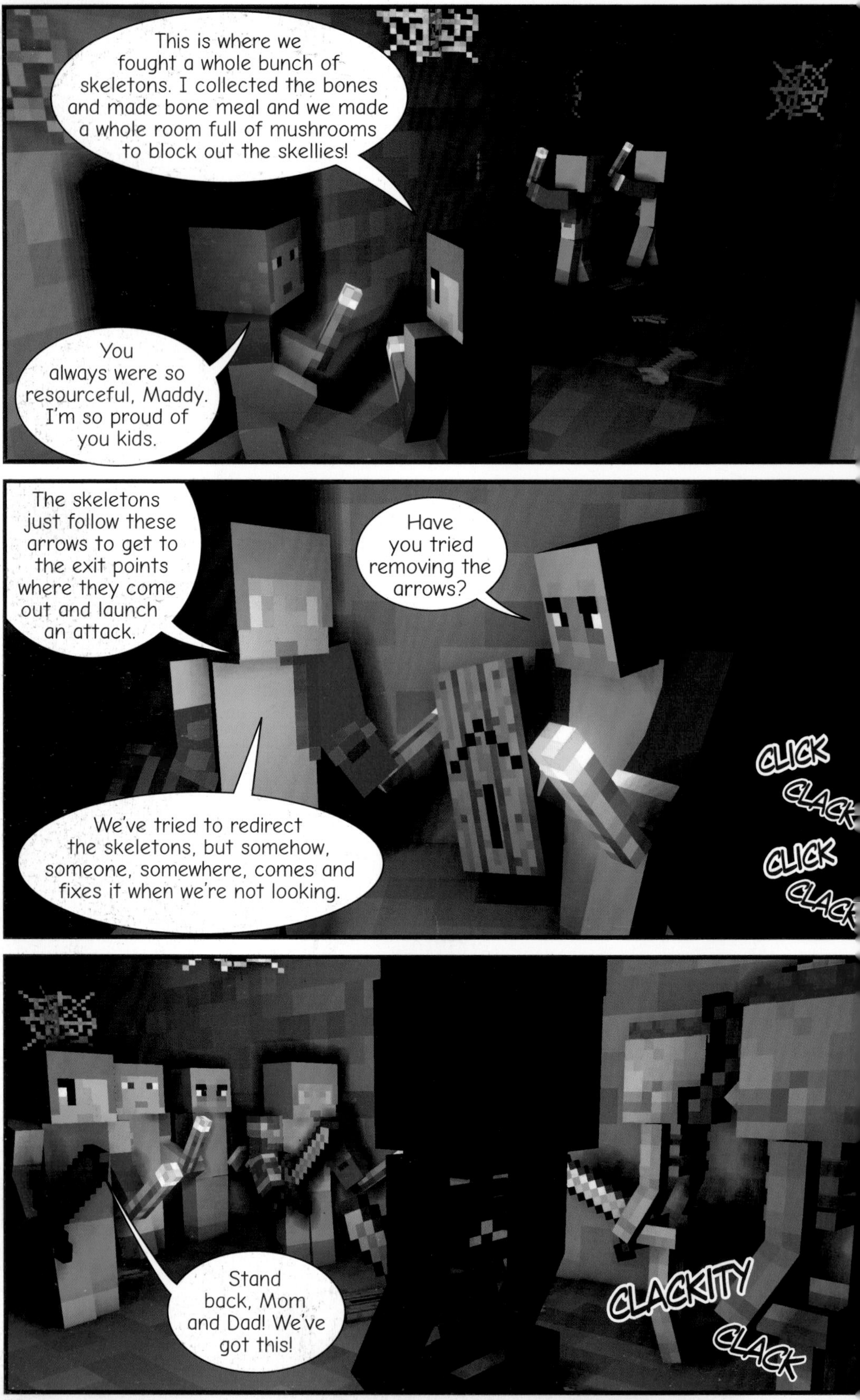
This is where we fought a whole bunch of skeletons. I collected the bones and made bone meal and we made a whole room full of mushrooms to block out the skellies!
You always were so resourceful, Maddy. I'm so proud of you kids.
The skeletons just follow these arrows to get to the exit points where they come out and launch an attack.
Have you tried removing the arrows?
We've tried to redirect the skeletons, but somehow, someone, somewhere, comes and fixes it when we're not looking.
CLICK
CLACK
CLICK
CLACK
Stand back, Mom and Dad! We've got this!
CLACKITY
CLACK

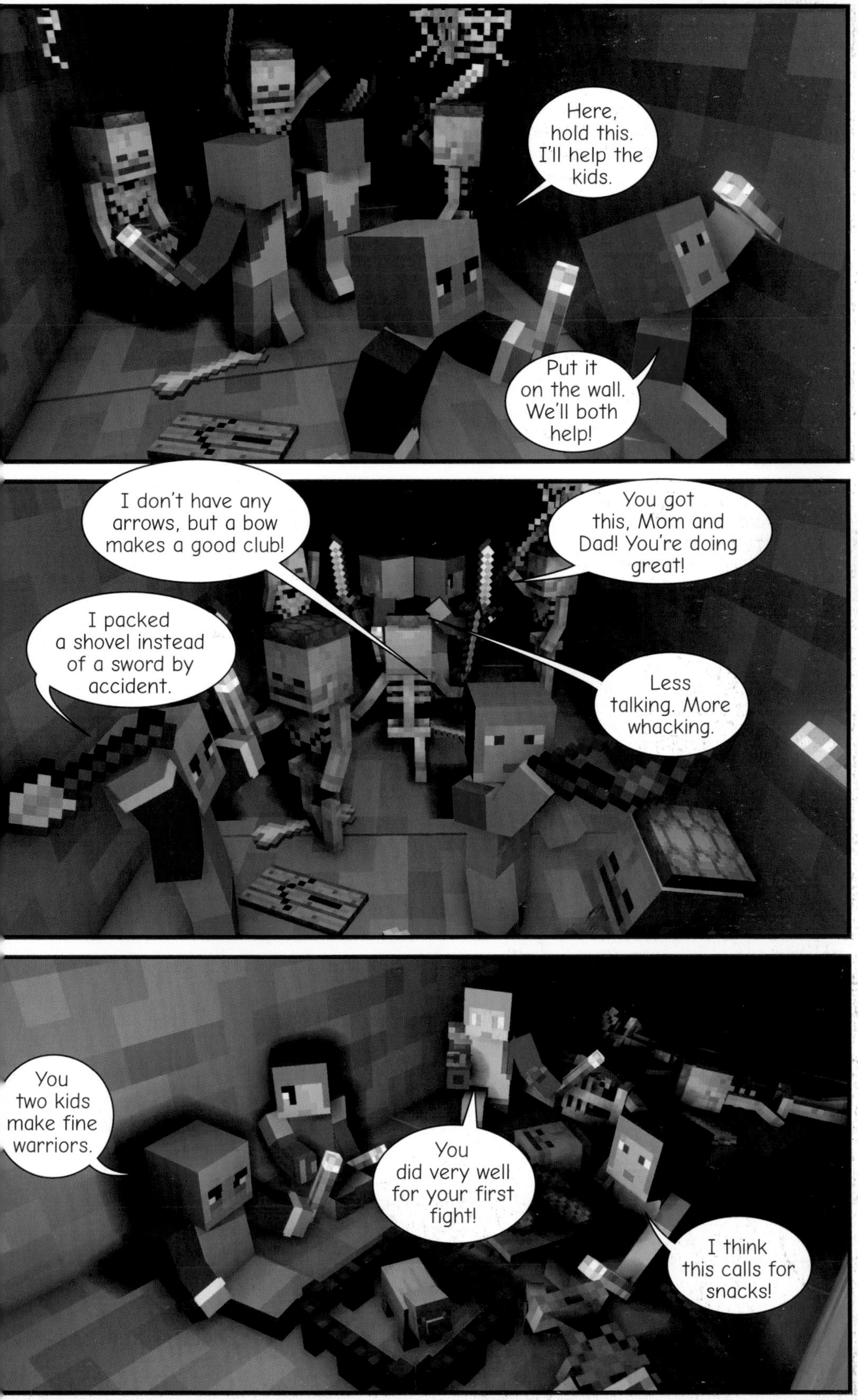
Here, hold this. I'll help the kids.
Put it on the wall. We'll both help!
I don't have any arrows, but a bow makes a good club!
You got this, Mom and Dad! You're doing great!
I packed a shovel instead of a sword by accident.
Less talking. More whacking.
You two kids make fine warriors.
You did very well for your first fight!
I think this calls for snacks!

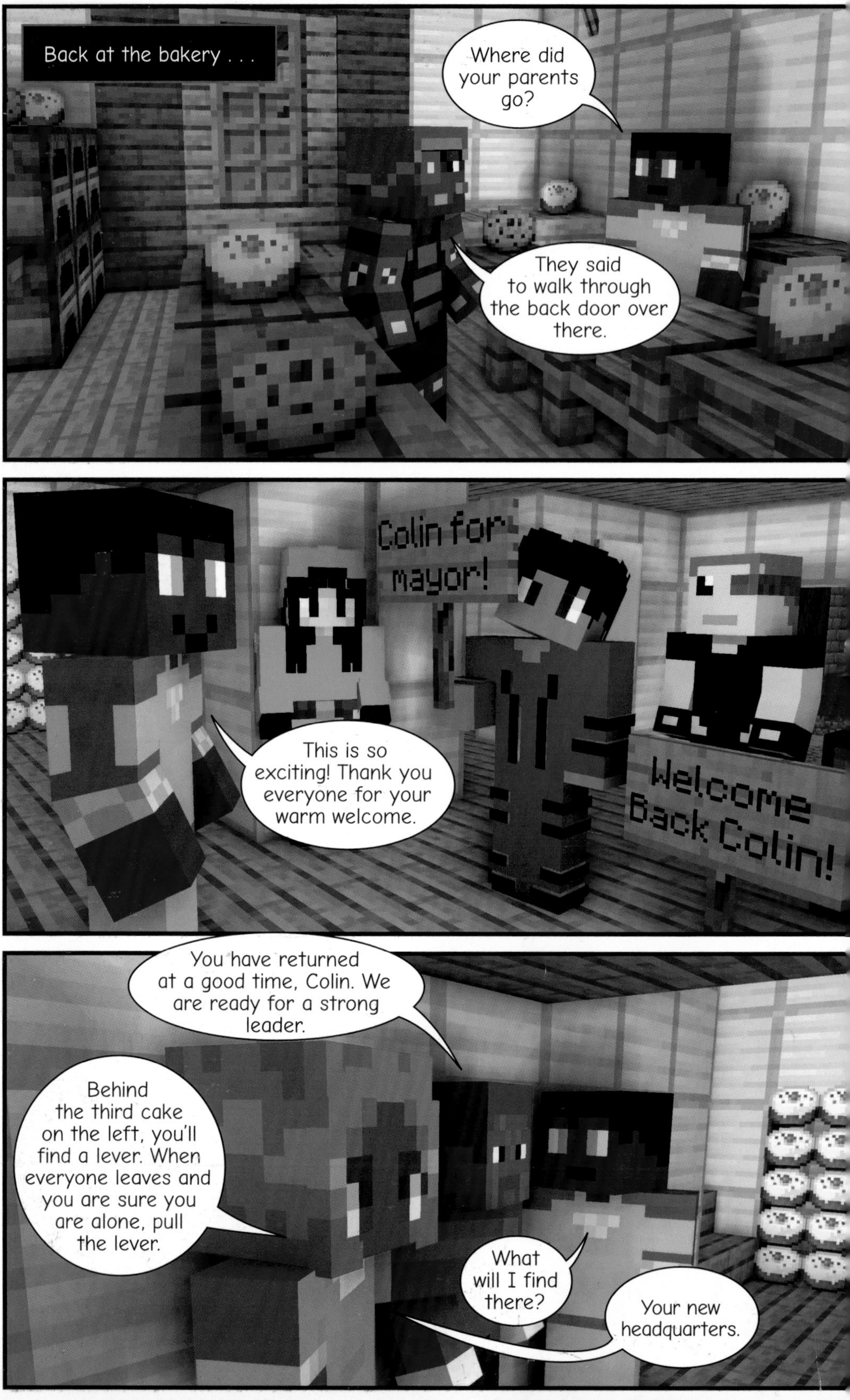
Back at the bakery . . .
Where did your parents go?
They said to walk through the back door over there.
Colin for mayor!
Welcome Back Colin!
This is so exciting! Thank you everyone for your warm welcome.
You have returned at a good time, Colin. We are ready for a strong leader.
Behind the third cake on the left, you'll find a lever. When everyone leaves and you are sure you are alone, pull the lever.
What will I find there?
Your new headquarters.

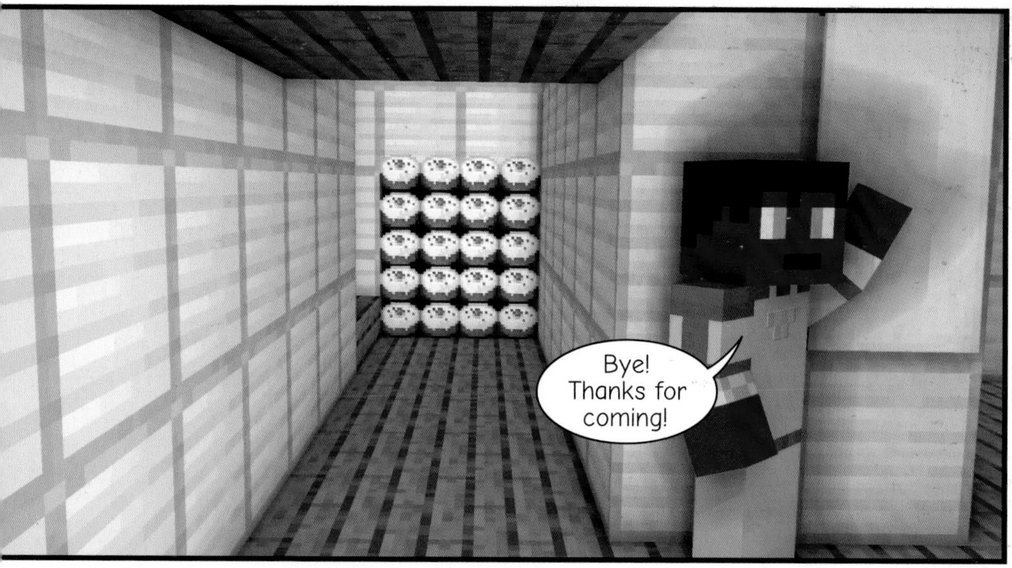
Bye! Thanks for coming!

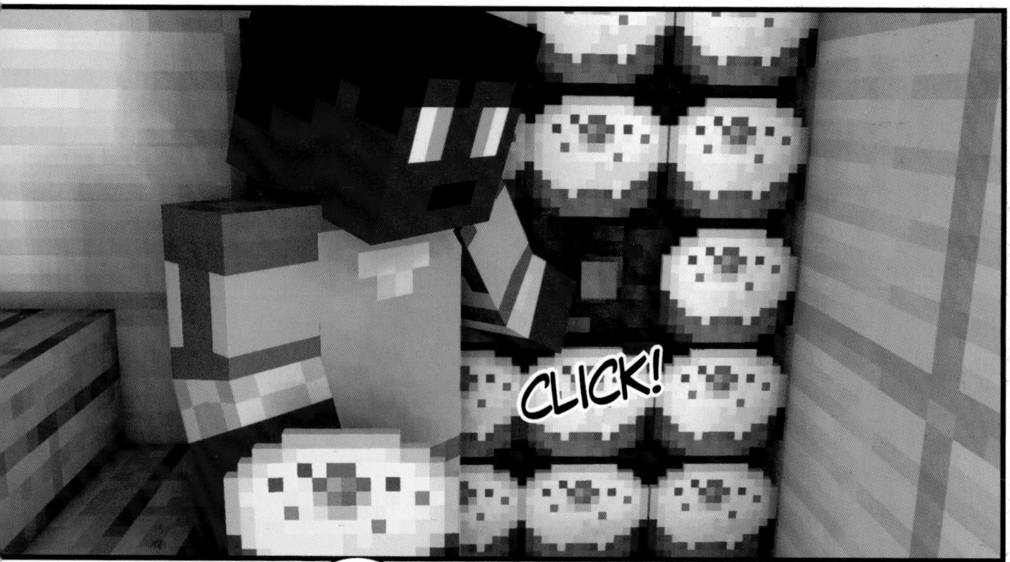
CLICK!

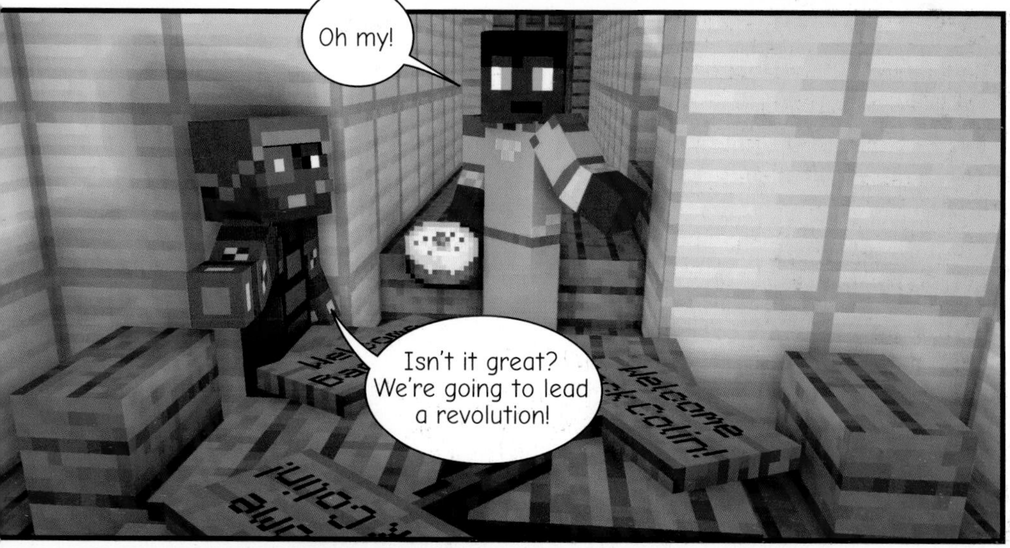
Oh my!
Isn't it great? We're going to lead a revolution!

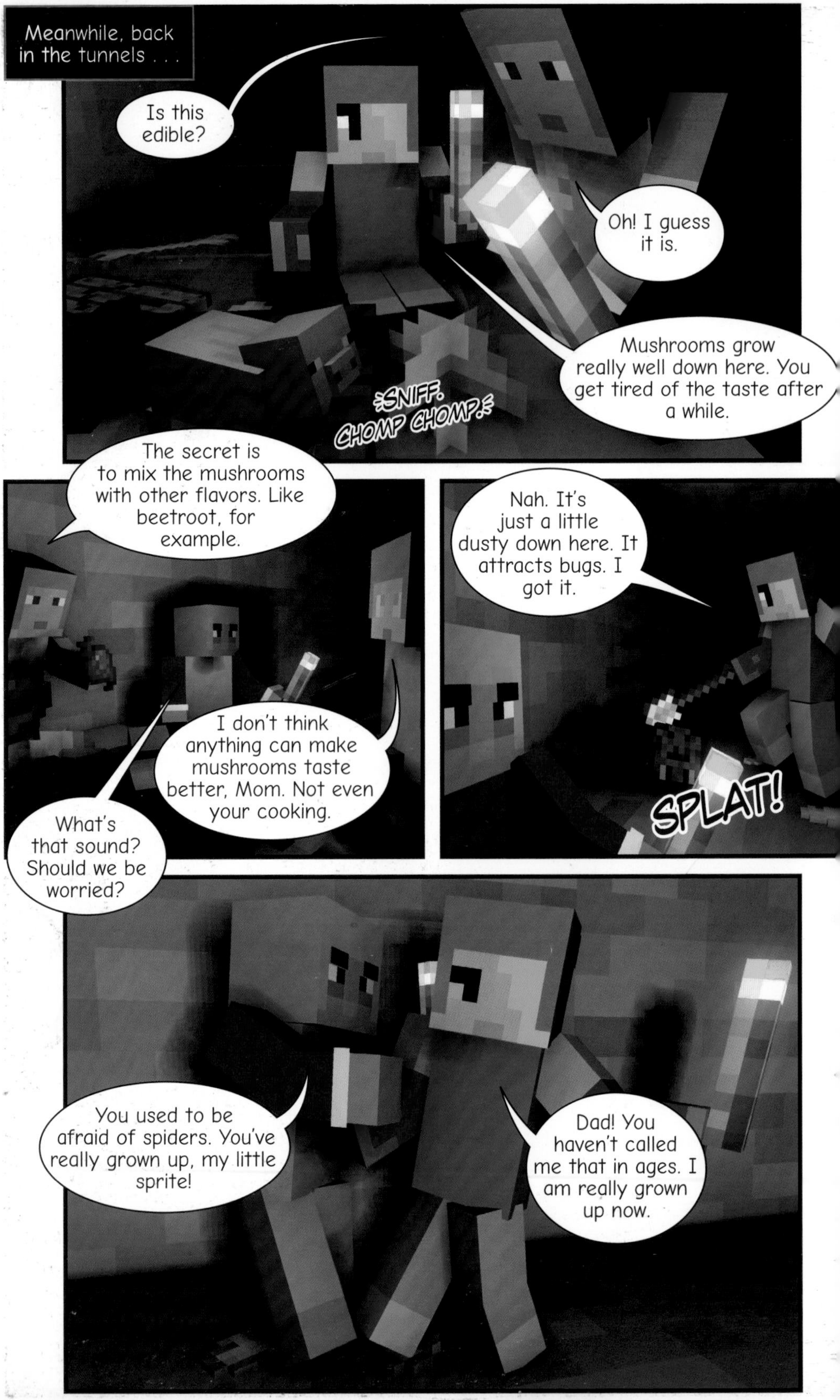

Meanwhile, back in the tunnels . . .
Is this edible?
Oh! I guess it is.
Mushrooms grow really well down here. You get tired of the taste after a while.
SNIFF. CHOMP CHOMP.
The secret is to mix the mushrooms with other flavors. Like beetroot, for example.
I don't think anything can make mushrooms taste better, Mom. Not even your cooking.
What's that sound? Should we be worried?
Nah. It's just a little dusty down here. It attracts bugs. I got it.
SPLAT!
You used to be afraid of spiders. You've really grown up, my little sprite!
Dad! You haven't called me that in ages. I am really grown up now.

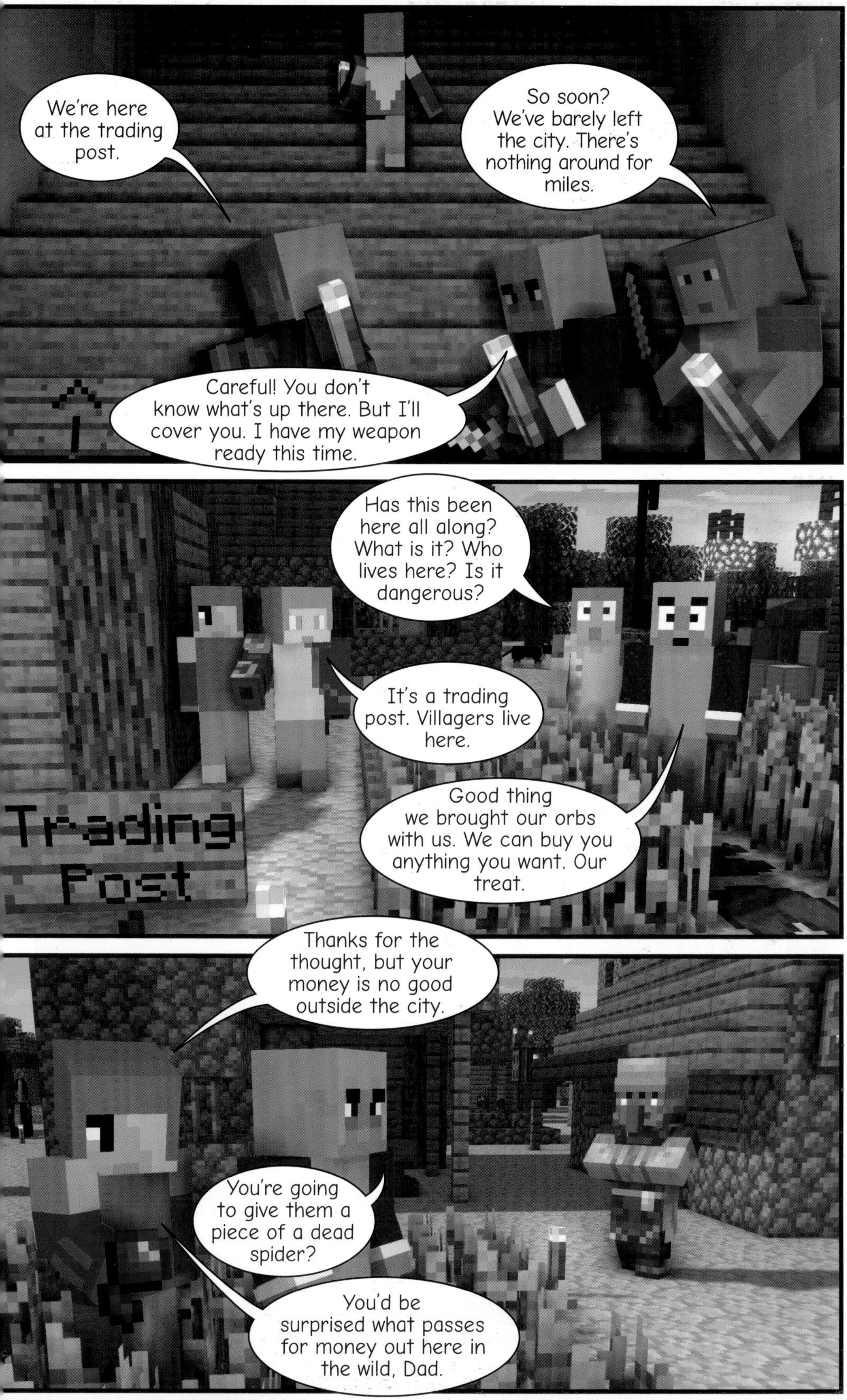
We're here at the trading post.
So soon? We've barely left the city. There's nothing around for miles.
Careful! You don't know what's up there. But I'll cover you. I have my weapon ready this time.
Has this been here all along? What is it? Who lives here? Is it dangerous?
It's a trading post. Villagers live here.
Good thing we brought our orbs with us. We can buy you anything you want. Our treat.
Trading Post
Thanks for the thought, but your money is no good outside the city.
You're going to give them a piece of a dead spider?
You'd be surprised what passes for money out here in the wild, Dad.

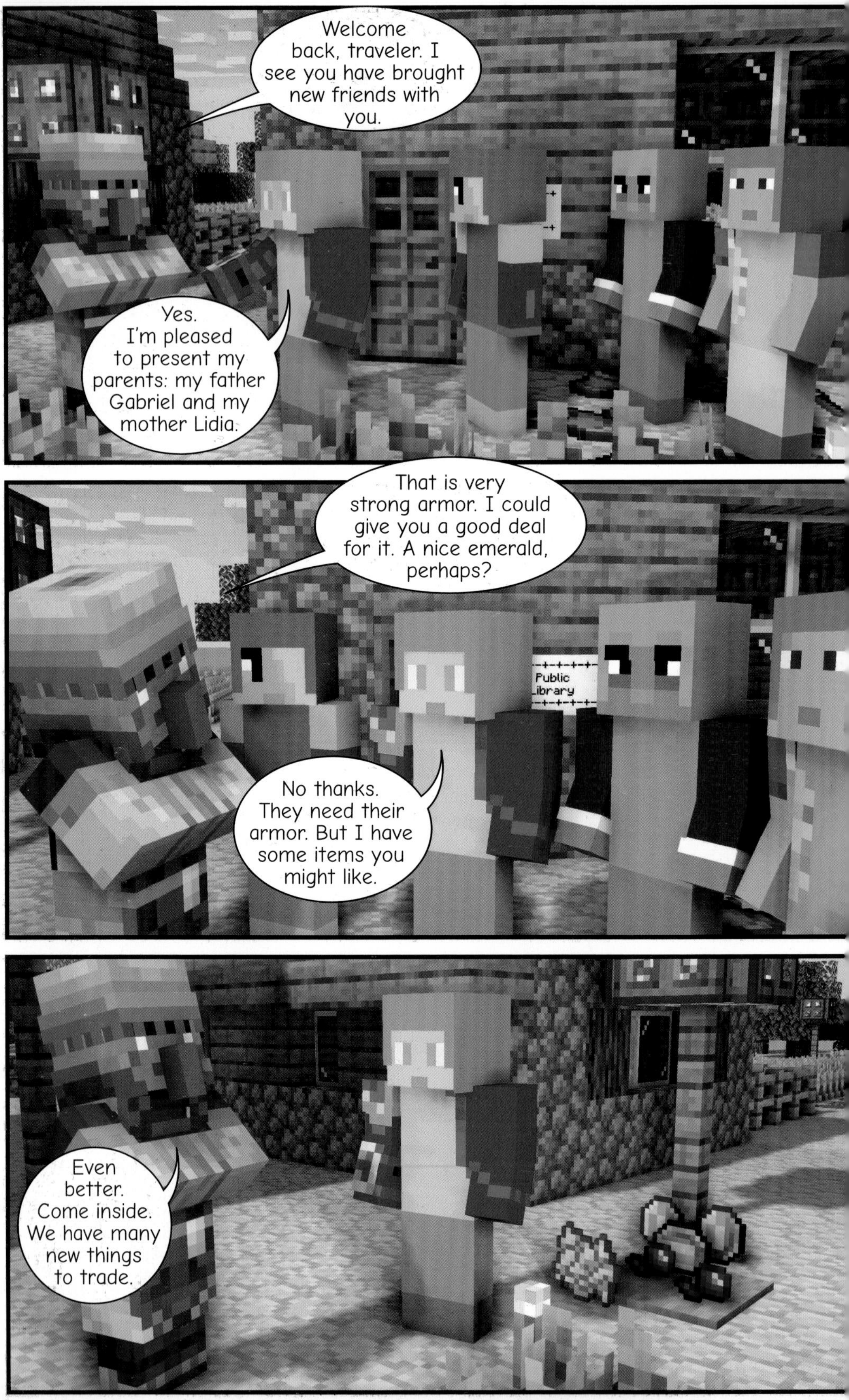
Welcome back, traveler. I see you have brought new friends with you.
Yes. I'm pleased to present my parents: my father Gabriel and my mother Lidia.
That is very strong armor. I could give you a good deal for it. A nice emerald, perhaps?
Public Library
No thanks. They need their armor. But I have some items you might like.
Even better. Come inside. We have many new things to trade.

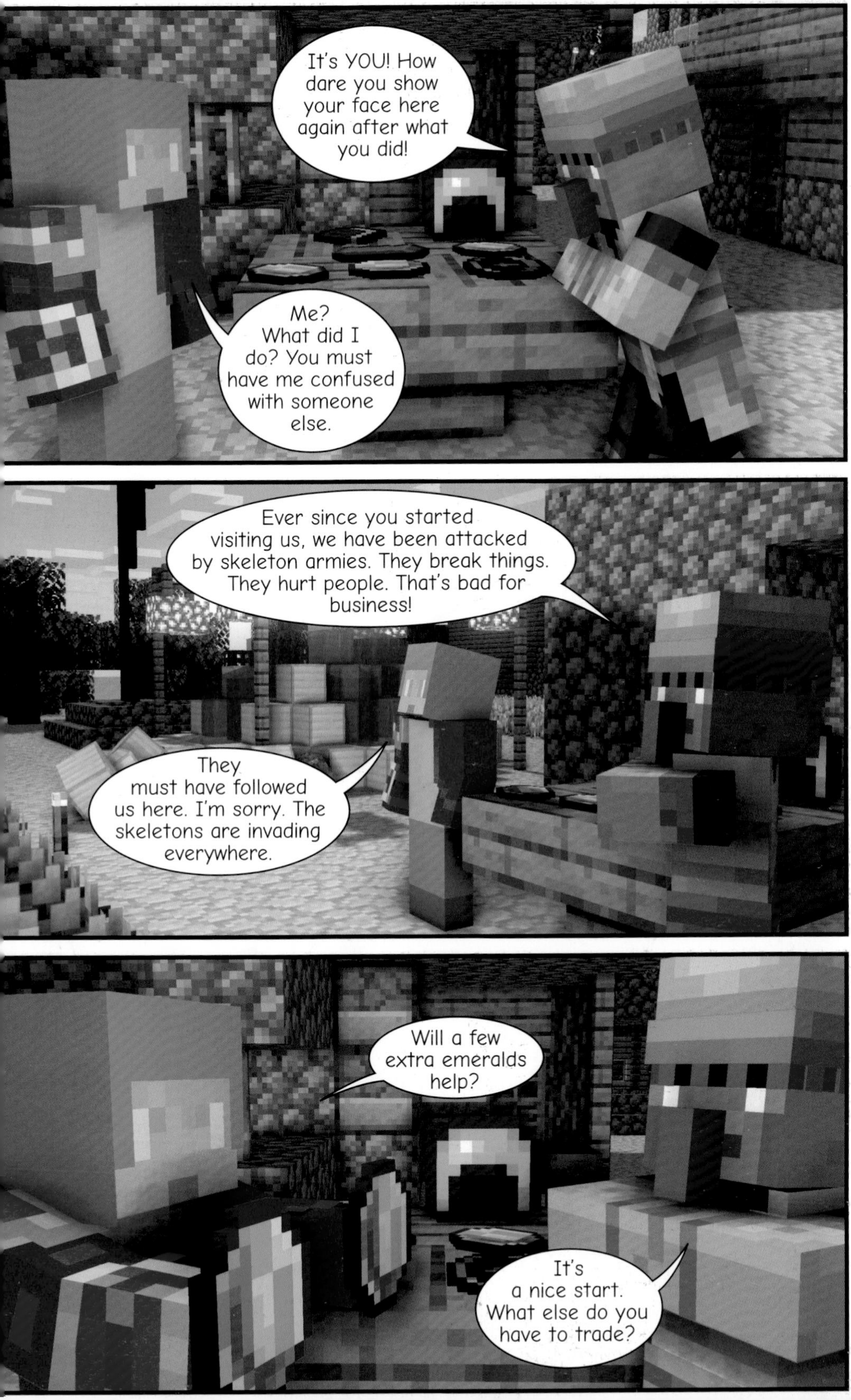
It's YOU! How dare you show your face here again after what you did!
Me? What did I do? You must have me confused with someone else.
Ever since you started visiting us, we have been attacked by skeleton armies. They break things. They hurt people. That's bad for business!
They must have followed us here. I'm sorry. The skeletons are invading everywhere.
Will a few extra emeralds help?
It's a nice start. What else do you have to trade?

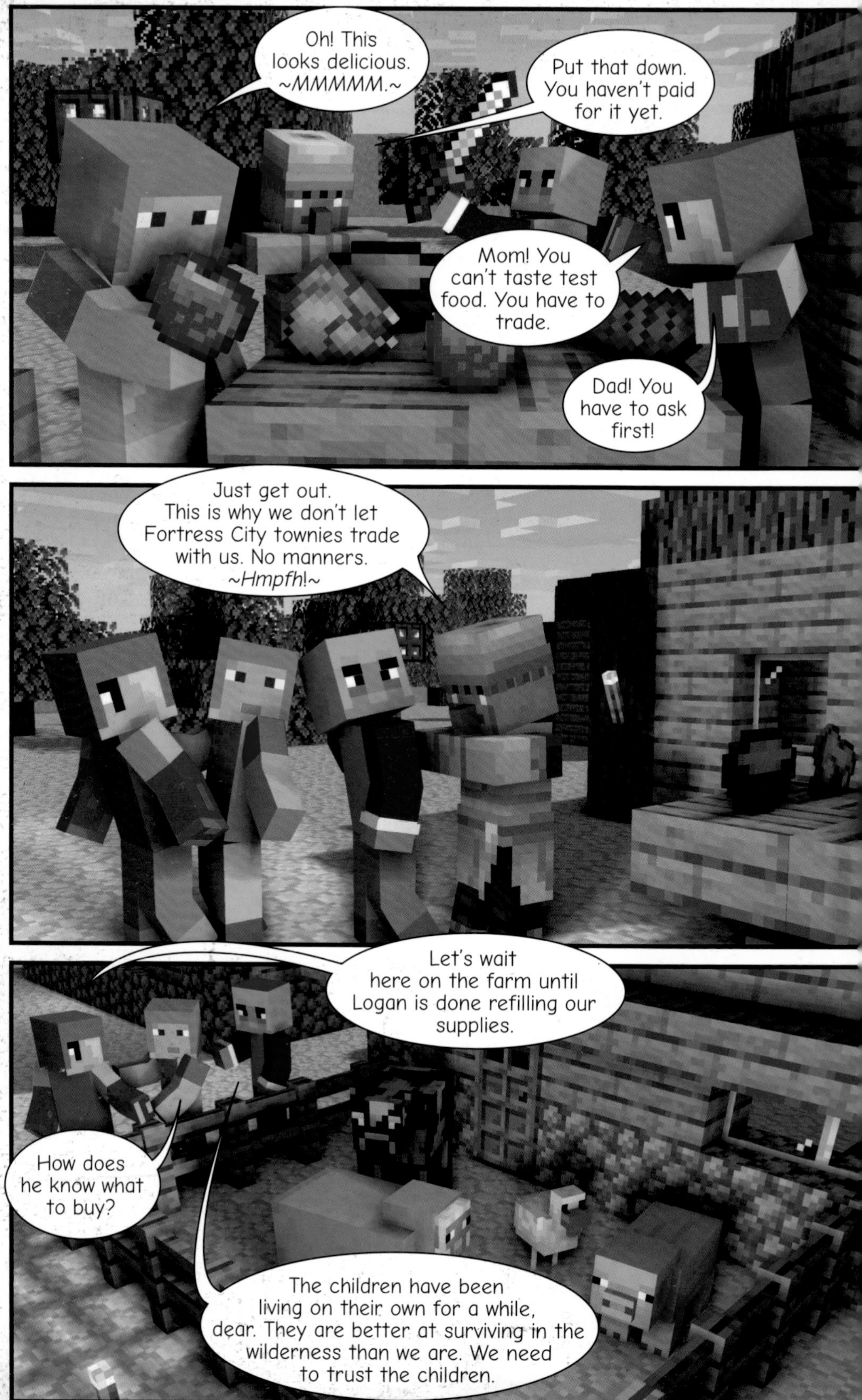
Oh! This looks delicious. ~MMMMM.~
Put that down. You haven't paid for it yet.
Mom! You can't taste test food. You have to trade.
Dad! You have to ask first!
Just get out. This is why we don't let Fortress City townies trade with us. No manners. ~Hmpfh!~
Let's wait here on the farm until Logan is done refilling our supplies.
How does he know what to buy?
The children have been living on their own for a while, dear. They are better at surviving in the wilderness than we are. We need to trust the children.

CHAPTER 6

AT THE EDGE
OF DANGER

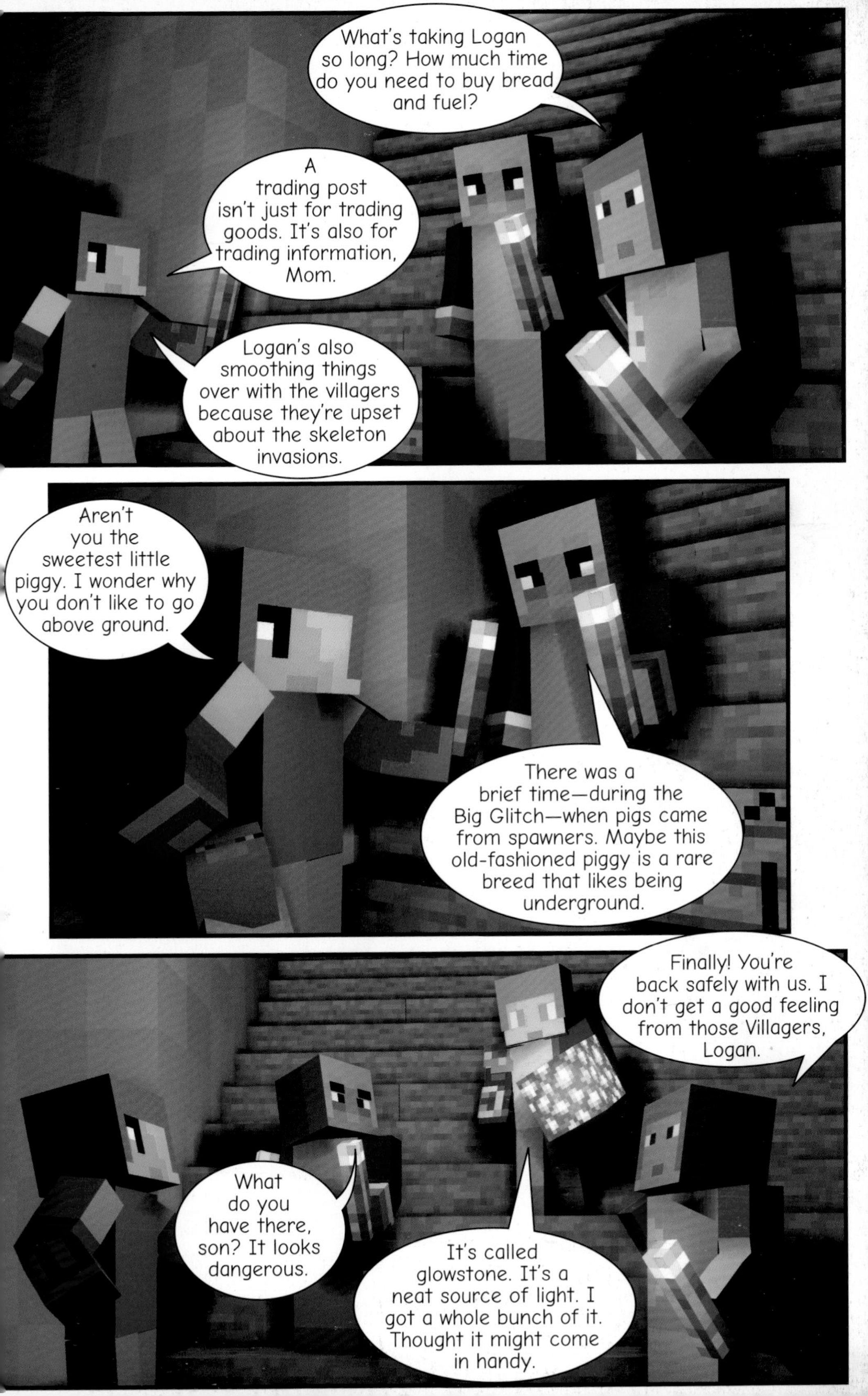
What's taking Logan so long? How much time do you need to buy bread and fuel?
A trading post isn't just for trading goods. It's also for trading information, Mom.
Logan's also smoothing things over with the villagers because they're upset about the skeleton invasions.
Aren't you the sweetest little piggy. I wonder why you don't like to go above ground.
There was a brief time—during the Big Glitch—when pigs came from spawners. Maybe this old-fashioned piggy is a rare breed that likes being underground.
Finally! You're back safely with us. I don't get a good feeling from those Villagers, Logan.
What do you have there, son? It looks dangerous.
It's called glowstone. It's a neat source of light. I got a whole bunch of it. Thought it might come in handy.

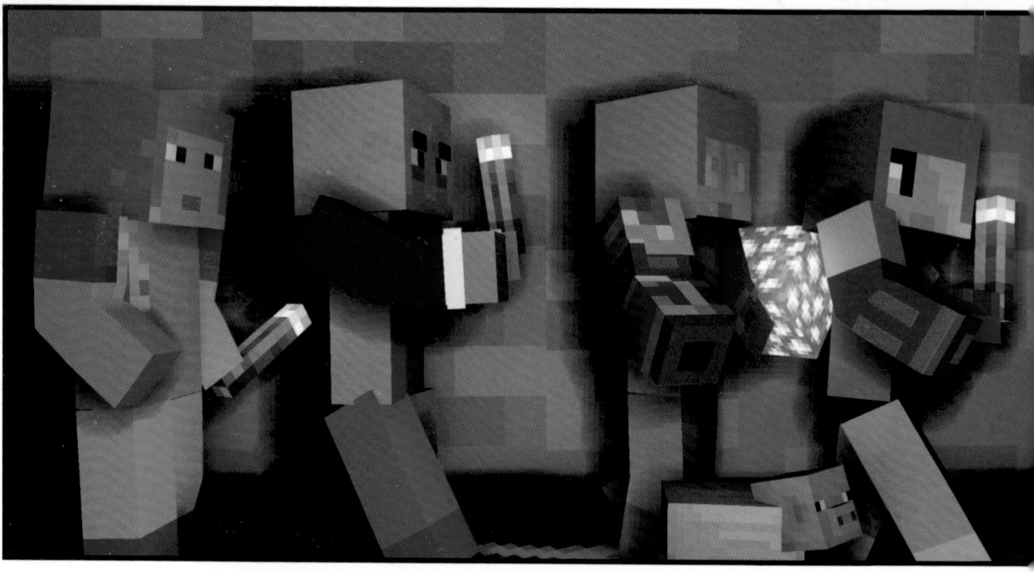

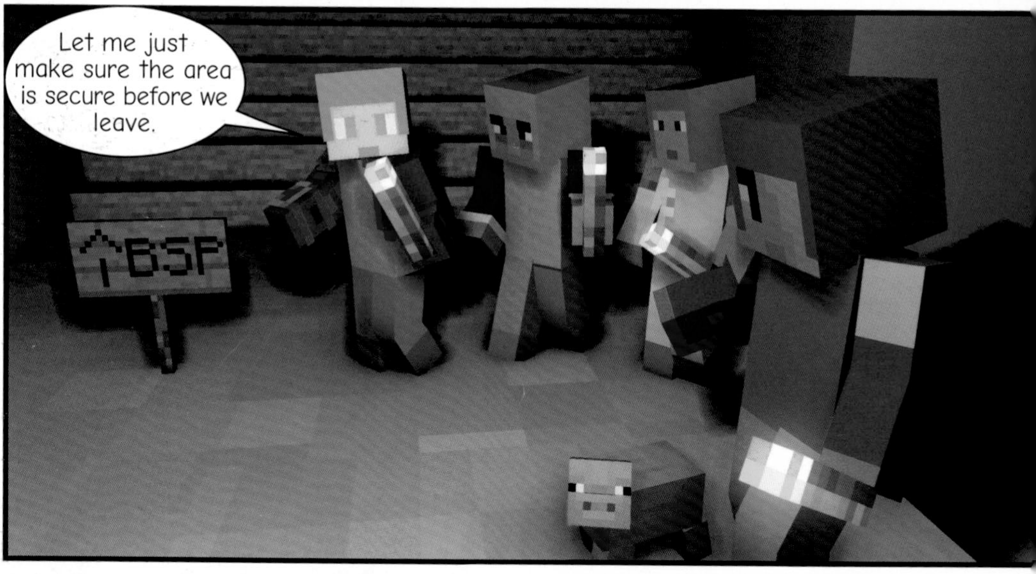
Let me just make sure the area is secure before we leave.
BSP

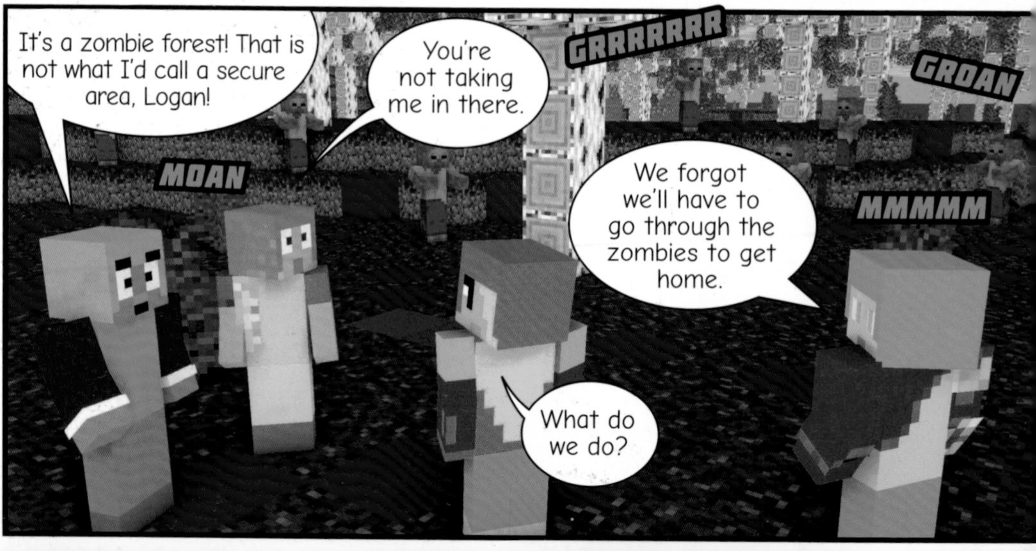
It's a zombie forest! That is not what I'd call a secure area, Logan!
You're not taking me in there.
GRRRRRRR
GROAN
MOAN
We forgot we'll have to go through the zombies to get home.
MMMMM
What do we do?

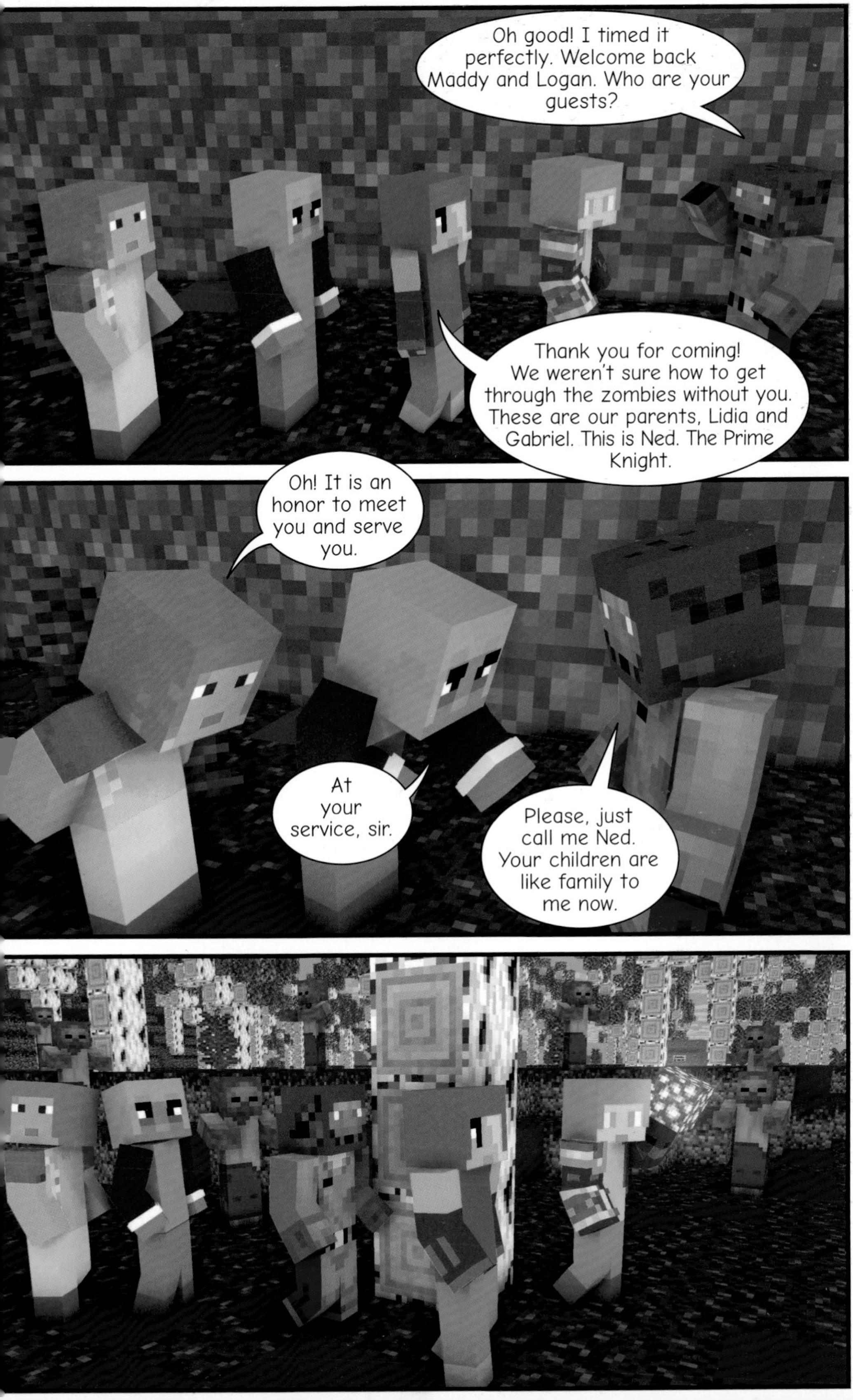
Oh good! I timed it perfectly. Welcome back Maddy and Logan. Who are your guests?
Thank you for coming! We weren't sure how to get through the zombies without you. These are our parents, Lidia and Gabriel. This is Ned. The Prime Knight.
Oh! It is an honor to meet you and serve you.
At your service, sir.
Please, just call me Ned. Your children are like family to me now.

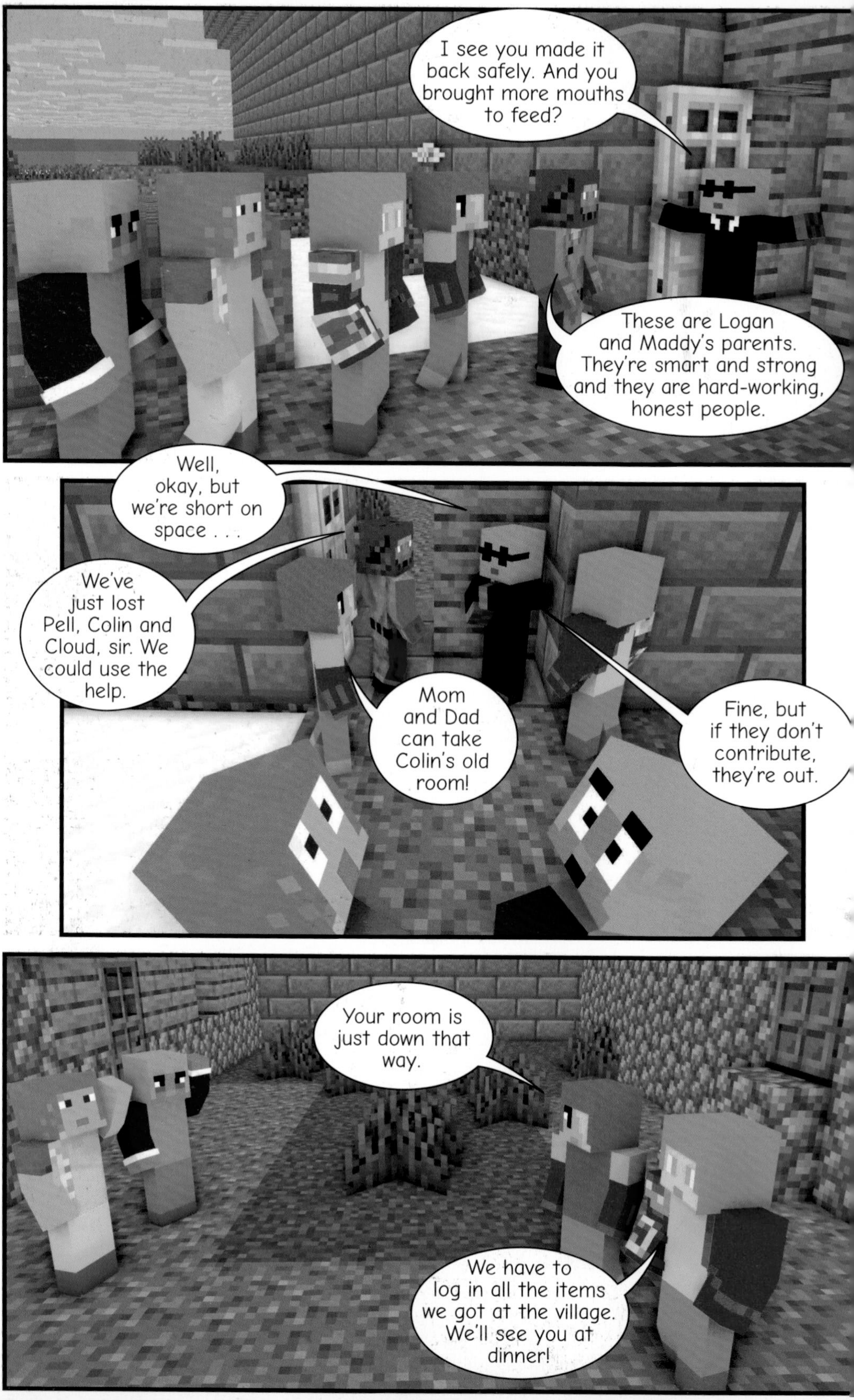
I see you made it back safely. And you brought more mouths to feed?
These are Logan and Maddy's parents. They're smart and strong and they are hard-working, honest people.
Well, okay, but we're short on space . . .
We've just lost Pell, Colin and Cloud, sir. We could use the help.
Mom and Dad can take Colin's old room!
Fine, but if they don't contribute, they're out.
Your room is just down that way.
We have to log in all the items we got at the village. We'll see you at dinner!

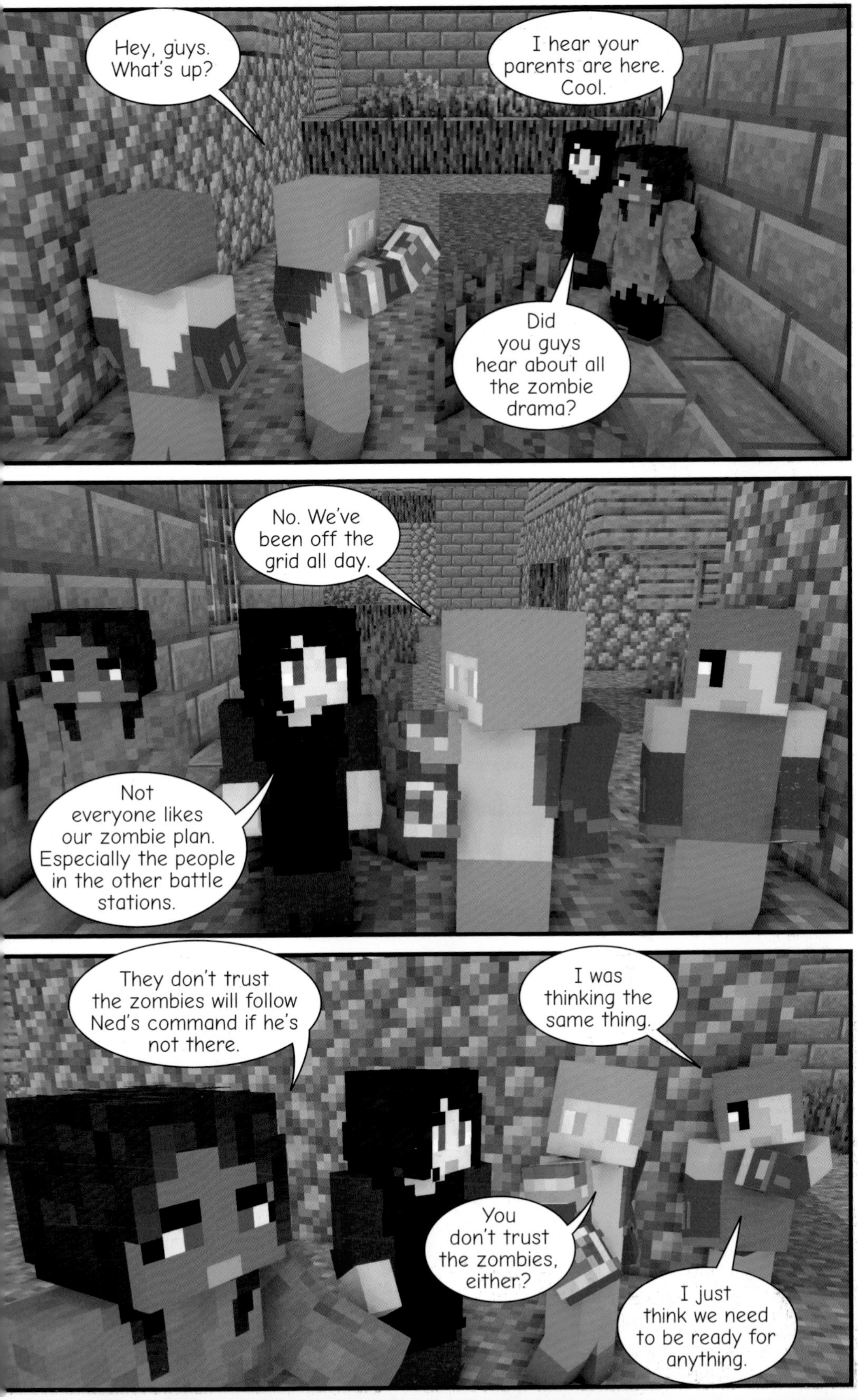
Hey, guys. What's up?
I hear your parents are here. Cool.
Did you guys hear about all the zombie drama?
No. We've been off the grid all day.
Not everyone likes our zombie plan. Especially the people in the other battle stations.
They don't trust the zombies will follow Ned's command if he's not there.
I was thinking the same thing.
You don't trust the zombies, either?
I just think we need to be ready for anything.

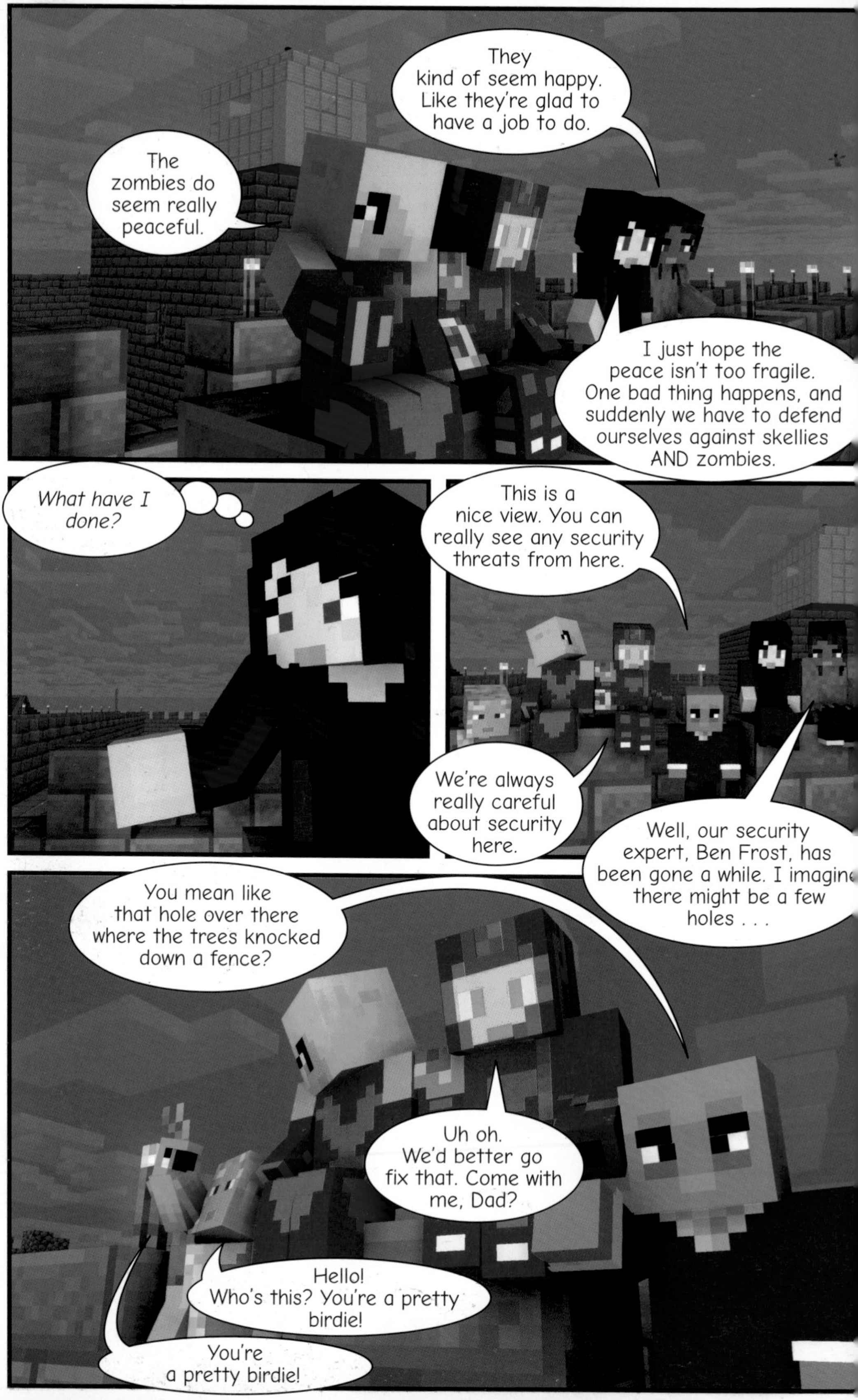
The zombies do seem really peaceful.
They kind of seem happy. Like they're glad to have a job to do.
I just hope the peace isn't too fragile. One bad thing happens, and suddenly we have to defend ourselves against skellies AND zombies.
What have I done?
This is a nice view. You can really see any security threats from here.
We're always really careful about security here.
Well, our security expert, Ben Frost, has been gone a while. I imagine there might be a few holes . . .
You mean like that hole over there where the trees knocked down a fence?
Uh oh. We'd better go fix that. Come with me, Dad?
Hello! Who's this? You're a pretty birdie!
You're a pretty birdie!

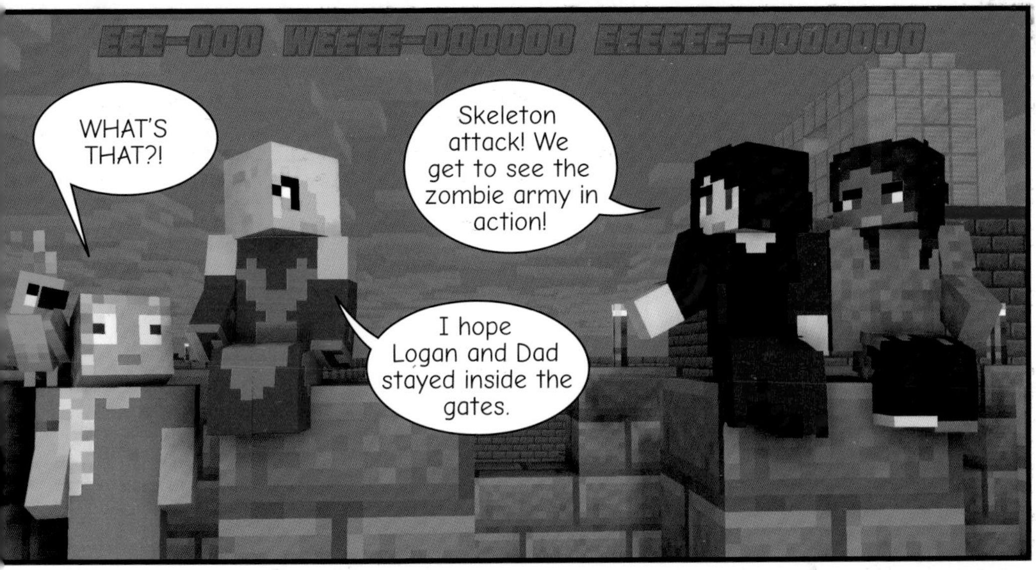
EEE-OOO WEEEE-OOOOOO EEEEEE-OOOOOOO
WHAT'S THAT?!
Skeleton attack! We get to see the zombie army in action!
I hope Logan and Dad stayed inside the gates.

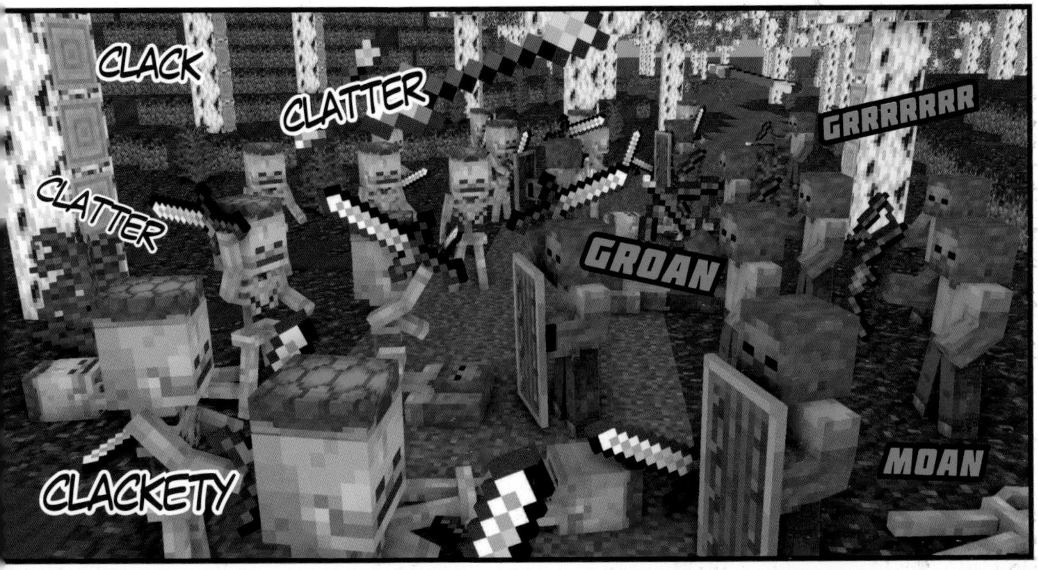
CLACK
CLATTER
GRRRRRRR
CLATTER
GROAN
MOAN
CLACKETY

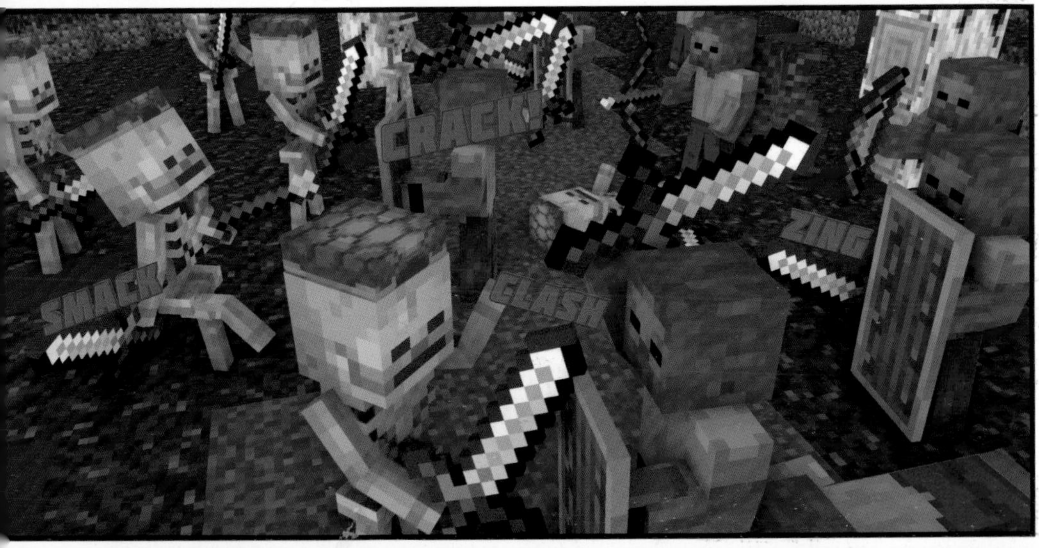
CRACK!
ZING
SMACK
CLASH

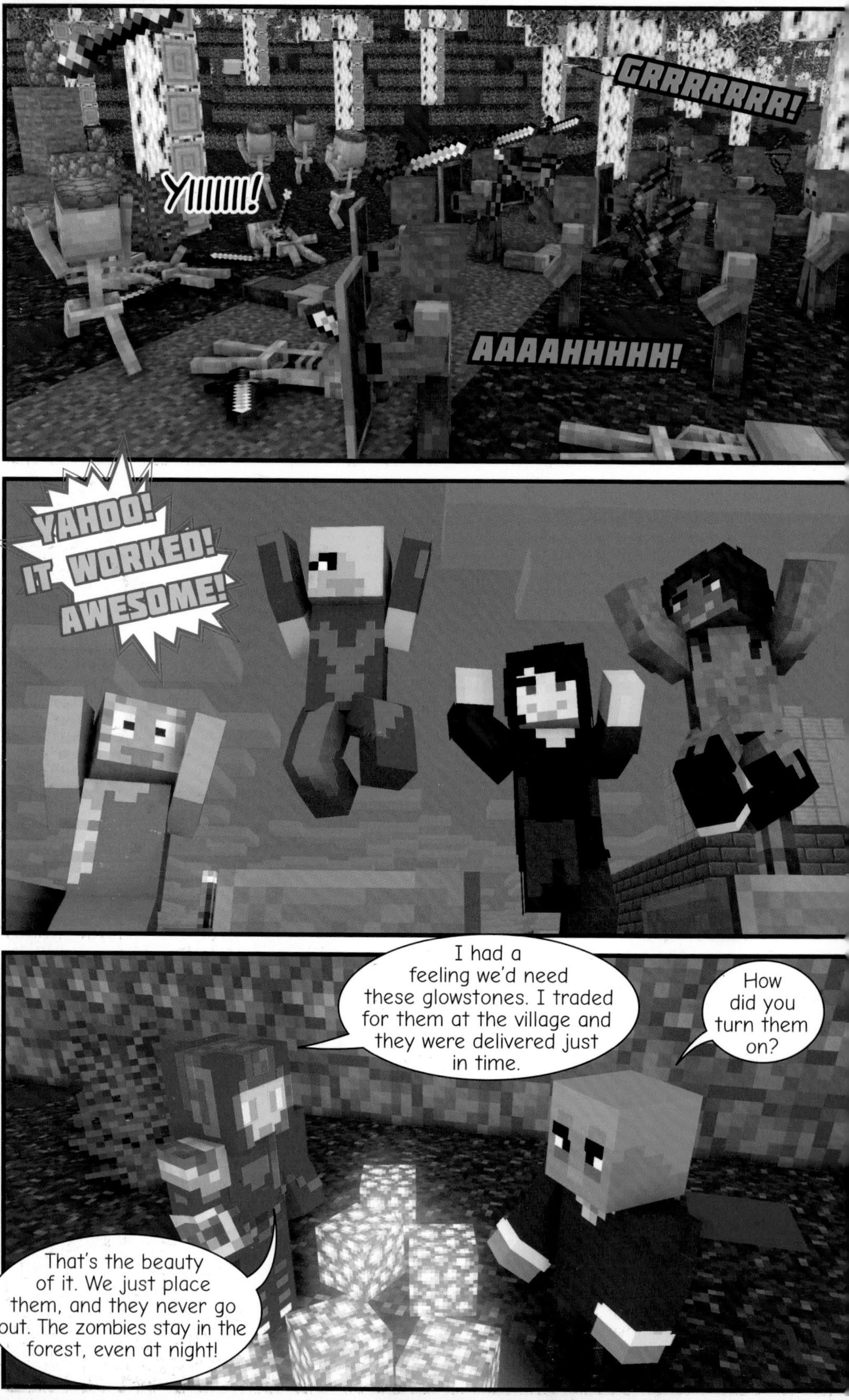
GRRRRRRR!
YIIIIIIII!
AAAAHHHHH!
YAHOO! IT WORKED! AWESOME!
I had a feeling we'd need these glowstones. I traded for them at the village and they were delivered just in time.
How did you turn them on?
That's the beauty of it. We just place them, and they never go out. The zombies stay in the forest, even at night!

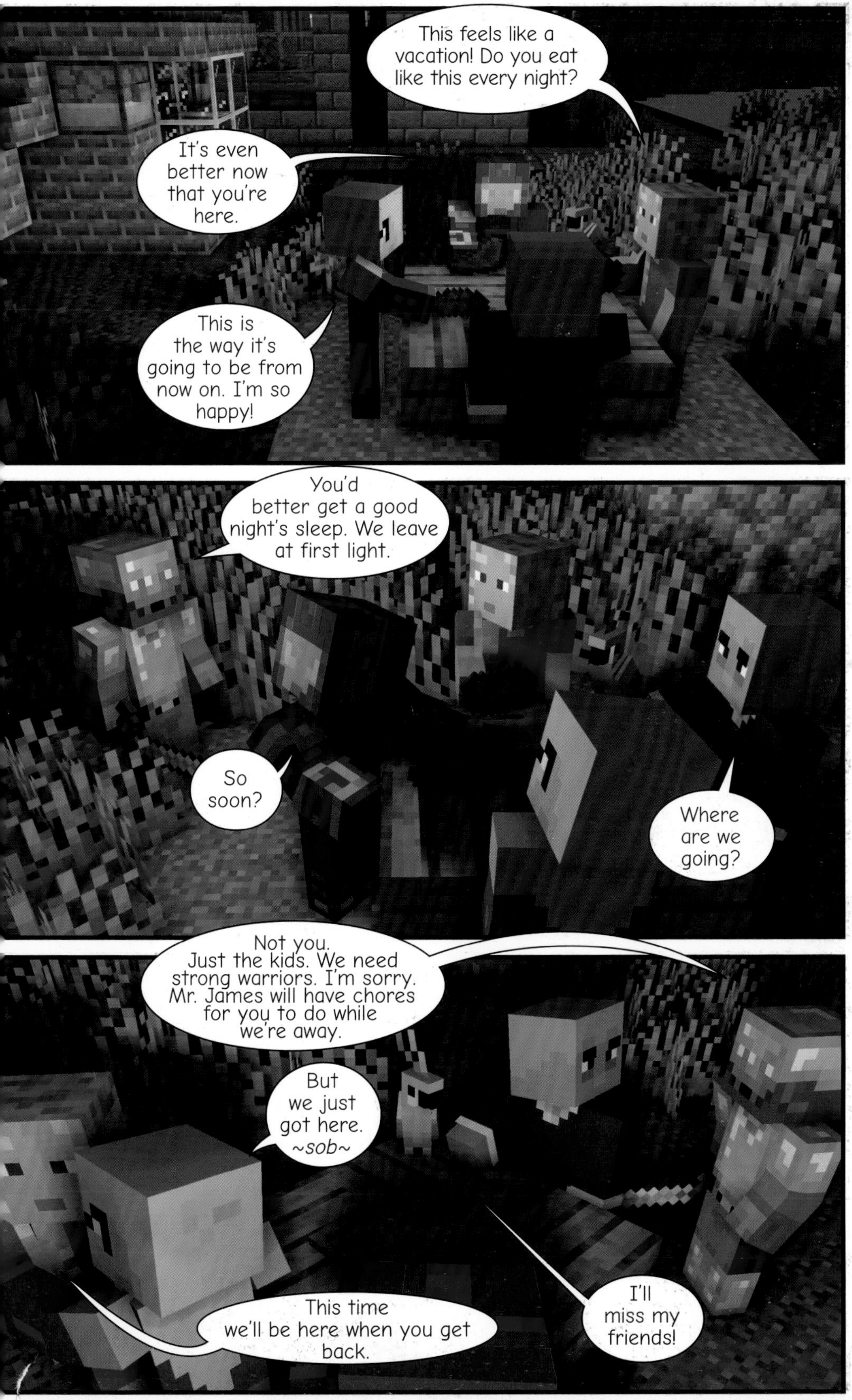
This feels like a vacation! Do you eat like this every night?
It's even better now that you're here.
This is the way it's going to be from now on. I'm so happy!
You'd better get a good night's sleep. We leave at first light.
So soon?
Where are we going?
Not you. Just the kids. We need strong warriors. I'm sorry. Mr. James will have chores for you to do while we're away.
But we just got here. ~sob~
This time we'll be here when you get back.
I'll miss my friends!

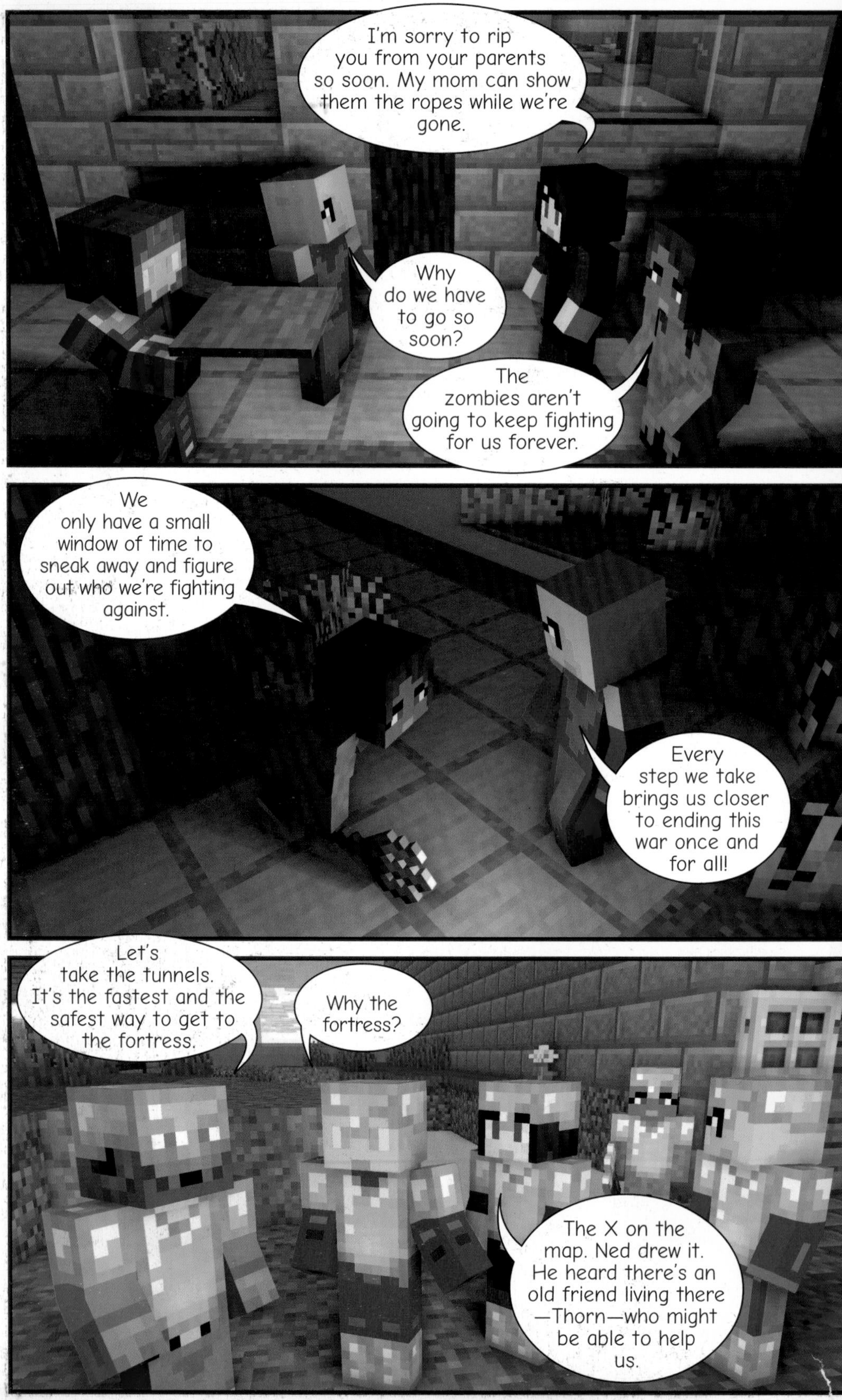
I'm sorry to rip you from your parents so soon. My mom can show them the ropes while we're gone.
Why do we have to go so soon?
The zombies aren't going to keep fighting for us forever.
We only have a small window of time to sneak away and figure out who we're fighting against.
Every step we take brings us closer to ending this war once and for all!
Let's take the tunnels. It's the fastest and the safest way to get to the fortress.
Why the fortress?
The X on the map. Ned drew it. He heard there's an old friend living there —Thorn—who might be able to help us.

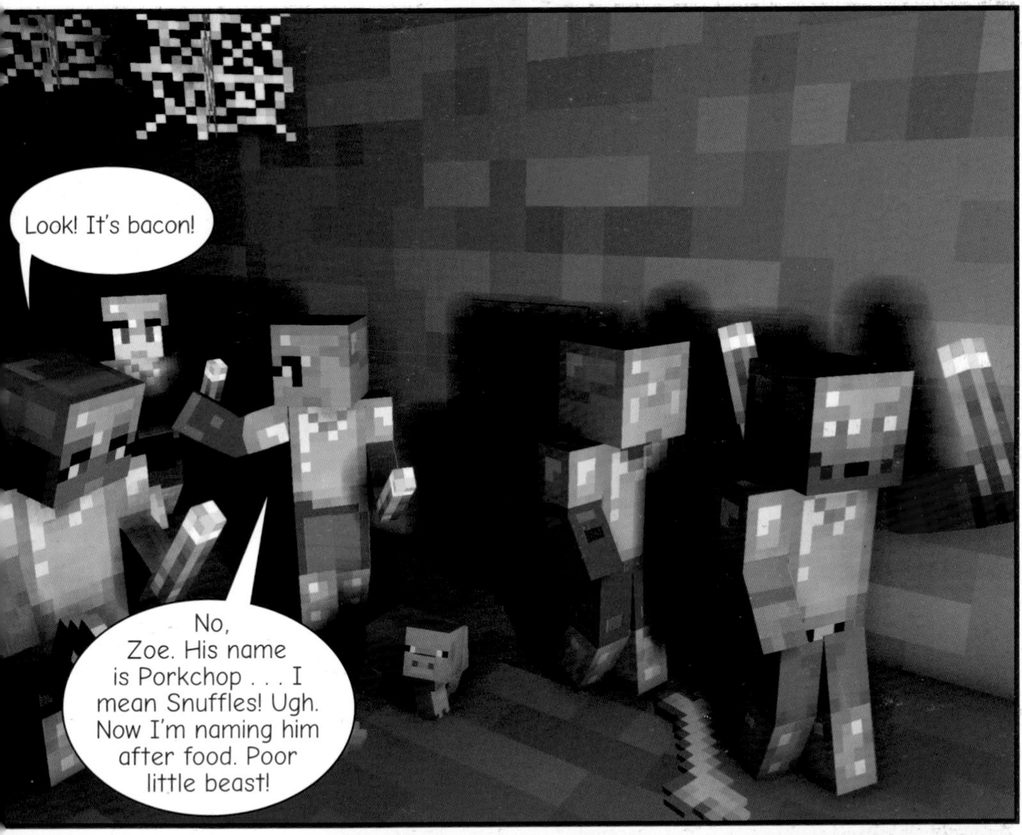
Look! It's bacon!
No, Zoe. His name is Porkchop . . . I mean Snuffles! Ugh. Now I'm naming him after food. Poor little beast!

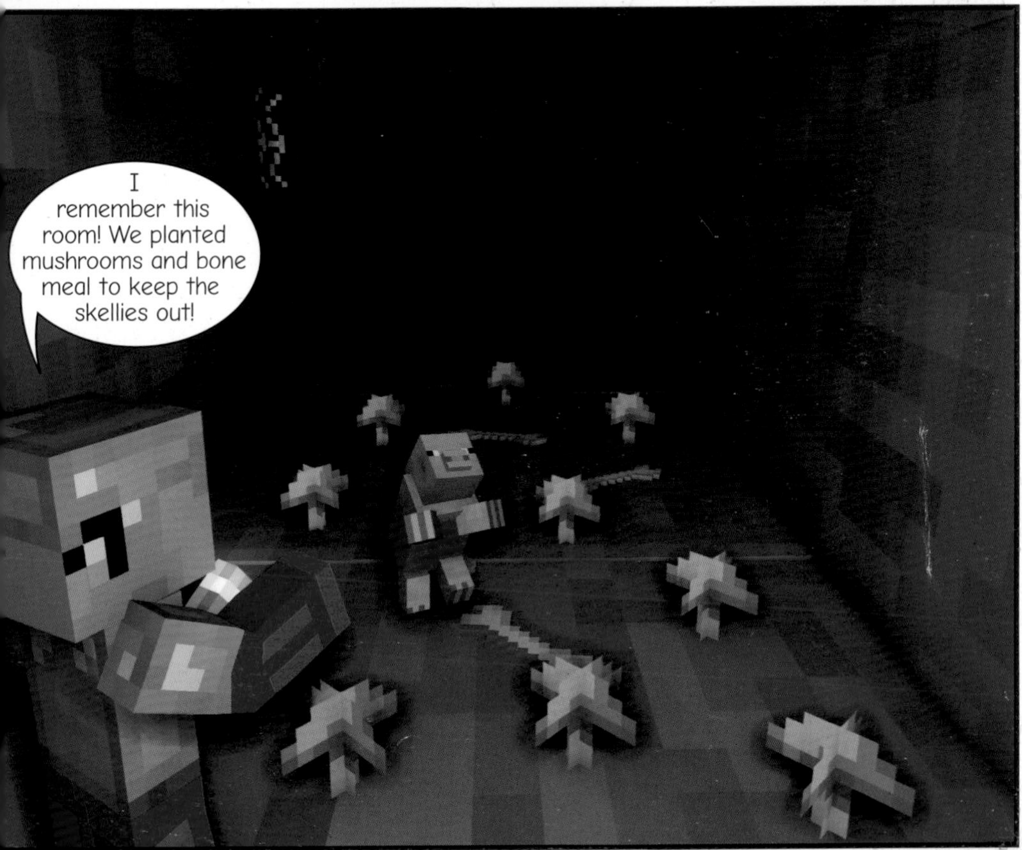
I remember this room! We planted mushrooms and bone meal to keep the skellies out!

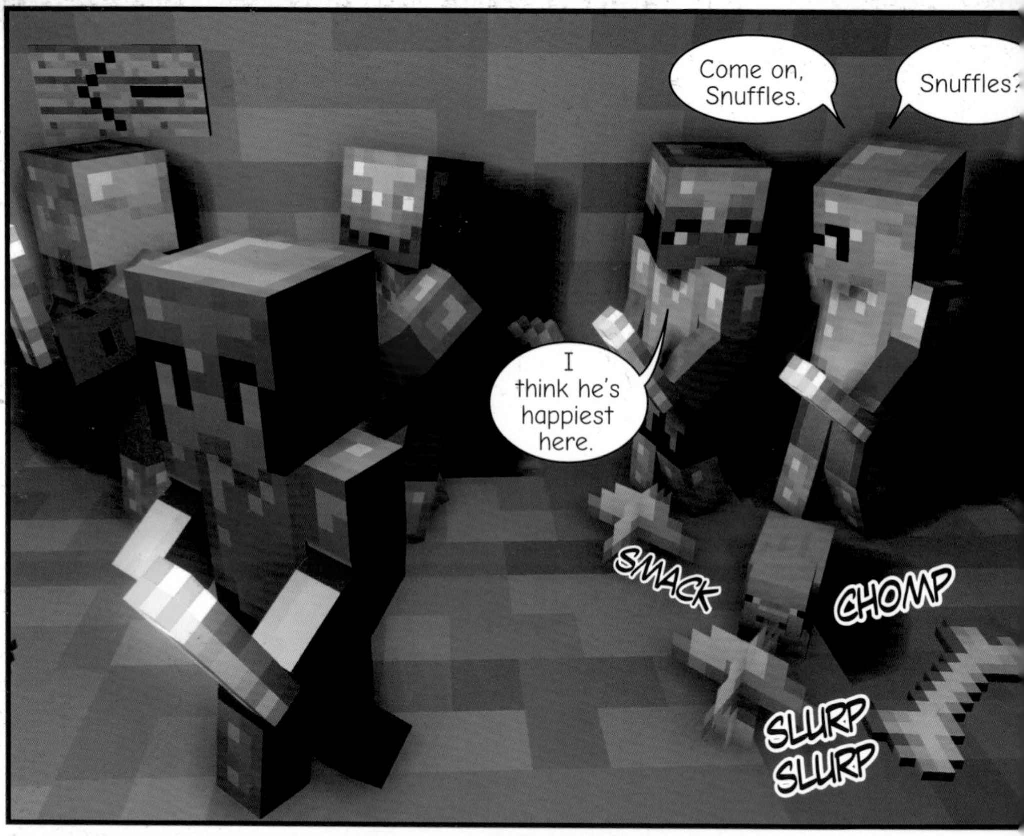
Come on, Snuffles.
Snuffles?
I think he's happiest here.
SMACK
CHOMP
SLURP SLURP

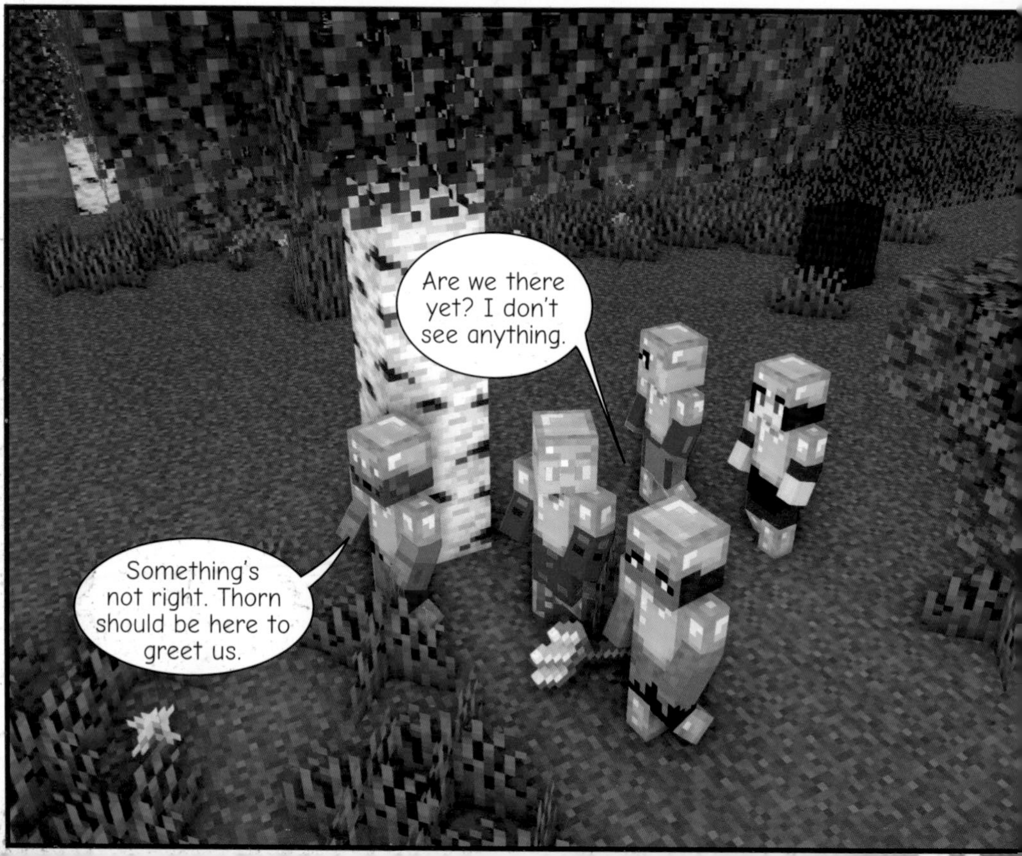
Are we there yet? I don't see anything.
Something's not right. Thorn should be here to greet us.

CHAPTER 7

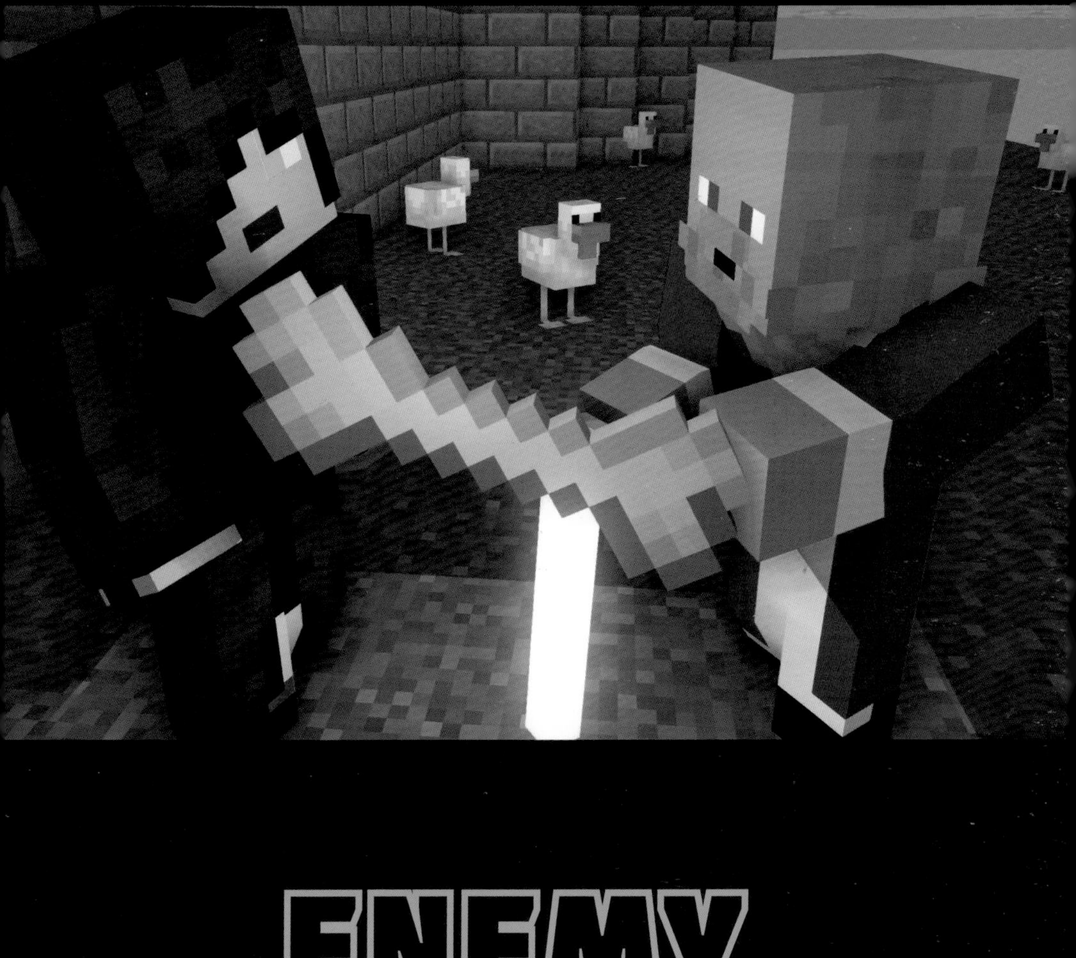

ENEMY SECRETS

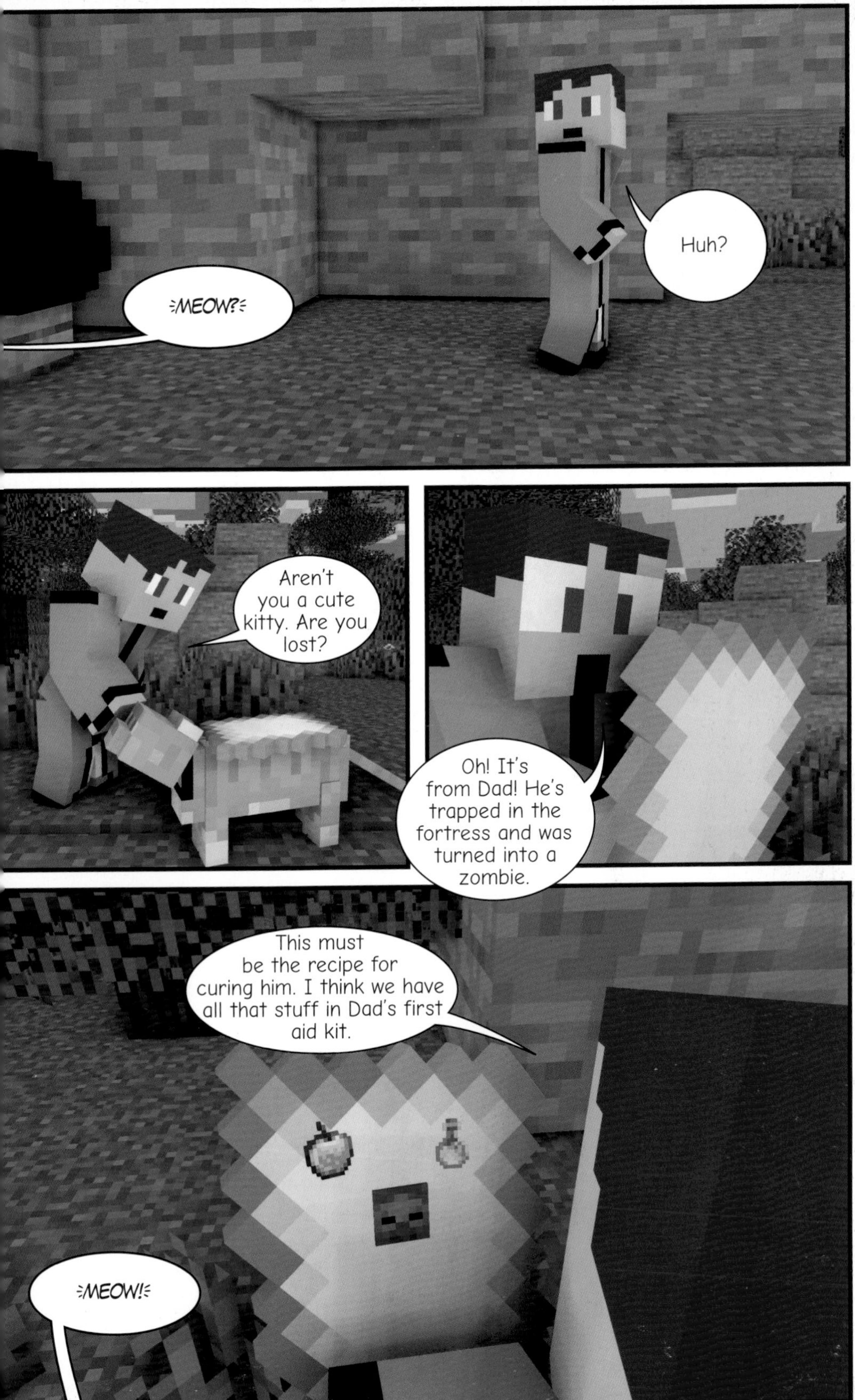
Huh?
MEOW?
Aren't you a cute kitty. Are you lost?
Oh! It's from Dad! He's trapped in the fortress and was turned into a zombie.
This must be the recipe for curing him. I think we have all that stuff in Dad's first aid kit.
MEOW!

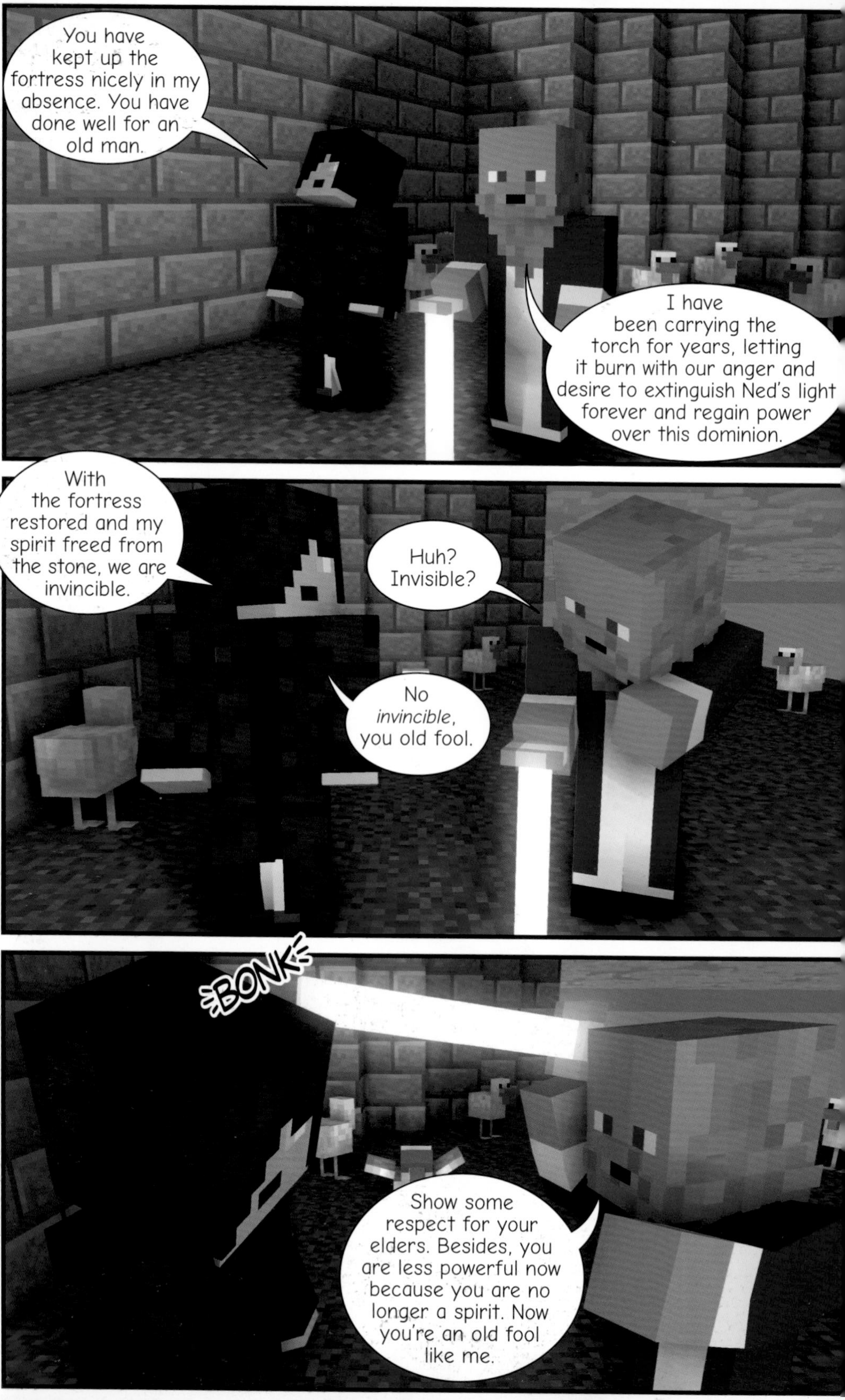
You have kept up the fortress nicely in my absence. You have done well for an old man.
I have been carrying the torch for years, letting it burn with our anger and desire to extinguish Ned's light forever and regain power over this dominion.
With the fortress restored and my spirit freed from the stone, we are invincible.
Huh? Invisible?
No *invincible*, you old fool.
BONK
Show some respect for your elders. Besides, you are less powerful now because you are no longer a spirit. Now you're an old fool like me.

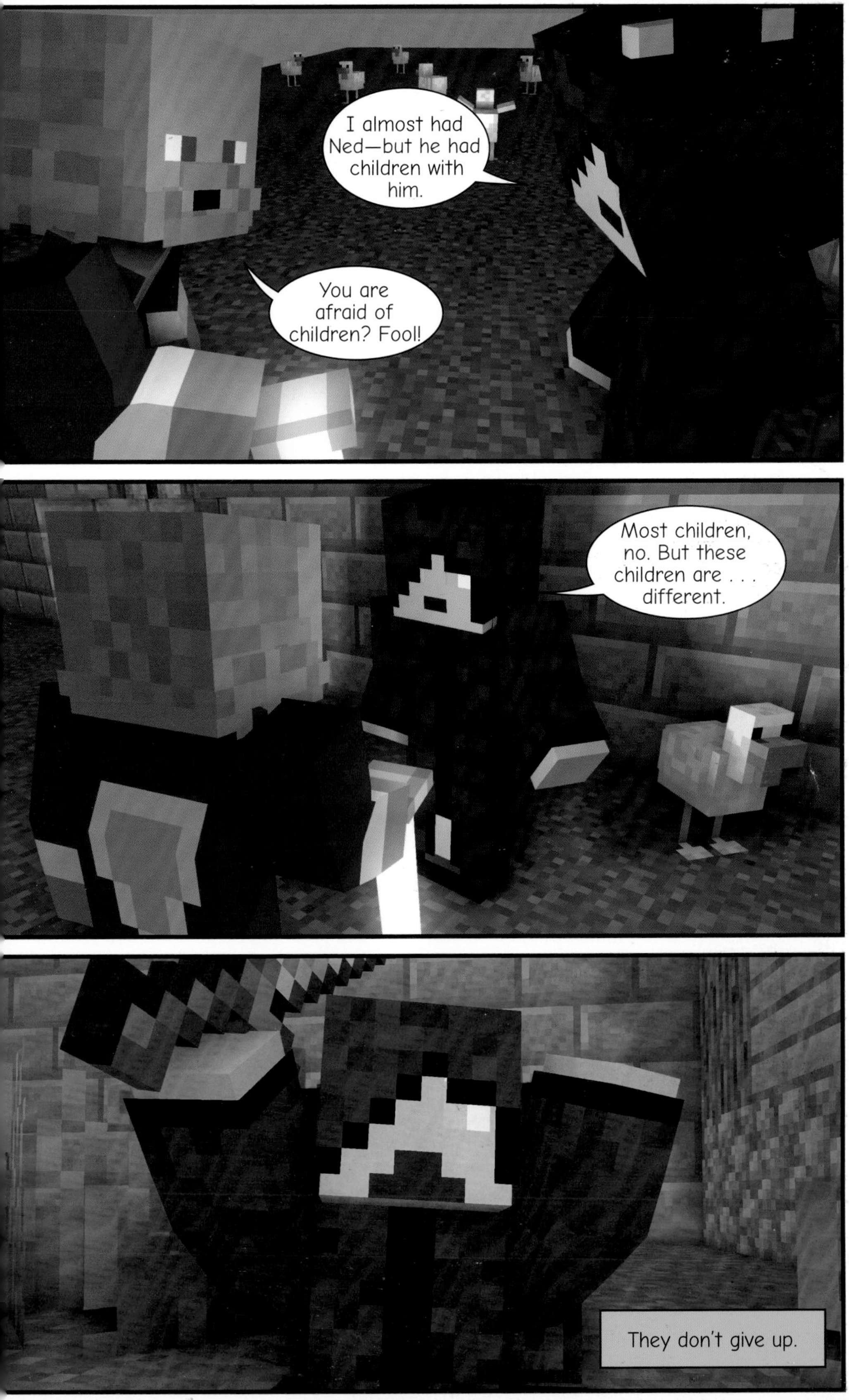
I almost had Ned—but he had children with him.
You are afraid of children? Fool!
Most children, no. But these children are . . . different.
They don't give up.

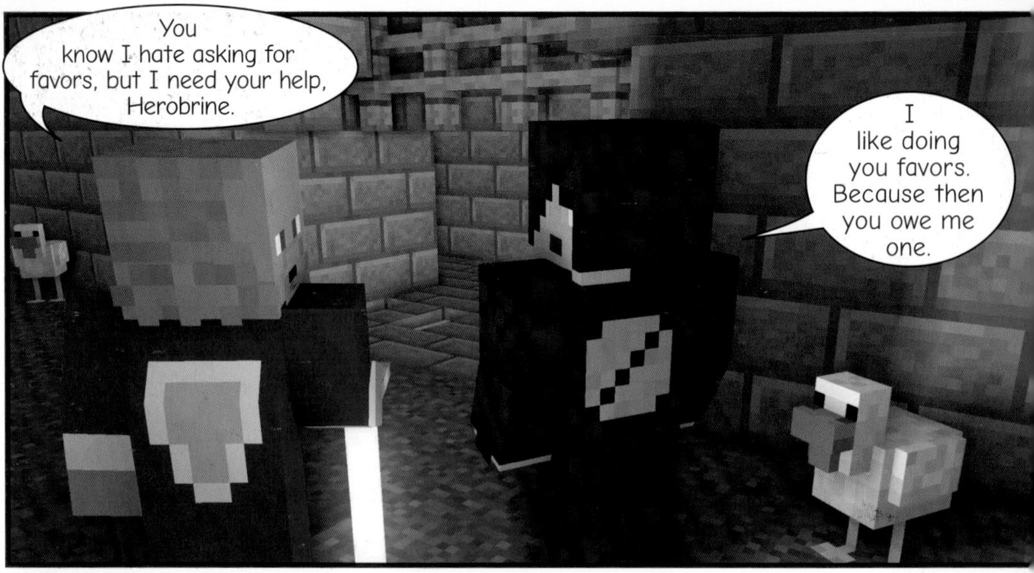
You know I hate asking for favors, but I need your help, Herobrine.
I like doing you favors. Because then you owe me one.

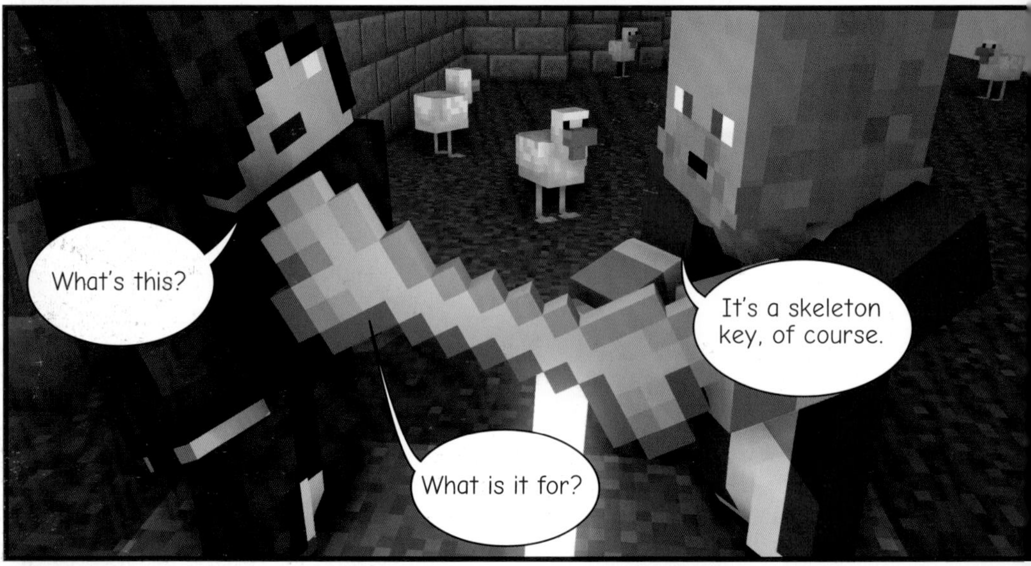
What's this?
It's a skeleton key, of course.
What is it for?

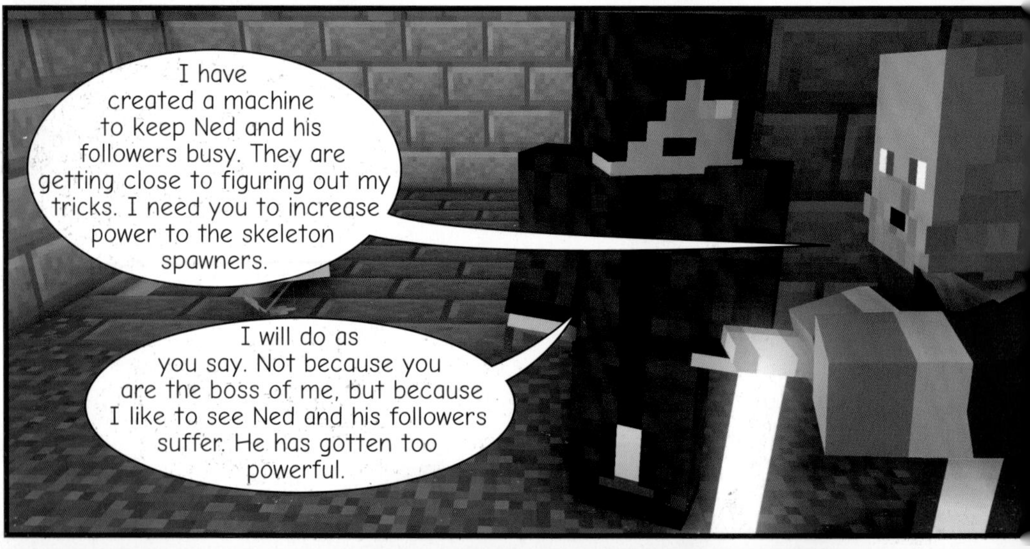
I have created a machine to keep Ned and his followers busy. They are getting close to figuring out my tricks. I need you to increase power to the skeleton spawners.
I will do as you say. Not because you are the boss of me, but because I like to see Ned and his followers suffer. He has gotten too powerful.

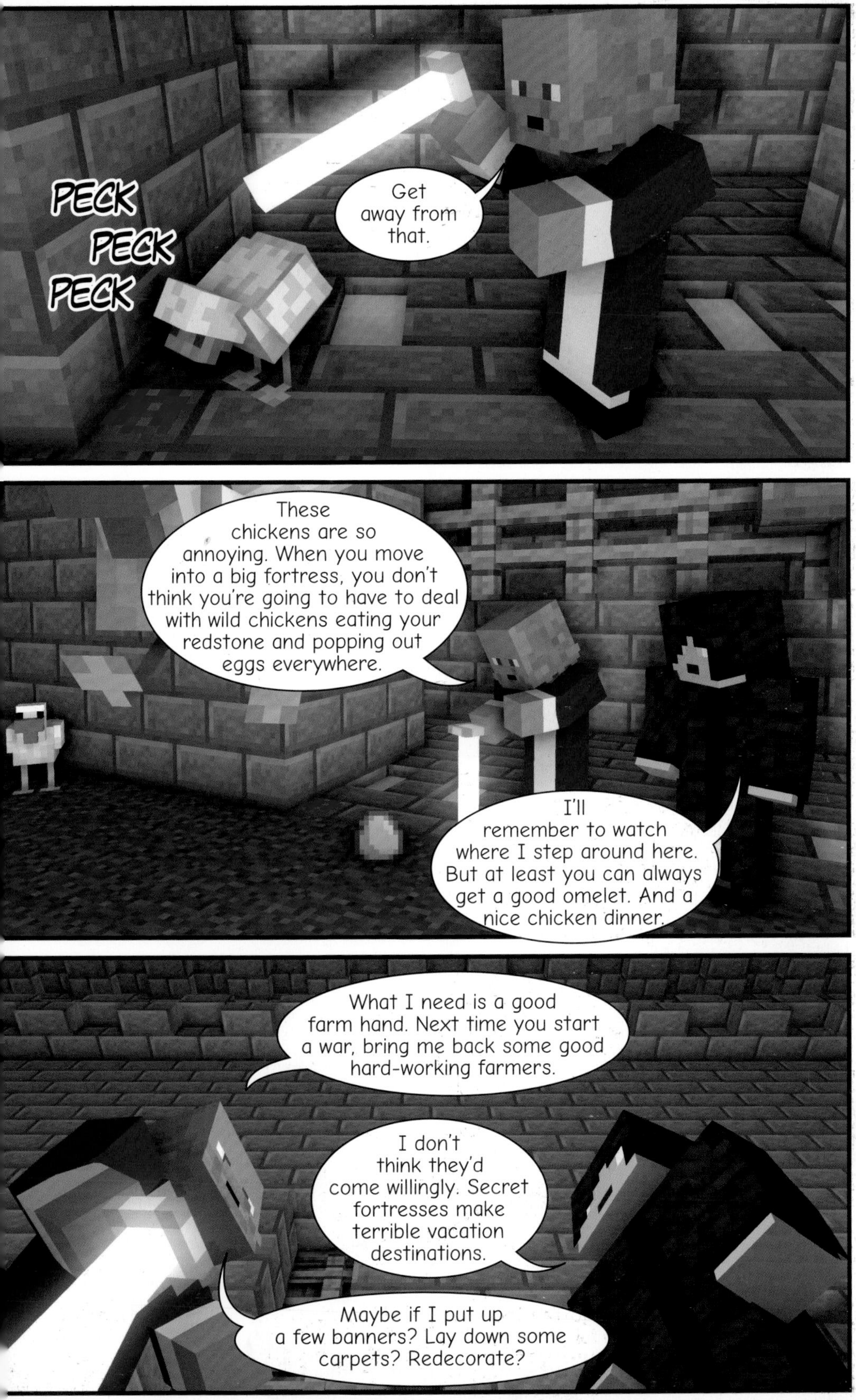
PECK
PECK
PECK
Get away from that.
These chickens are so annoying. When you move into a big fortress, you don't think you're going to have to deal with wild chickens eating your redstone and popping out eggs everywhere.
I'll remember to watch where I step around here. But at least you can always get a good omelet. And a nice chicken dinner.
What I need is a good farm hand. Next time you start a war, bring me back some good hard-working farmers.
I don't think they'd come willingly. Secret fortresses make terrible vacation destinations.
Maybe if I put up a few banners? Lay down some carpets? Redecorate?

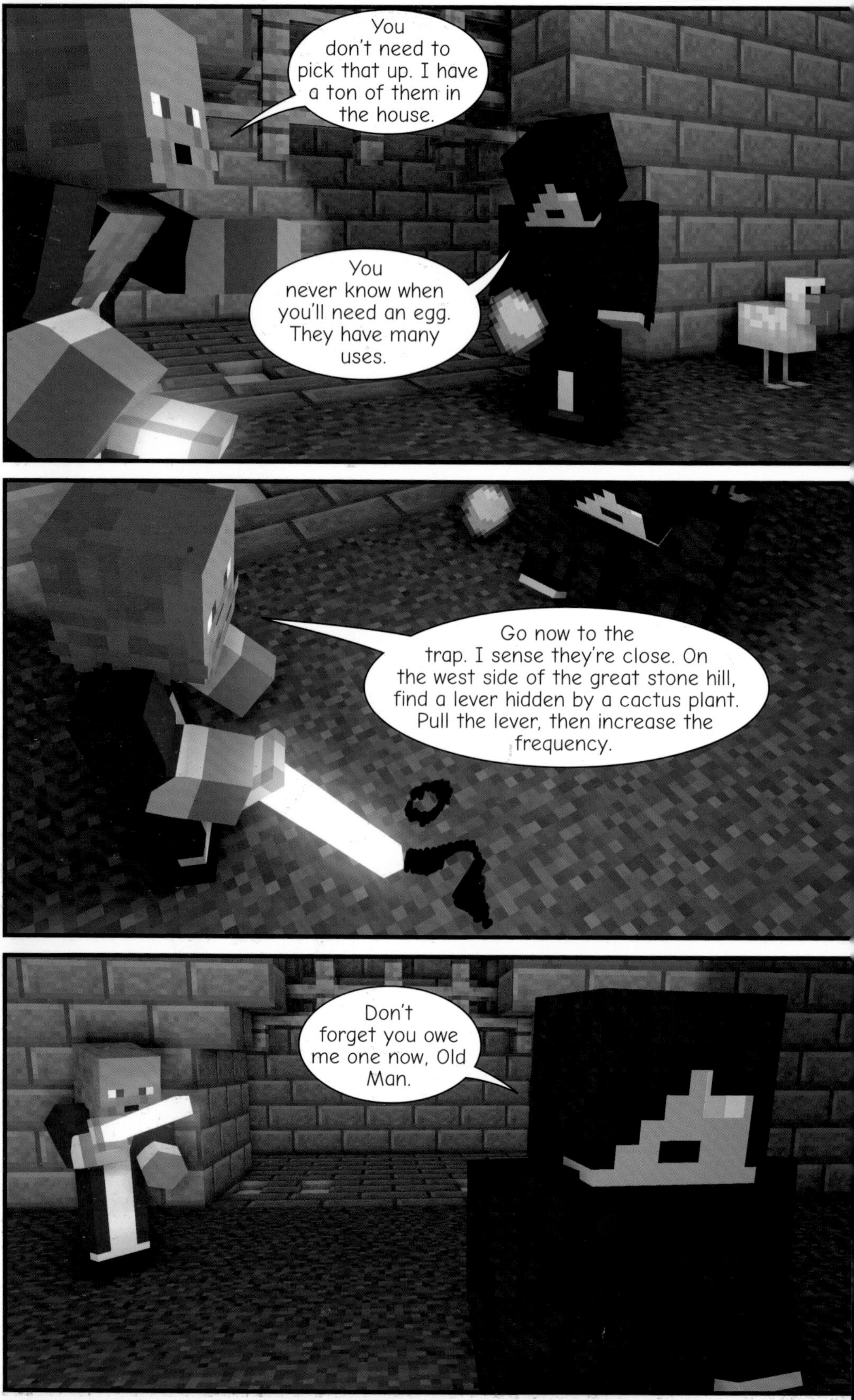
You don't need to pick that up. I have a ton of them in the house.
You never know when you'll need an egg. They have many uses.
Go now to the trap. I sense they're close. On the west side of the great stone hill, find a lever hidden by a cactus plant. Pull the lever, then increase the frequency.
Don't forget you owe me one now, Old Man.

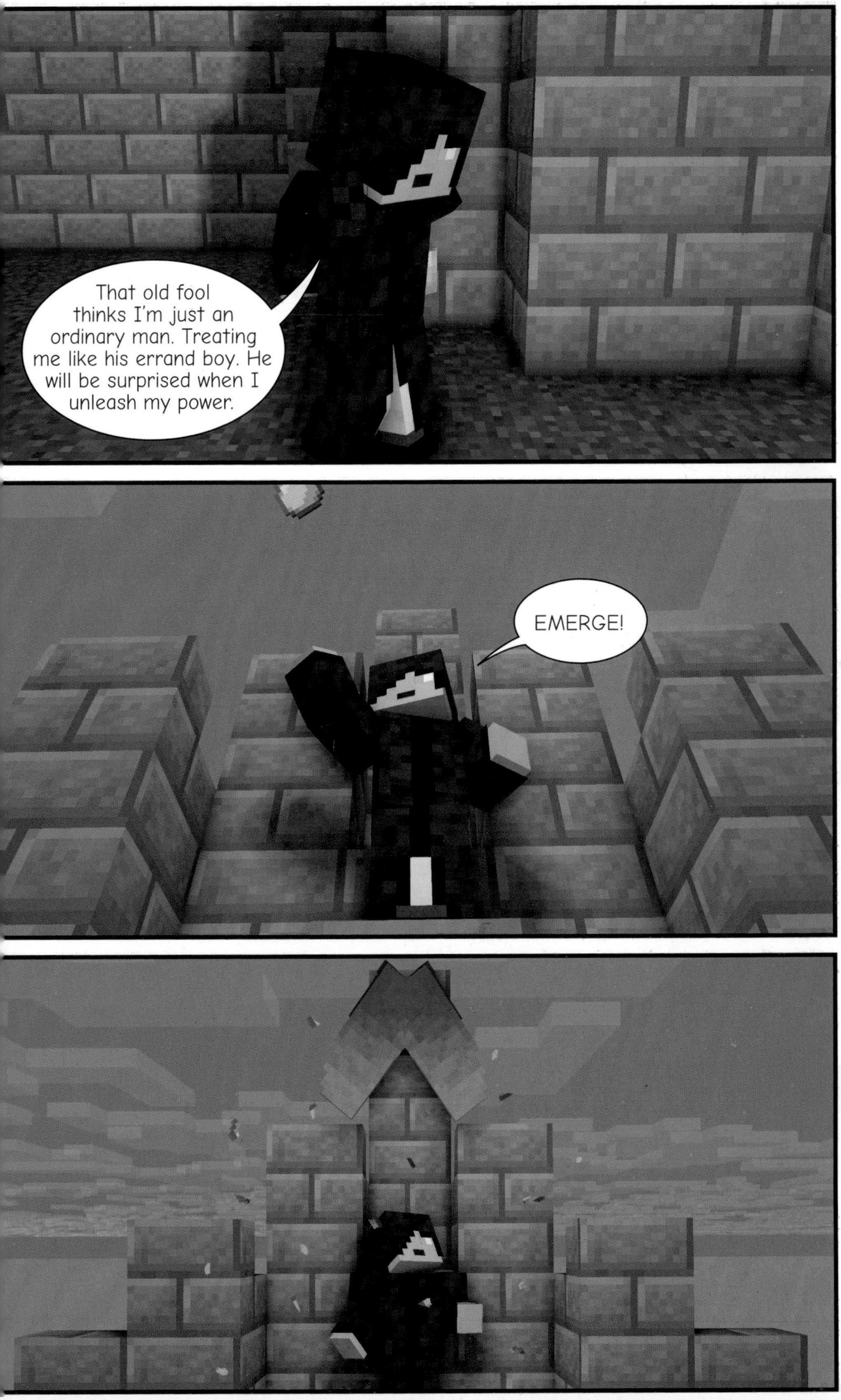
That old fool thinks I'm just an ordinary man. Treating me like his errand boy. He will be surprised when I unleash my power.
EMERGE!

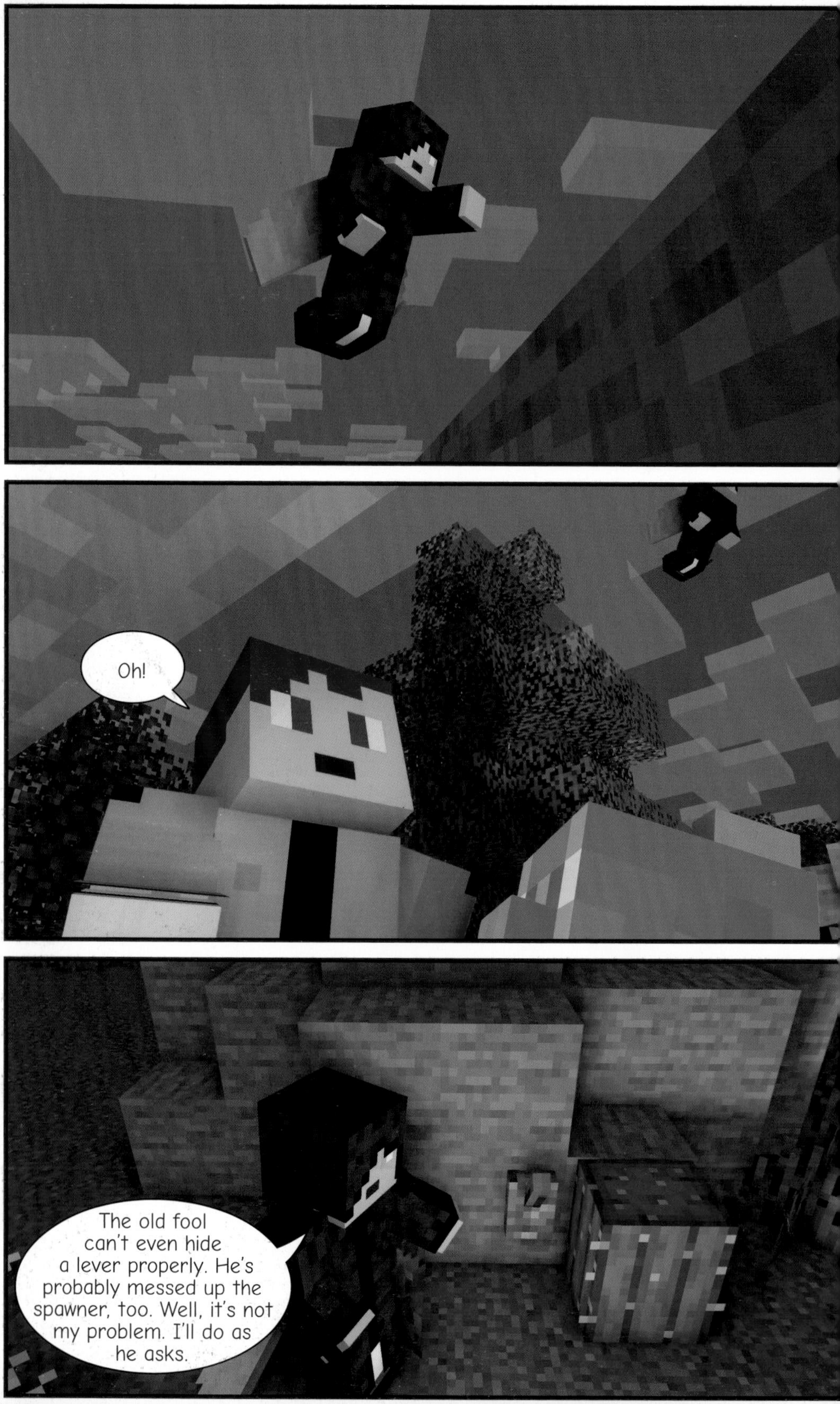
Oh!
The old fool can't even hide a lever properly. He's probably messed up the spawner, too. Well, it's not my problem. I'll do as he asks.

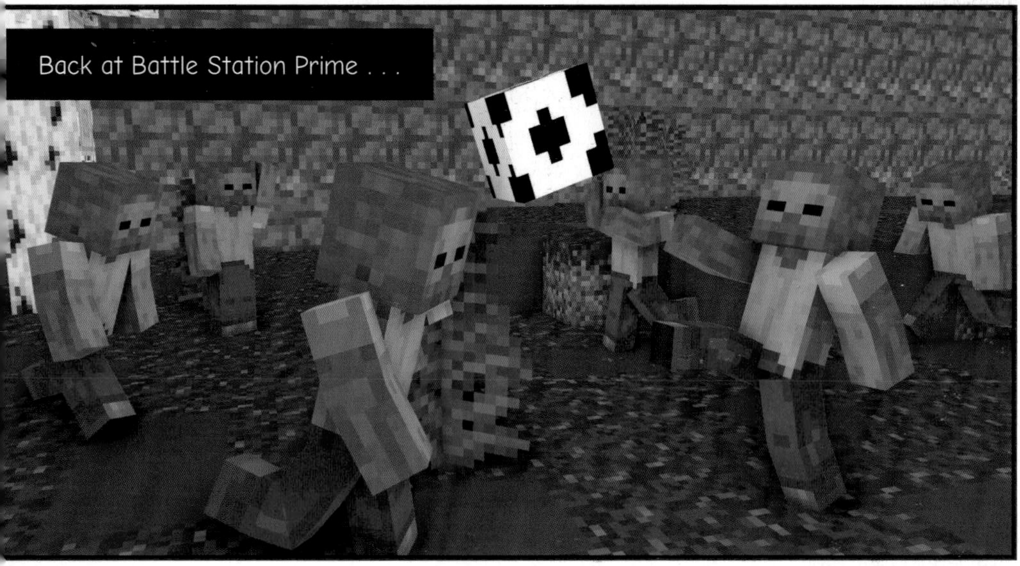
Back at Battle Station Prime . . .

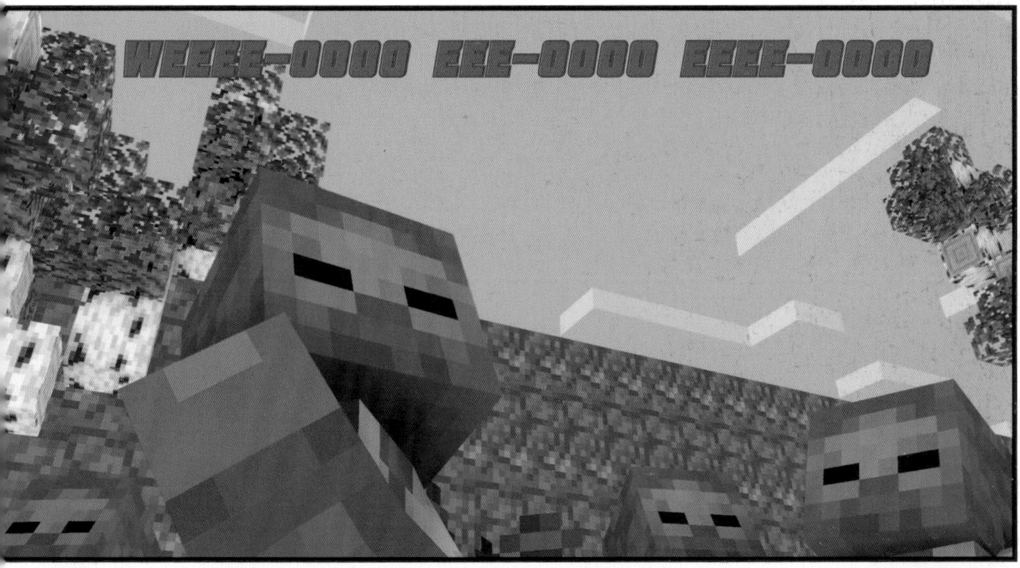
WEEEE-OOOO EEE-OOOO EEEE-OOOO

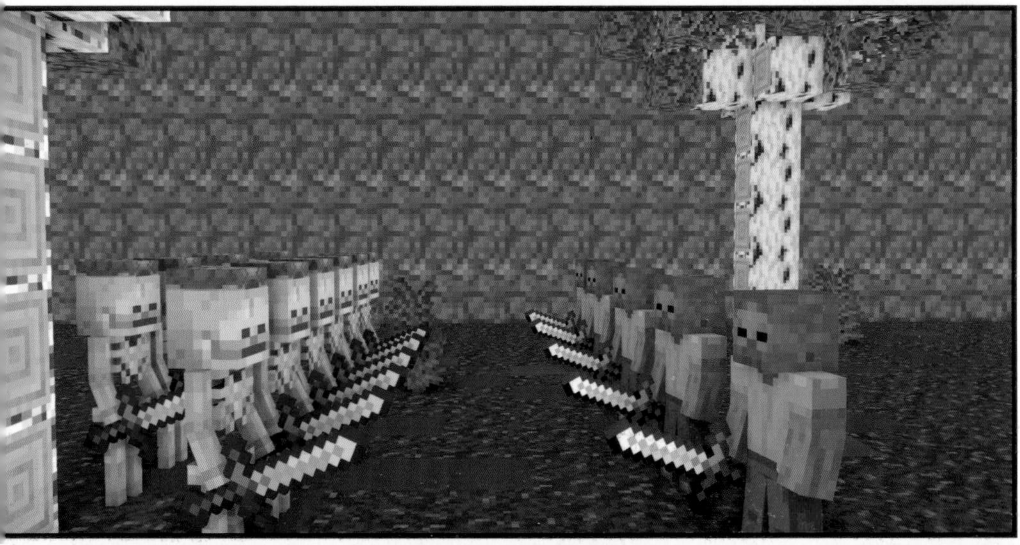

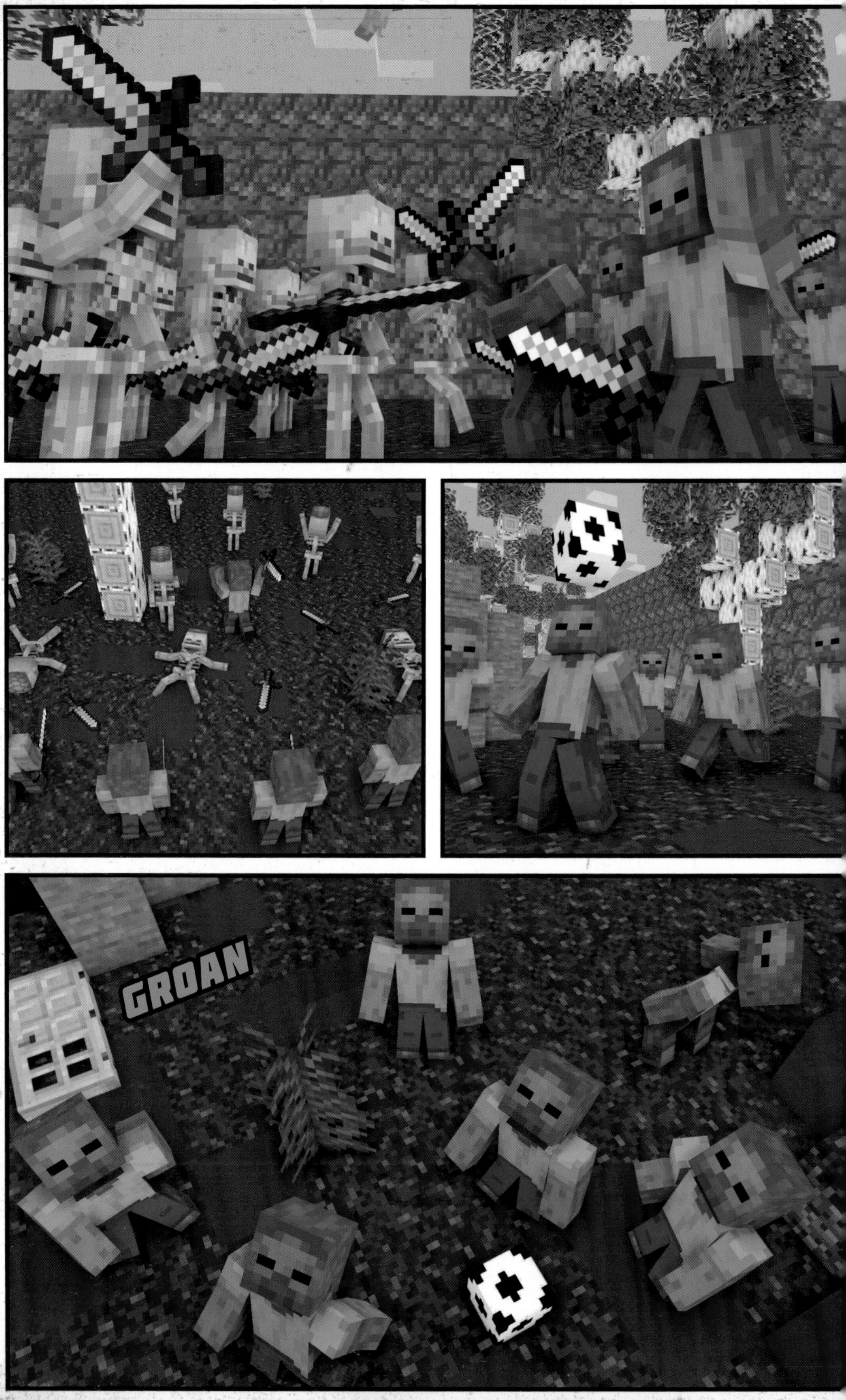
GROAN

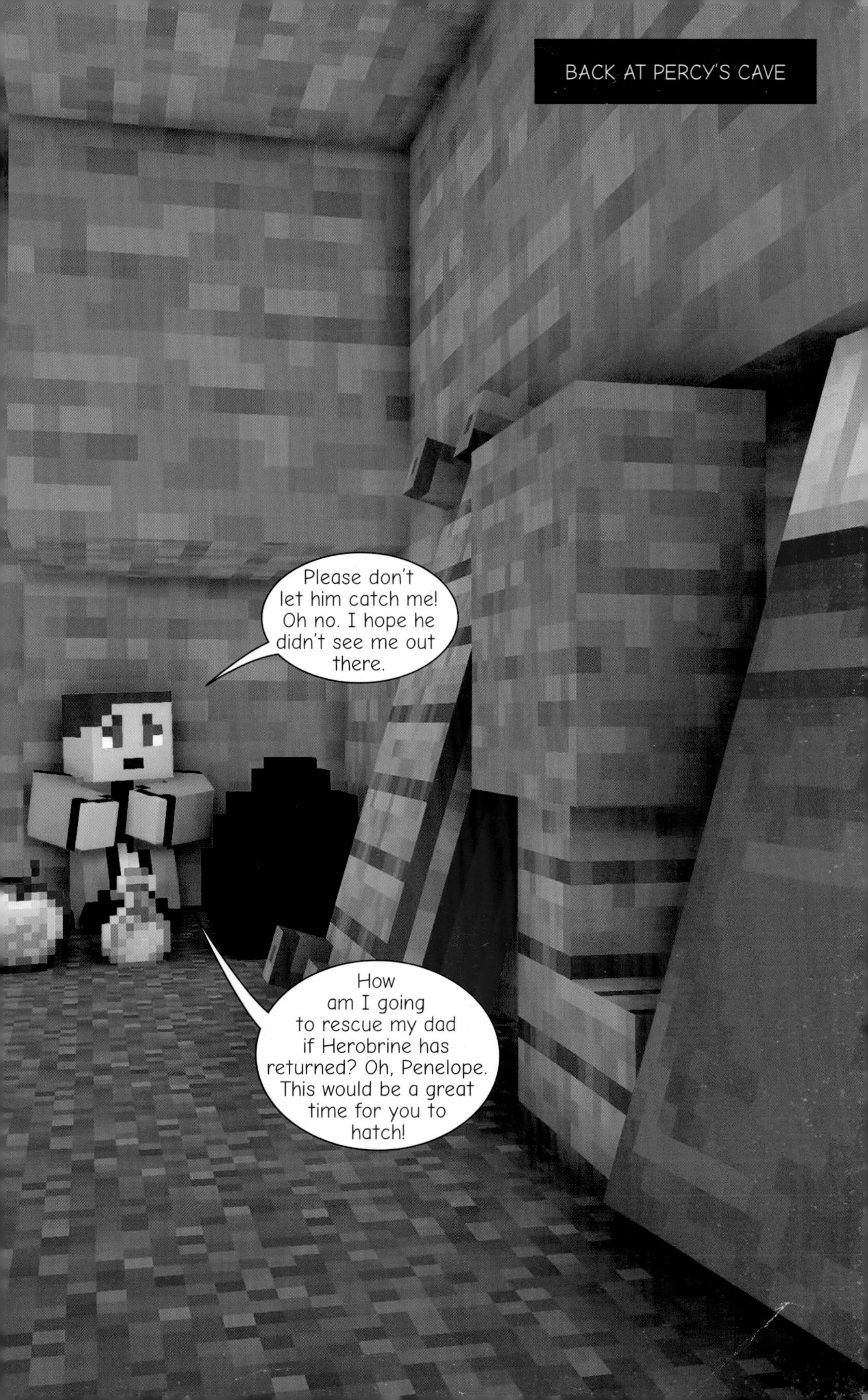
BACK AT PERCY'S CAVE
Please don't let him catch me! Oh no. I hope he didn't see me out there.
How am I going to rescue my dad if Herobrine has returned? Oh, Penelope. This would be a great time for you to hatch!

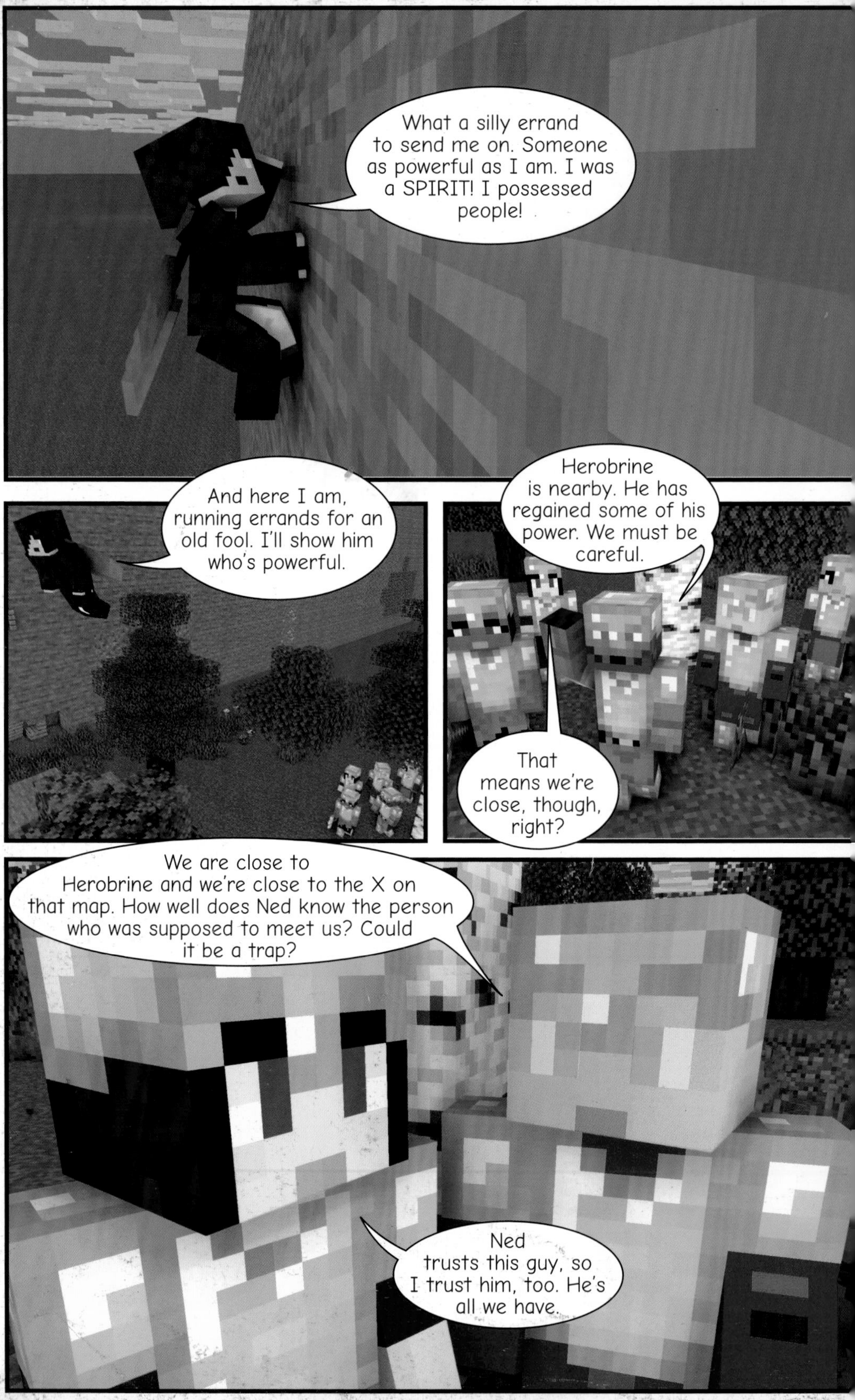
What a silly errand to send me on. Someone as powerful as I am. I was a SPIRIT! I possessed people!
And here I am, running errands for an old fool. I'll show him who's powerful.
Herobrine is nearby. He has regained some of his power. We must be careful.
That means we're close, though, right?
We are close to Herobrine and we're close to the X on that map. How well does Ned know the person who was supposed to meet us? Could it be a trap?
Ned trusts this guy, so I trust him, too. He's all we have.

CHAPTER 8

COURAGE UNDER FIRE

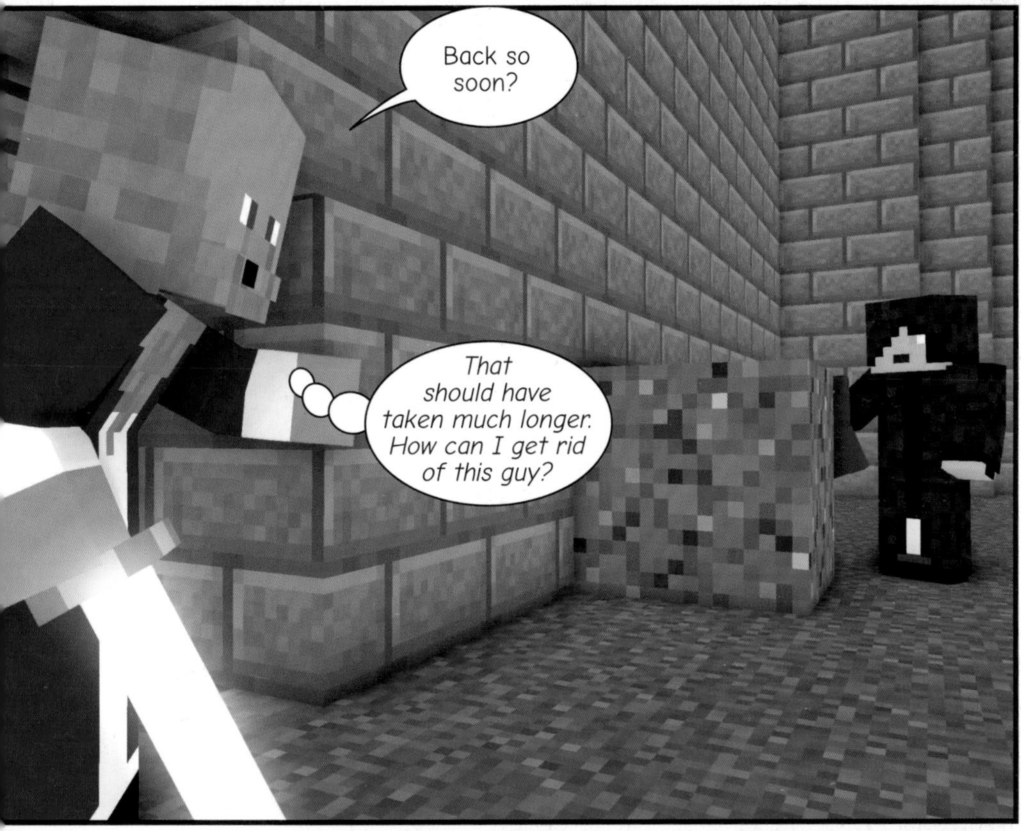
Back so soon?
That should have taken much longer. How can I get rid of this guy?

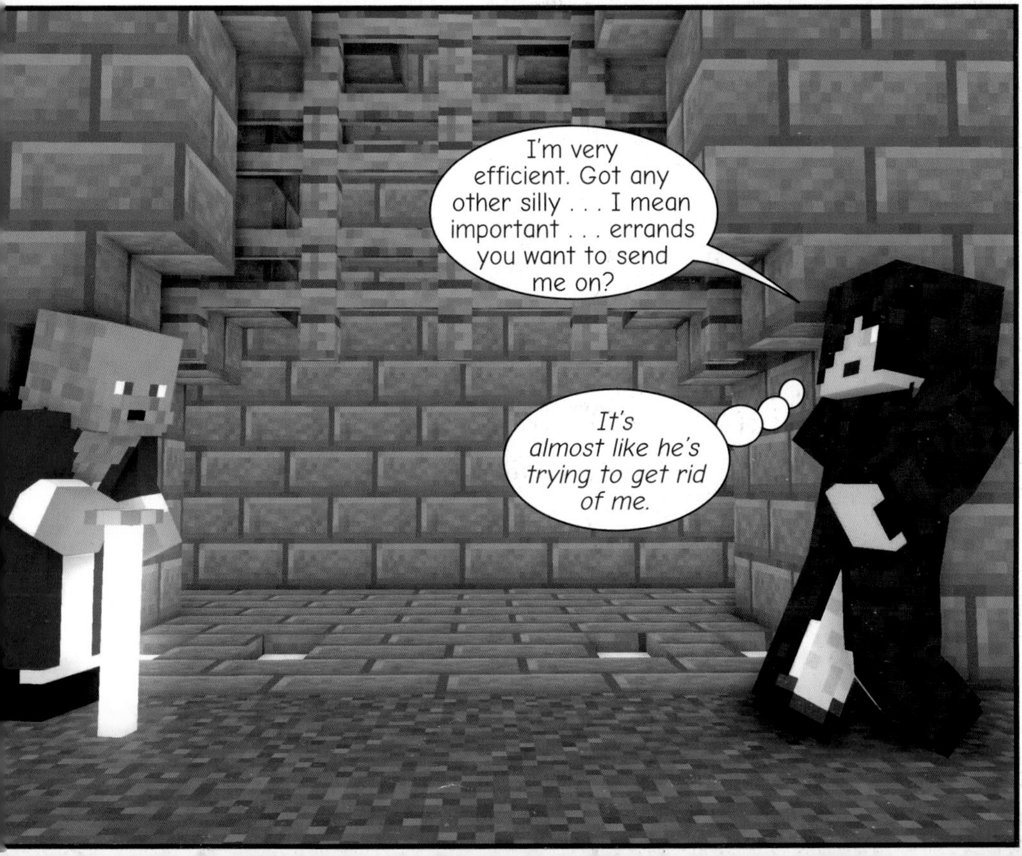
I'm very efficient. Got any other silly . . . I mean important . . . errands you want to send me on?
It's almost like he's trying to get rid of me.

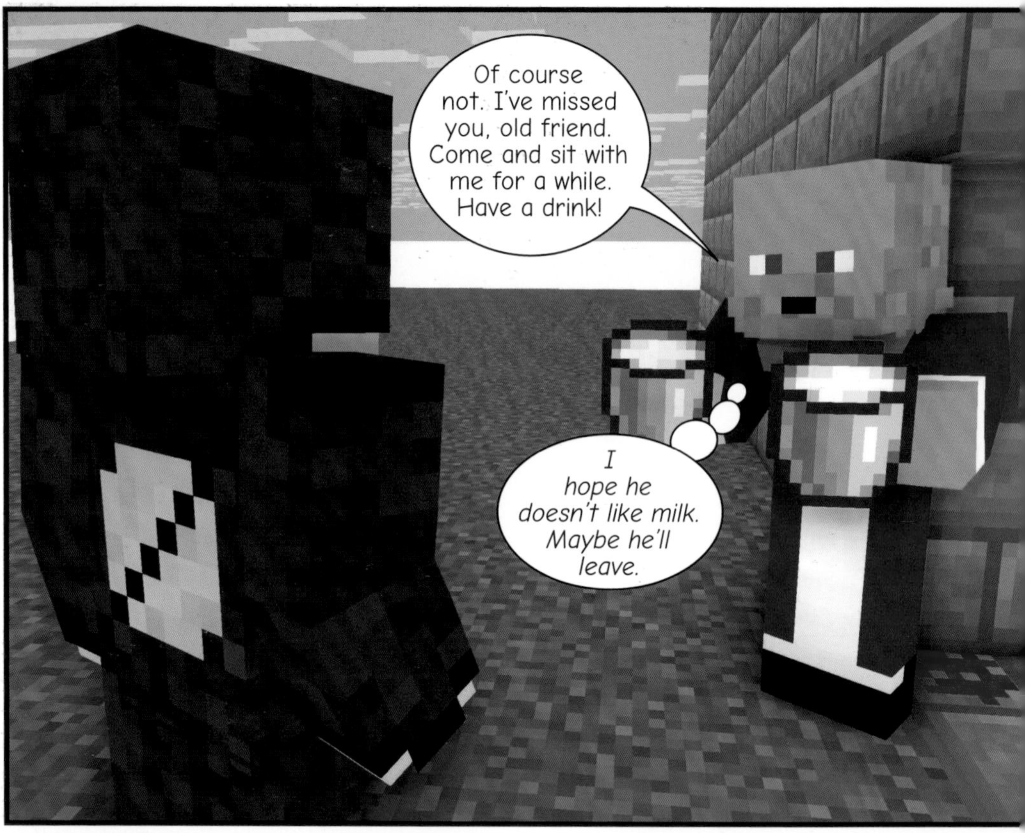
Of course not. I've missed you, old friend. Come and sit with me for a while. Have a drink!
I hope he doesn't like milk. Maybe he'll leave.

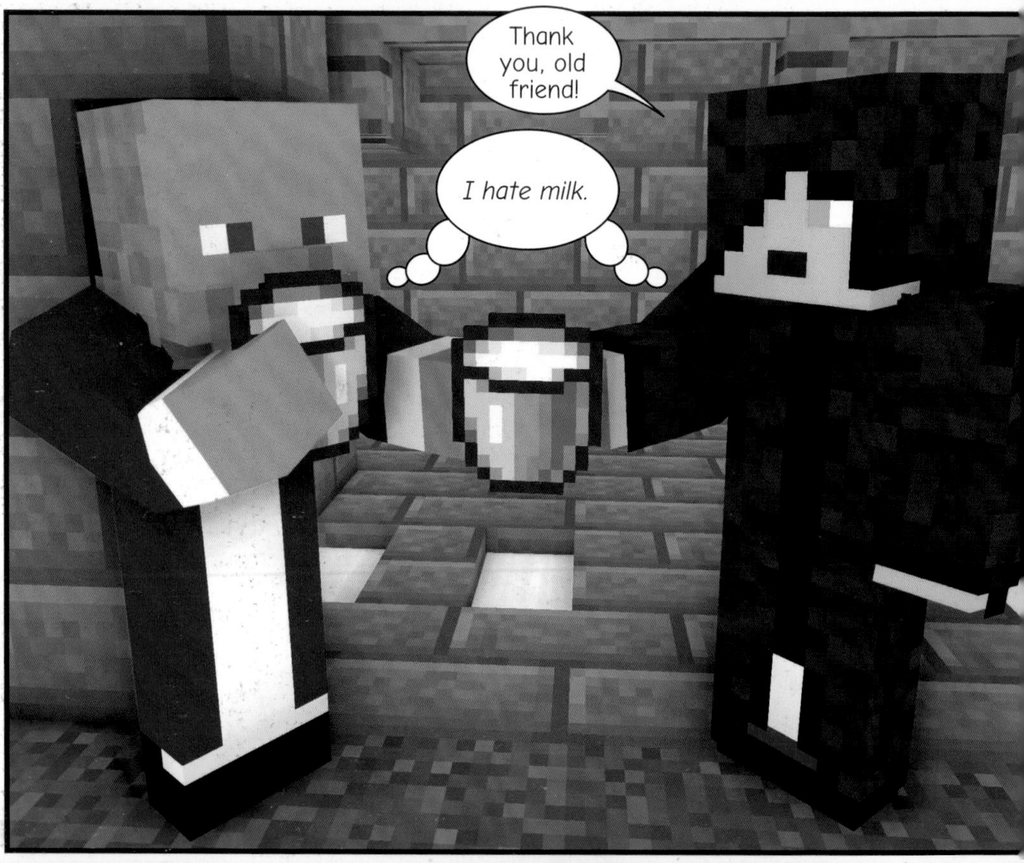
Thank you, old friend!
I hate milk.

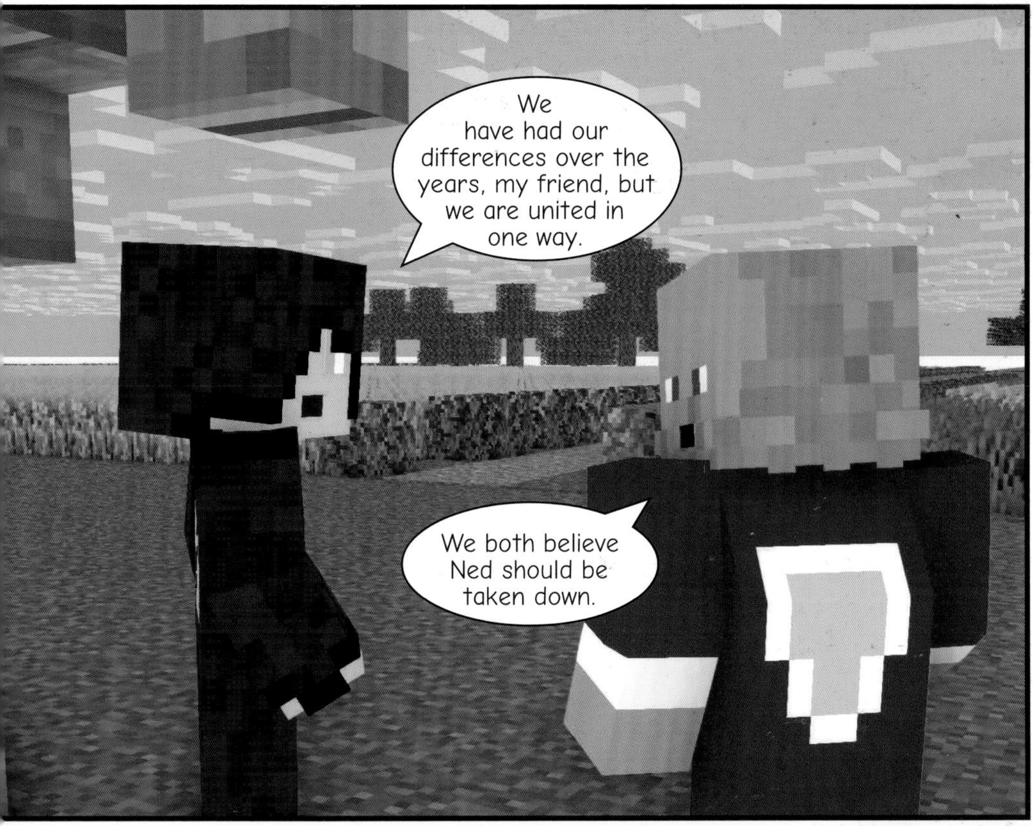
We have had our differences over the years, my friend, but we are united in one way.
We both believe Ned should be taken down.

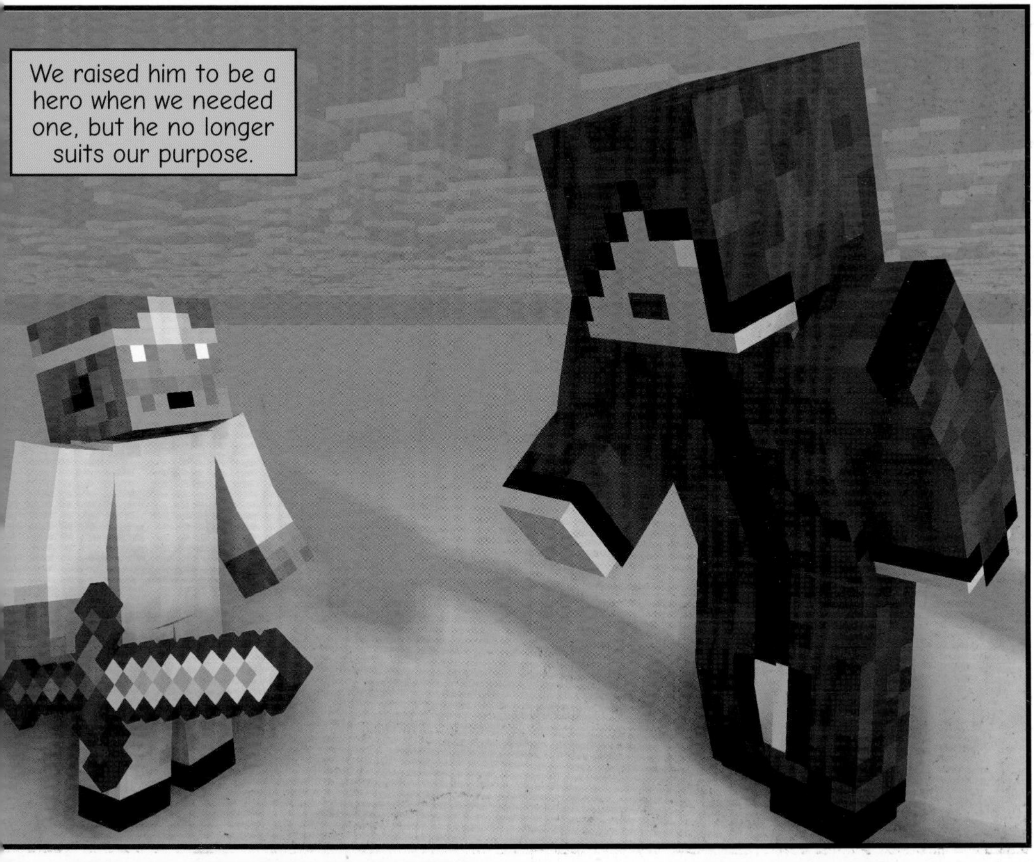
We raised him to be a hero when we needed one, but he no longer suits our purpose.

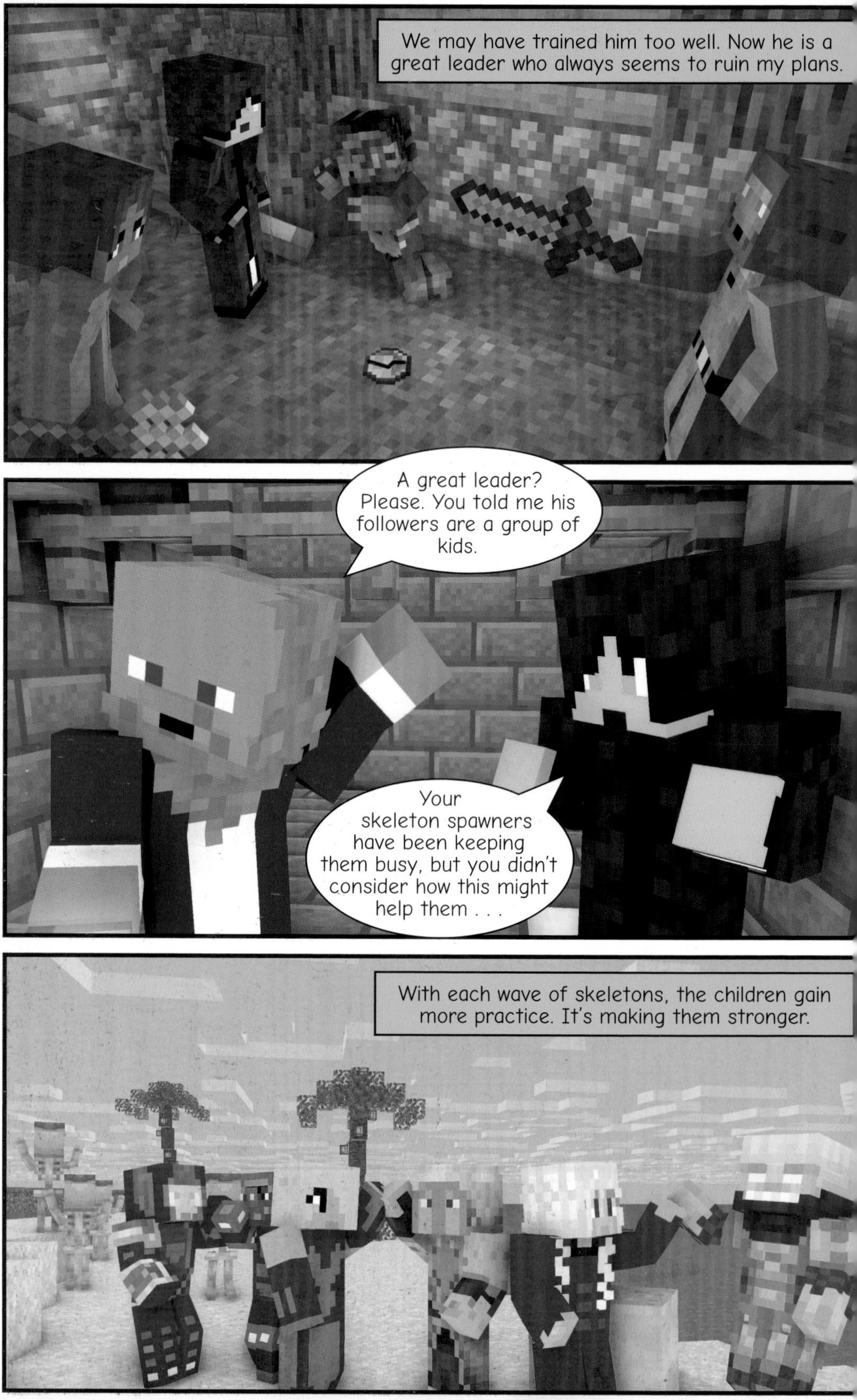
We may have trained him too well. Now he is a great leader who always seems to ruin my plans.
A great leader? Please. You told me his followers are a group of kids.
Your skeleton spawners have been keeping them busy, but you didn't consider how this might help them . . .
With each wave of skeletons, the children gain more practice. It's making them stronger.

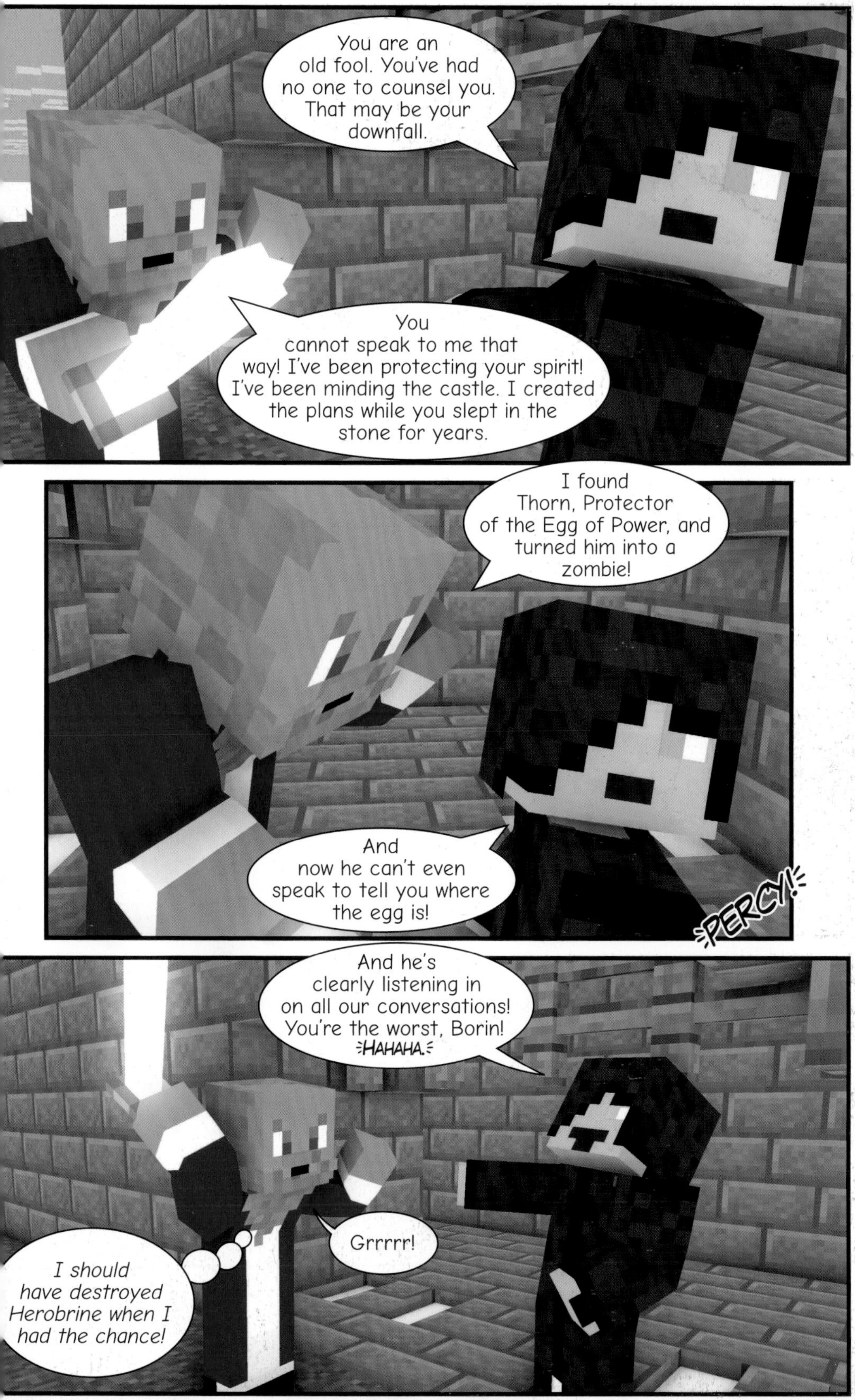
You are an old fool. You've had no one to counsel you. That may be your downfall.
You cannot speak to me that way! I've been protecting your spirit! I've been minding the castle. I created the plans while you slept in the stone for years.
I found Thorn, Protector of the Egg of Power, and turned him into a zombie!
And now he can't even speak to tell you where the egg is!
PERCY!
And he's clearly listening in on all our conversations! You're the worst, Borin! HAHAHA.
Grrrrr!
I should have destroyed Herobrine when I had the chance!

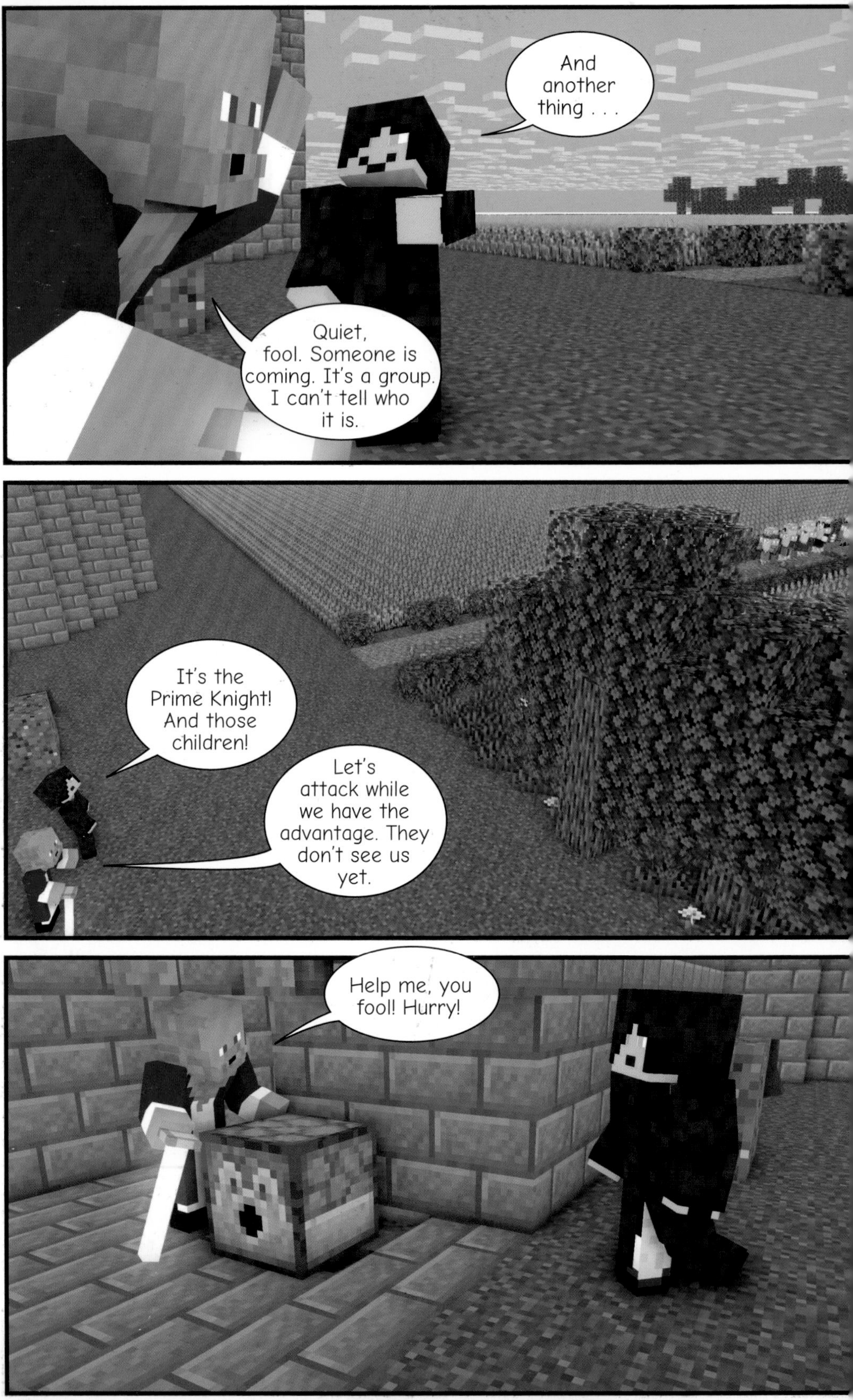
And another thing . . .
Quiet, fool. Someone is coming. It's a group. I can't tell who it is.
It's the Prime Knight! And those children!
Let's attack while we have the advantage. They don't see us yet.
Help me, you fool! Hurry!

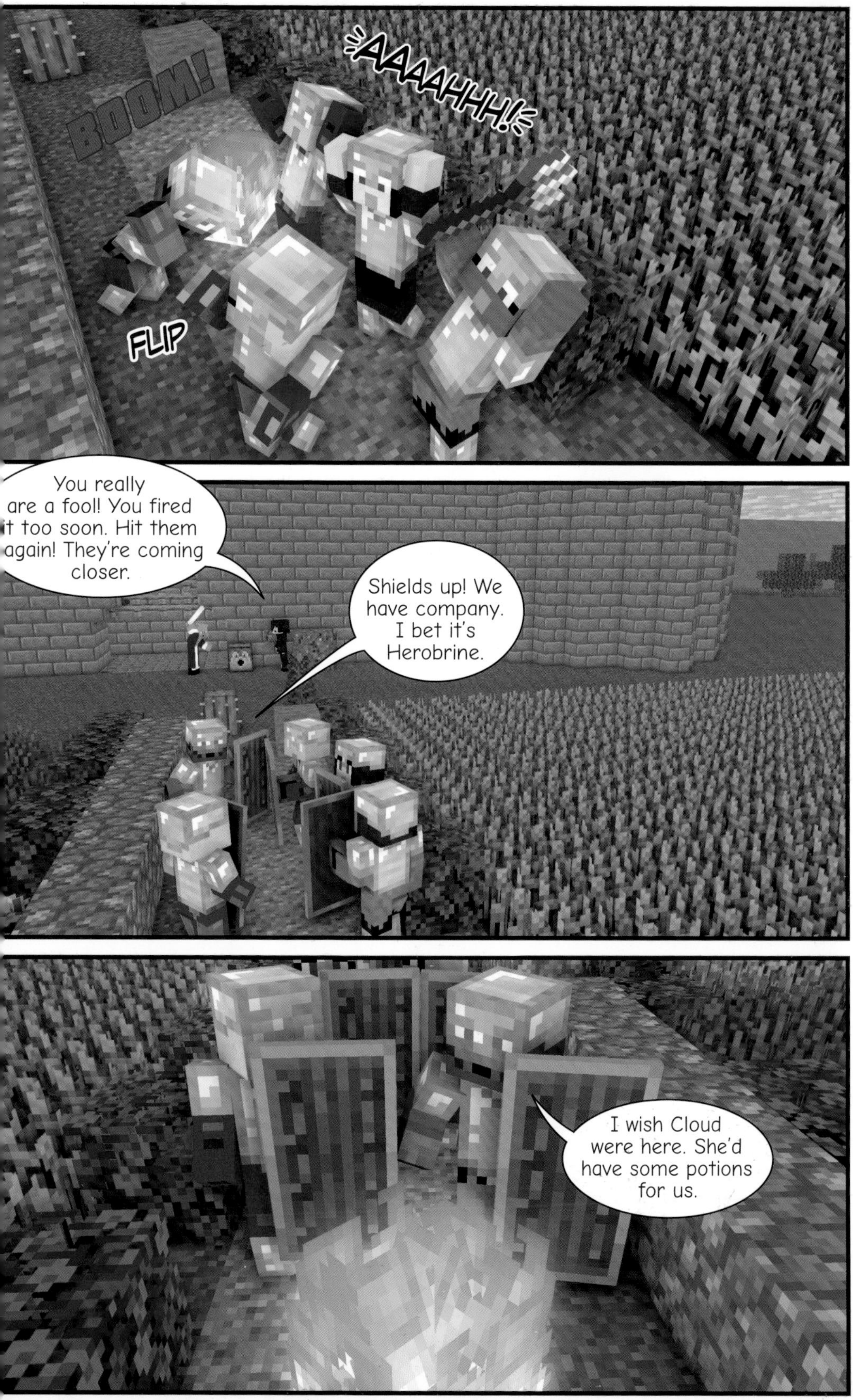
BOOM!
AAAAHHH!
FLIP
You really are a fool! You fired it too soon. Hit them again! They're coming closer.
Shields up! We have company. I bet it's Herobrine.
I wish Cloud were here. She'd have some potions for us.

She left some behind.
I took a few with us. I don't
know what's in them, but they're
worth a try!

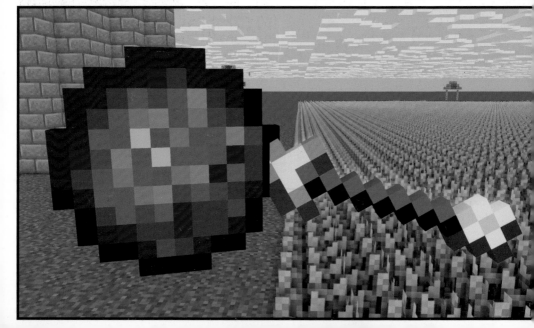

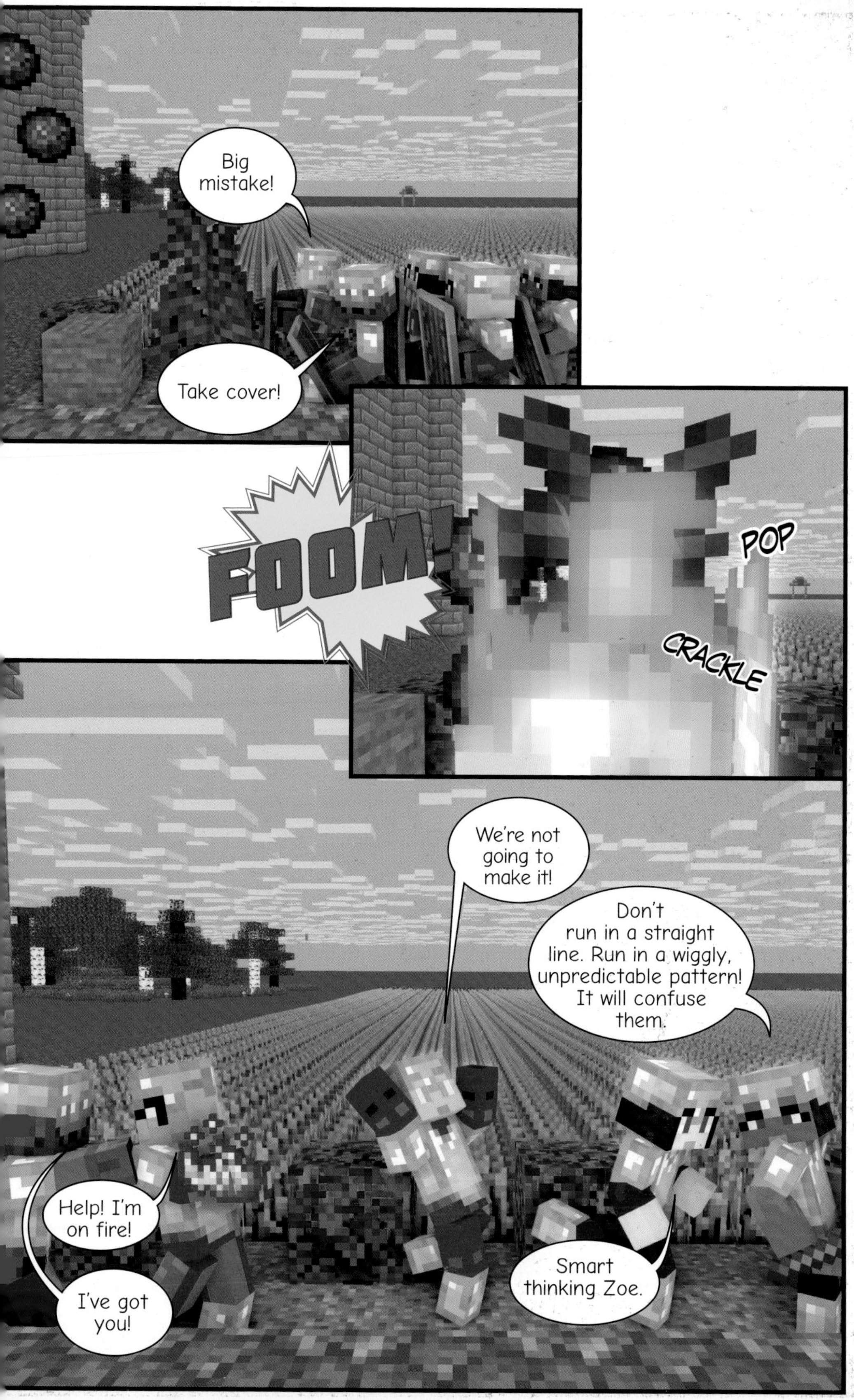

Big mistake!
Take cover!
FOOM!
POP
CRACKLE
We're not going to make it!
Don't run in a straight line. Run in a wiggly, unpredictable pattern! It will confuse them.
Help! I'm on fire!
I've got you!
Smart thinking Zoe.

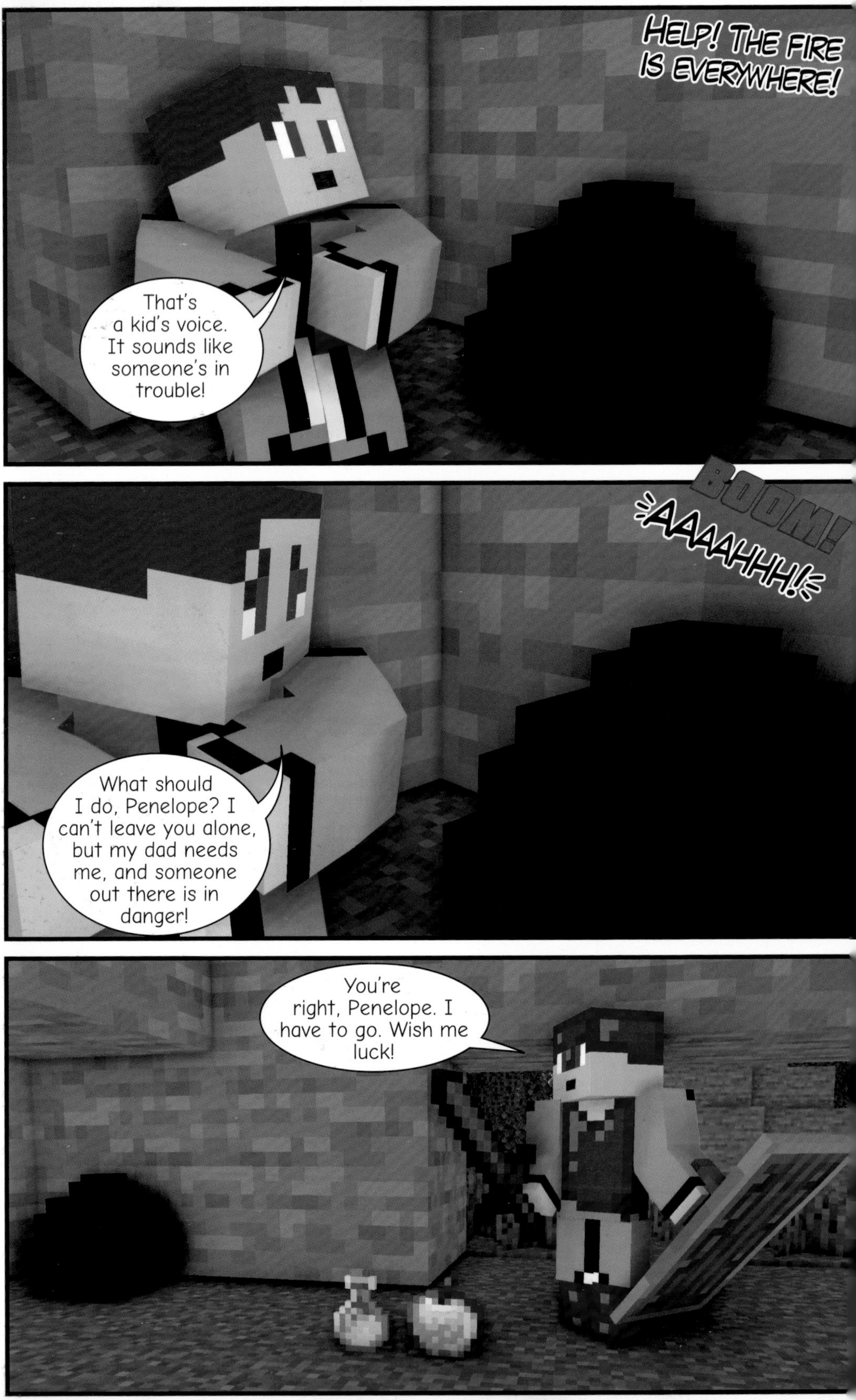
HELP! THE FIRE IS EVERYWHERE!
That's a kid's voice. It sounds like someone's in trouble!
BOOM!
AAAAHHH!
What should I do, Penelope? I can't leave you alone, but my dad needs me, and someone out there is in danger!
You're right, Penelope. I have to go. Wish me luck!

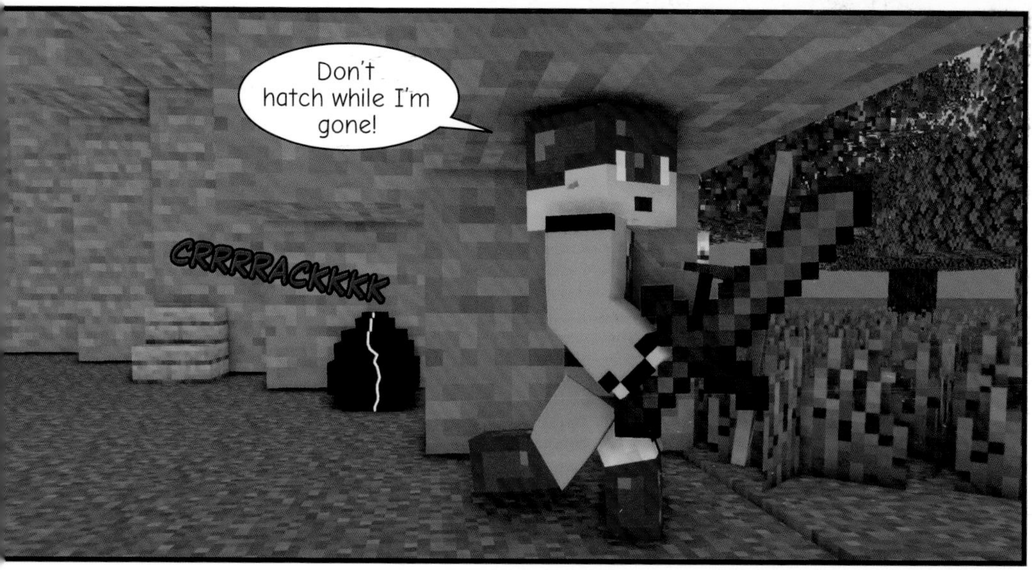
Don't hatch while I'm gone!
CRRRRACKKKK

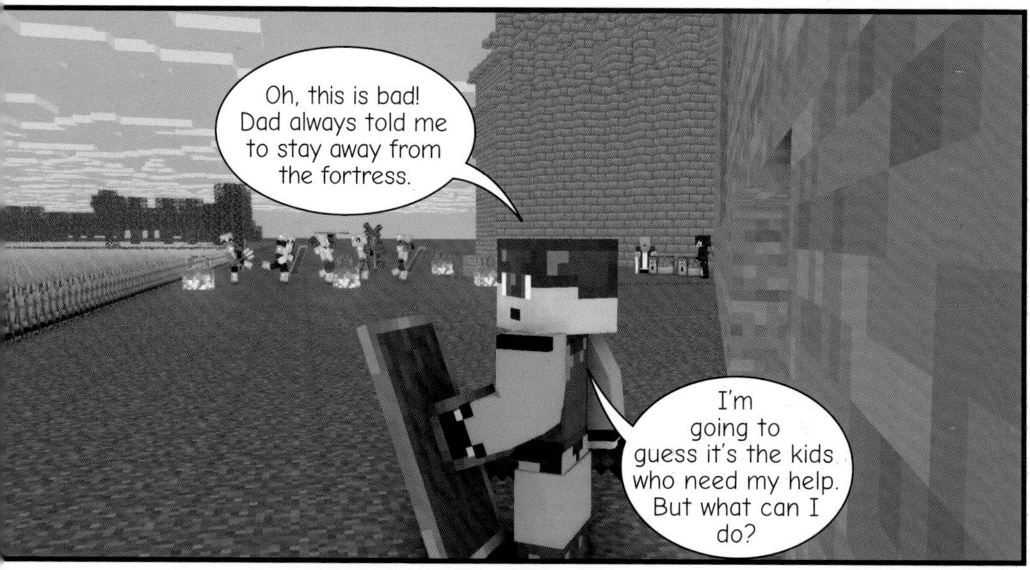
Oh, this is bad! Dad always told me to stay away from the fortress.
I'm going to guess it's the kids who need my help. But what can I do?

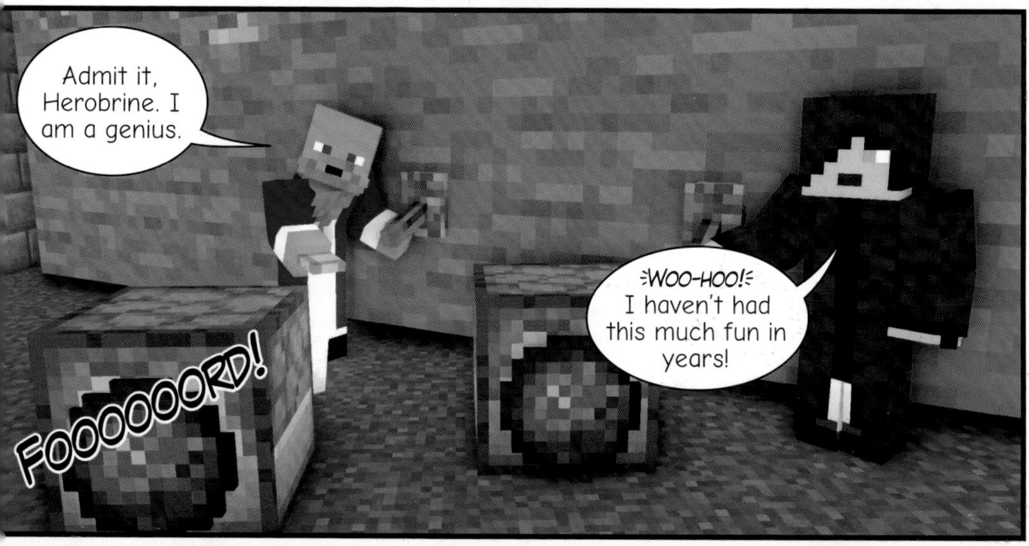
Admit it, Herobrine. I am a genius.
WOO-HOO! I haven't had this much fun in years!
FOOOOOORD!

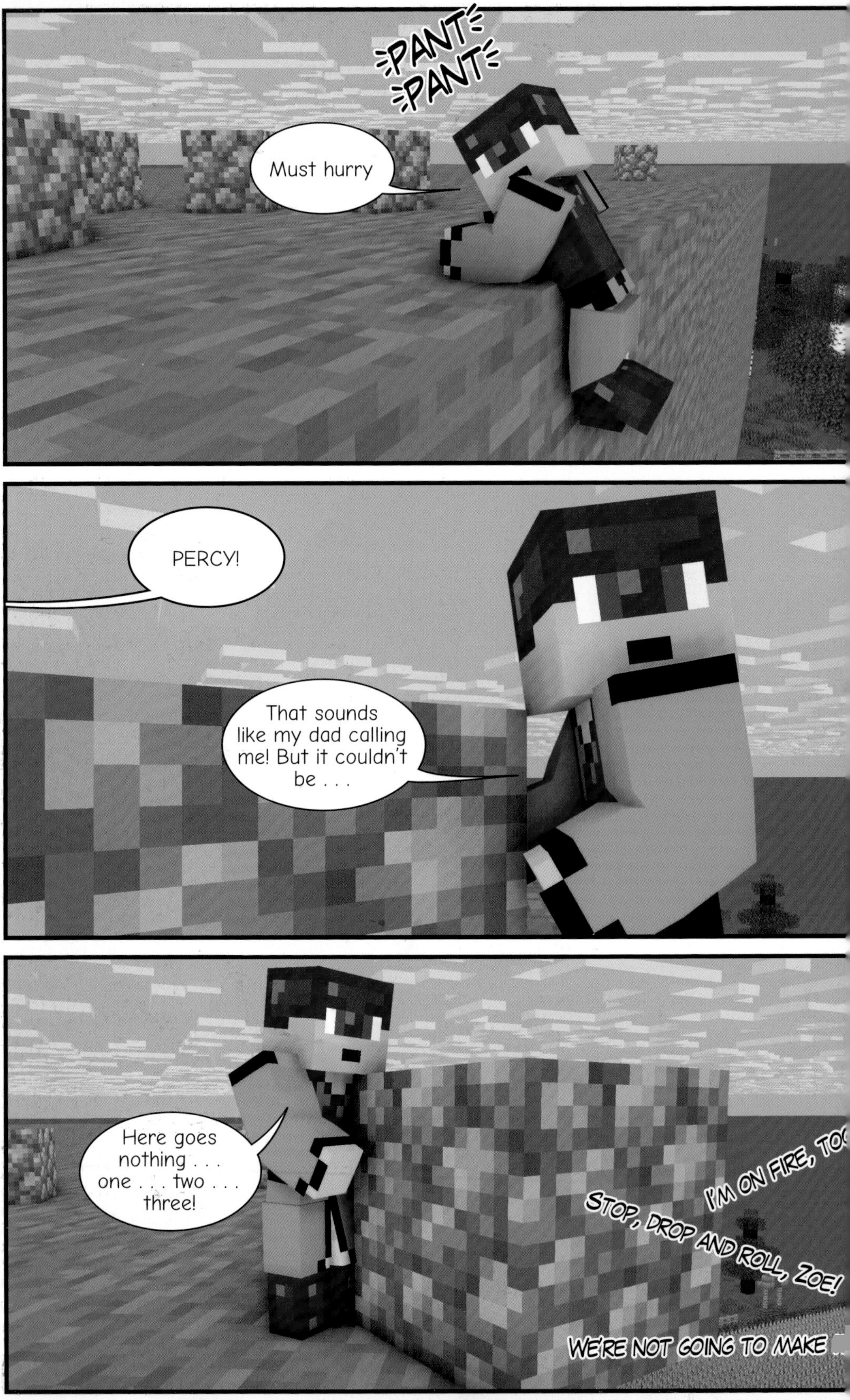
PANT
PANT
Must hurry
PERCY!
That sounds like my dad calling me! But it couldn't be . . .
Here goes nothing . . . one . . . two . . . three!
I'M ON FIRE, TO
STOP, DROP AND ROLL, ZOE!
WE'RE NOT GOING TO MAKE

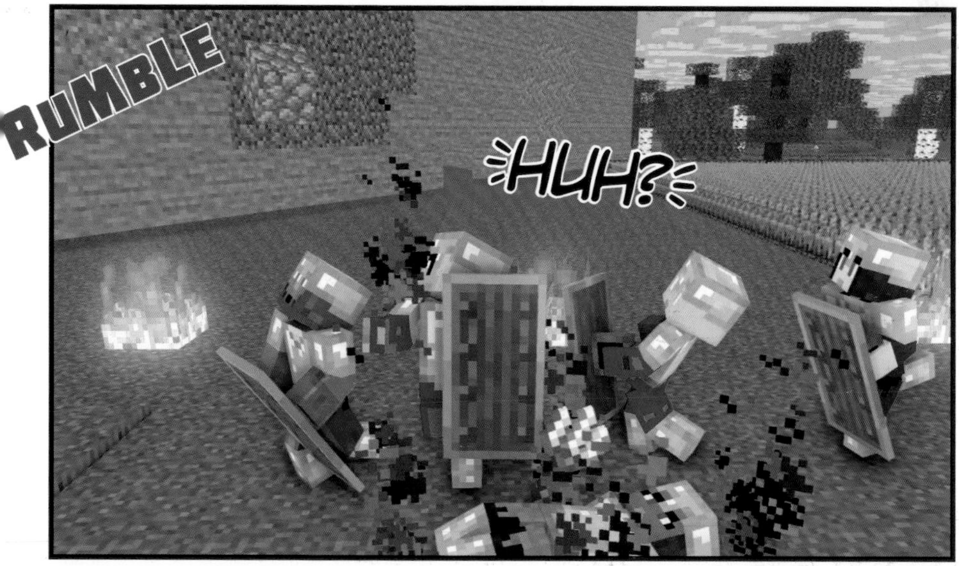
RUMBLE
HUH?

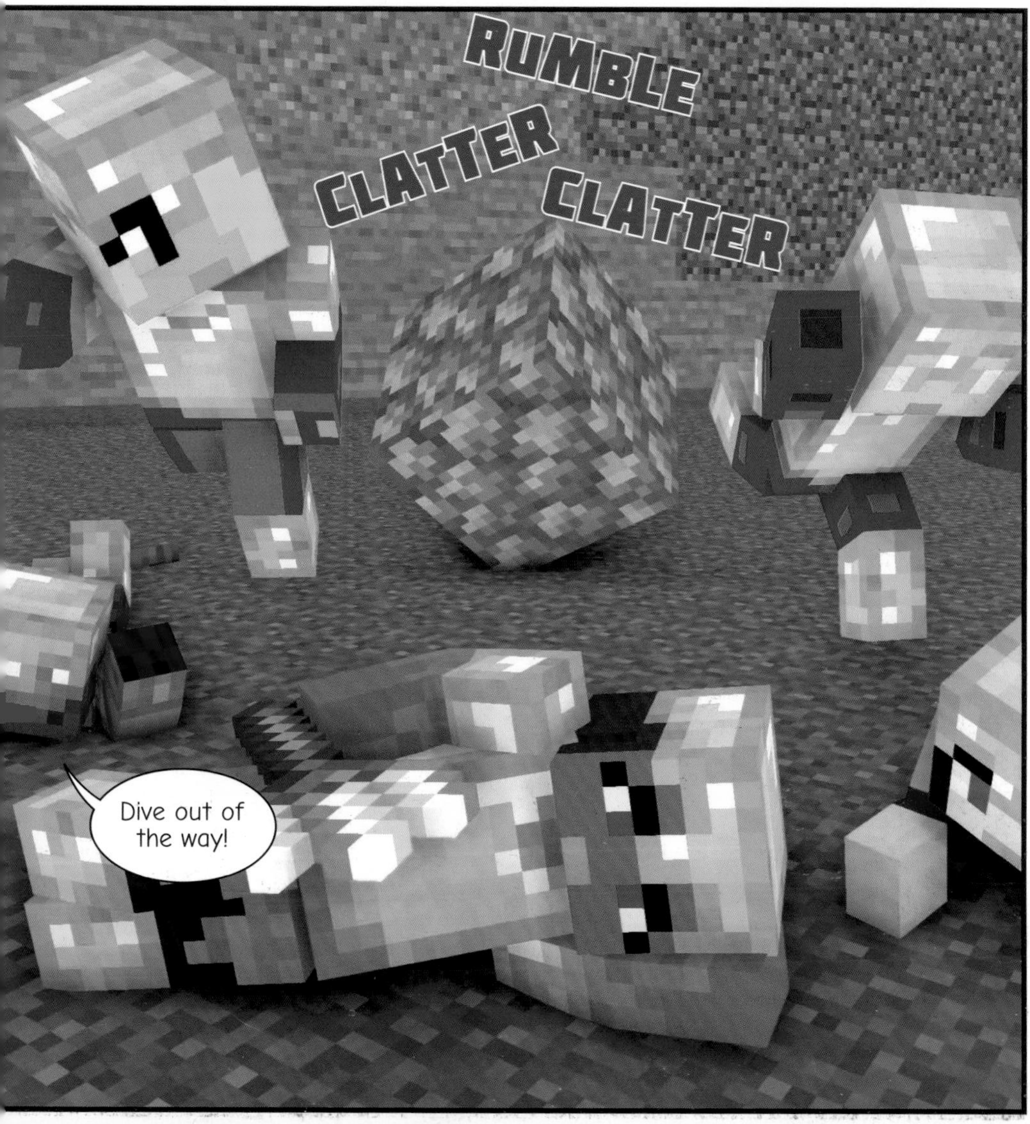
RUMBLE
CLATTER
CLATTER
Dive out of the way!

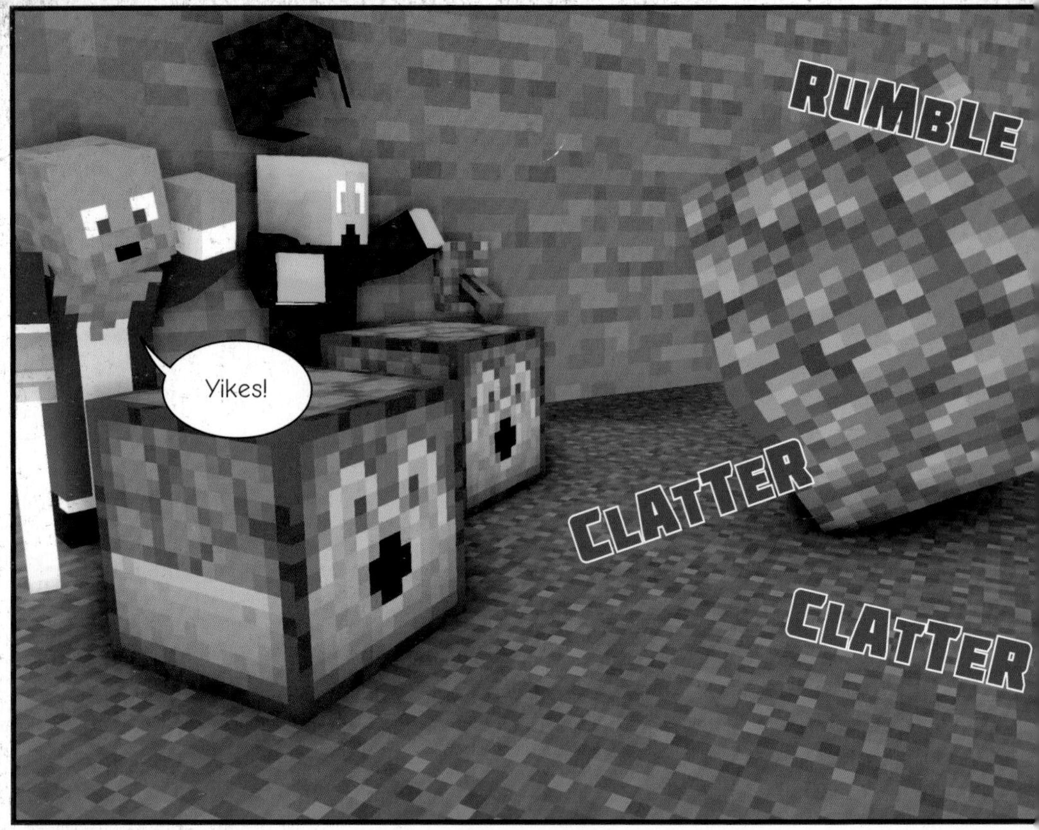
RUMBLE
Yikes!
CLATTER
CLATTER

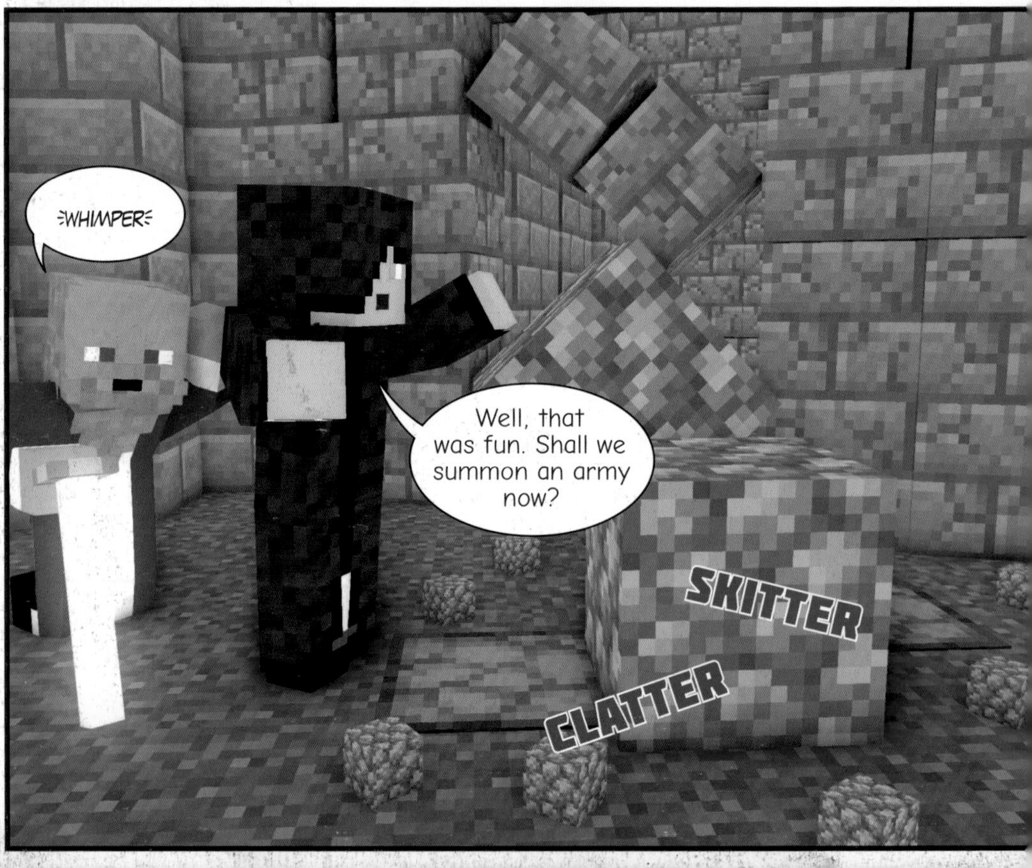
WHIMPER
Well, that was fun. Shall we summon an army now?
SKITTER
CLATTER

CHAPTER 9

THE SKELETONS ARE COMING!

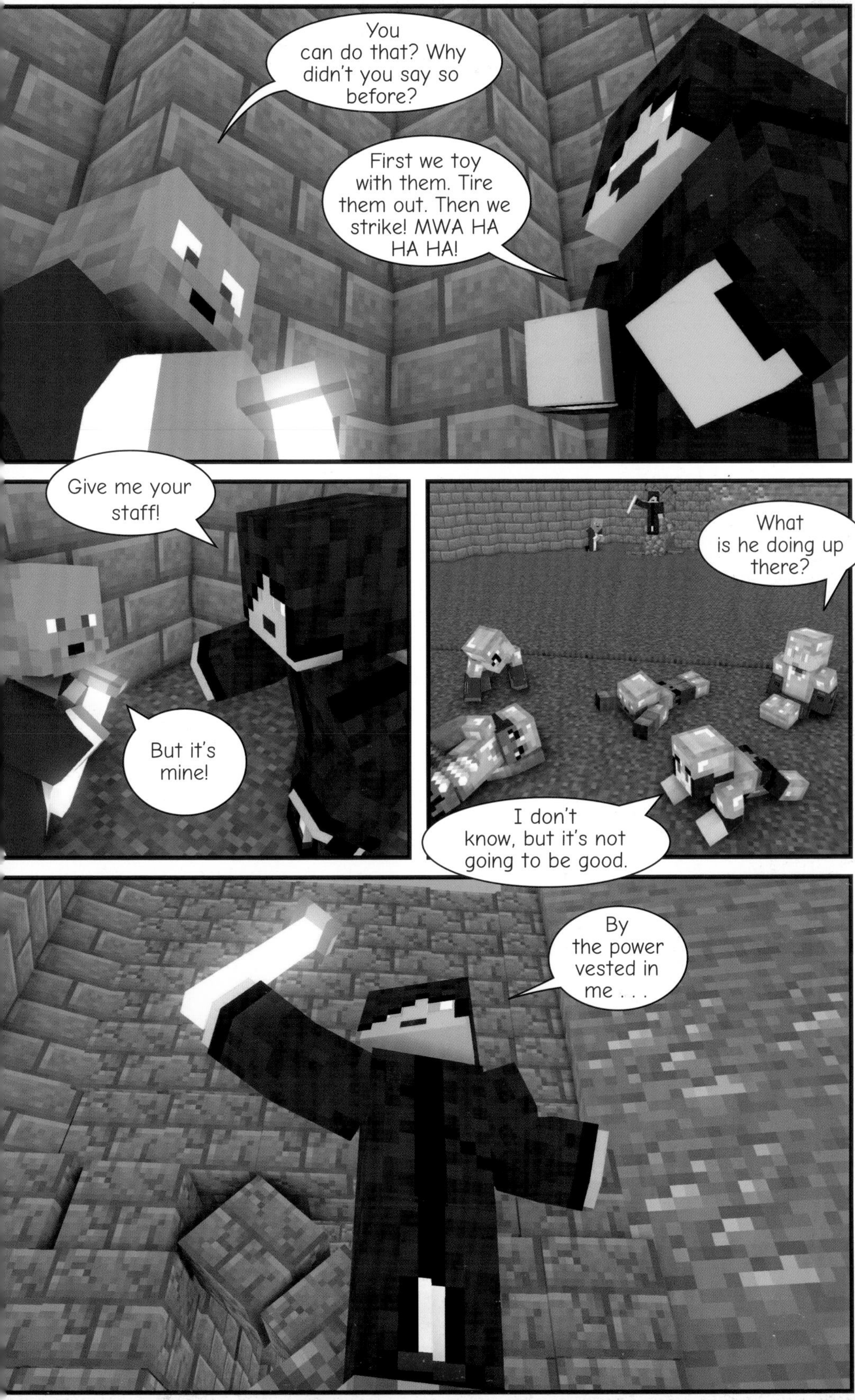
You can do that? Why didn't you say so before?
First we toy with them. Tire them out. Then we strike! MWA HA HA HA!
Give me your staff!
But it's mine!
What is he doing up there?
I don't know, but it's not going to be good.
By the power vested in me . . .

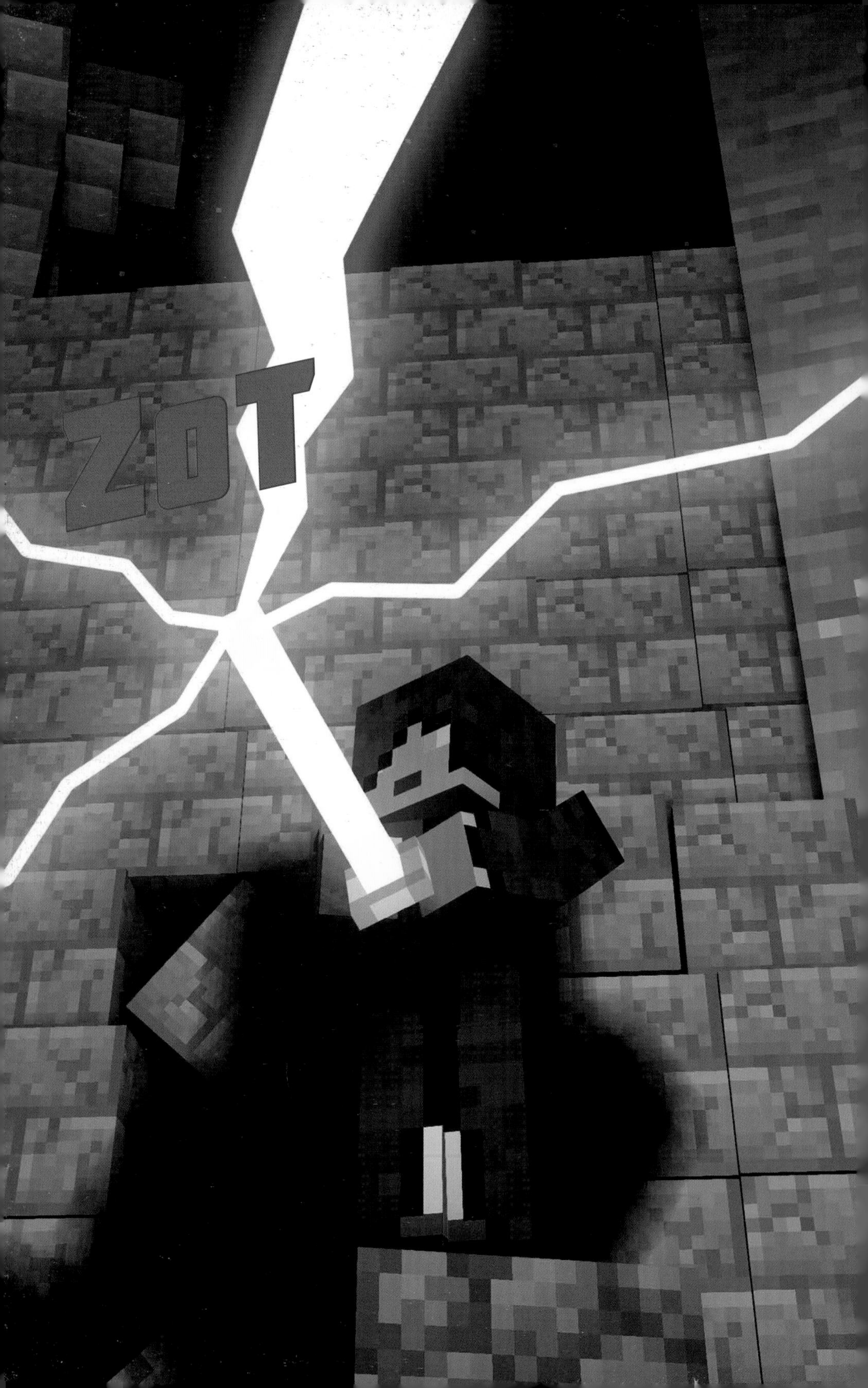
ZOT

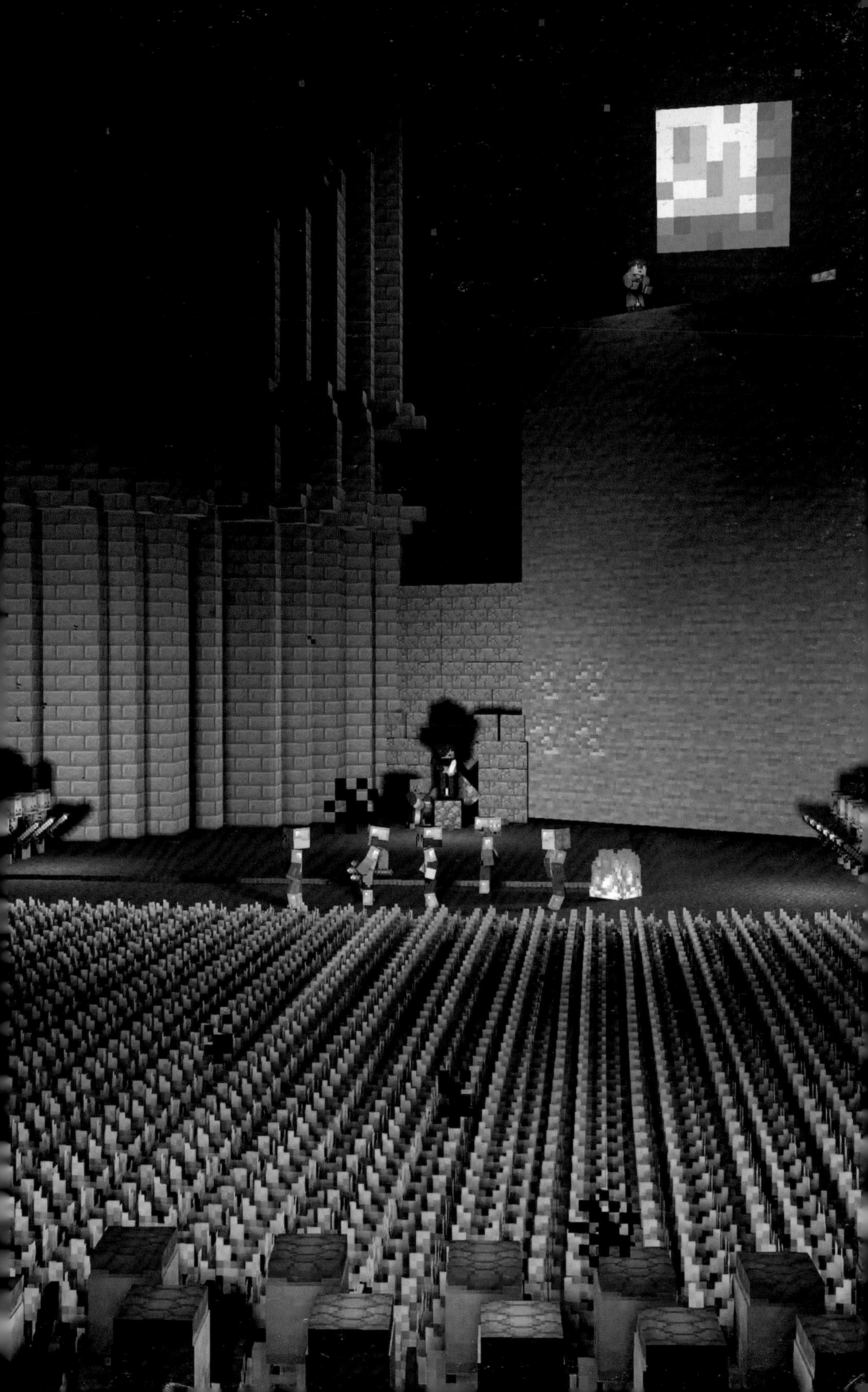

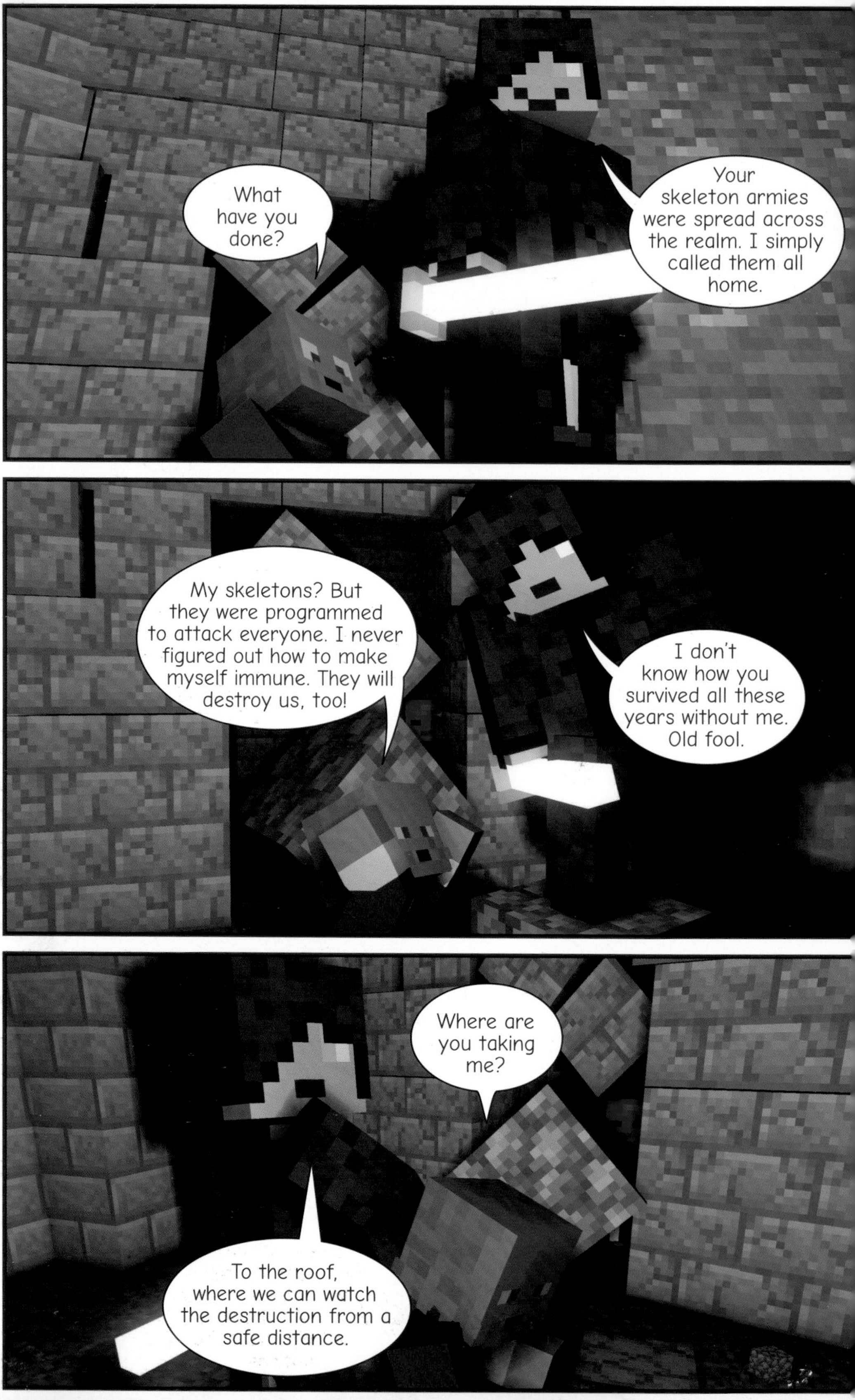
What have you done?
Your skeleton armies were spread across the realm. I simply called them all home.
My skeletons? But they were programmed to attack everyone. I never figured out how to make myself immune. They will destroy us, too!
I don't know how you survived all these years without me. Old fool.
Where are you taking me?
To the roof, where we can watch the destruction from a safe distance.

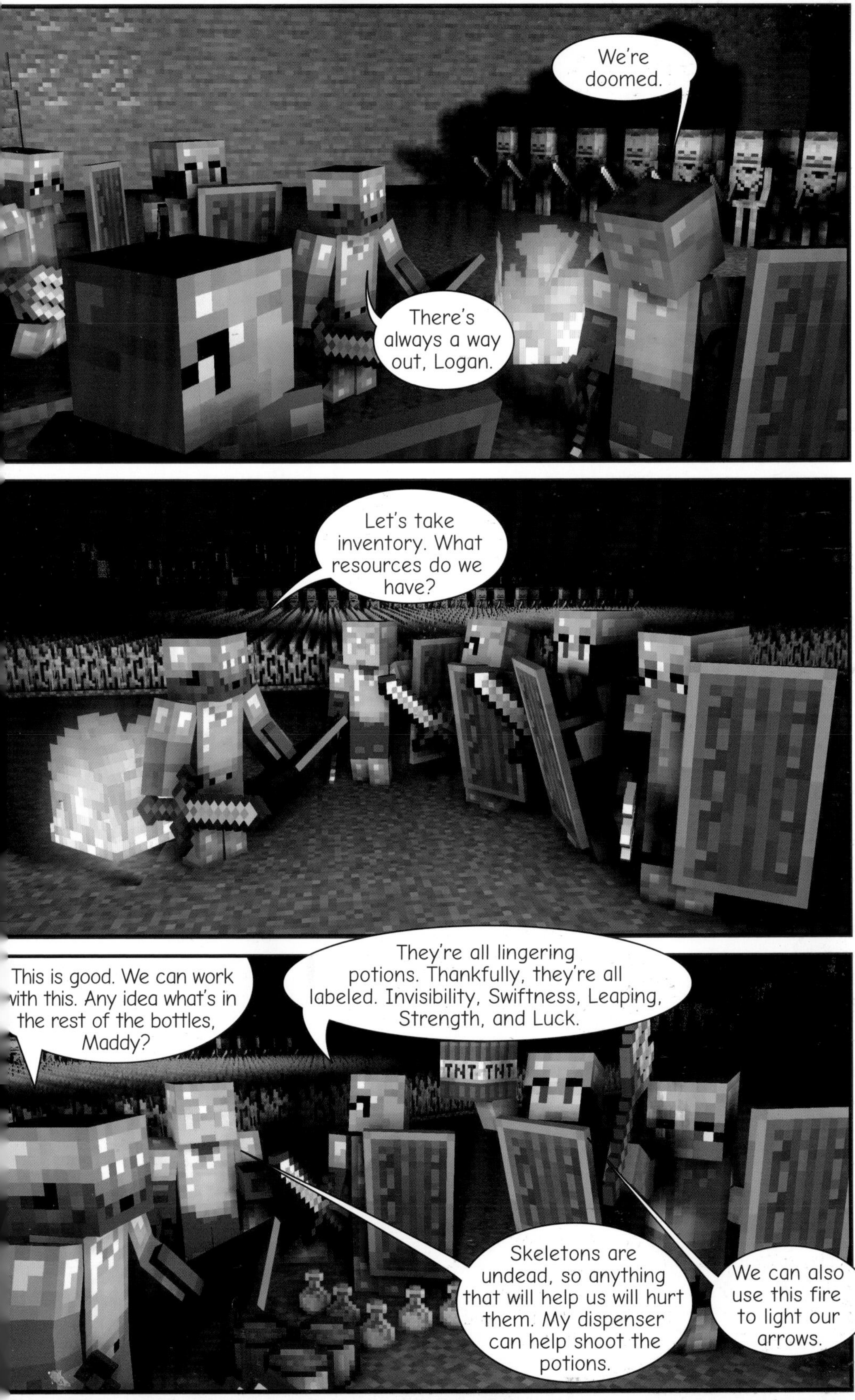

We're doomed.
There's always a way out, Logan.
Let's take inventory. What resources do we have?
This is good. We can work with this. Any idea what's in the rest of the bottles, Maddy?
They're all lingering potions. Thankfully, they're all labeled. Invisibility, Swiftness, Leaping, Strength, and Luck.
TNT TNT
Skeletons are undead, so anything that will help us will hurt them. My dispenser can help shoot the potions.
We can also use this fire to light our arrows.

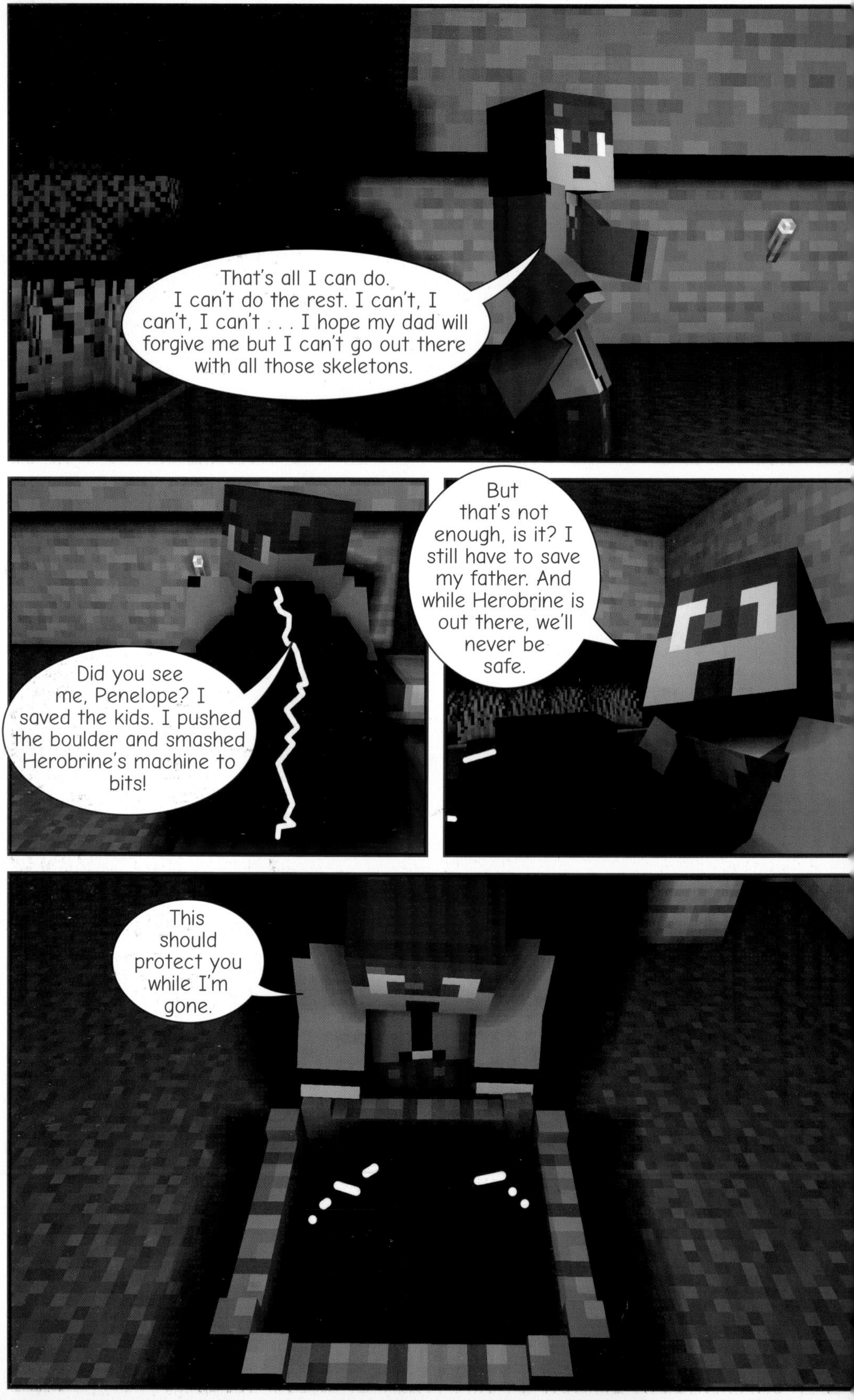
That's all I can do. I can't do the rest. I can't, I can't, I can't . . . I hope my dad will forgive me but I can't go out there with all those skeletons.
Did you see me, Penelope? I saved the kids. I pushed the boulder and smashed Herobrine's machine to bits!
But that's not enough, is it? I still have to save my father. And while Herobrine is out there, we'll never be safe.
This should protect you while I'm gone.

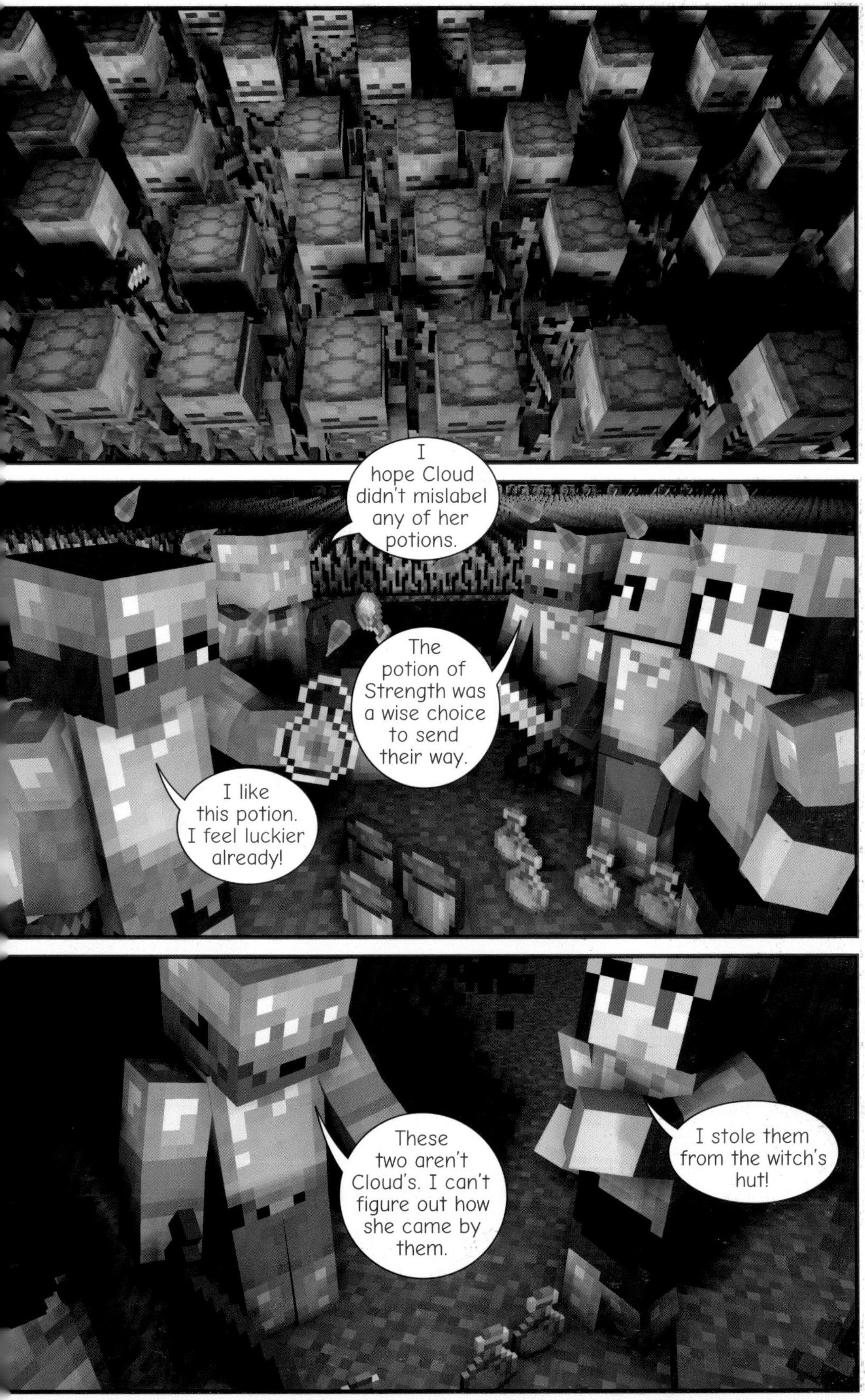
I hope Cloud didn't mislabel any of her potions.
The potion of Strength was a wise choice to send their way.
I like this potion. I feel luckier already!
These two aren't Cloud's. I can't figure out how she came by them.
I stole them from the witch's hut!

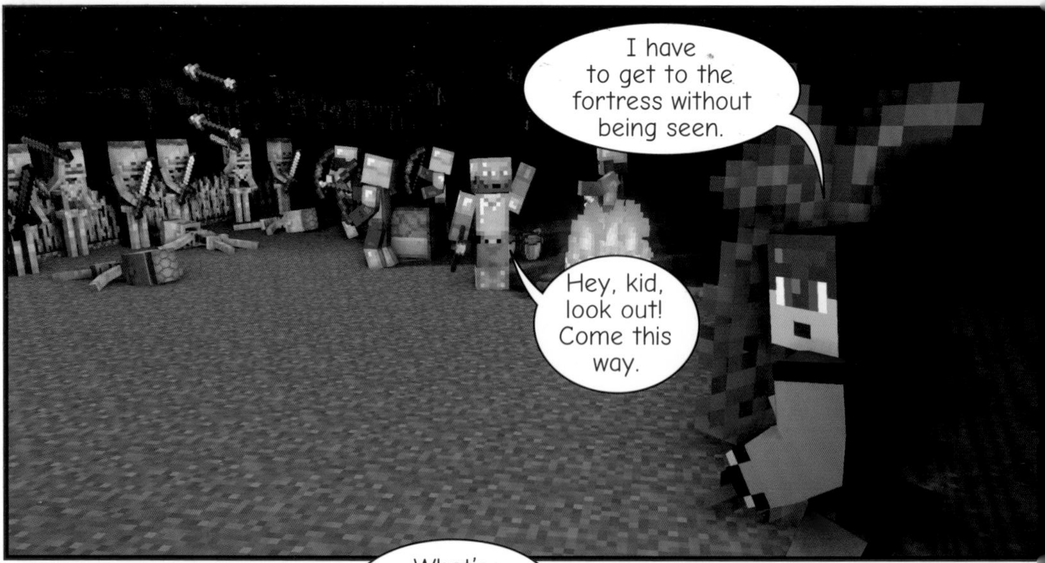
I have to get to the fortress without being seen.
Hey, kid, look out! Come this way.
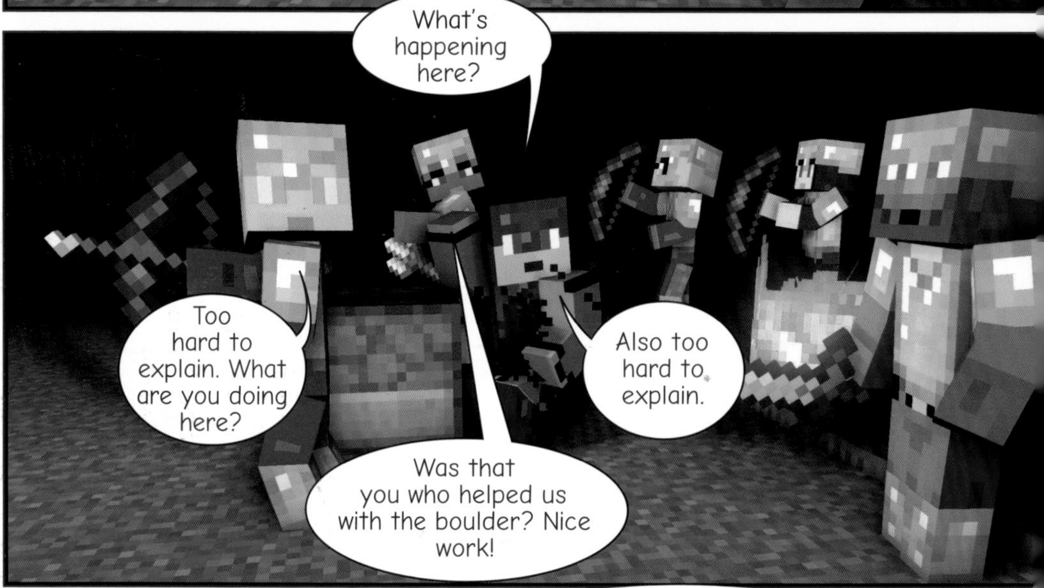
What's happening here?
Too hard to explain. What are you doing here?
Also too hard to explain.
Was that you who helped us with the boulder? Nice work!
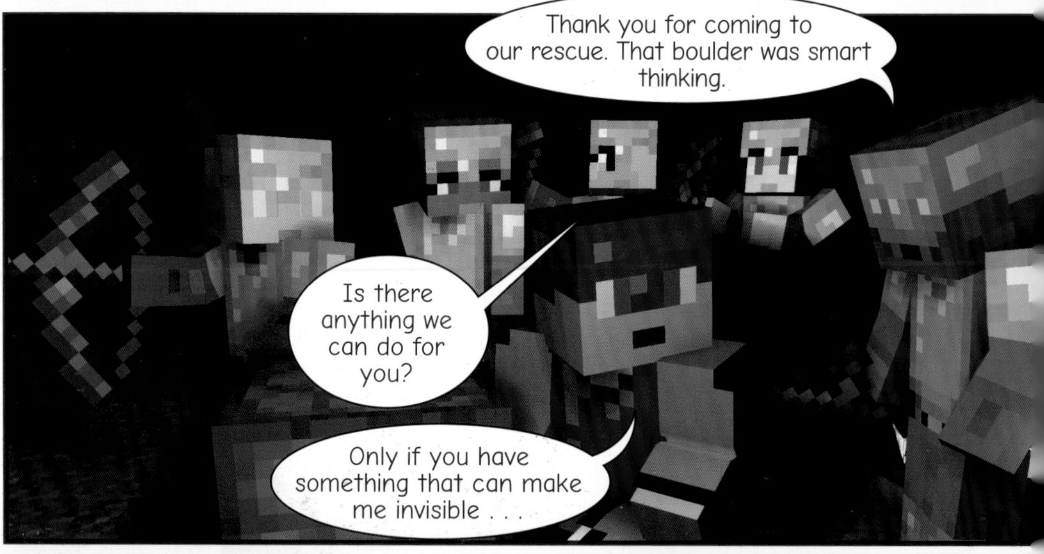
Thank you for coming to our rescue. That boulder was smart thinking.
Is there anything we can do for you?
Only if you have something that can make me invisible . . .

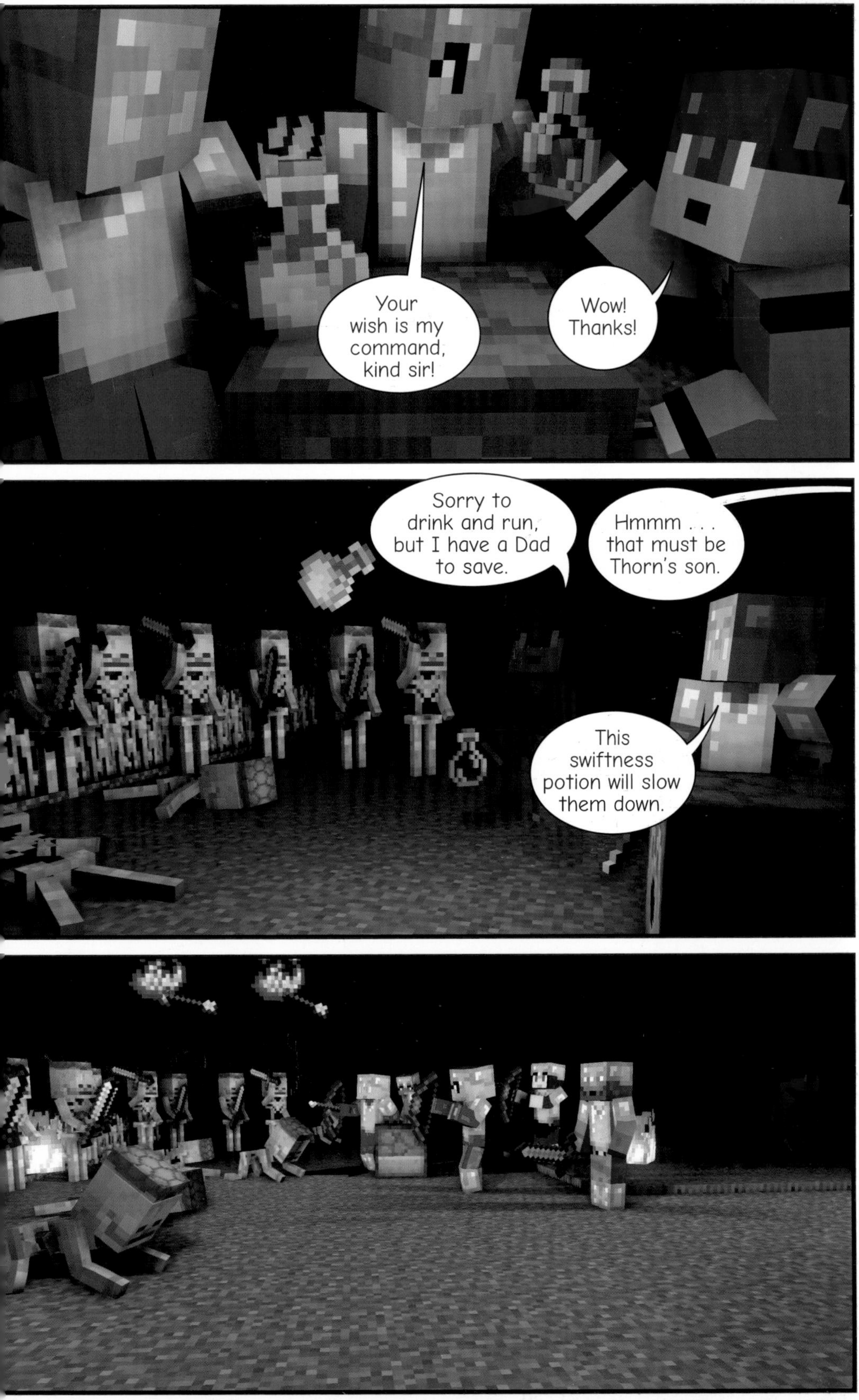
Your wish is my command, kind sir!
Wow! Thanks!
Sorry to drink and run, but I have a Dad to save.
Hmmm . . . that must be Thorn's son.
This swiftness potion will slow them down.

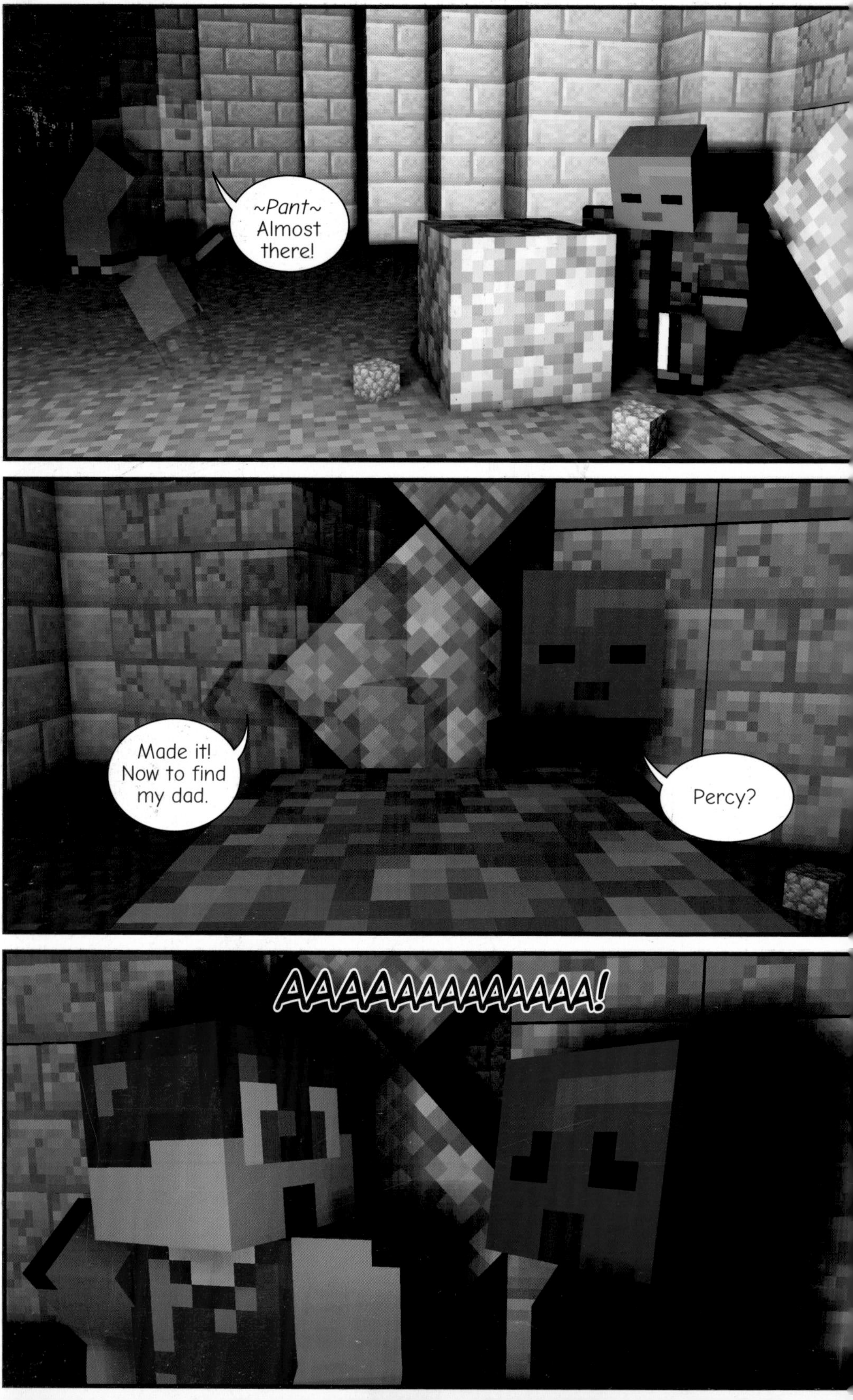

~Pant~ Almost there!
Made it! Now to find my dad.
Percy?
AAAAAAAAAAAAA!

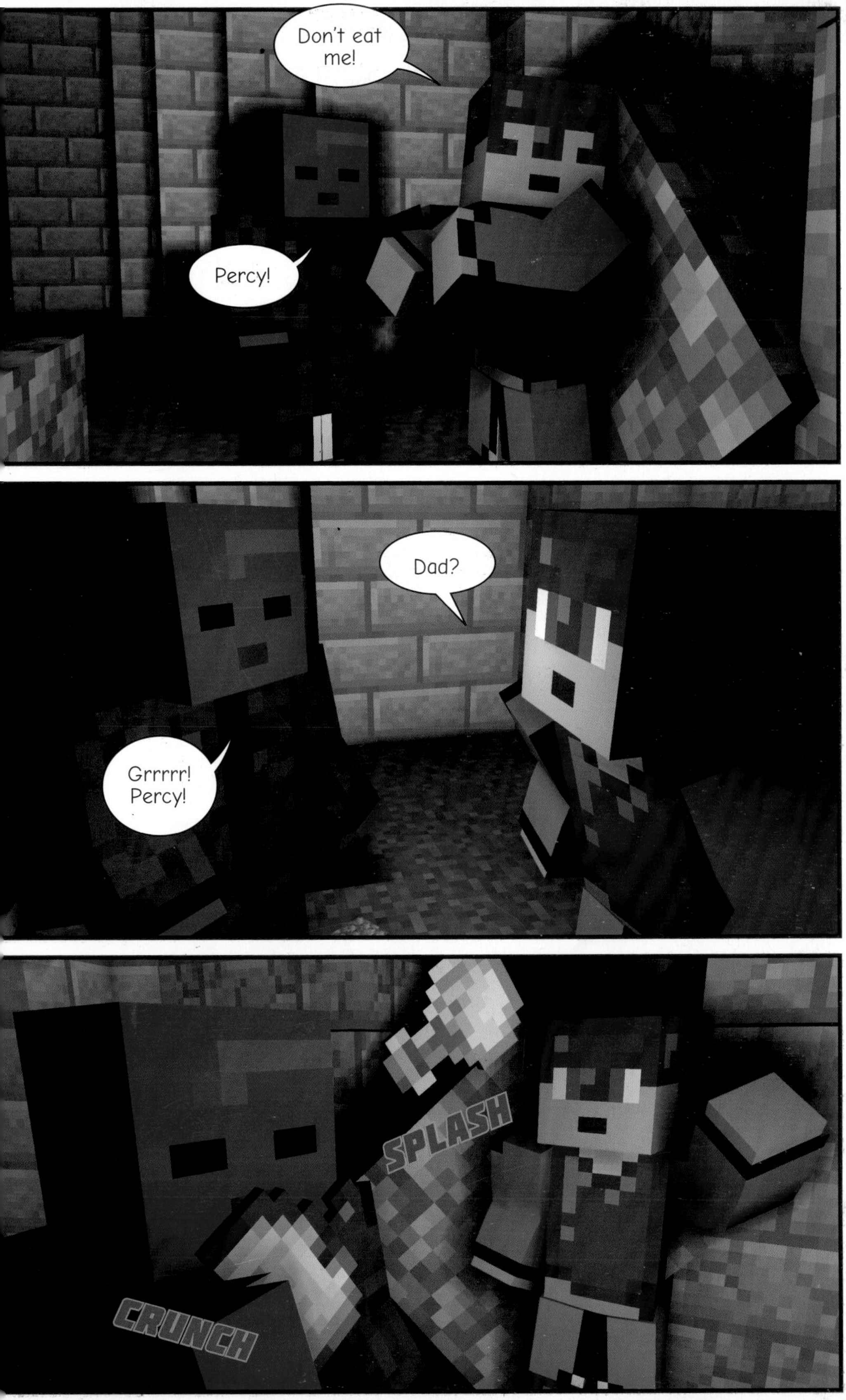
Don't eat me!
Percy!
Dad?
Grrrrr! Percy!
SPLASH
CRUNCH

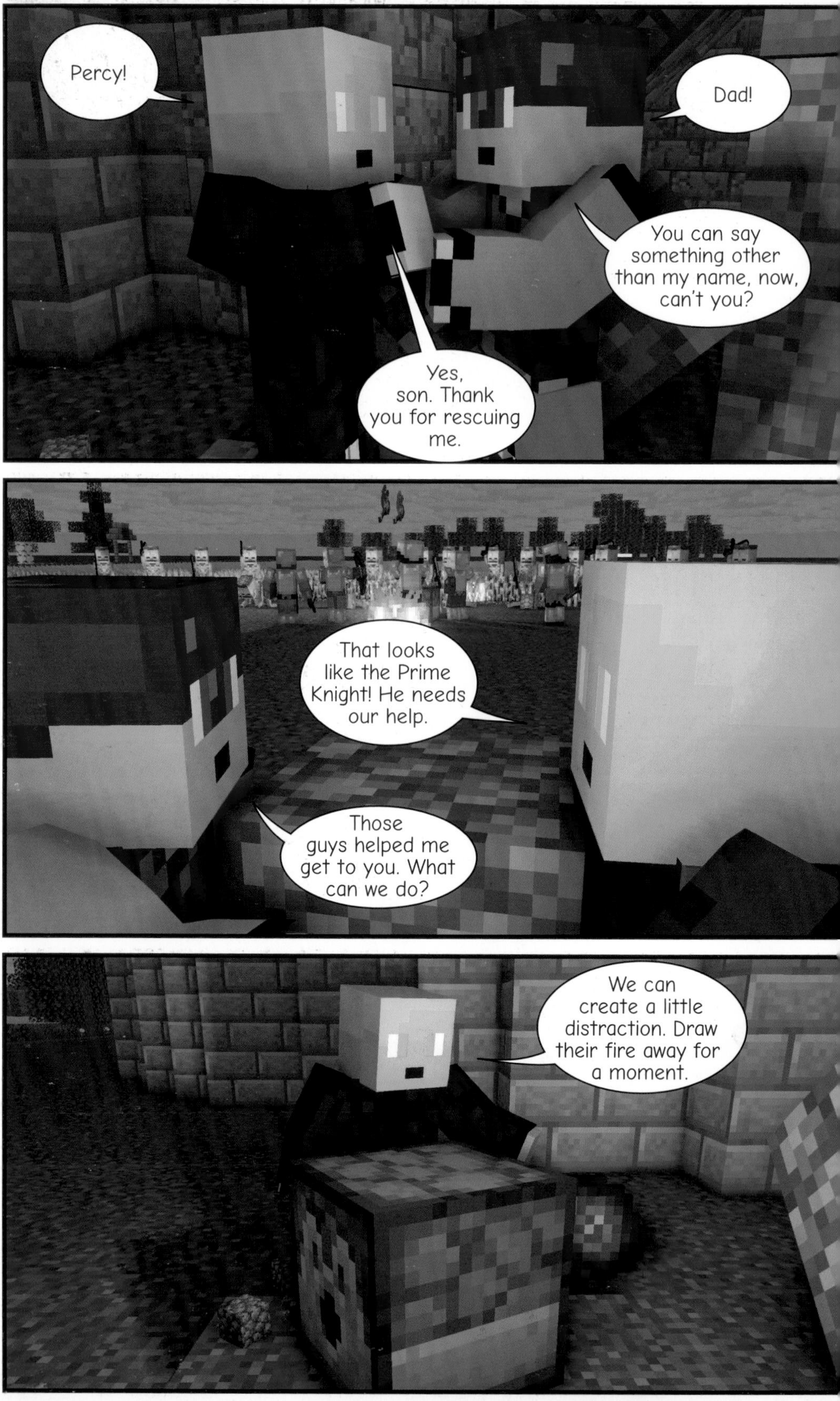
Percy!
Dad!
You can say something other than my name, now, can't you?
Yes, son. Thank you for rescuing me.
That looks like the Prime Knight! He needs our help.
Those guys helped me get to you. What can we do?
We can create a little distraction. Draw their fire away for a moment.

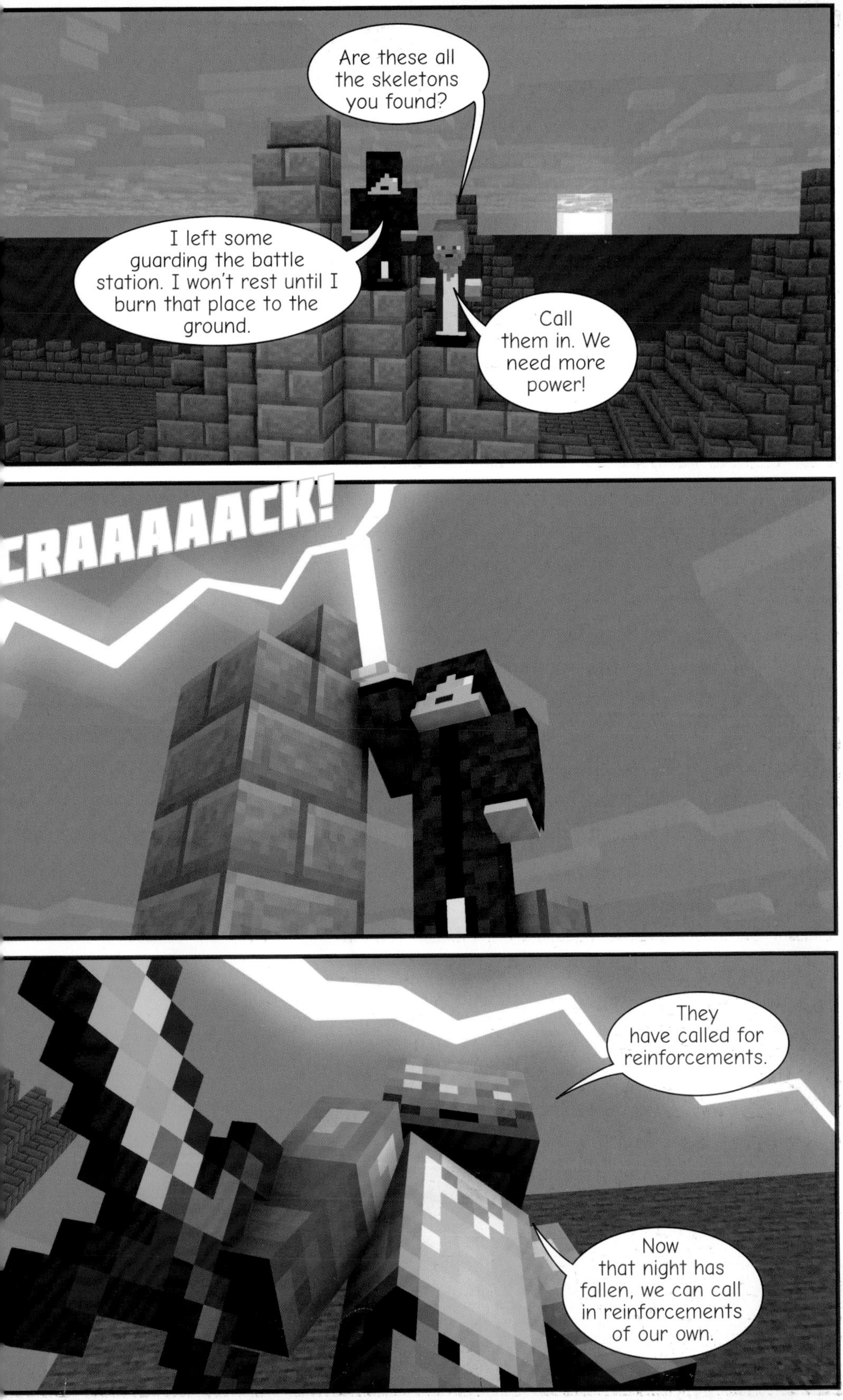
Are these all the skeletons you found?
I left some guarding the battle station. I won't rest until I burn that place to the ground.
Call them in. We need more power!
CRAAAAACK!
They have called for reinforcements.
Now that night has fallen, we can call in reinforcements of our own.

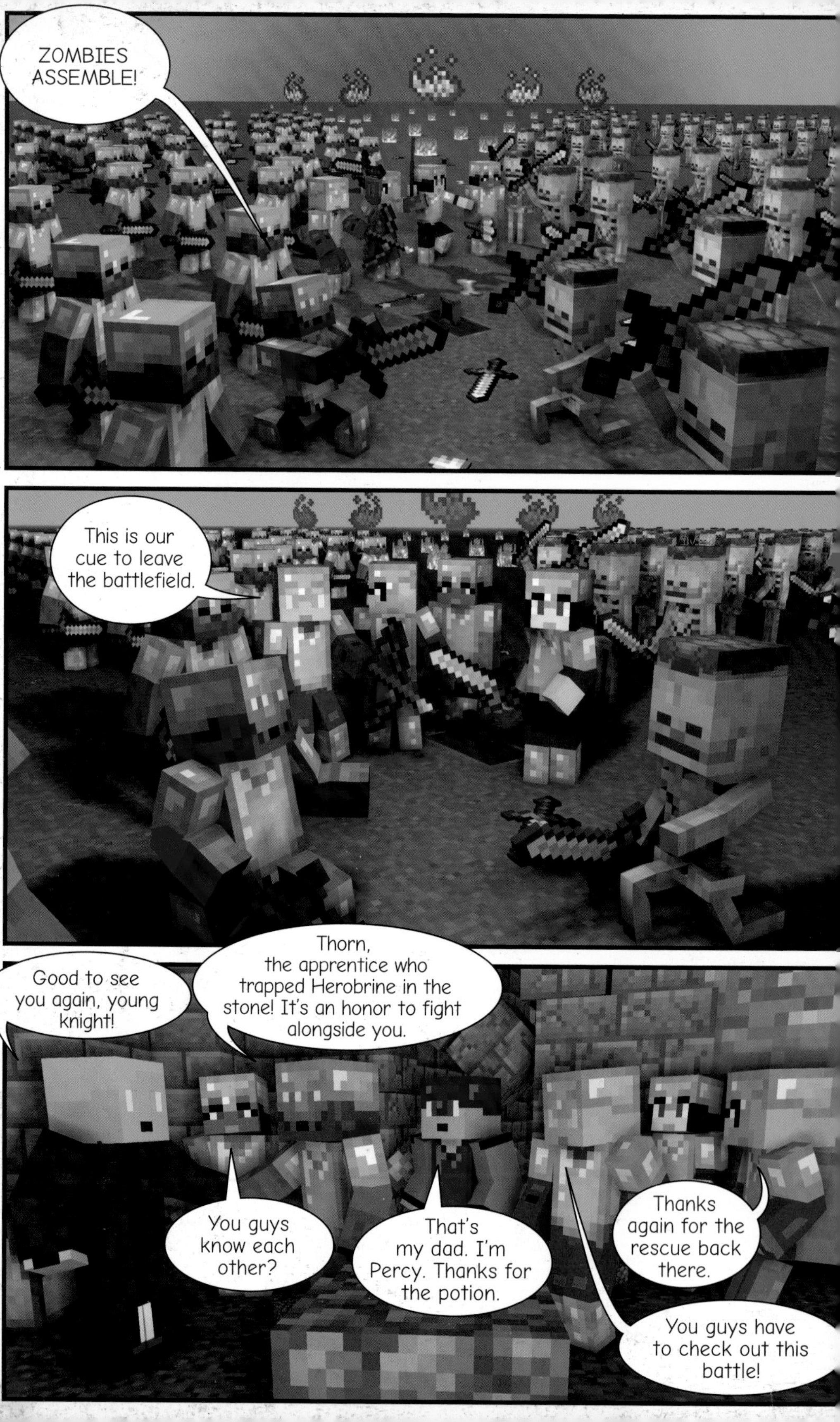
ZOMBIES ASSEMBLE!
This is our cue to leave the battlefield.
Good to see you again, young knight!
Thorn, the apprentice who trapped Herobrine in the stone! It's an honor to fight alongside you.
You guys know each other?
That's my dad. I'm Percy. Thanks for the potion.
Thanks again for the rescue back there.
You guys have to check out this battle!

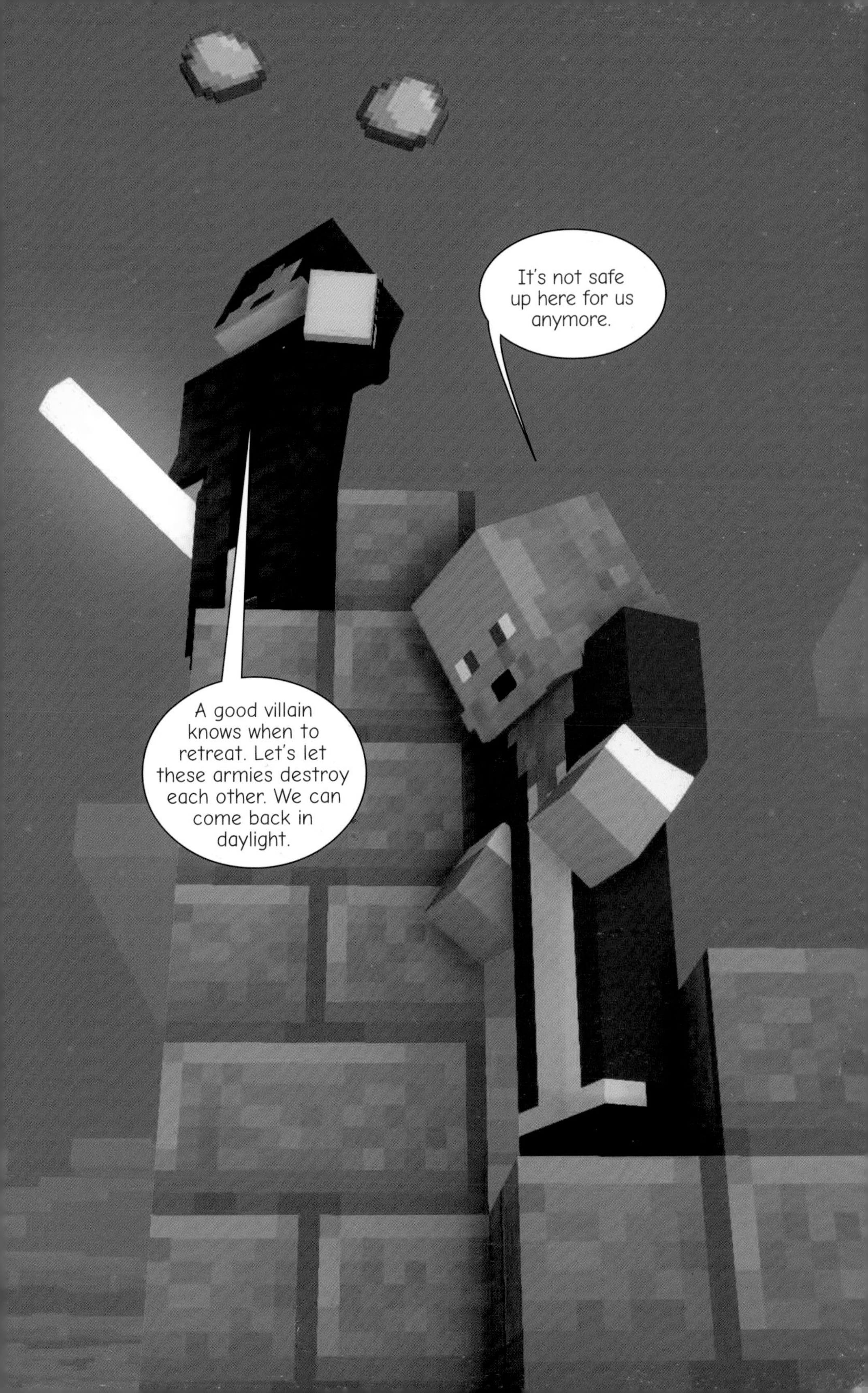
It's not safe up here for us anymore.
A good villain knows when to retreat. Let's let these armies destroy each other. We can come back in daylight.

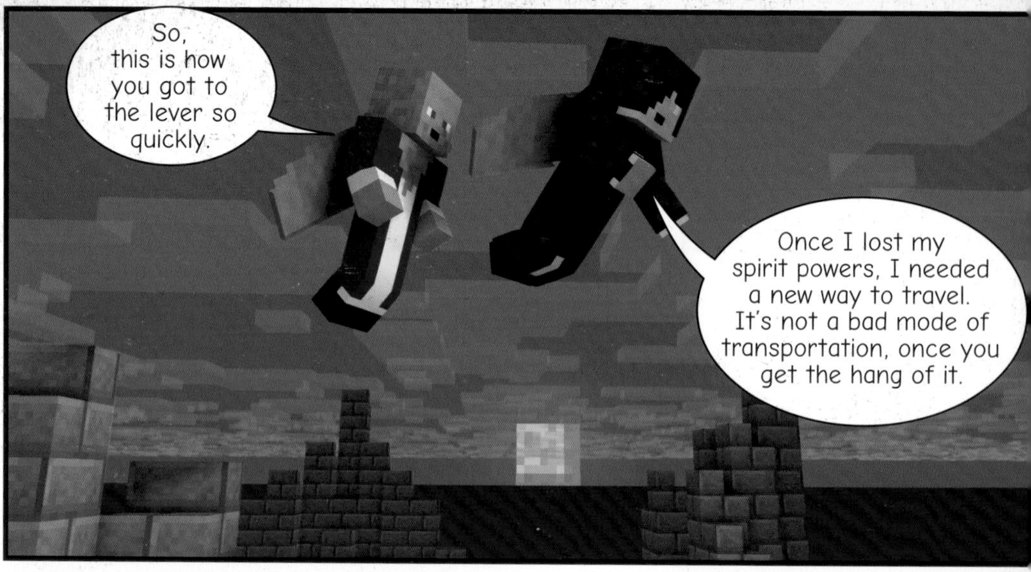
So, this is how you got to the lever so quickly.
Once I lost my spirit powers, I needed a new way to travel. It's not a bad mode of transportation, once you get the hang of it.

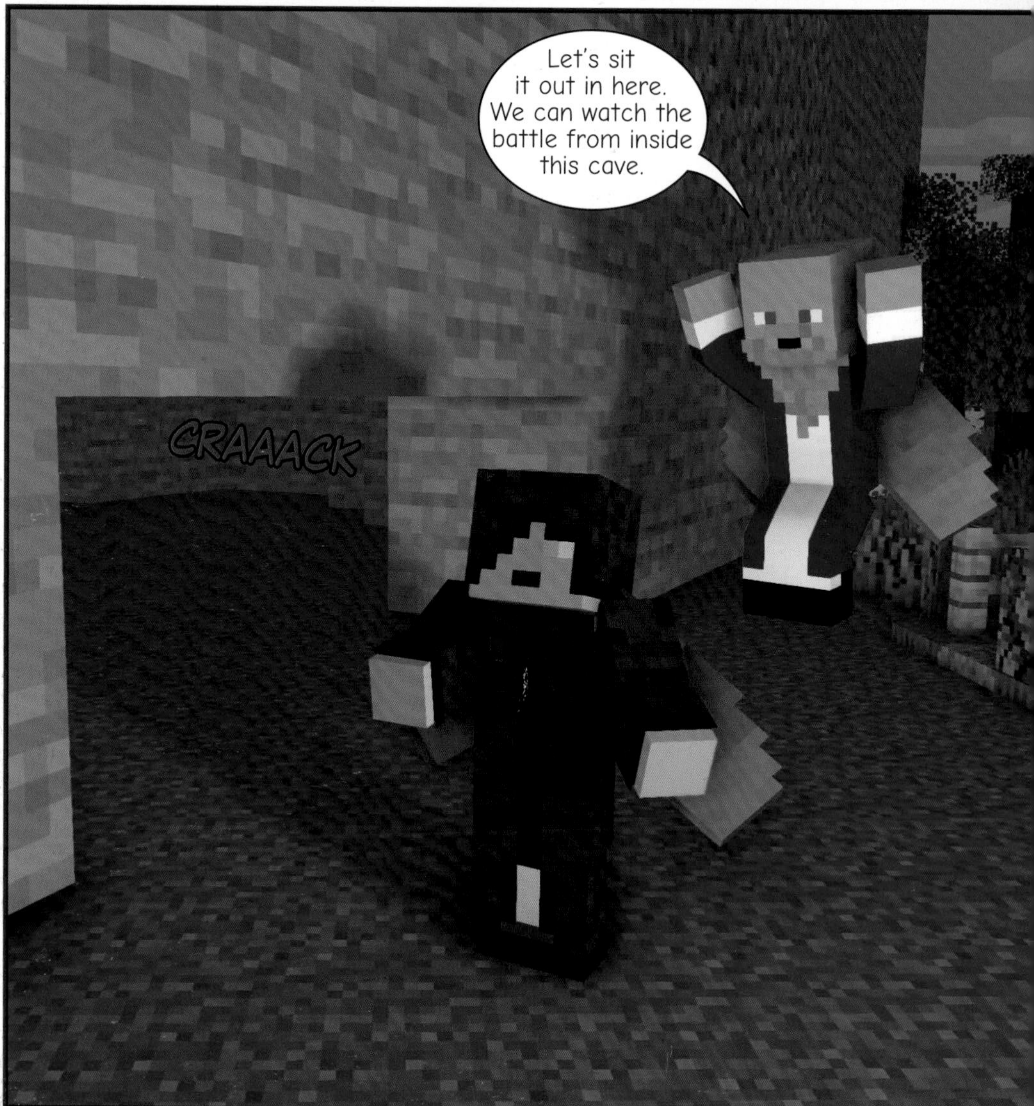
Let's sit it out in here. We can watch the battle from inside this cave.
CRAAACK

CHAPTER 10

PANIC AT THE BEACH

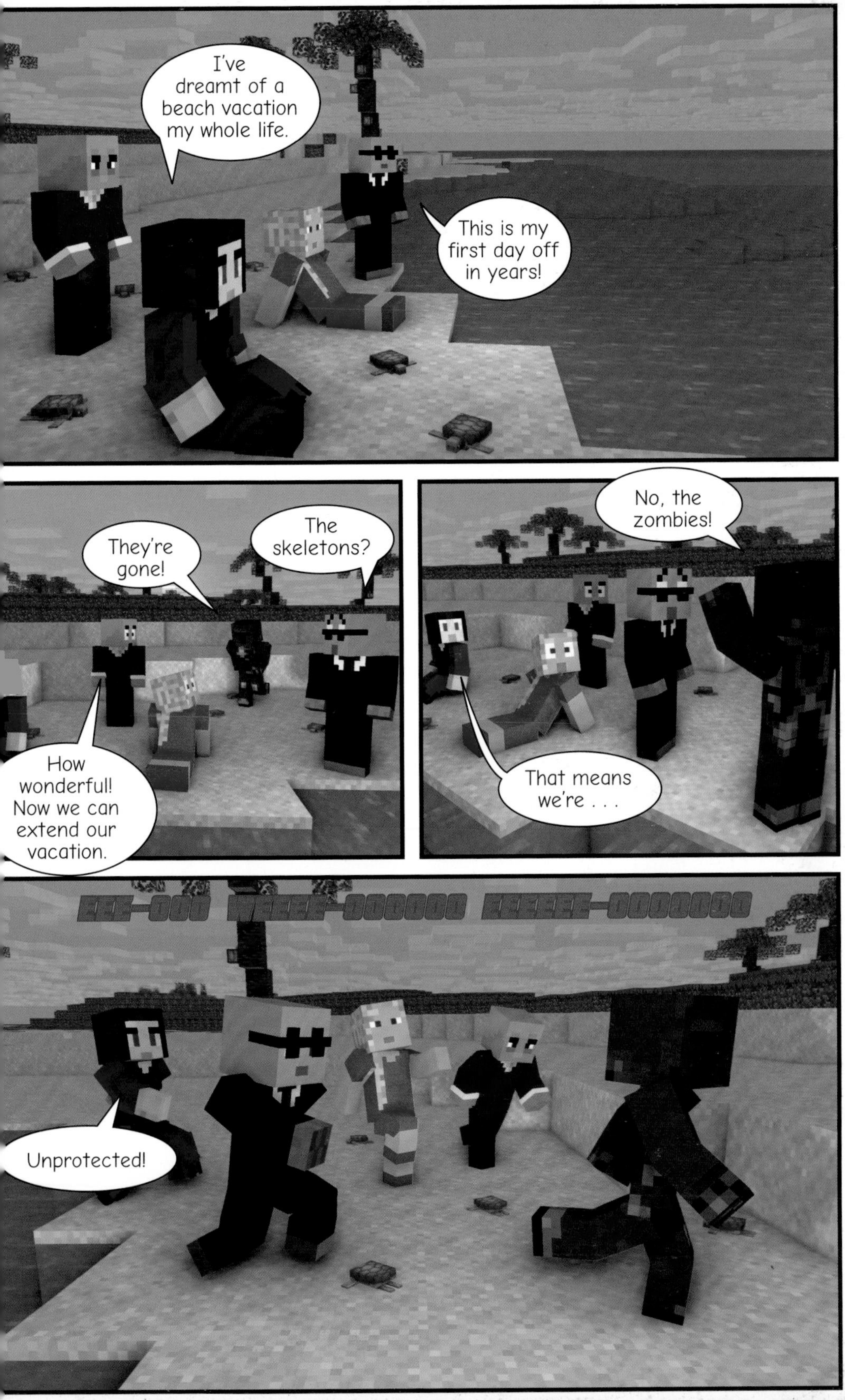

I've dreamt of a beach vacation my whole life.
This is my first day off in years!
They're gone!
The skeletons?
How wonderful! Now we can extend our vacation.
No, the zombies!
That means we're . . .
EEE-OOO WEEEE-OOOOOO EEEEEE-OOOOOOO
Unprotected!

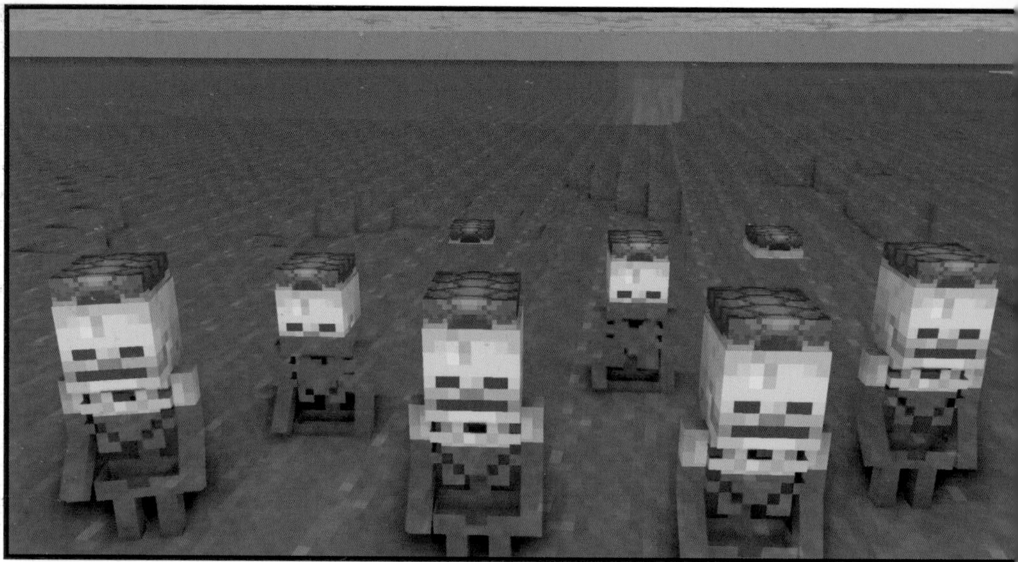

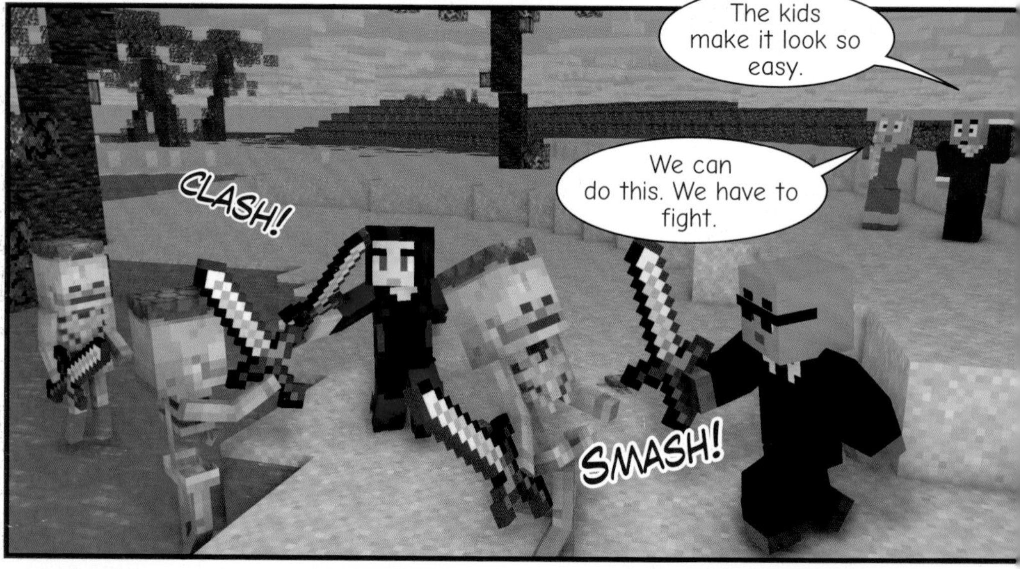
The kids make it look so easy.
We can do this. We have to fight.
CLASH!
SMASH!

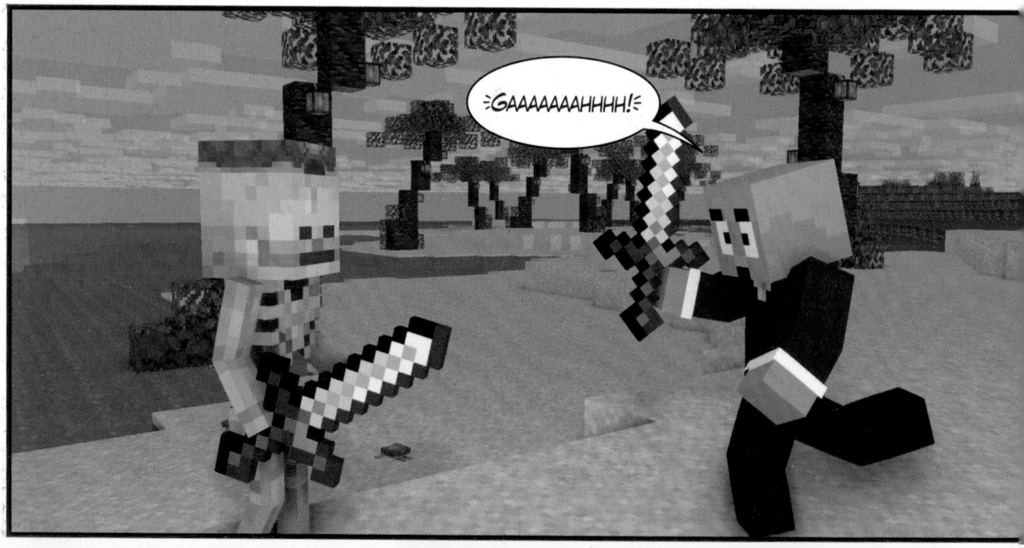
GAAAAAAAHHHH!

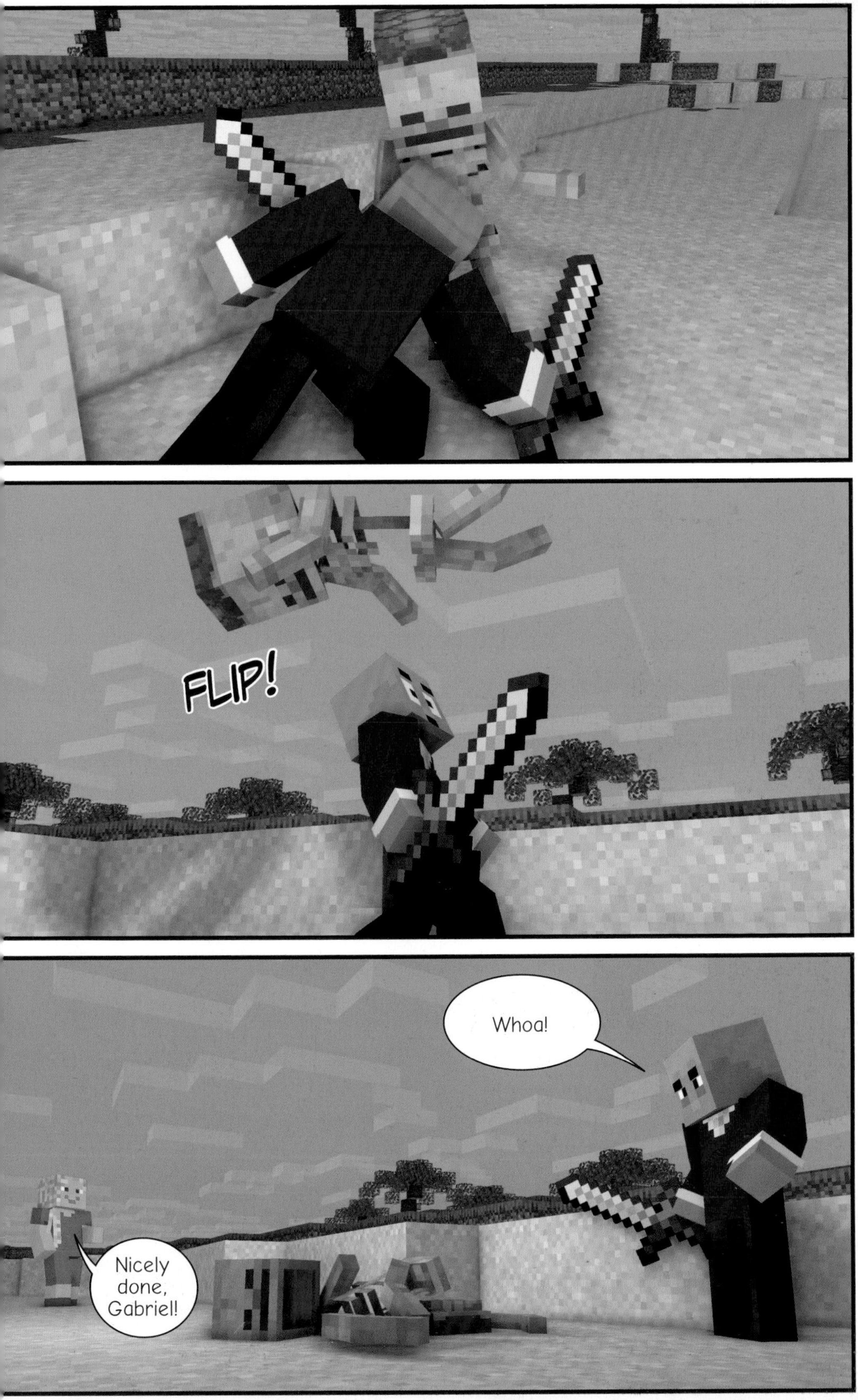
FLIP!
Whoa!
Nicely done, Gabriel!

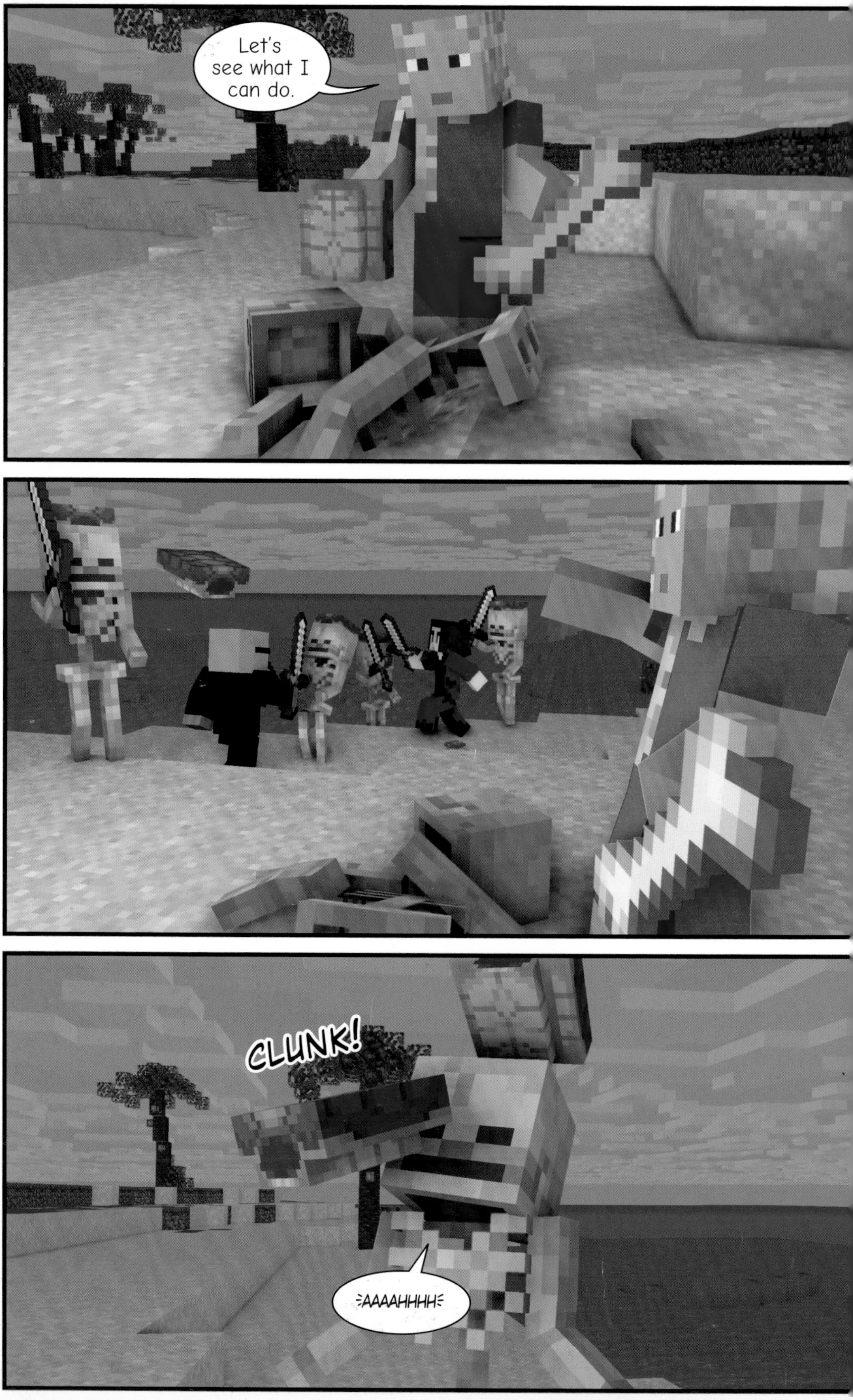
Let's see what I can do.
CLUNK!
AAAAHHHH

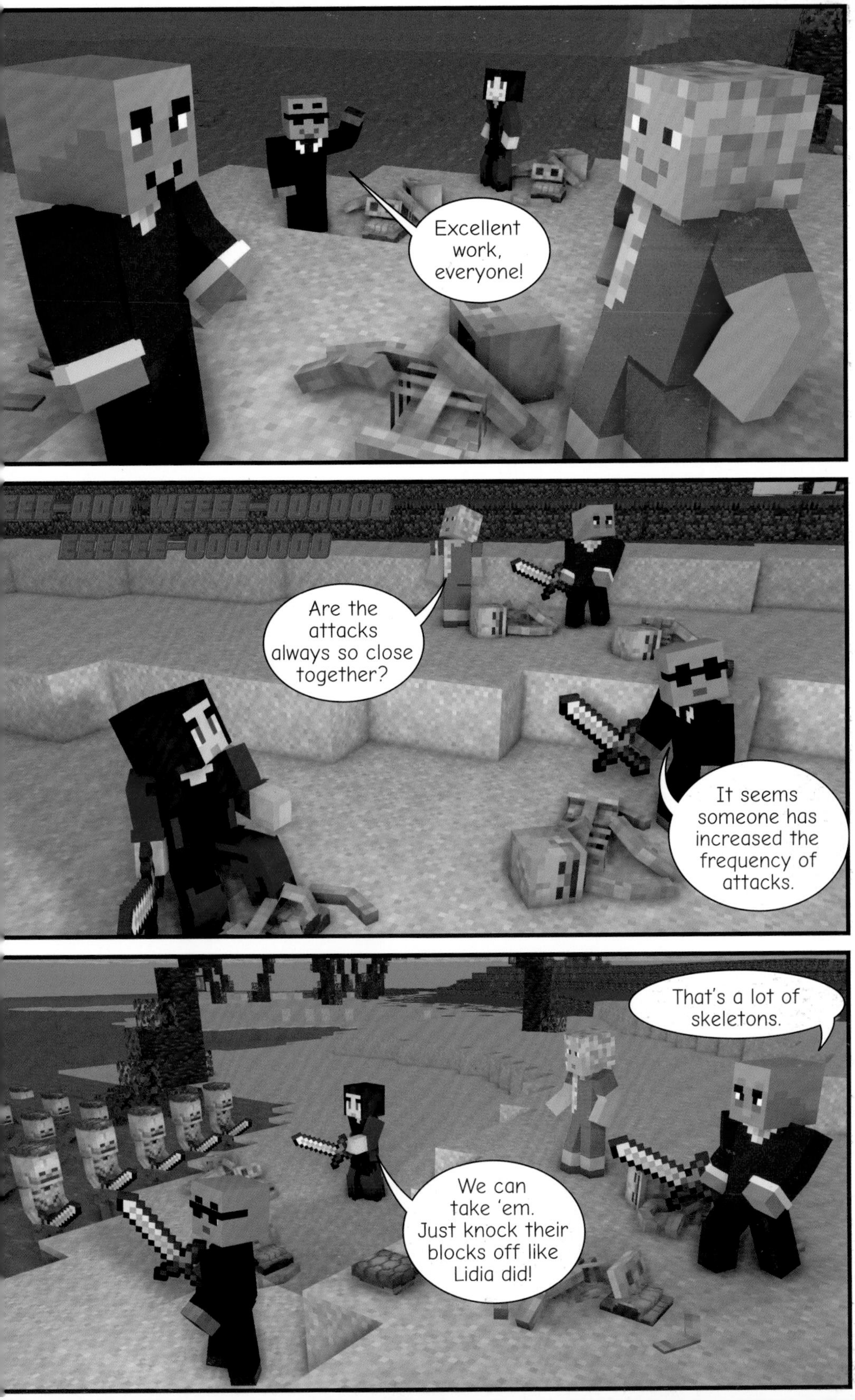
Excellent work, everyone!
EEE-OOO WEEEE-OOOOOO
EEEEE-OOOOOOO
Are the attacks always so close together?
It seems someone has increased the frequency of attacks.
That's a lot of skeletons.
We can take 'em. Just knock their blocks off like Lidia did!

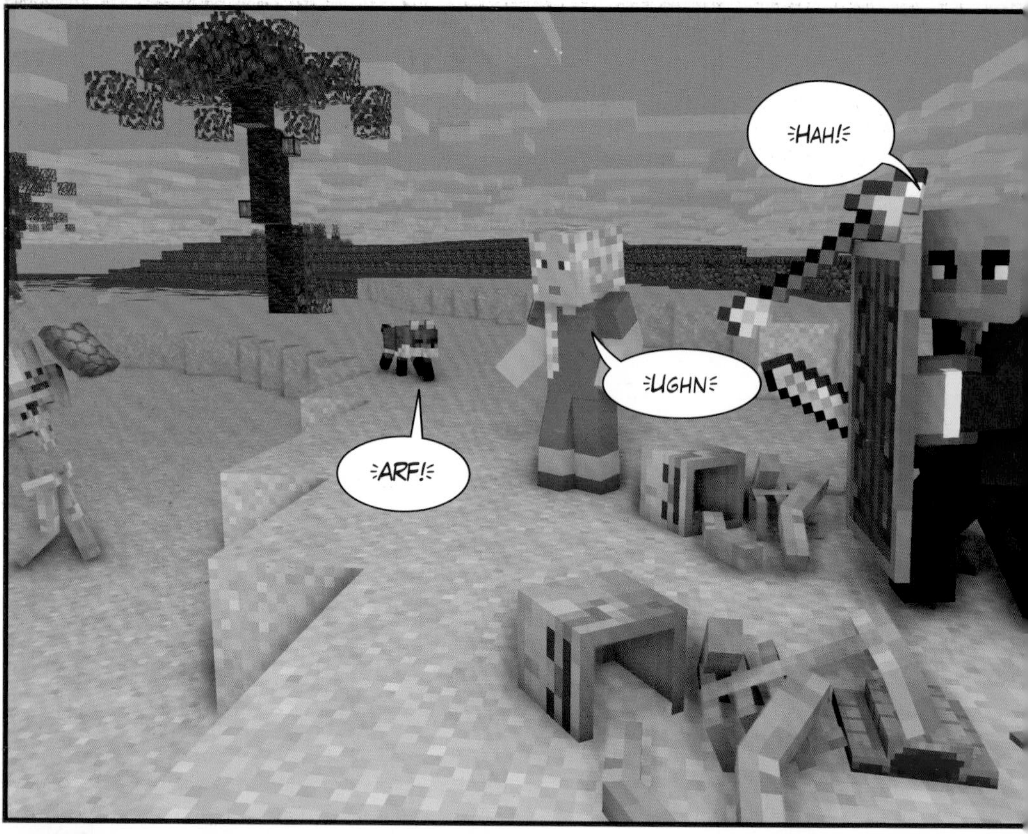
HAH!
UGHN
ARF!

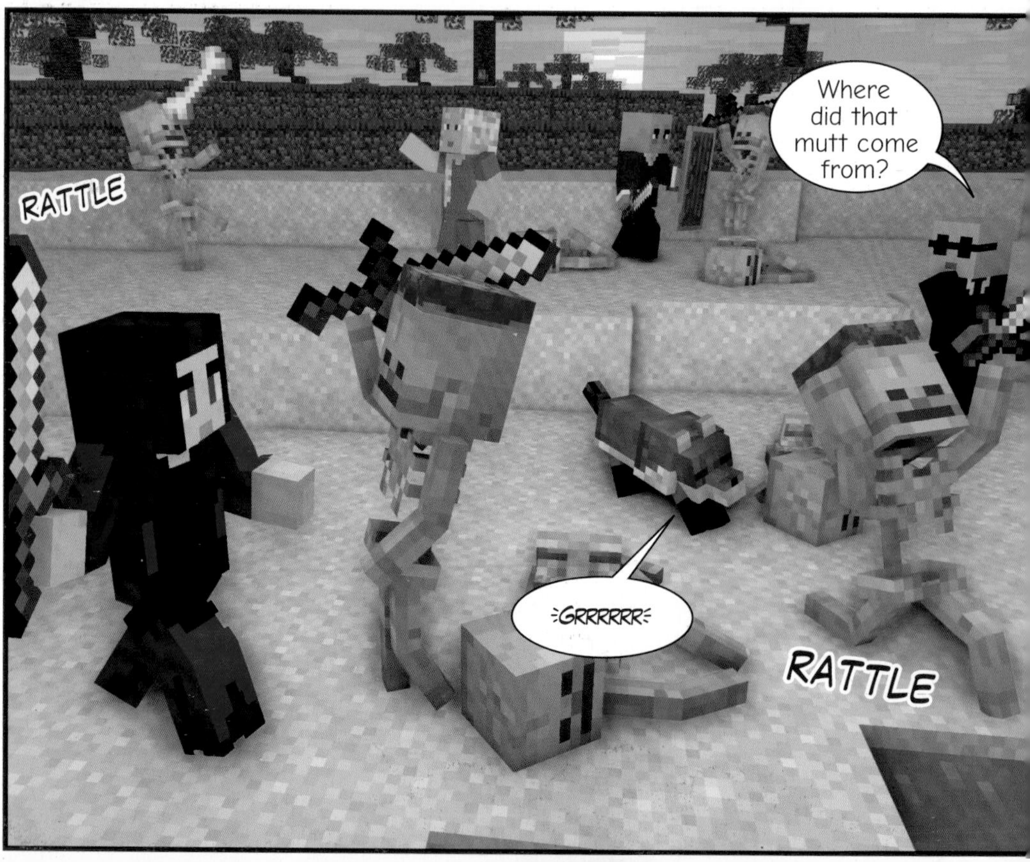
RATTLE
Where did that mutt come from?
GRRRRRR
RATTLE

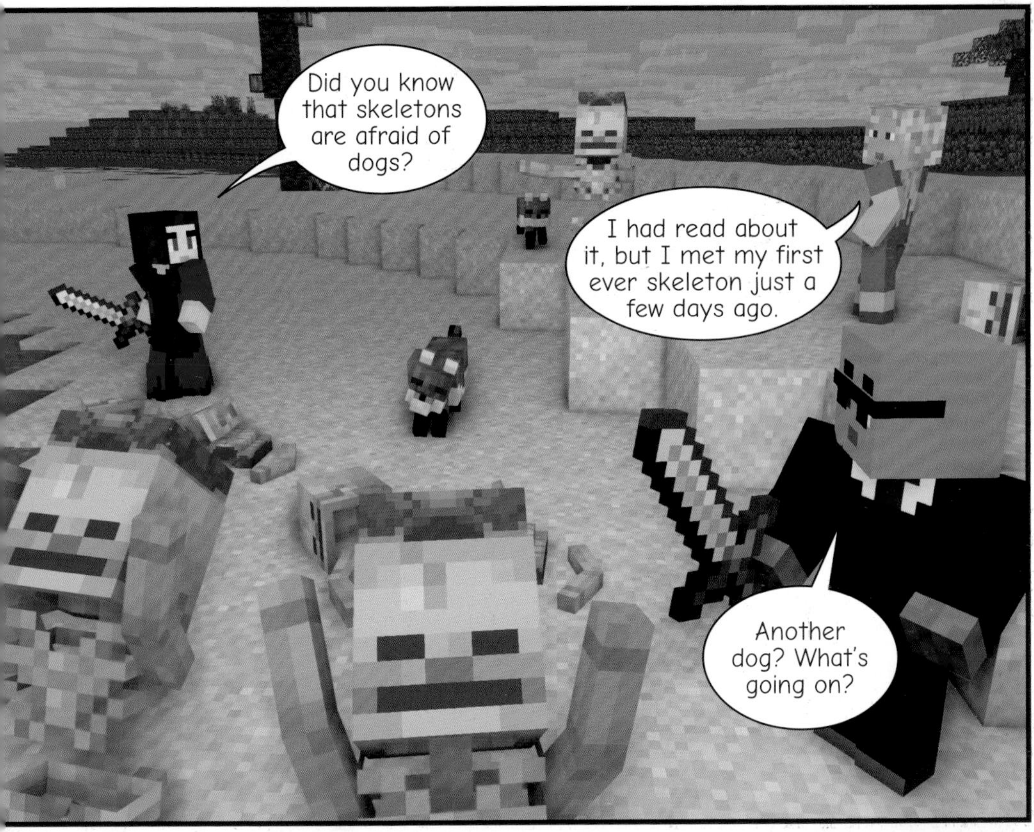
Did you know that skeletons are afraid of dogs?
I had read about it, but I met my first ever skeleton just a few days ago.
Another dog? What's going on?

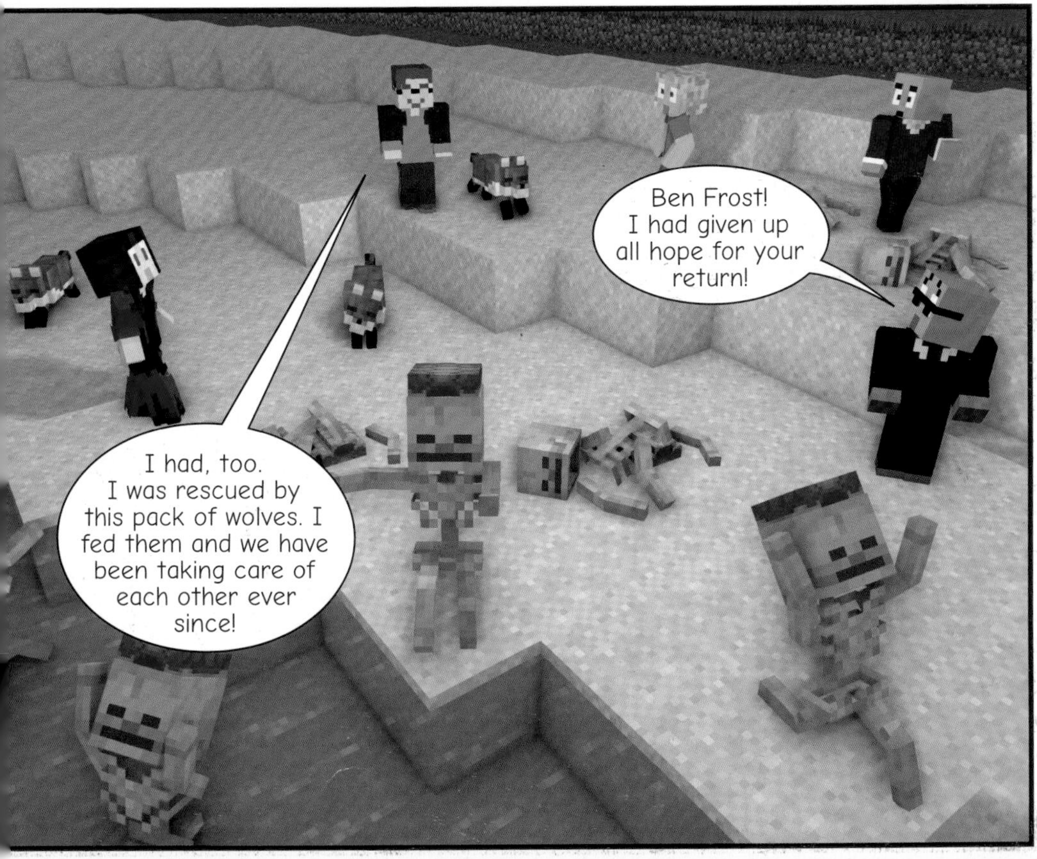
Ben Frost! I had given up all hope for your return!
I had, too. I was rescued by this pack of wolves. I fed them and we have been taking care of each other ever since!

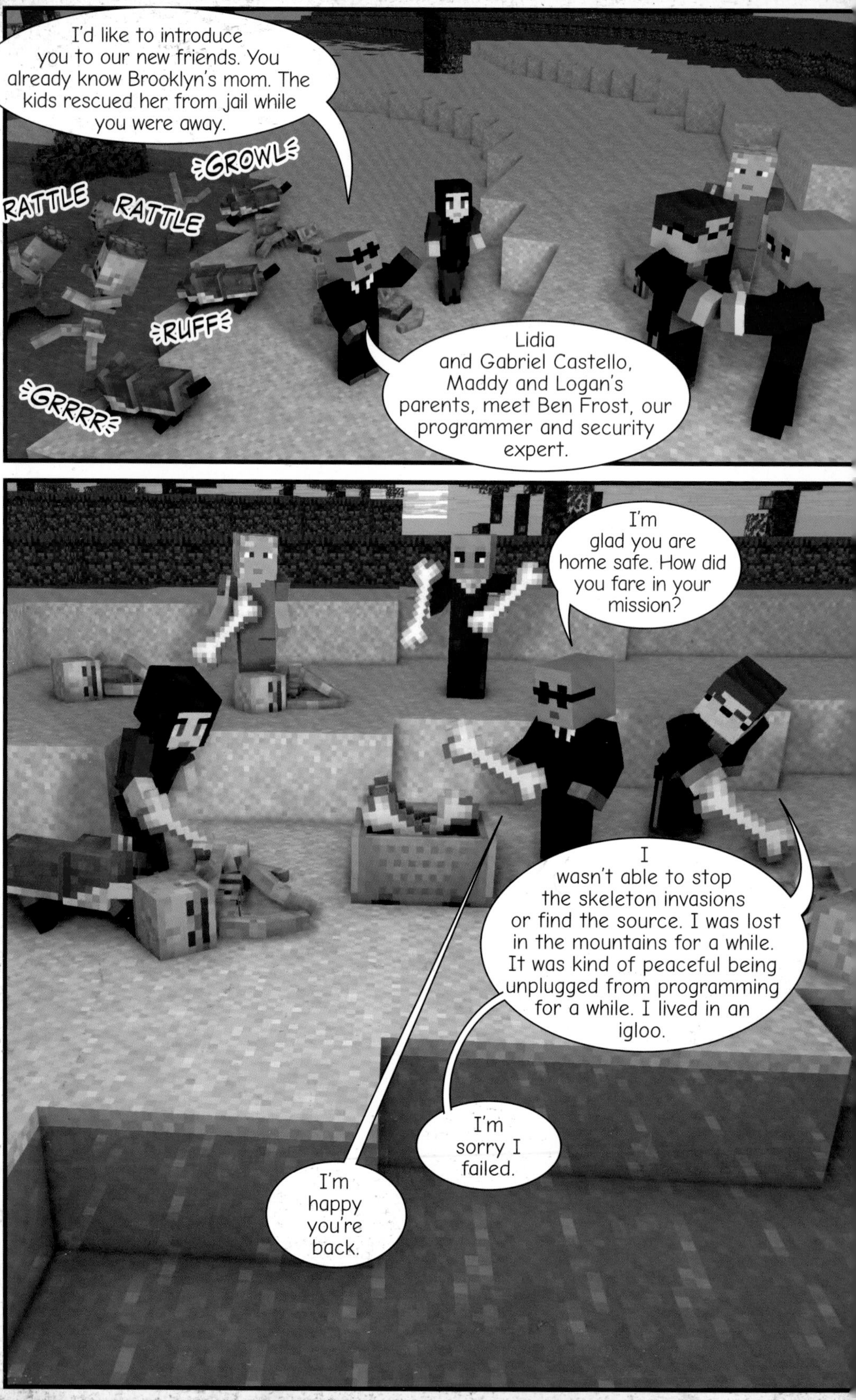
I'd like to introduce you to our new friends. You already know Brooklyn's mom. The kids rescued her from jail while you were away.
GROWL
RATTLE
RATTLE
RUFF
GRRRR
Lidia and Gabriel Castello, Maddy and Logan's parents, meet Ben Frost, our programmer and security expert.
I'm glad you are home safe. How did you fare in your mission?
I wasn't able to stop the skeleton invasions or find the source. I was lost in the mountains for a while. It was kind of peaceful being unplugged from programming for a while. I lived in an igloo.
I'm sorry I failed.
I'm happy you're back.

CHAPTER 11

HEROES OF
THE REALM
UNITE

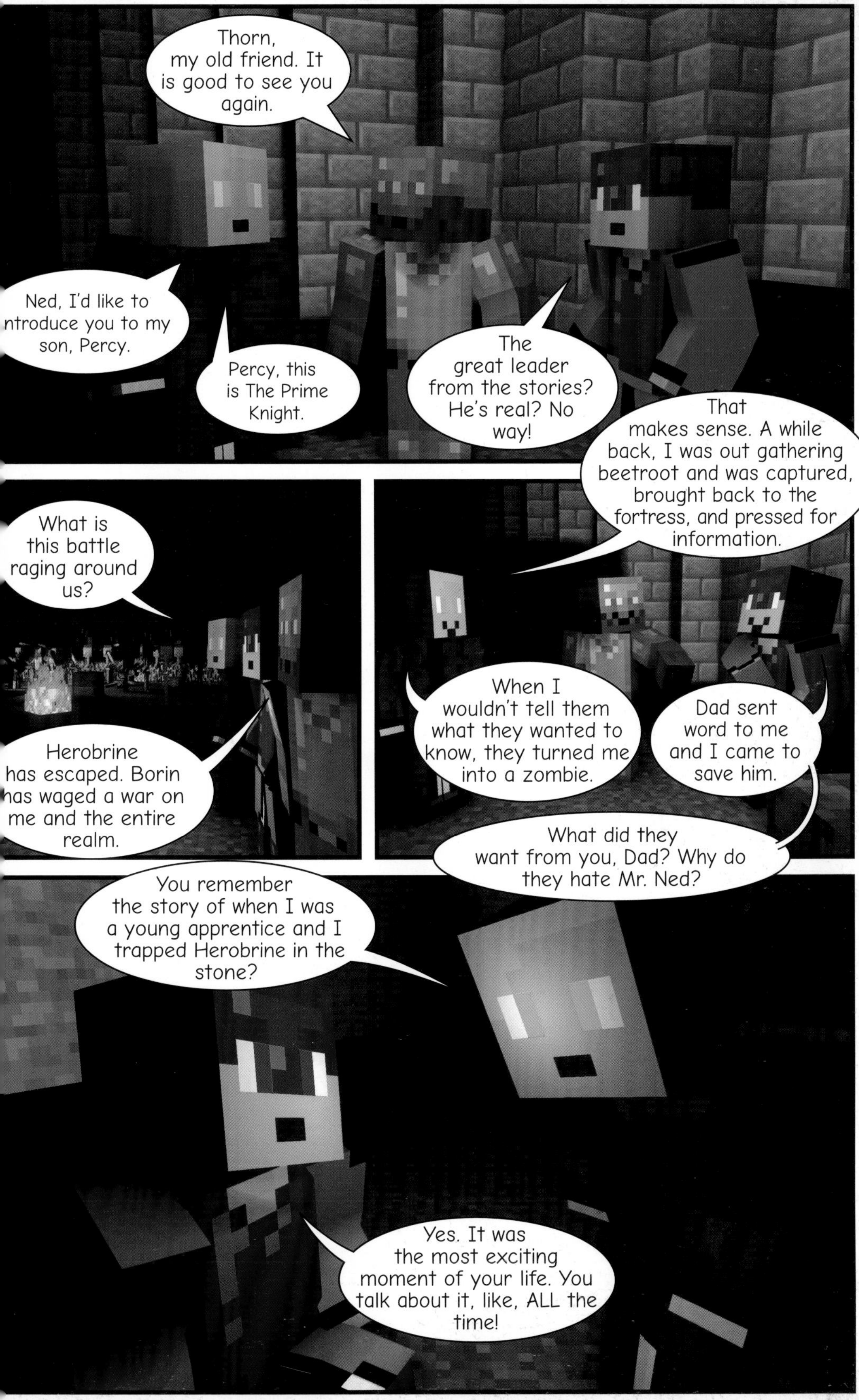
Thorn, my old friend. It is good to see you again.
Ned, I'd like to ntroduce you to my son, Percy.
Percy, this is The Prime Knight.
The great leader from the stories? He's real? No way!
What is this battle raging around us?
Herobrine has escaped. Borin has waged a war on me and the entire realm.
That makes sense. A while back, I was out gathering beetroot and was captured, brought back to the fortress, and pressed for information.
When I wouldn't tell them what they wanted to know, they turned me into a zombie.
Dad sent word to me and I came to save him.
What did they want from you, Dad? Why do they hate Mr. Ned?
You remember the story of when I was a young apprentice and I trapped Herobrine in the stone?
Yes. It was the most exciting moment of your life. You talk about it, like, ALL the time!

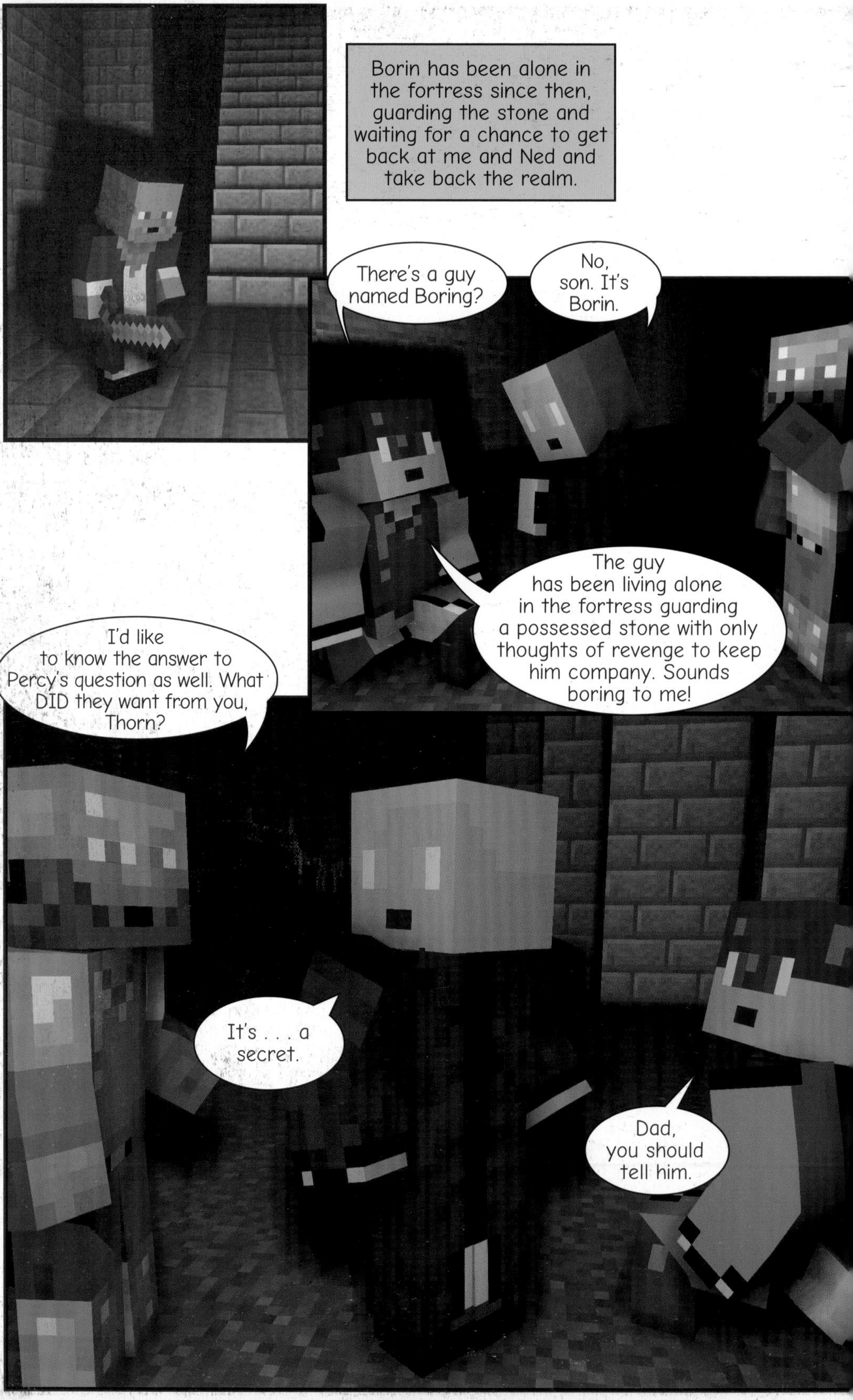

Borin has been alone in the fortress since then, guarding the stone and waiting for a chance to get back at me and Ned and take back the realm.
There's a guy named Boring?
No, son. It's Borin.
The guy has been living alone in the fortress guarding a possessed stone with only thoughts of revenge to keep him company. Sounds boring to me!
I'd like to know the answer to Percy's question as well. What DID they want from you, Thorn?
It's . . . a secret.
Dad, you should tell him.

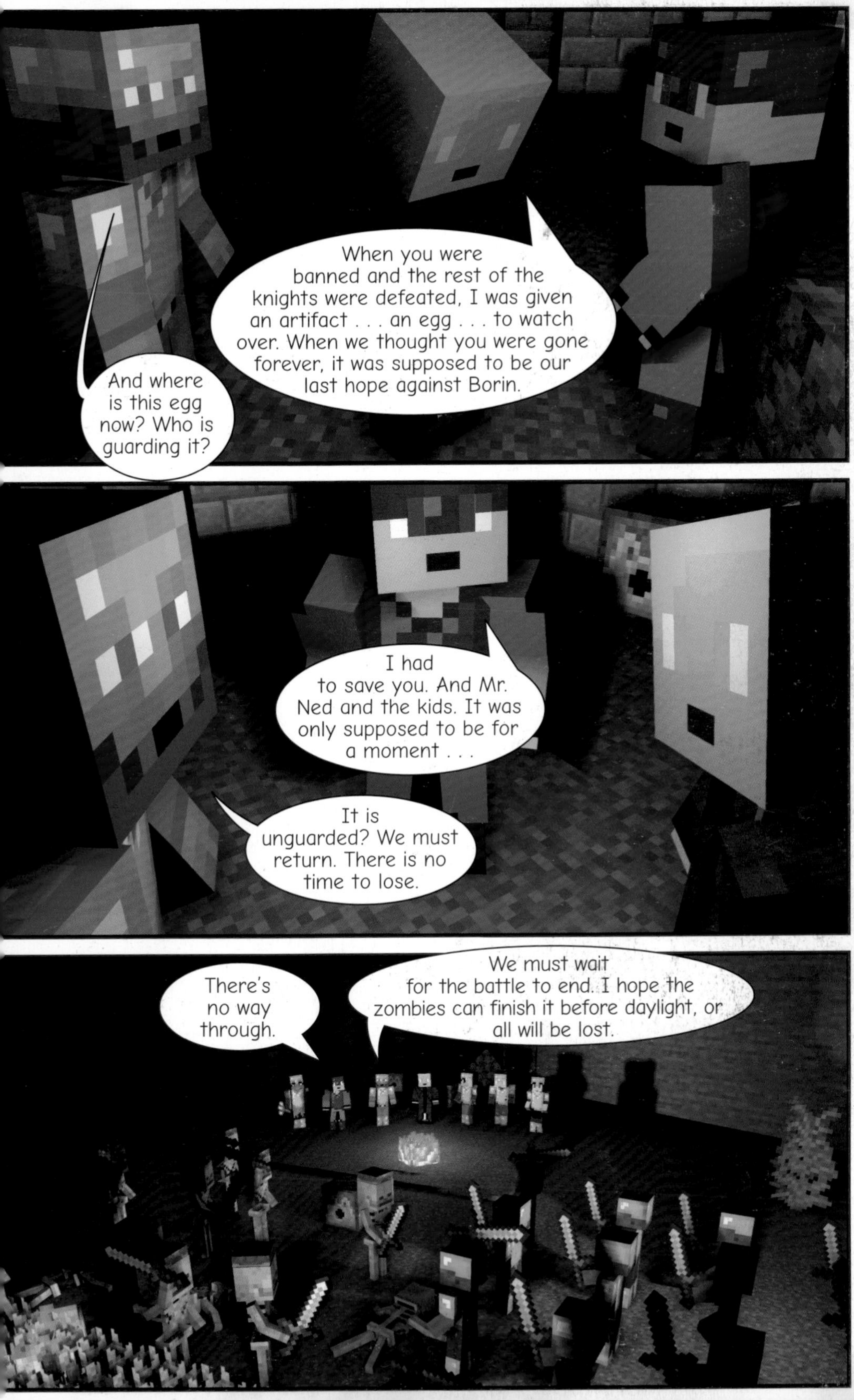
When you were banned and the rest of the knights were defeated, I was given an artifact . . . an egg . . . to watch over. When we thought you were gone forever, it was supposed to be our last hope against Borin.
And where is this egg now? Who is guarding it?
I had to save you. And Mr. Ned and the kids. It was only supposed to be for a moment . . .
It is unguarded? We must return. There is no time to lose.
There's no way through.
We must wait for the battle to end. I hope the zombies can finish it before daylight, or all will be lost.

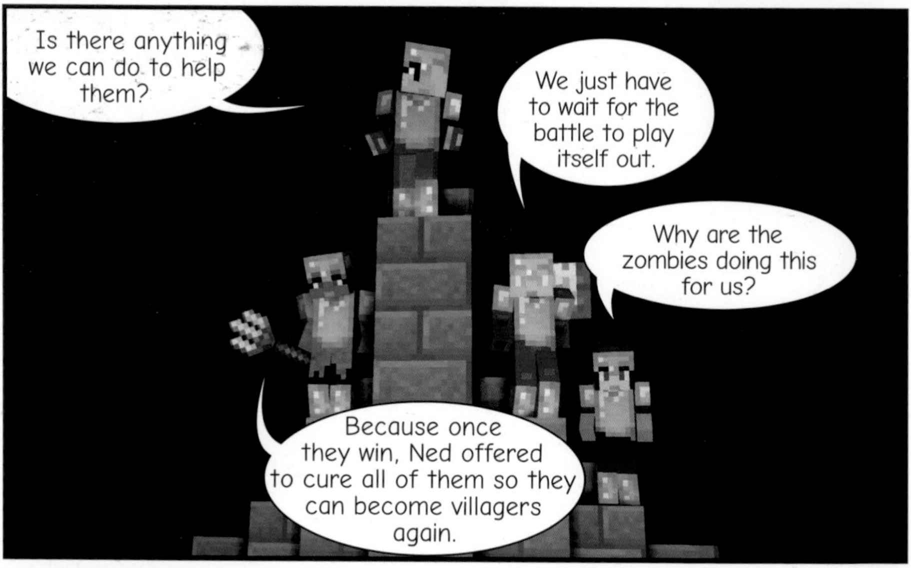
Is there anything we can do to help them?
We just have to wait for the battle to play itself out.
Why are the zombies doing this for us?
Because once they win, Ned offered to cure all of them so they can become villagers again.

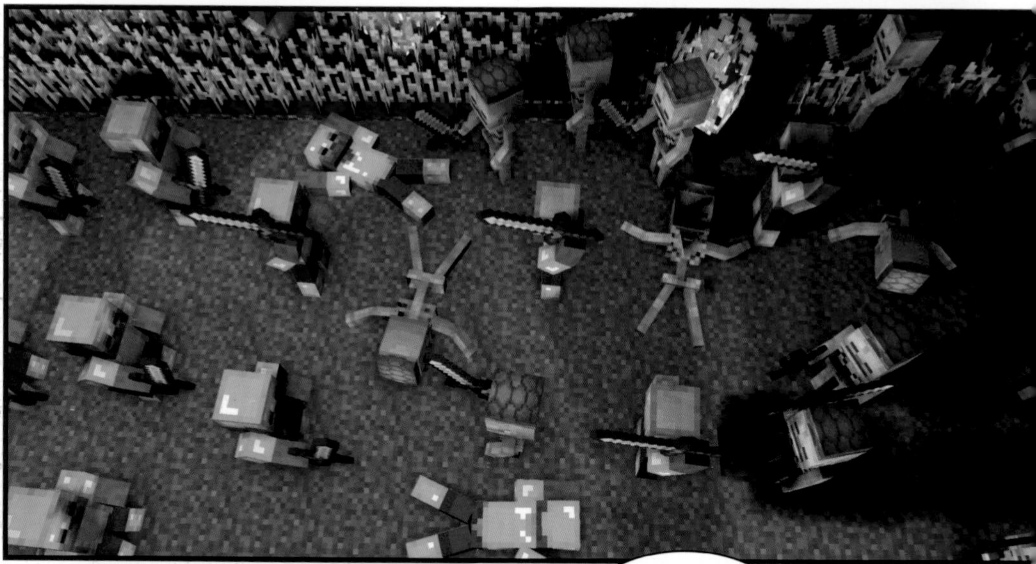

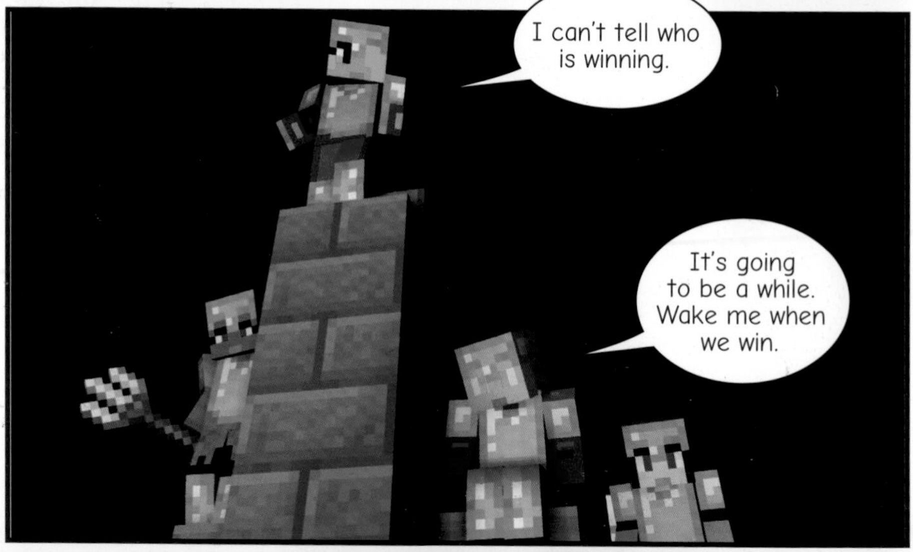
I can't tell who is winning.
It's going to be a while. Wake me when we win.

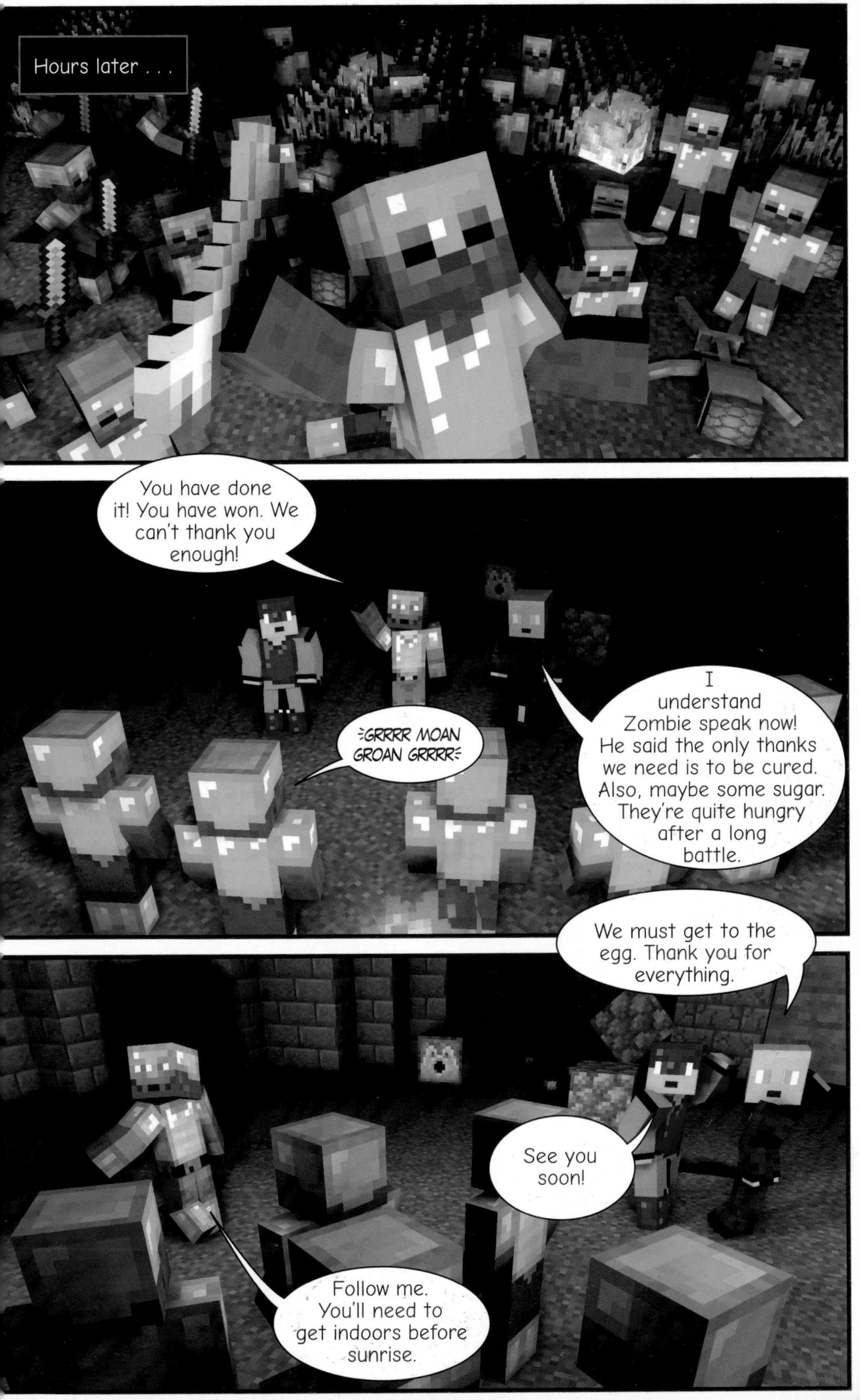
Hours later . . .
You have done it! You have won. We can't thank you enough!
GRRRR MOAN GROAN GRRRR
I understand Zombie speak now! He said the only thanks we need is to be cured. Also, maybe some sugar. They're quite hungry after a long battle.
We must get to the egg. Thank you for everything.
See you soon!
Follow me. You'll need to get indoors before sunrise.

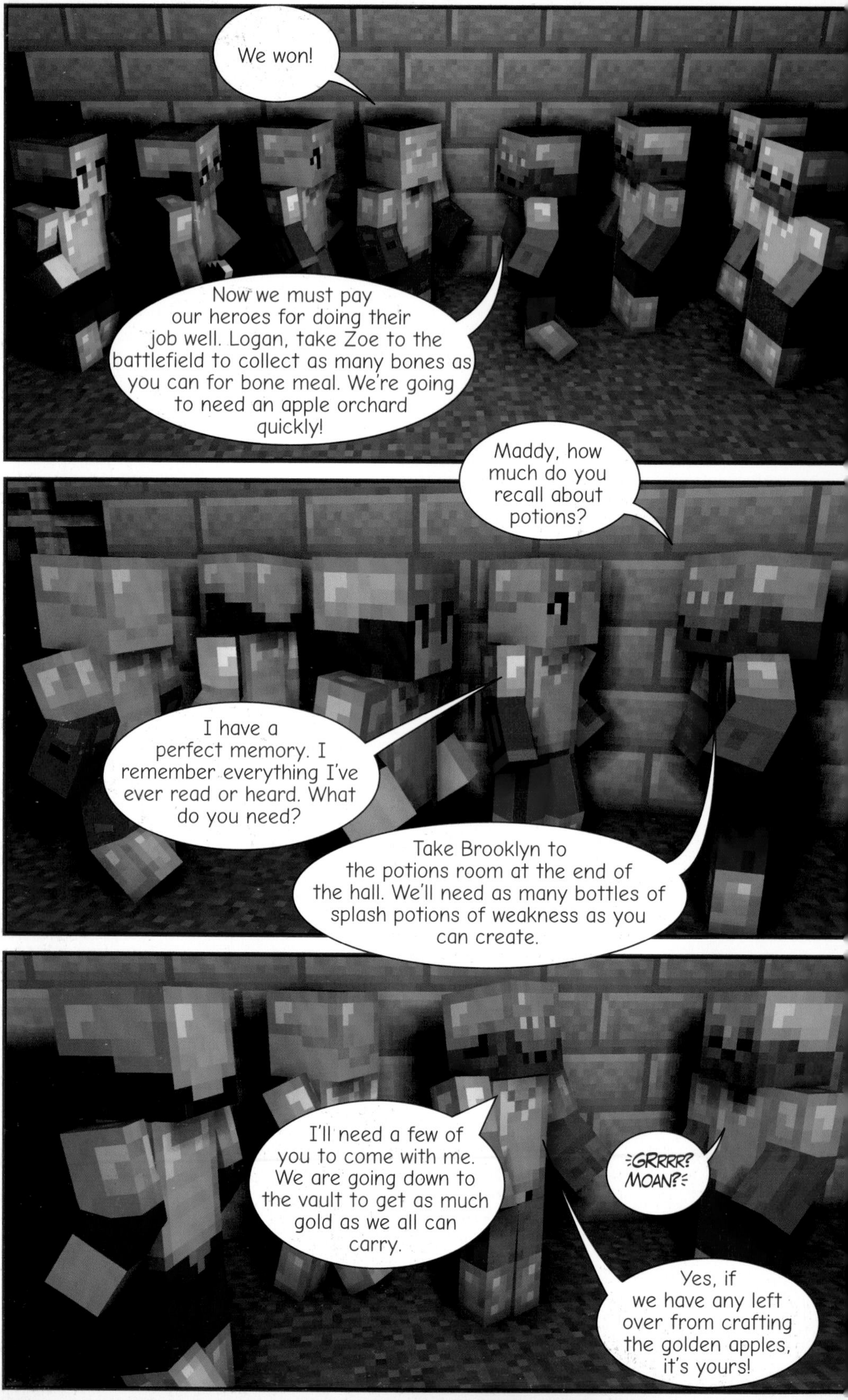
We won!
Now we must pay our heroes for doing their job well. Logan, take Zoe to the battlefield to collect as many bones as you can for bone meal. We're going to need an apple orchard quickly!
Maddy, how much do you recall about potions?
I have a perfect memory. I remember everything I've ever read or heard. What do you need?
Take Brooklyn to the potions room at the end of the hall. We'll need as many bottles of splash potions of weakness as you can create.
I'll need a few of you to come with me. We are going down to the vault to get as much gold as we all can carry.
GRRRR? MOAN?
Yes, if we have any left over from crafting the golden apples, it's yours!

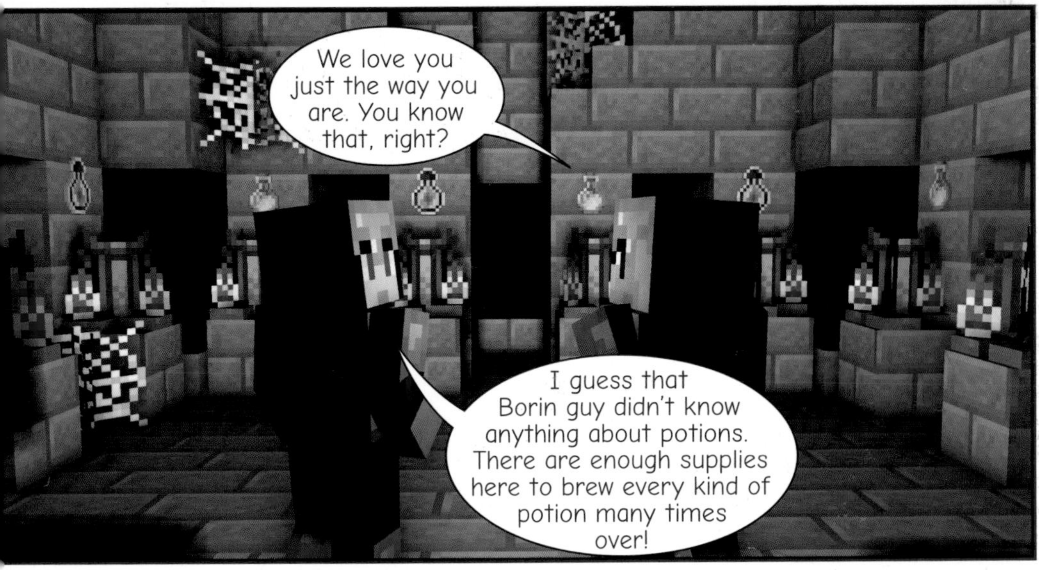
We love you just the way you are. You know that, right?
I guess that Borin guy didn't know anything about potions. There are enough supplies here to brew every kind of potion many times over!

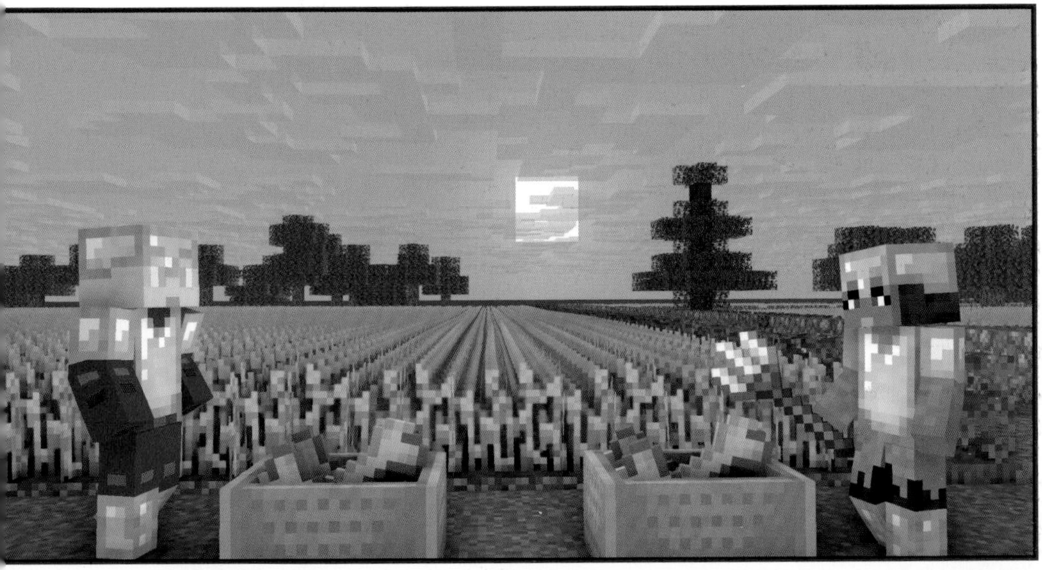

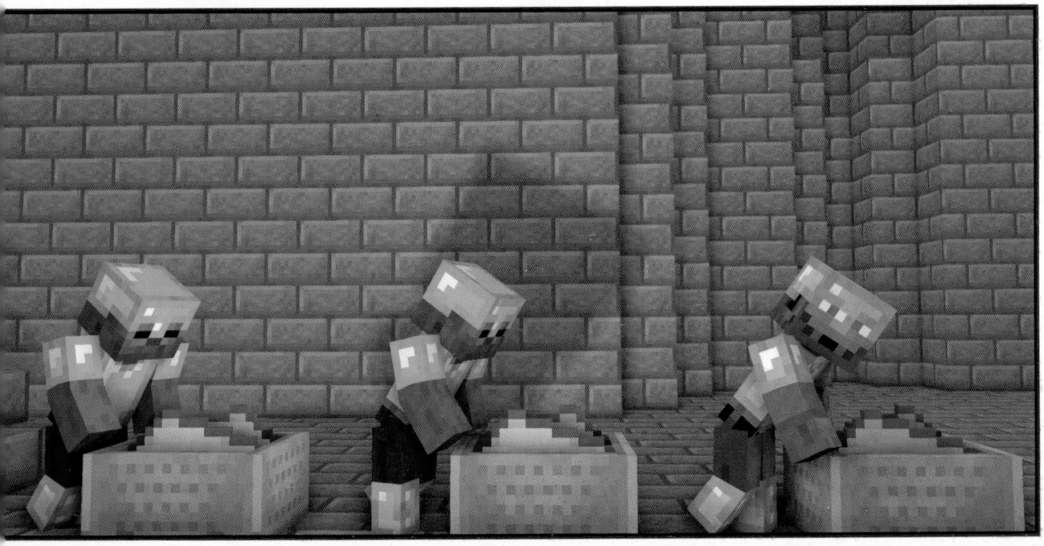

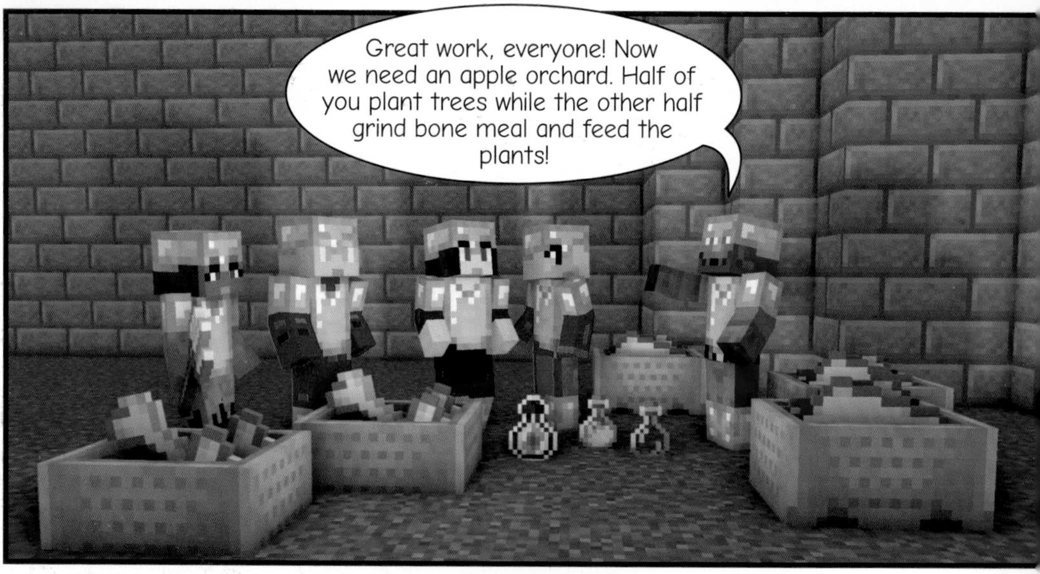
Great work, everyone! Now we need an apple orchard. Half of you plant trees while the other half grind bone meal and feed the plants!

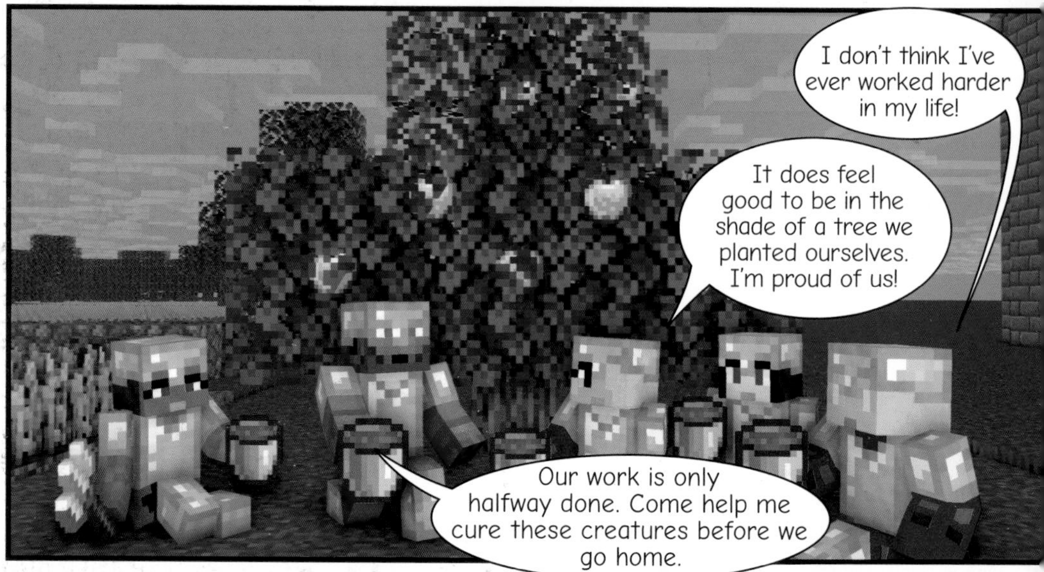
I don't think I've ever worked harder in my life!
It does feel good to be in the shade of a tree we planted ourselves. I'm proud of us!
Our work is only halfway done. Come help me cure these creatures before we go home.

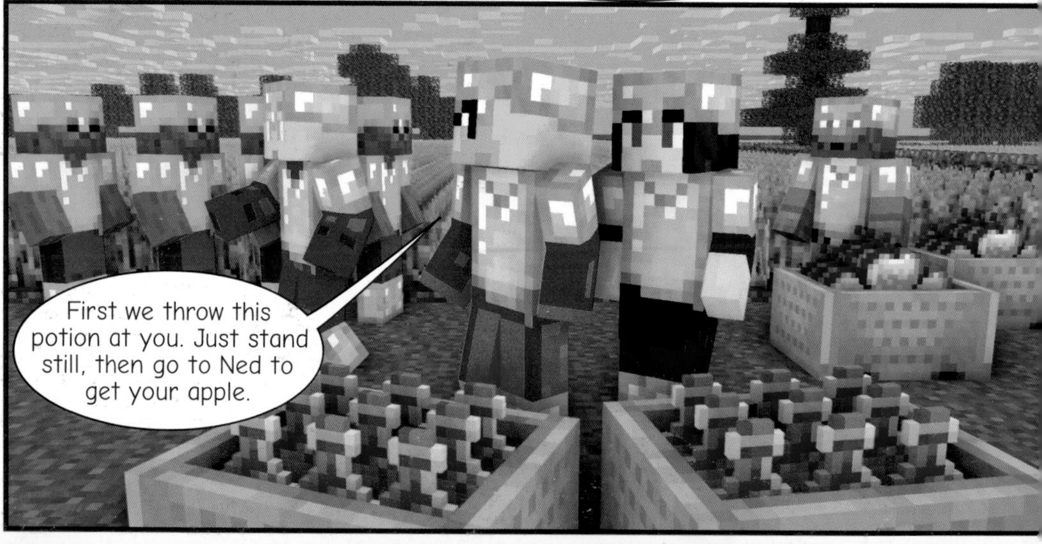
First we throw this potion at you. Just stand still, then go to Ned to get your apple.

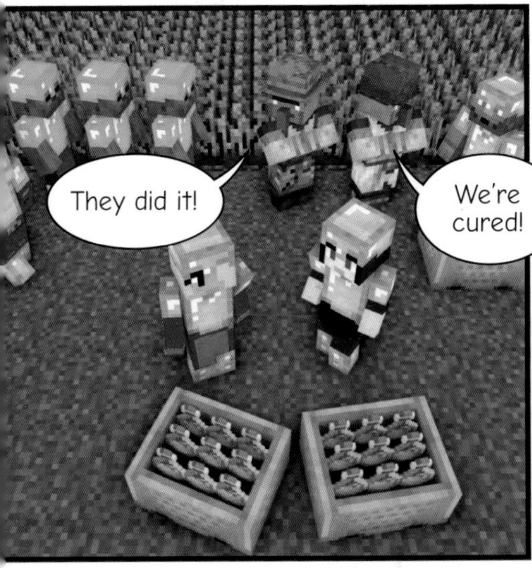
They did it!
We're cured!

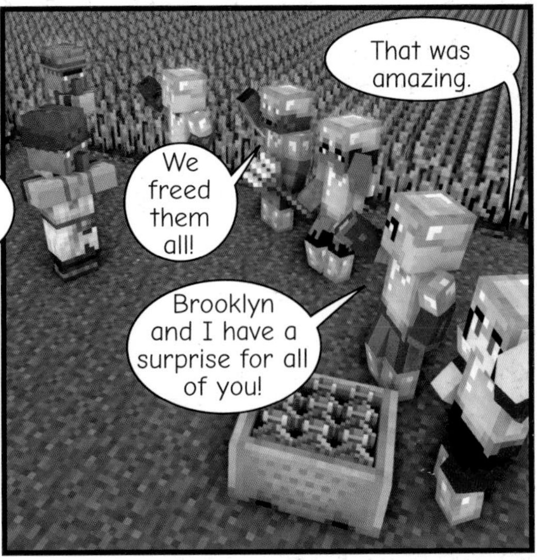
That was amazing.
We freed them all!
Brooklyn and I have a surprise for all of you!

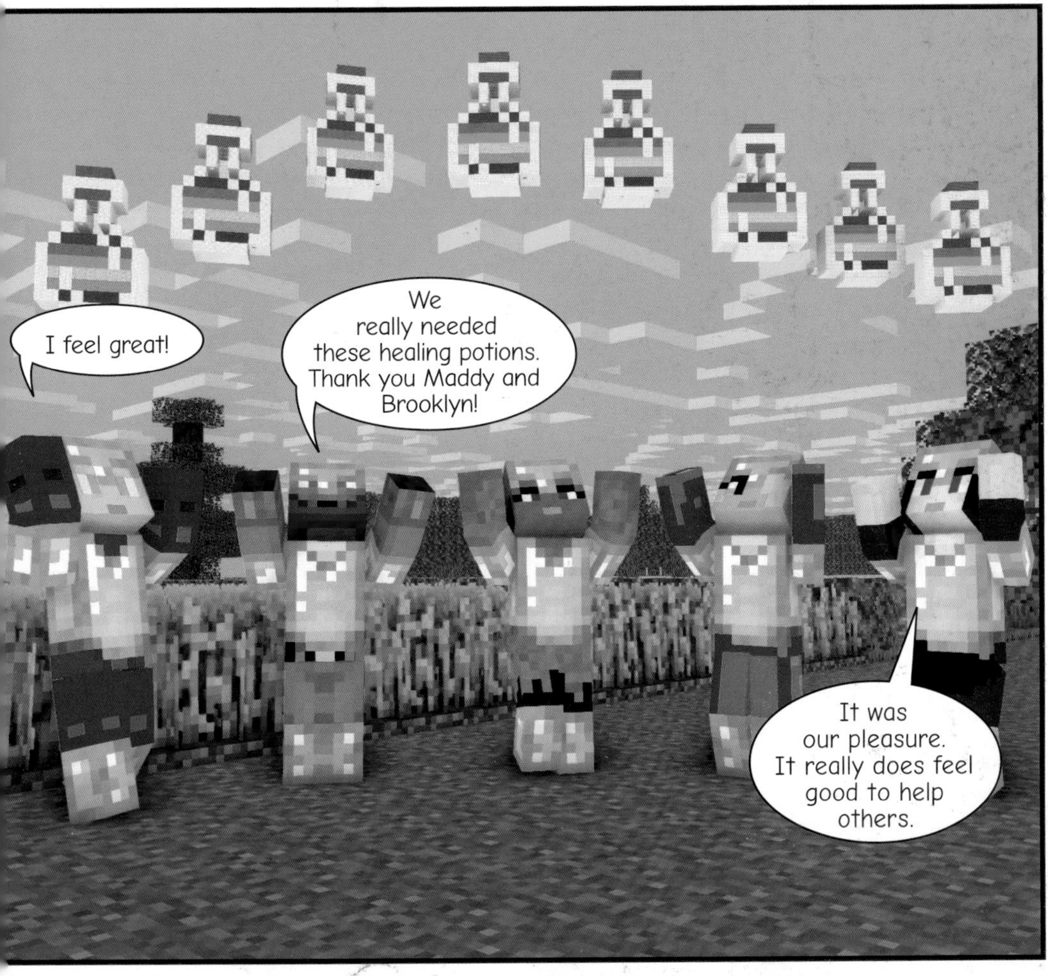
I feel great!
We really needed these healing potions. Thank you Maddy and Brooklyn!
It was our pleasure. It really does feel good to help others.

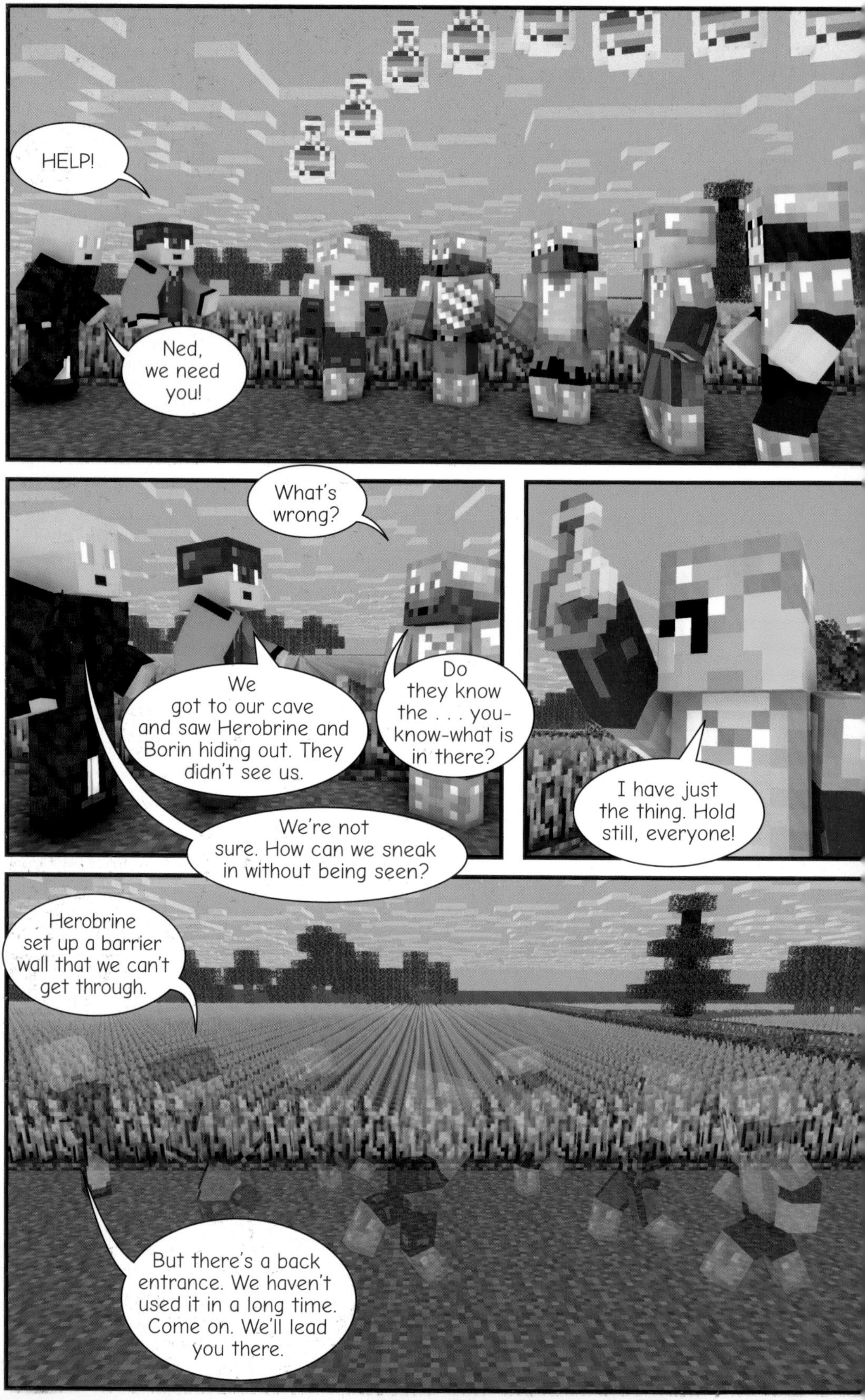

HELP!
Ned, we need you!
What's wrong?
We got to our cave and saw Herobrine and Borin hiding out. They didn't see us.
Do they know the . . . you-know-what is in there?
We're not sure. How can we sneak in without being seen?
I have just the thing. Hold still, everyone!
Herobrine set up a barrier wall that we can't get through.
But there's a back entrance. We haven't used it in a long time. Come on. We'll lead you there.

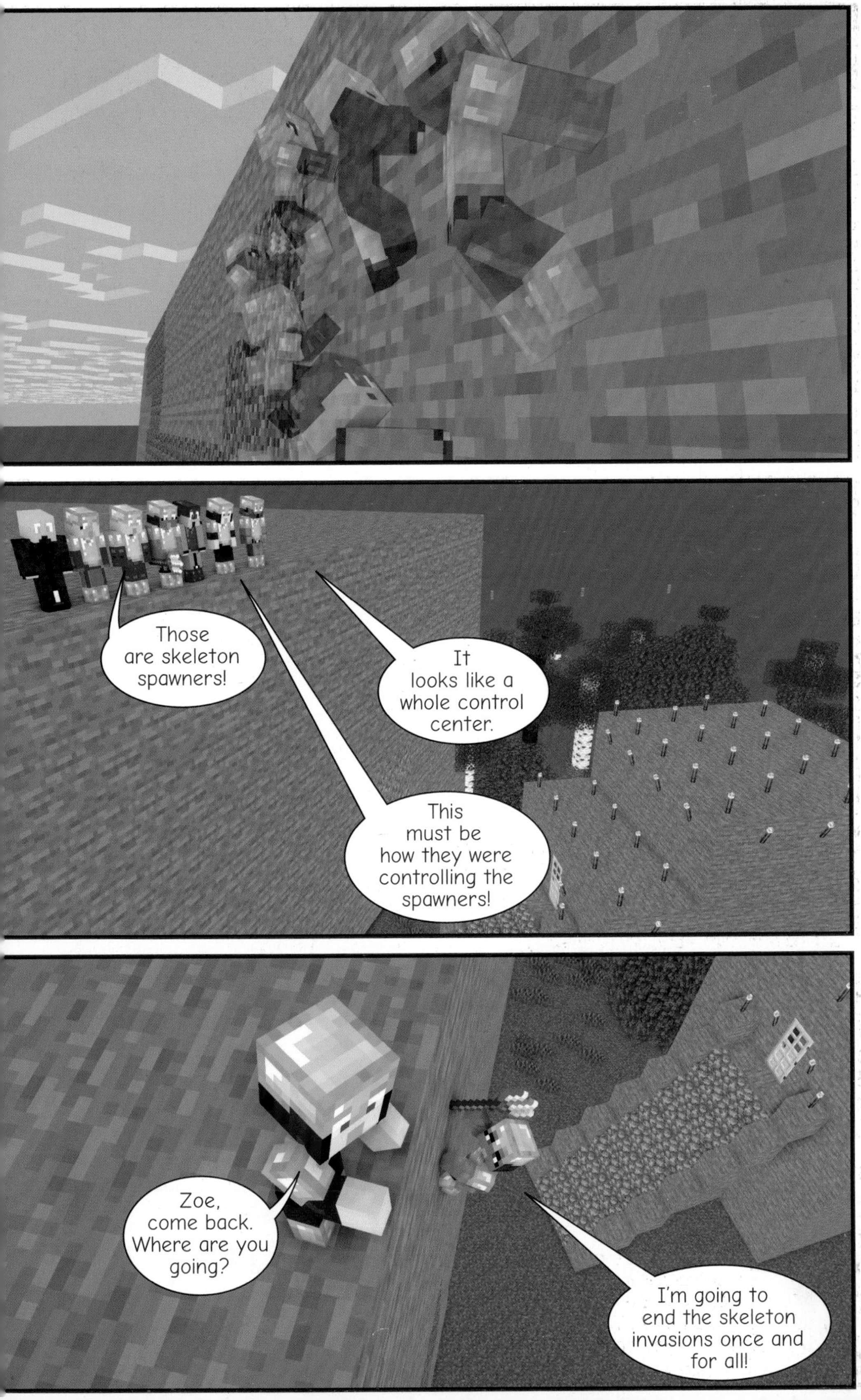
Those are skeleton spawners!
It looks like a whole control center.
This must be how they were controlling the spawners!
Zoe, come back. Where are you going?
I'm going to end the skeleton invasions once and for all!

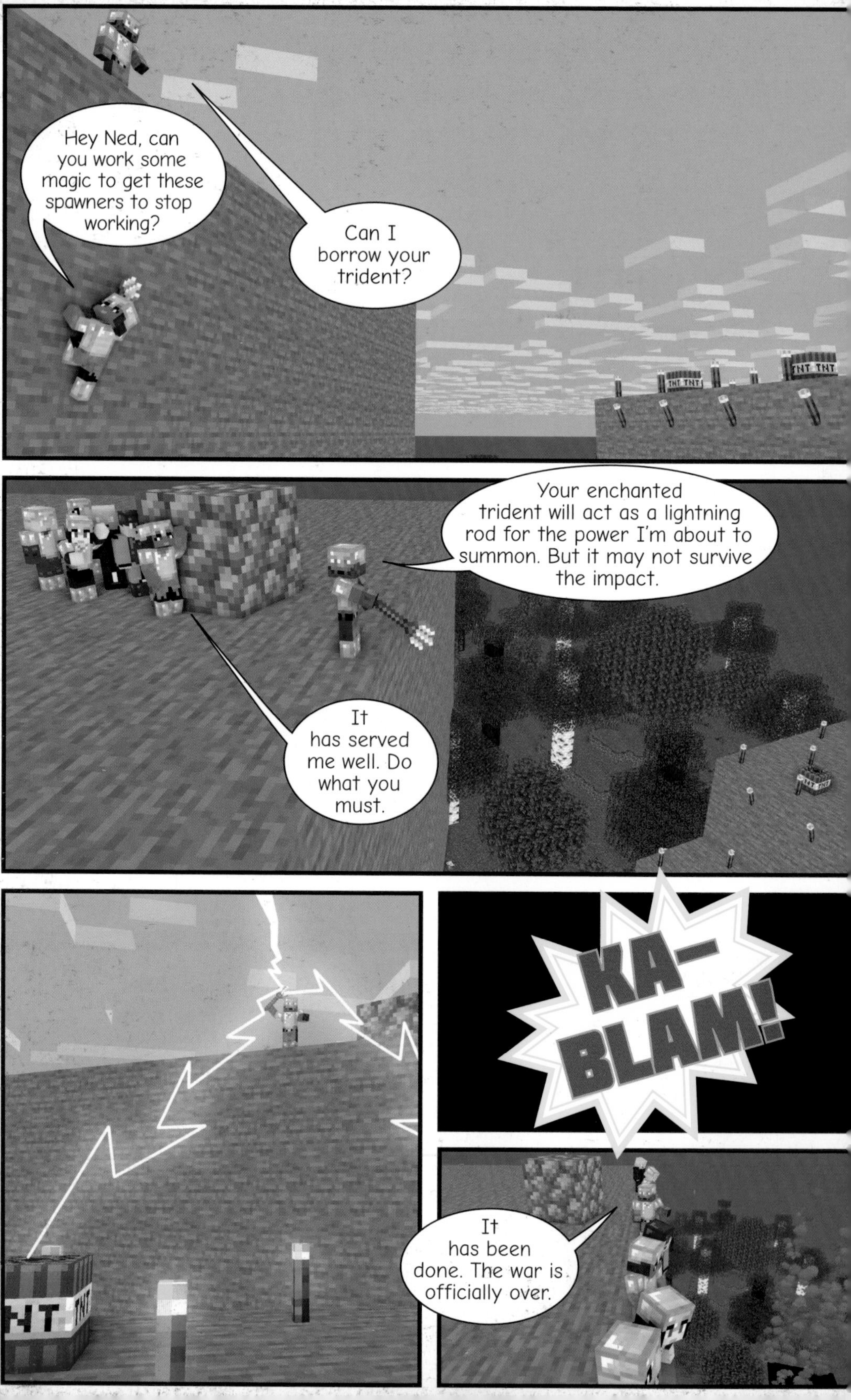
Hey Ned, can you work some magic to get these spawners to stop working?
Can I borrow your trident?
Your enchanted trident will act as a lightning rod for the power I'm about to summon. But it may not survive the impact.
It has served me well. Do what you must.
KA-BLAM!
It has been done. The war is officially over.

CHAPTER 12

A NEW SENSE OF PURPOSE

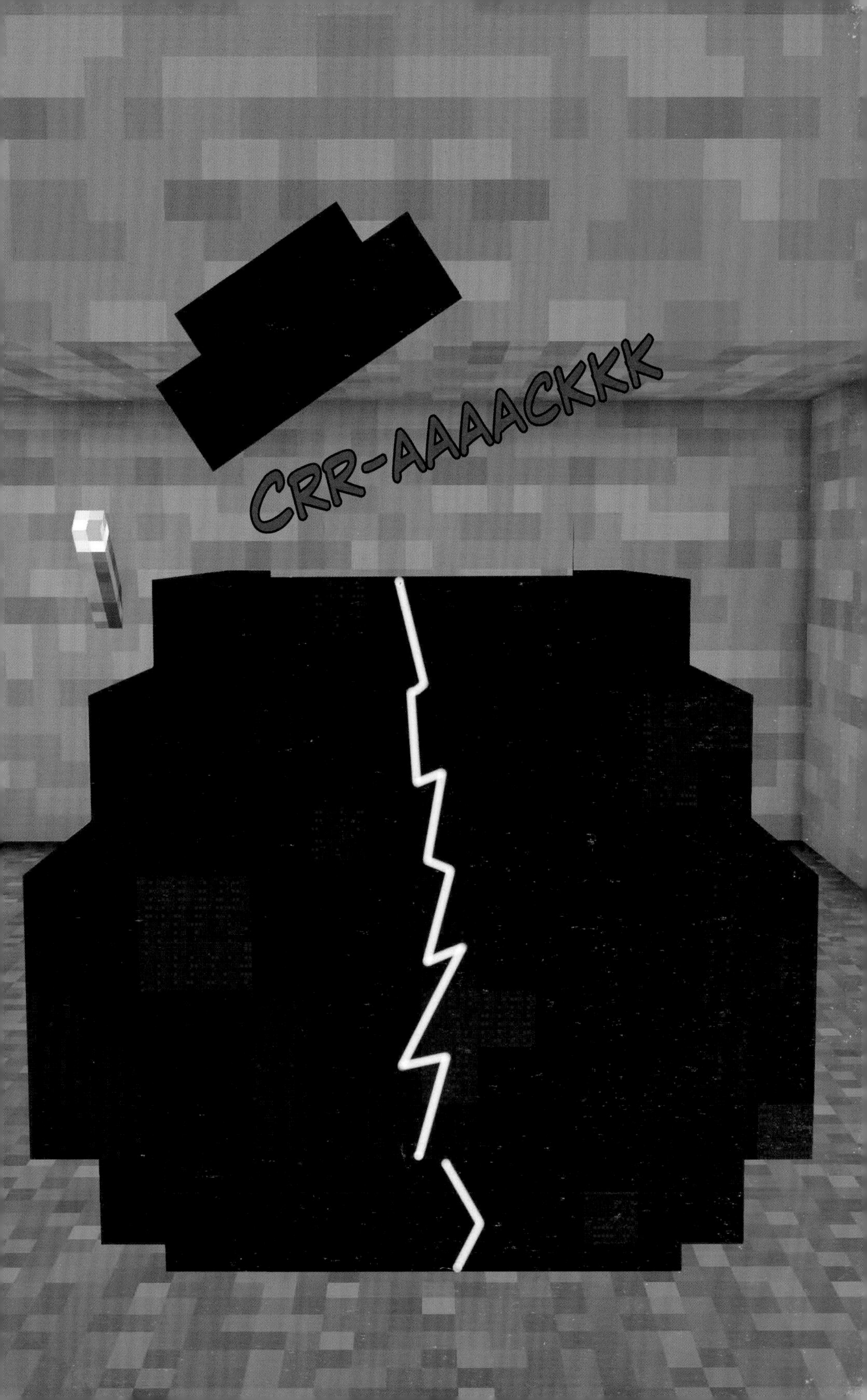
CRR-AAAACKKK

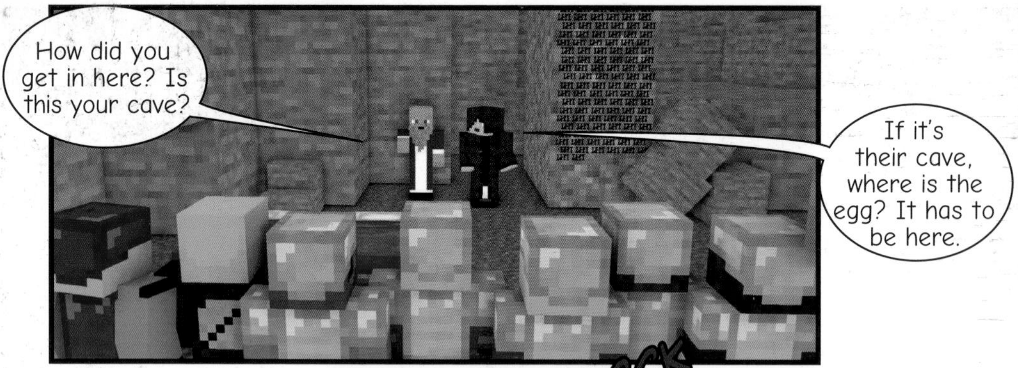
How did you get in here? Is this your cave?
If it's their cave, where is the egg? It has to be here.

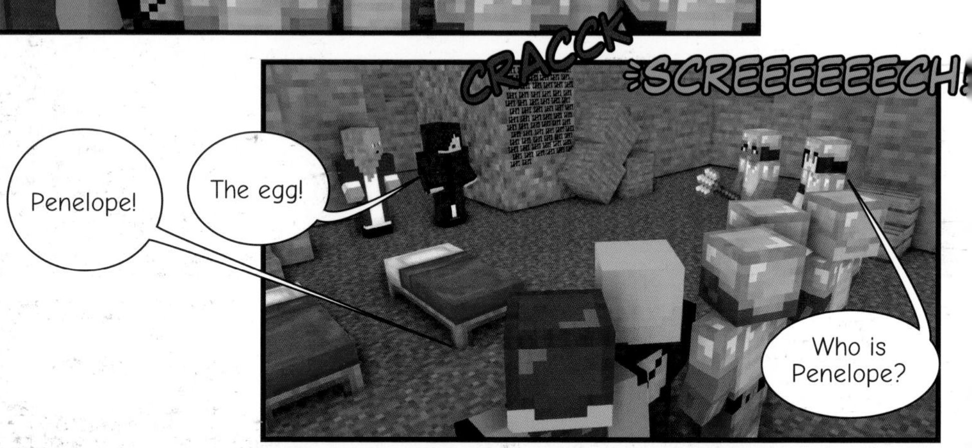
CRACCK!
SCREEEEEEECH!
Penelope!
The egg!
Who is Penelope?

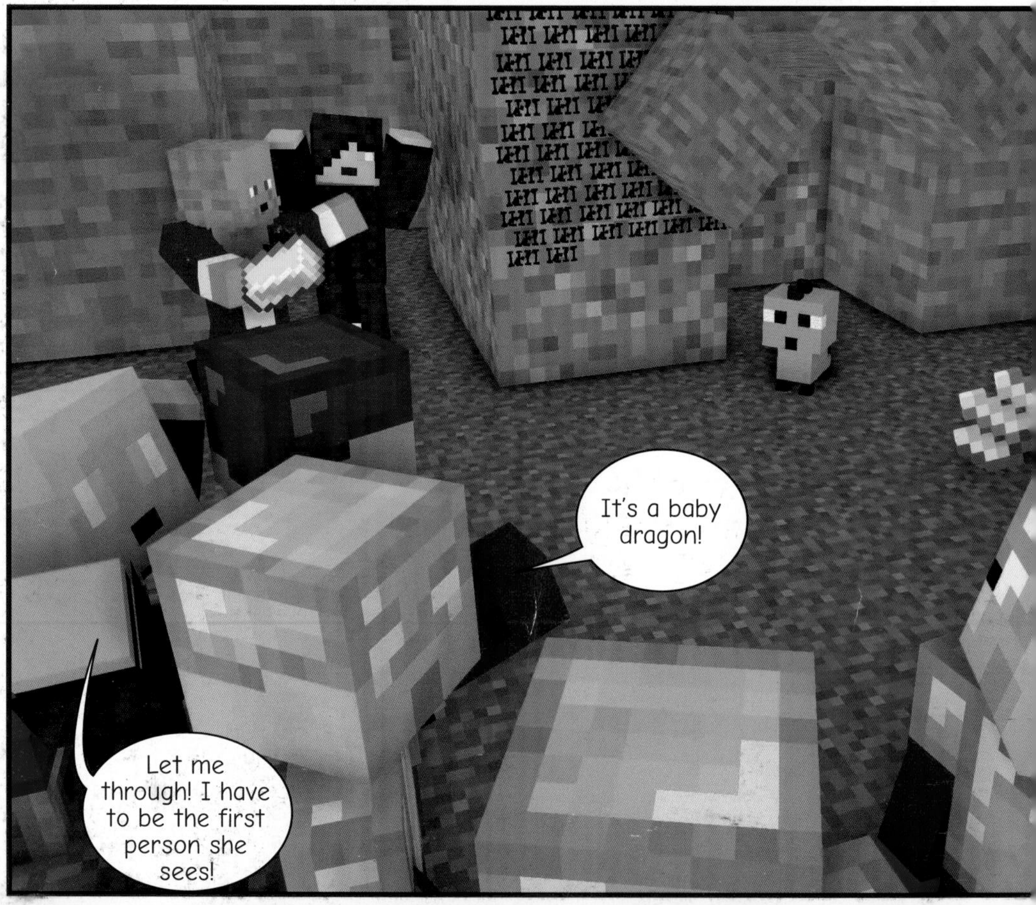
It's a baby dragon!
Let me through! I have to be the first person she sees!

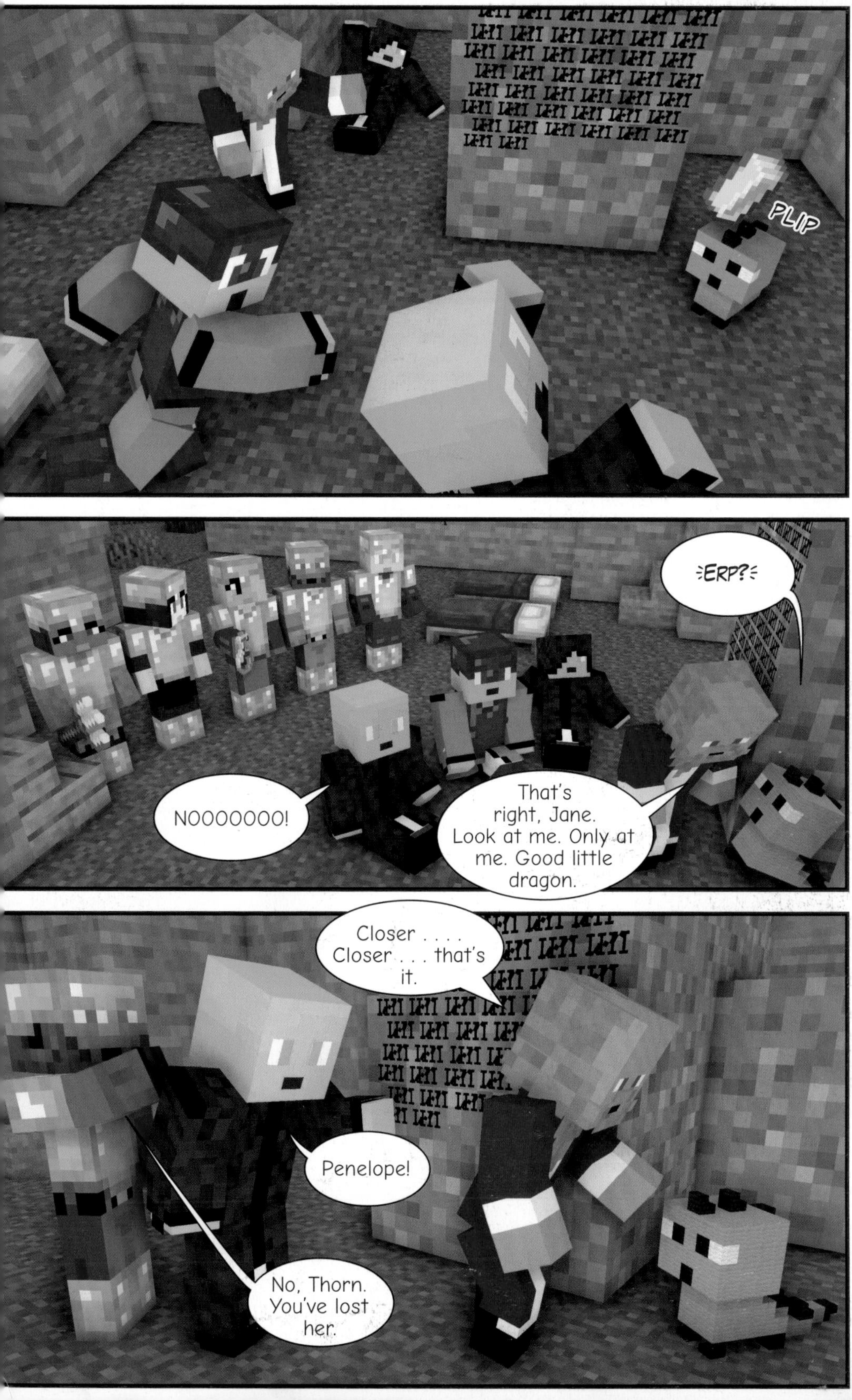
PLIP
ERP?
NOOOOOOO!
That's right, Jane. Look at me. Only at me. Good little dragon.
Closer . . . . Closer . . . that's it.
Penelope!
No, Thorn. You've lost her.

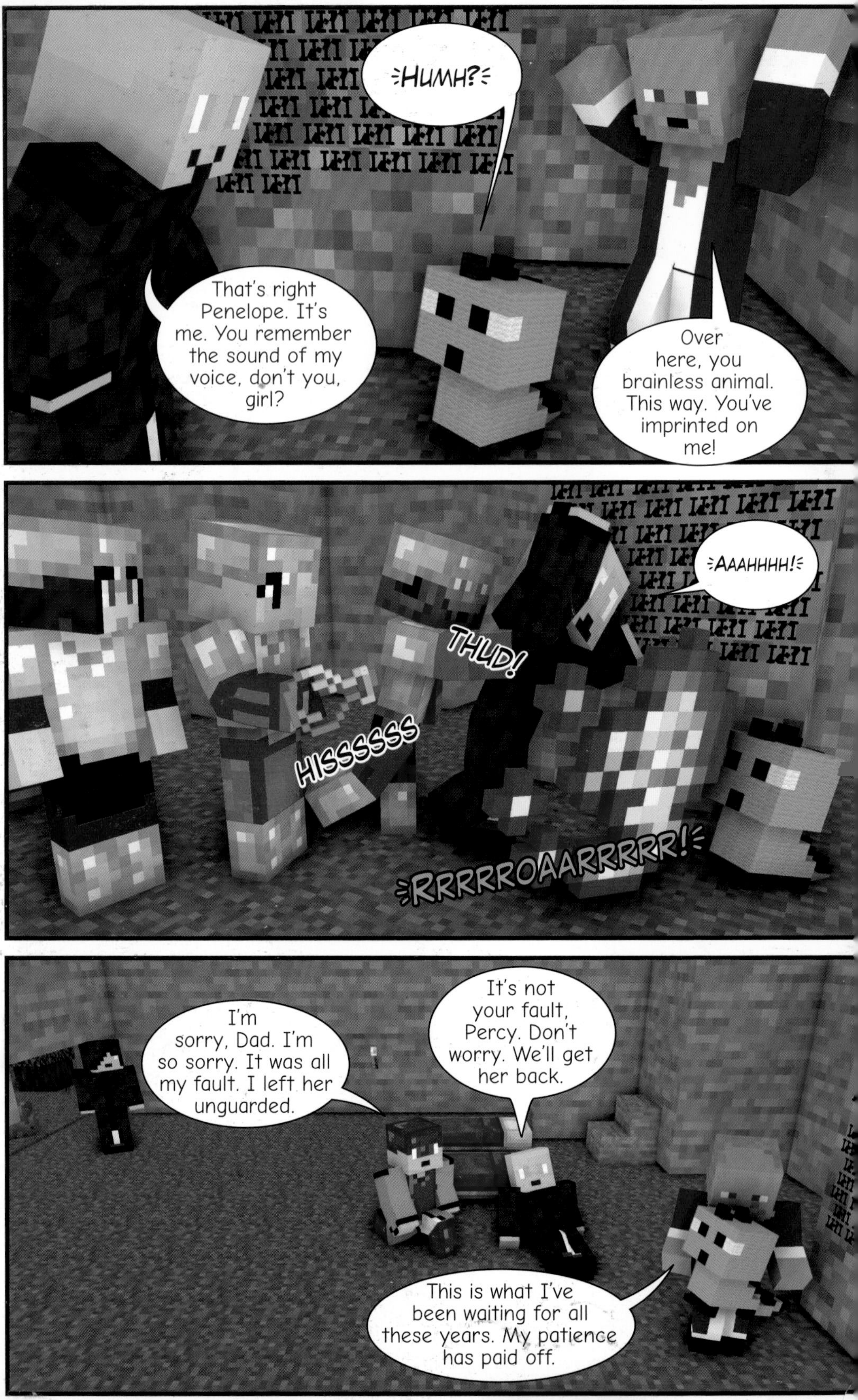
HUMH?
That's right Penelope. It's me. You remember the sound of my voice, don't you, girl?
Over here, you brainless animal. This way. You've imprinted on me!
AAAHHHH!
THUD!
HISSSSSS
RRRRROAARRRRR!
I'm sorry, Dad. I'm so sorry. It was all my fault. I left her unguarded.
It's not your fault, Percy. Don't worry. We'll get her back.
This is what I've been waiting for all these years. My patience has paid off.

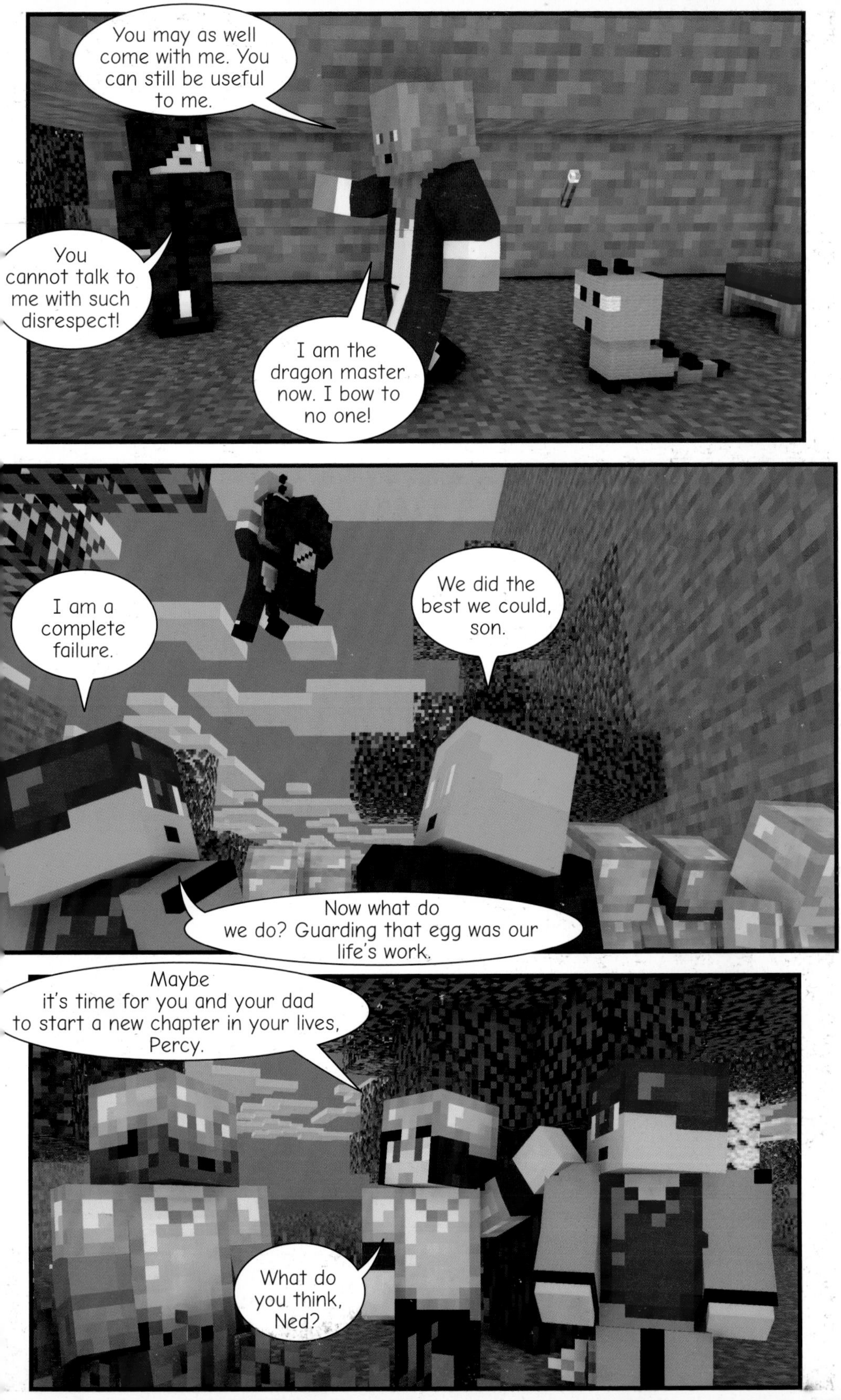
You may as well come with me. You can still be useful to me.
You cannot talk to me with such disrespect!
I am the dragon master now. I bow to no one!
I am a complete failure.
We did the best we could, son.
Now what do we do? Guarding that egg was our life's work.
Maybe it's time for you and your dad to start a new chapter in your lives, Percy.
What do you think, Ned?

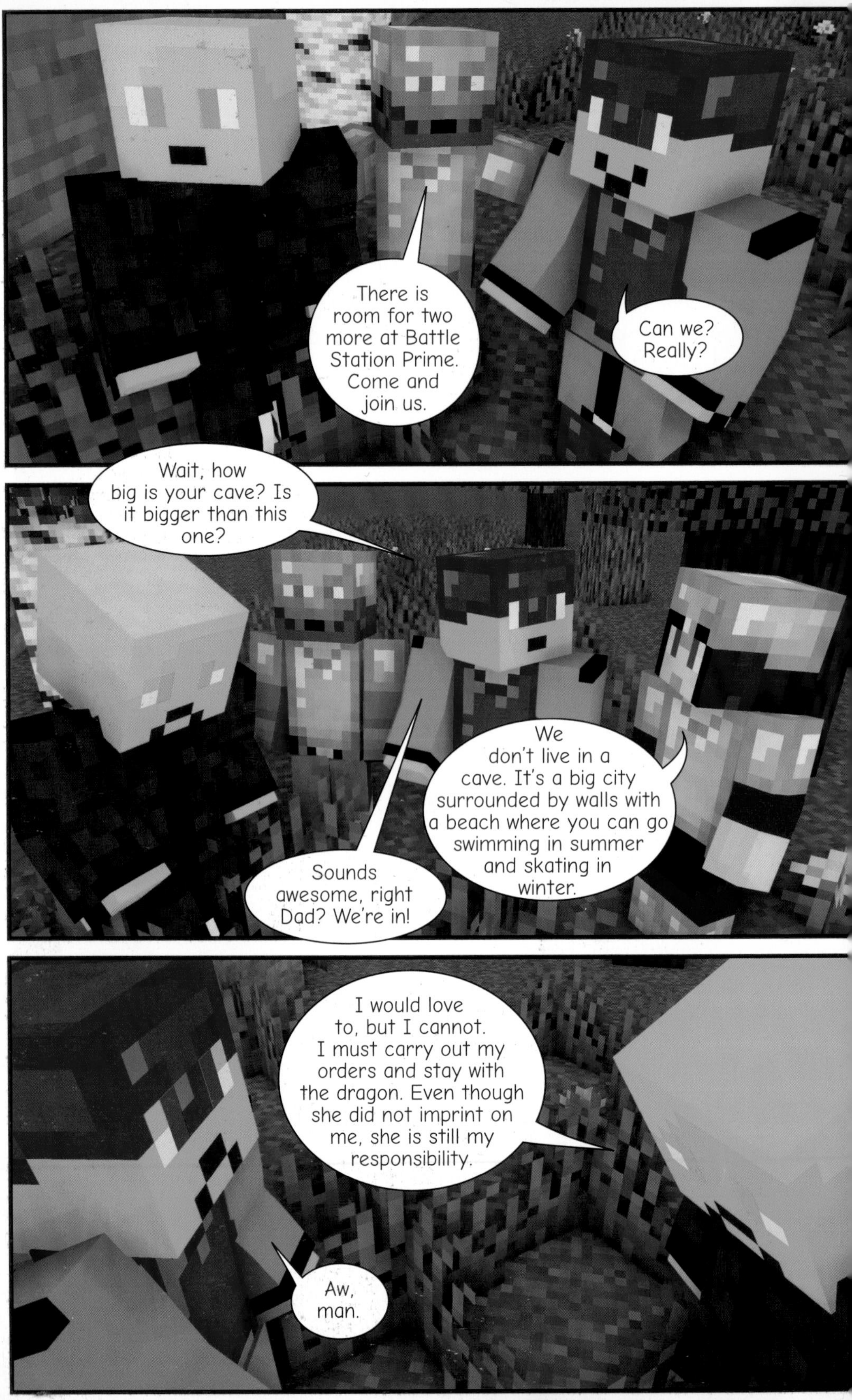
There is room for two more at Battle Station Prime. Come and join us.
Can we? Really?
Wait, how big is your cave? Is it bigger than this one?
We don't live in a cave. It's a big city surrounded by walls with a beach where you can go swimming in summer and skating in winter.
Sounds awesome, right Dad? We're in!
I would love to, but I cannot. I must carry out my orders and stay with the dragon. Even though she did not imprint on me, she is still my responsibility.
Aw, man.

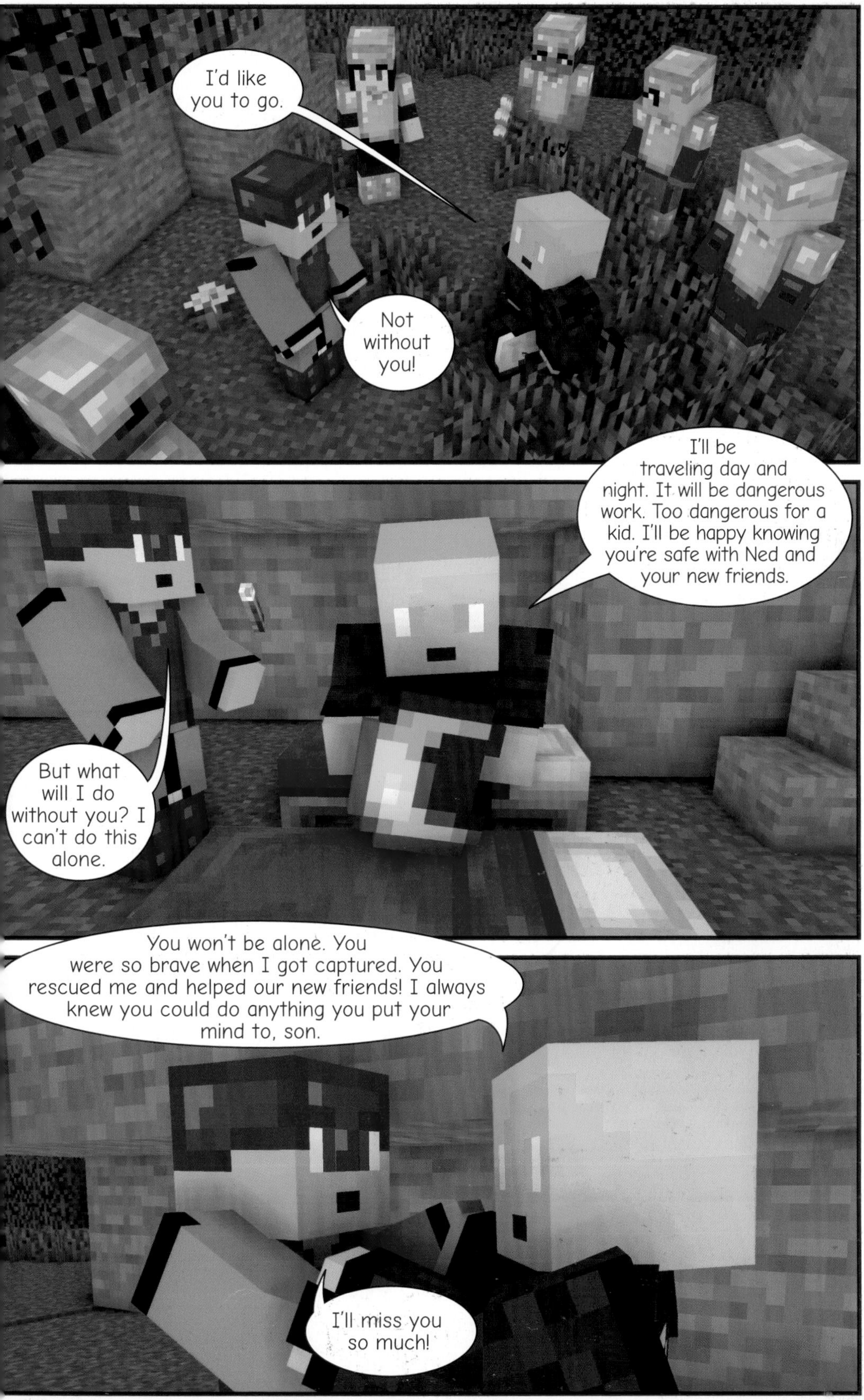
I'd like you to go.
Not without you!
I'll be traveling day and night. It will be dangerous work. Too dangerous for a kid. I'll be happy knowing you're safe with Ned and your new friends.
But what will I do without you? I can't do this alone.
You won't be alone. You were so brave when I got captured. You rescued me and helped our new friends! I always knew you could do anything you put your mind to, son.
I'll miss you so much!

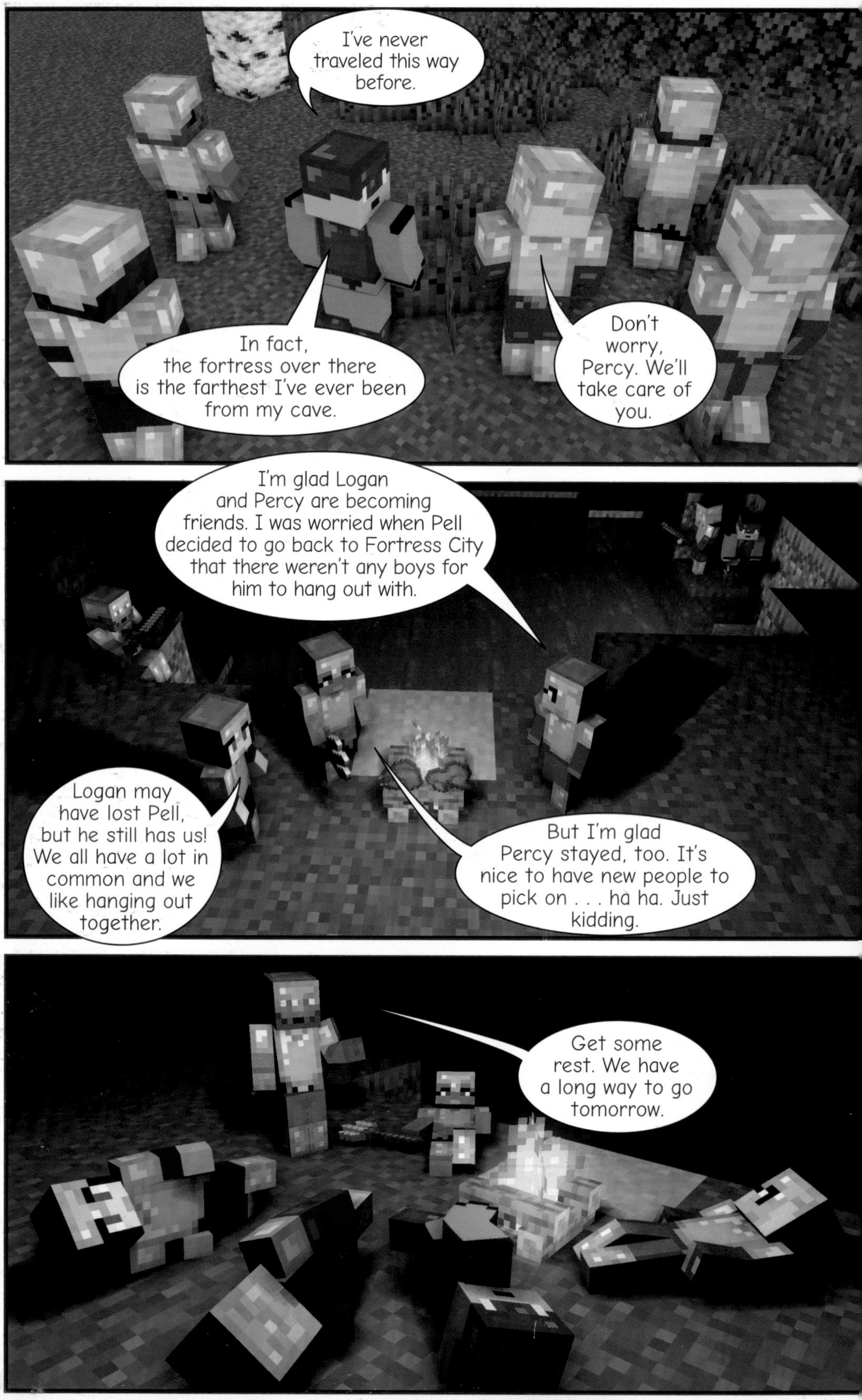
I've never traveled this way before.
In fact, the fortress over there is the farthest I've ever been from my cave.
Don't worry, Percy. We'll take care of you.
I'm glad Logan and Percy are becoming friends. I was worried when Pell decided to go back to Fortress City that there weren't any boys for him to hang out with.
Logan may have lost Pell, but he still has us! We all have a lot in common and we like hanging out together.
But I'm glad Percy stayed, too. It's nice to have new people to pick on . . . ha ha. Just kidding.
Get some rest. We have a long way to go tomorrow.

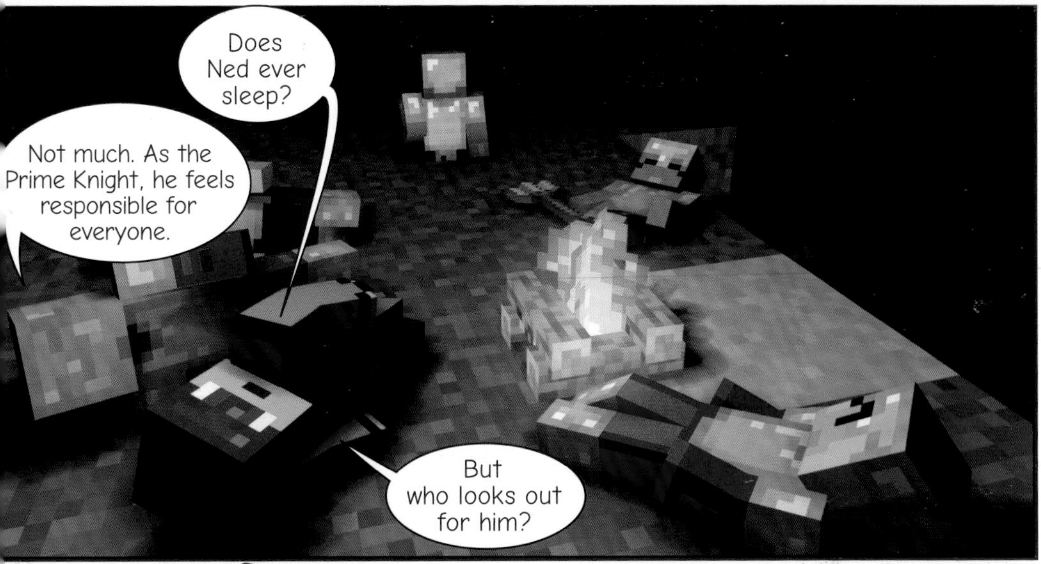
Does Ned ever sleep?
Not much. As the Prime Knight, he feels responsible for everyone.
But who looks out for him?

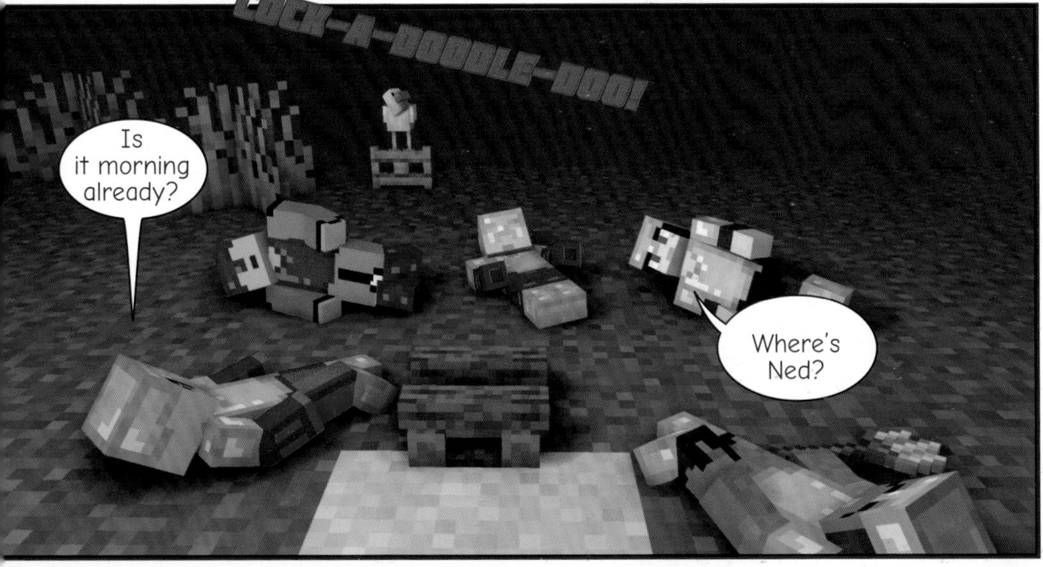
COCK-A-DOODLE-DOO!
Is it morning already?
Where's Ned?

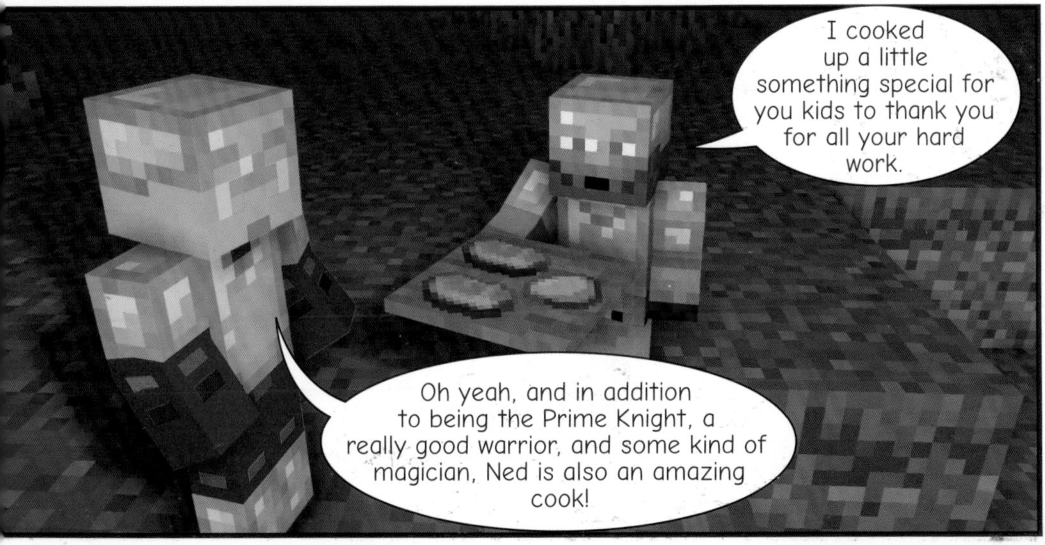
I cooked up a little something special for you kids to thank you for all your hard work.
Oh yeah, and in addition to being the Prime Knight, a really good warrior, and some kind of magician, Ned is also an amazing cook!

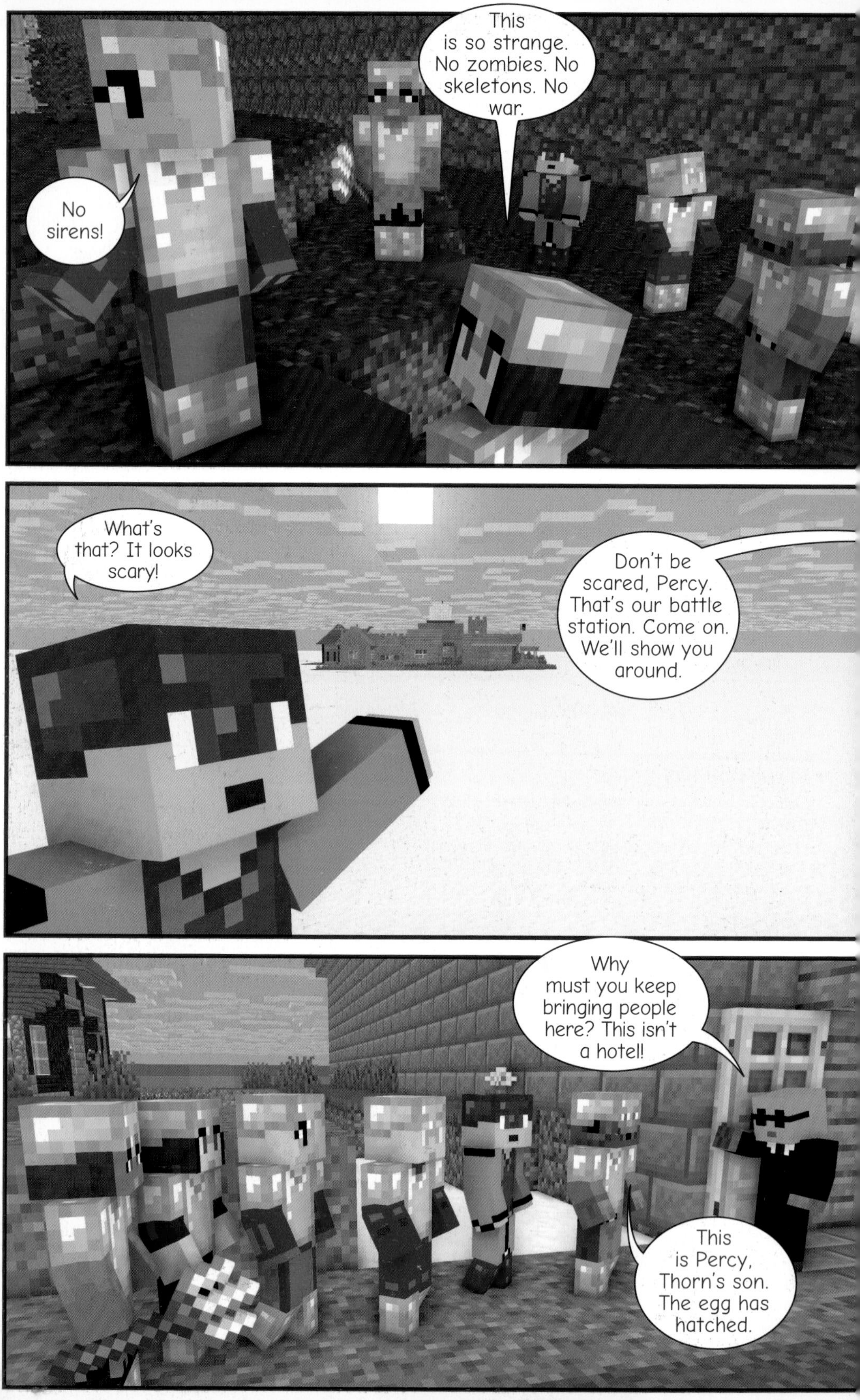
No sirens!
This is so strange. No zombies. No skeletons. No war.
What's that? It looks scary!
Don't be scared, Percy. That's our battle station. Come on. We'll show you around.
Why must you keep bringing people here? This isn't a hotel!
This is Percy, Thorn's son. The egg has hatched.

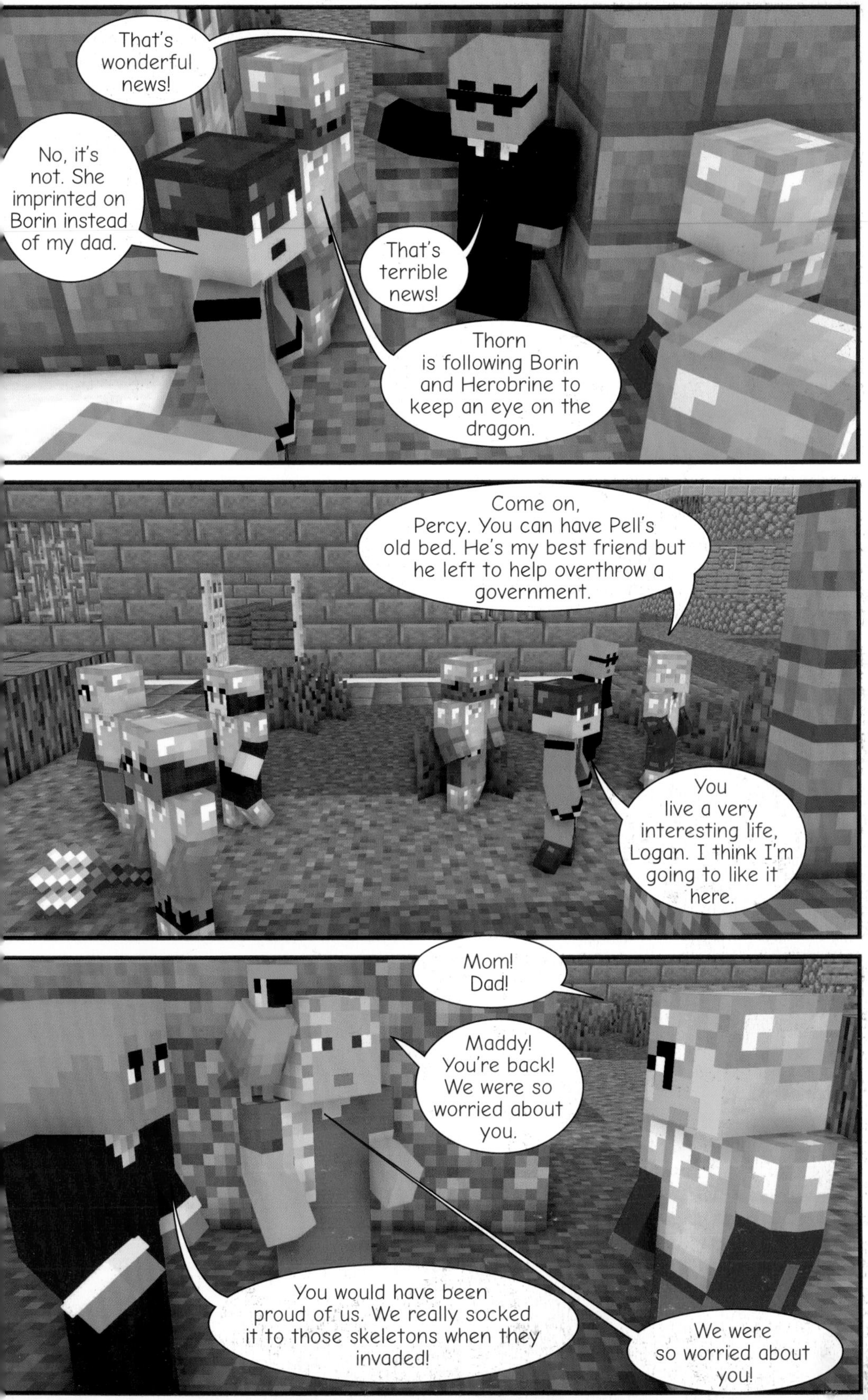
That's wonderful news!
No, it's not. She imprinted on Borin instead of my dad.
That's terrible news!
Thorn is following Borin and Herobrine to keep an eye on the dragon.
Come on, Percy. You can have Pell's old bed. He's my best friend but he left to help overthrow a government.
You live a very interesting life, Logan. I think I'm going to like it here.
Mom! Dad!
Maddy! You're back! We were so worried about you.
You would have been proud of us. We really socked it to those skeletons when they invaded!
We were so worried about you!

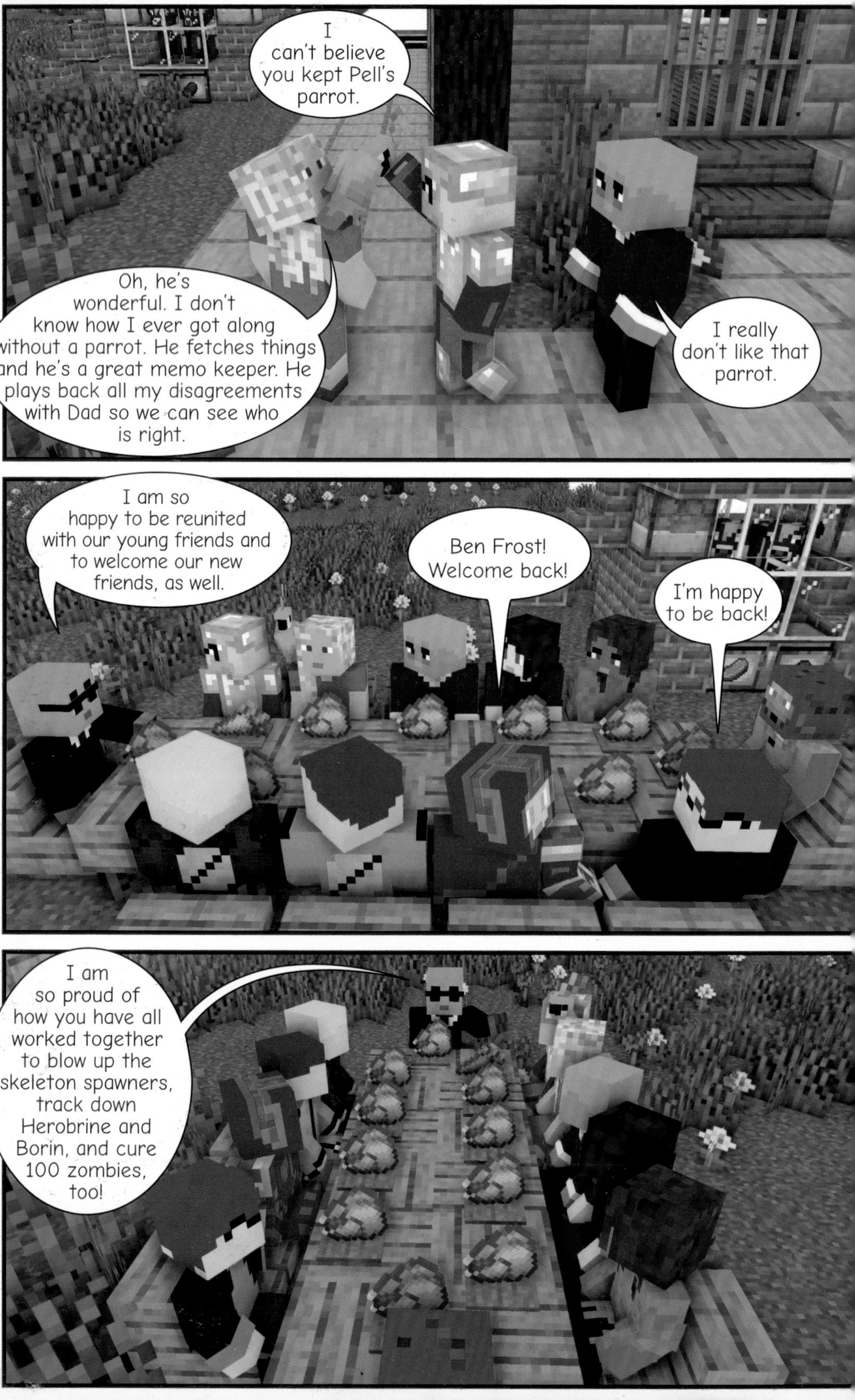
I can't believe you kept Pell's parrot.
Oh, he's wonderful. I don't know how I ever got along without a parrot. He fetches things and he's a great memo keeper. He plays back all my disagreements with Dad so we can see who is right.
I really don't like that parrot.
I am so happy to be reunited with our young friends and to welcome our new friends, as well.
Ben Frost! Welcome back!
I'm happy to be back!
I am so proud of how you have all worked together to blow up the skeleton spawners, track down Herobrine and Borin, and cure 100 zombies, too!

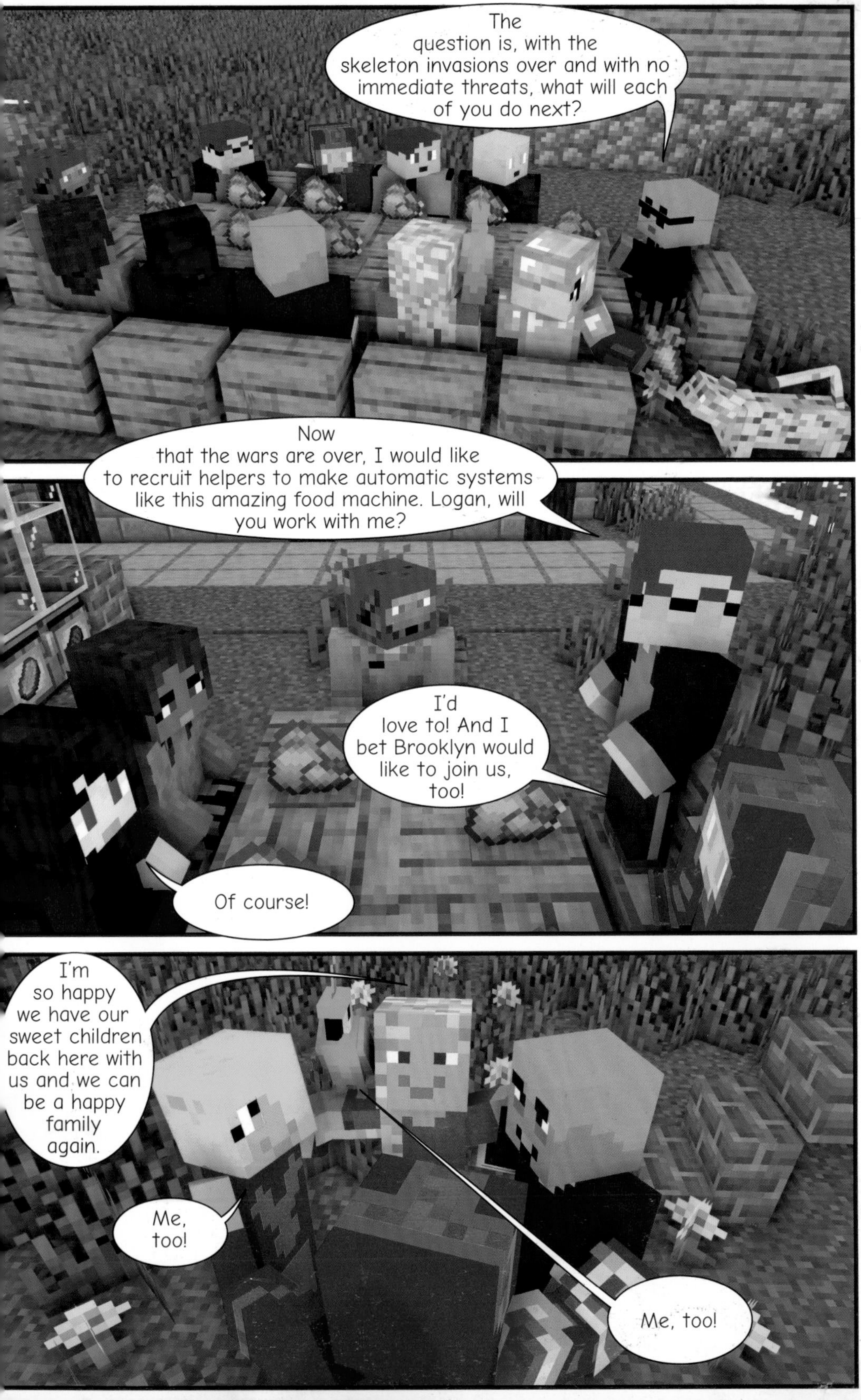
The question is, with the skeleton invasions over and with no immediate threats, what will each of you do next?
Now that the wars are over, I would like to recruit helpers to make automatic systems like this amazing food machine. Logan, will you work with me?
I'd love to! And I bet Brooklyn would like to join us, too!
Of course!
I'm so happy we have our sweet children back here with us and we can be a happy family again.
Me, too!
Me, too!

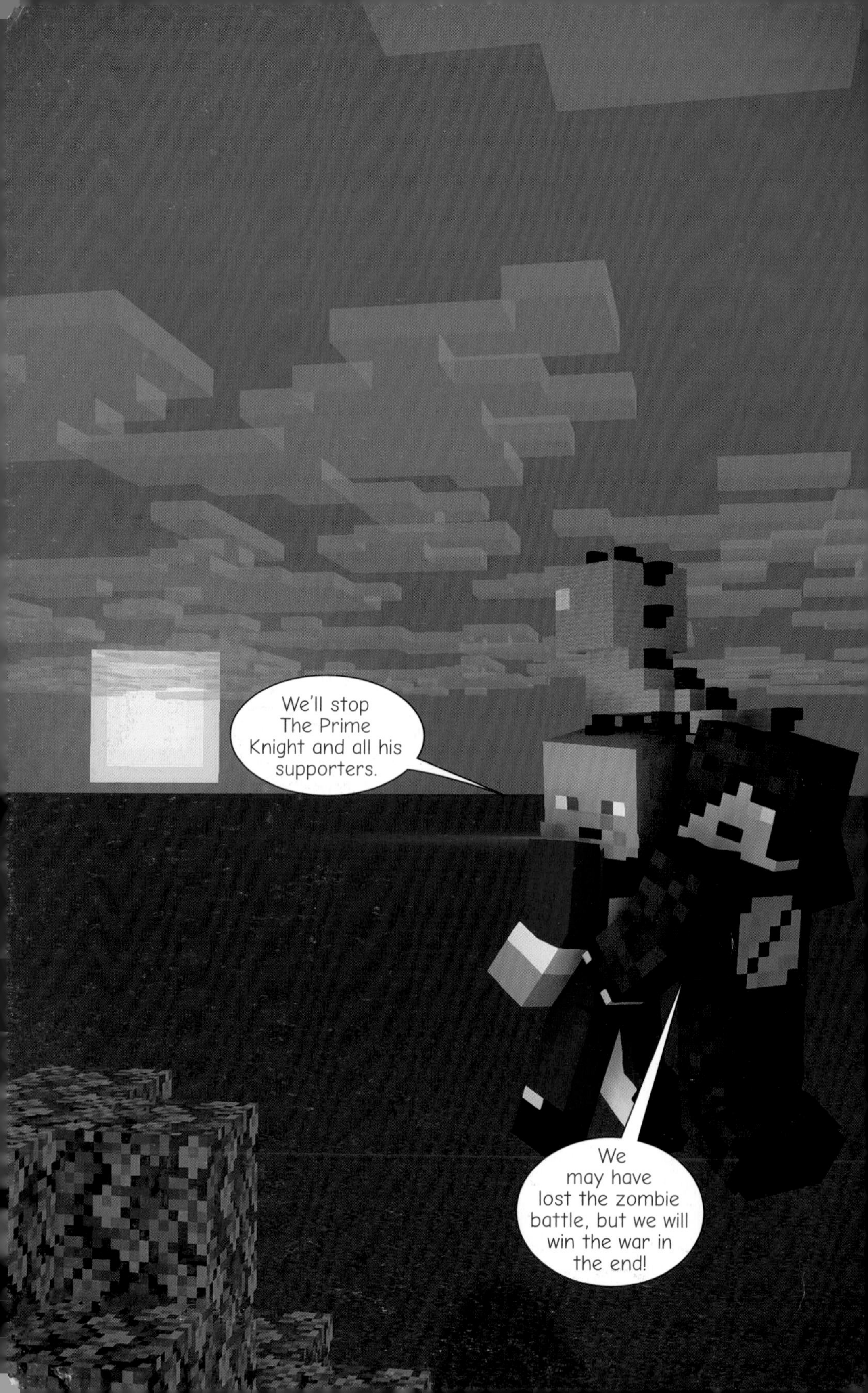
We'll stop The Prime Knight and all his supporters.
We may have lost the zombie battle, but we will win the war in the end!

ALSO AVAILABLE FROM THE BATTLE STATION PRIME SERIES!

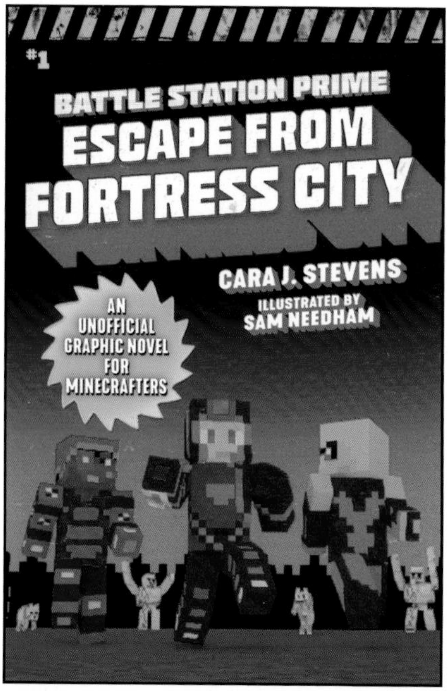
#1
BATTLE STATION PRIME
ESCAPE FROM FORTRESS CITY
CARA J. STEVENS
ILLUSTRATED BY SAM NEEDHAM
AN UNOFFICIAL GRAPHIC NOVEL FOR MINECRAFTERS

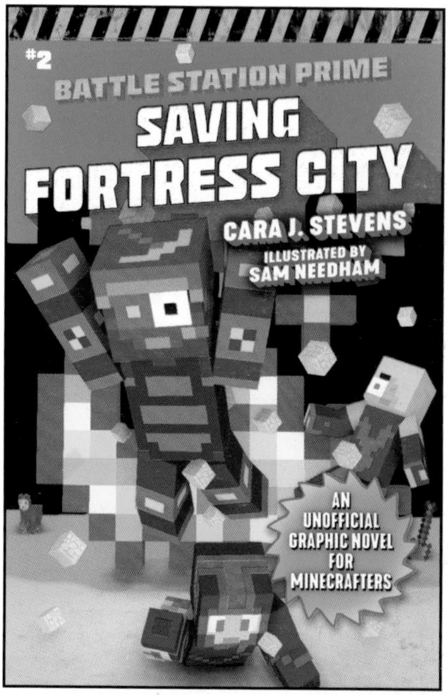
#2
BATTLE STATION PRIME
SAVING FORTRESS CITY
CARA J. STEVENS
ILLUSTRATED BY SAM NEEDHAM
AN UNOFFICIAL GRAPHIC NOVEL FOR MINECRAFTERS

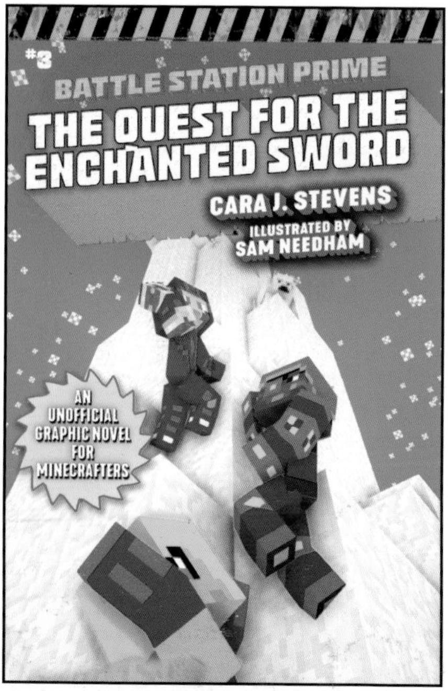
#3
BATTLE STATION PRIME
THE QUEST FOR THE ENCHANTED SWORD
CARA J. STEVENS
ILLUSTRATED BY SAM NEEDHAM
AN UNOFFICIAL GRAPHIC NOVEL FOR MINECRAFTERS

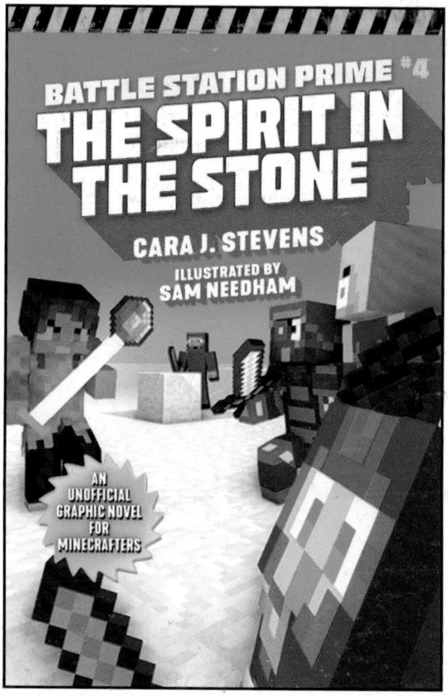
BATTLE STATION PRIME #4
THE SPIRIT IN THE STONE
CARA J. STEVENS
ILLUSTRATED BY SAM NEEDHAM
AN UNOFFICIAL GRAPHIC NOVEL FOR MINECRAFTERS

COMING SOON FROM THE BATTLE STATION PRIME SERIES!

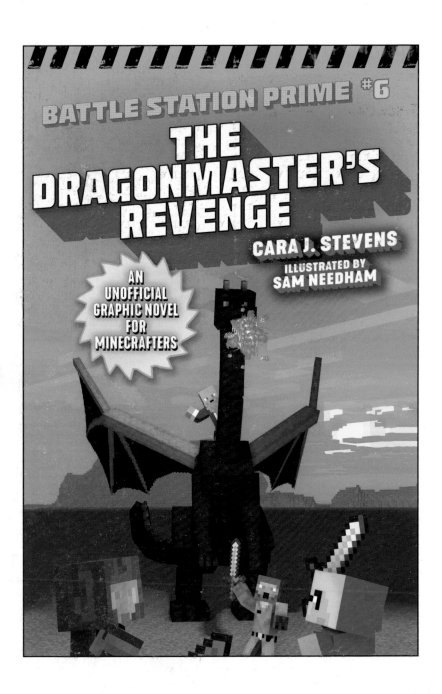

BATTLE STATION PRIME #6

THE DRAGONMASTER'S REVENGE

CARA J. STEVENS

ILLUSTRATED BY SAM NEEDHAM

AN UNOFFICIAL GRAPHIC NOVEL FOR MINECRAFTERS